THE LONELY HOUSE

THE LONELY HOUSE

MARIE BELLOC LOWNDES

Originally published in 1920.
Published by Wildside Press LLC.

WILDSIDE PRESS

Originally published in 1920.
Published by Wildside Press LLC.
wildsidepress.com

INTRODUCTION

KARL WURF

Marie Belloc Lowndes (1868–1947) was a British novelist and journalist whose work helped shape early psychological crime fiction. Born in London to a prominent Anglo-French family, she was the daughter of feminist writer Bessie Rayner Parkes and the sister of author and political commentator Hilaire Belloc. Educated partly in Paris, she began her literary career as a biographer and historical novelist, but her lasting reputation rests on her suspense fiction.

Her breakthrough came with *The Lodger* (1913), inspired by the Jack the Ripper murders. It was a sensation, selling widely and adapted multiple times for stage and screen—most notably in Alfred Hitchcock's 1927 silent film, which marked his first thriller. That novel established Lowndes as a master of domestic suspense, particularly skilled in exploring fear, guilt, and repression within middle-class households.

The Lonely House, published in 1920, is one of her most compelling works from this period. It introduced her recurring French detective, Hercules Popeau, who appeared in several subsequent novels. Popeau, a thoughtful and quiet figure, predates Hercule Poirot and helped popularize the European detective in English fiction. The novel was later adapted for the stage in 1924.

Lowndes wrote more than forty novels over her career, along with short stories and essays. Her fiction is marked by psychological depth, sharp social observation, and a focus on women navigating danger in seemingly ordinary settings. While she often worked within the structure of crime stories, her real interest lay in character: the private anxieties, moral compromises, and emotional costs of her protagonists.

In *The Lonely House*, Lowndes weaves themes of isolation and mistrust into a story that is as much about the inner life of her characters as it is about external suspense—a hallmark of her distinctive legacy.

CHAPTER 1

Lily Fairfield seemed to be rushing along a dark tunnel. It was as if she were being borne on wings. A keen, delicately perfumed air was blowing in her face. Far ahead of her there was a pin-point gleam of bright light—that surely must be the end of the tunnel? But as she swept on and on, farther and farther, the gleam did not grow larger or brighter. It seemed to remain, a white fixed star of light, infinitely far away.

Though the experience was intensely vivid, in a sense the girl was conscious that she was experiencing one of the strange, curious dreams, not wholly unpleasant, though sometimes verging on nightmare, which had haunted her at certain intervals during the whole of her not very long life.

With dreadful suddenness, out of the dark void above there leapt on her a huge black and white cat. She could see its phosphorescent eyes glaring at her in the darkness; she could feel its stifling weight on her breast.

She awoke with a strangled cry—to realise that the nightmare cat had materialised from a book which had fallen out of the net-rack of the swaying French railway carriage in which she was traveling!

She looked round her, still a little dazed by her strange dream. And then she grew very pink, for the only other two occupants of the railway carriage were smiling at her broadly.

There was unveiled admiration and eager interest in the face of the older man, a middle-aged Frenchman named Hercules Popeau, and a kind of unwilling admiration in that of his companion. And yet Angus Stuart, captain in the London Scottish, was repeating to himself the quaint, moving Scotch phrase, "A guid sight for sair e'en."

Lily Fairfield was certainly an agreeable example of what the cynics tell you will soon be a vision of the past—a delightfully pretty, happy-hearted, simple-natured, old-fashioned English girl—a girl who had "done her bit" in the Great War, and yet who was as unsophisticated as her grandmother might have been—though eager for any fun or pleasure that might come her way.

Lily's horrid nightmare faded into nothingness. It seemed so wonderful, after having left a London dark in fog and rain, to find herself in this fairyland of beauty. On her left a brilliant sun gleamed on the softly lapping waters of the Mediterranean, while to her right the train was rushing past lovely gardens full of the exquisite colouring which belongs to the French Riviera alone.

Could it really be only four days since Uncle Tom had seen her off at Victoria?

Though neither of them had said much, each had known it to be a solemn parting, the end of a happy chapter which had begun when Lily was five years old. Sixteen years had gone by since the orphan child had arrived at The Nest, Epsom, to become the charge, and in time the beloved adopted daughter, of her father's brother, a retired member of the Indian Medical Service, and his prim but kindly wife.

At first the war had not made much difference to The Nest and its occupants. Uncle Tom had taken over the practice of a resident doctor who had gone off to the front; and after the war had lasted two years Aunt Emmeline had at last allowed Lily to do some war work. This was not an amusing, exciting job of the kind so many of her young friends were doing, for it consisted in the dull business of looking after some Belgian refugees. Incidentally, she had thus acquired a good colloquial knowledge of French, a knowledge which should now prove useful.

The Great War closed a chapter in many a British girl's life, but in Lily's case it was death, not the war, that had done so. Aunt Emmeline, always so prudent and fussy, had caught influenza just after the Armistice, and had died in four days.

To the surprise of all those about her, the sudden ending of the war and her aunt's death coming together had been too much for the girl. She was ordered a complete change of scene, and it was then that Uncle Tom bethought himself of a certain clever, good-natured, and energetic lady, the Countess Polda, who had been what old-fashioned people would call a connection of his wife's.

It all hung on what was now very old family history. The Countess had been the daughter, by a first wife, of an Italian who had become, some forty years ago, Aunt Emmeline's stepfather. Thus, while entirely unrelated, she and Countess Polda had for a while called each other sister. Each of them had married—the one an Englishman, Tom Fairfield, and the other a certain Count Polda, who belonged to what had seemed to her English connections a very extraordinary nationality, for he was a subject of the Prince of Monaco.

Some twelve years ago the Countess had written to know if she might come and stay at The Nest for a few days while paying a business visit to London.

Uncle Tom, who was more forthcoming than his wife, had declared heartily that of course they must have her. And so she had arrived, to become in a sense the romance of Lily's childhood. "Aunt Cosy," as the little girl had been taught to call her, had about her something so hearty, so vivid, and so affectionate! Also she dressed beautifully, and wore lovely jewels. Everything about her appeared rich and rare to the English child.

Aunt Cosy had taken a great deal of notice of the little girl. She often said how much she wished that Lily could make friends with her beloved son, Beppo.

Beppo was the Poldas' only child. To him the Countess was passionately devoted; he was never far from her thoughts, and his name was constantly on her lips. Even now, after all these years, Lily remembered a miniature of Beppo which his mother had worn in a locket round her neck under her dress. It showed a pale, rather sickly-looking boy. Lily had sometimes wondered idly into what sort of a man he had grown up. Beppo had been sixteen or seventeen when the Countess had paid her memorable visit to England—he must be nearly thirty now.

At intervals the Countess would write the Englishwoman whom she called sister a letter which was at once formal and gushing. Two years after her visit to Epsom she had written to say that she and her husband, after spending most of their married life in Italy, had gone back to his native place, Monaco, where they had bought a small property, and where they hoped to spend a peaceful old age.

It was to La Solitude that Lily Fairfield was now on her way, to become Aunt Cosy's "paying guest" for three months.

* * * *

Lily took a little black leather case out of her pocket. It was the first time she had opened it since she had put in it the £50 in £5 notes which had been her Uncle Tom's parting gift. It had seemed to the girl an enormous sum of money, but, "it will melt much sooner than you think," he had said, smiling, but all the same he had told her not to let any strangers know that she had it.

The notes now lay safe in an envelope on one side of the letter-case. From the other flap she drew out a letter which she had never held in her hand before, though Uncle Tom had read it aloud to her the morning it had arrived, about ten days ago.

On a large and rather common-looking sheet of notepaper was written in a sloping hand, with what must have been an almost pin-point nib, the following letter:

LA SOLITUDE, MONACO.

My Dear Thomas,

I offer you sincere condolence on the death of the beloved Emmeline.

In answer to your kind inquiries I am glad to say our son is in excellent health, serving his country as a patriot should do in these dark days. He did not fight, for he has always been delicate; also very intelligent. He was of more use to Italy by staying in Rome than he would have been at the front.

And now, dear friend, to business and pleasure both. We shall be delighted to take your sweet Lily for the winter. You say "round about four pounds a week." In old days willingly would we have taken her for less than that, but now, alas, everything is very expensive. I suggest, therefore, five pounds a week, hoping that will not seem to you exaggerated. You say she should be much out of doors—that will be easy; we are surrounded by orange trees and olive groves; there is also a garden to which the Count gives much thought and care. We are quiet people and seldom go down into Monte Carlo. We neither of us frequent the Casino. The fact that we are householders in Monaco would make it illegal for us to gamble, even were we drawn to do so, which we are not. But I will see that Lily does not lead too dull and sad a life with her Aunt Cosy and Uncle Angelo.

If the terms, five pounds a week, suit you, may I suggest that you telegraph? Letters take so long coming and going. Perhaps you will add the approximate date of Lily's welcome arrival.

Receive, dear Thomas, the assurance of my affectionate and grateful memory.

                                                            Cosima Polda.

Lily folded the letter up again. It told a good deal, and yet it seemed to tell her nothing real of the writer. She knew that Uncle Tom had liked the Countess far more than Aunt Emmeline had done. Aunt Emmeline always sniffed when her step-sister was mentioned, and yet the Countess had appeared to be so very fond of her.

Turning back the flap of the little case, Lily noticed there was something else there. What a methodical man Uncle Tom was, to be sure! In addition to the Countess's letter, he had put the telegram which had arrived just as they were starting for the station—the telegram which asked Lily to postpone her arrival for two days. Uncle Tom had wired back that that was impossible, as all arrangements had been made, and he had again given the exact hour of her arrival at Monte Carlo.

Both Lily and Angus Stuart realised that they owed their very comfortable journey from Paris to their kindly, quaint fellow-traveller, Hercules Popeau.

A party of South Americans had made a determined effort to turn Lily out of the first-class carriage where she had settled herself with some difficulty in Paris. It was this at the time unpleasant episode which had made her acquainted with both Captain Stuart and M. Popeau. Captain Stuart had come forward and taken her part, but with very little result. And then, suddenly, there had emerged from the big crowd of travellers a short, stout, quiet-looking man, accompanied by an official with the magic letters P.L.M. on his cap. He had made very short work of the blustering South Americans, and had settled the three—Captain Stuart, Lily Fairfield, and the stout elderly Frenchman—into the carriage. Then, with a bow, he had handed the key of the door leading into the corridor to the man who Lily now knew was Hercules Popeau. Theirs had been the only airy, half-empty compartment in the long, dirty train.

As was natural, the three had become very friendly during the journey, and both Lily's fellow-travellers, the cheerful, talkative Frenchman, and the silent, quiet Scotsman, had vied with one another to make Miss Fairfield comfortable.

"We shall be at Monte Carlo in a very few minutes!" exclaimed M. Popeau. He spoke good English, but with a strong French accent.

The train went into a tunnel. Then, with a series of groans and squeaks, drew up at what Lily knew must be her final destination, Monte Carlo Station.

They all stepped down from the high railway carriage and waited till the comparatively small crowd of travellers had been seized by the smart-looking hotel porters who had come to meet them. But though Lily glanced eagerly this way and that, she could see no one who in the least reminded her of the Countess Polda, or, indeed, of any person who could be looking out for her.

M. Popeau saw the growing look of discomfiture on his pretty companion's face. He turned to Captain Stuart: "Mademoiselle must have lunch with us at the Hôtel de Paris, eh?" But Lily shook her head very decidedly, and so, "Very well. Then I will look after our young lady," he exclaimed in his decided, good-humoured way. "I know what you would call 'the ropes' of Monte Carlo. We will now find a nice carriage, and I will accompany her to her destination."

"I thought of doing that," said Captain Stuart, a little awkwardly.

M. Popeau shook his head. "No, no! It is more right, more *convenable*, that I should go. Am I not our friend's temporary guardian?"

They all three smiled at what had become by now a special little joke, and gratefully Lily followed the two men up the broad steps which looked more like those in a palace than in a railway station, till they reached the road running through the beautiful, tropical-looking gardens, which always seem to have an unreal touch of fairyland about them.

M. Popeau again turned to Captain Stuart: "You will not require a carriage," he said briskly. "The Hôtel de Paris is close by. Tell the manager that you are with me, and ask him to give you a good room, with the same view as mine. Say I am joining you at déjeuner. Oh, and Mon Capitaine? One word more—"

Captain Stuart turned round. He had not been listening to M. Popeau, for his mind was full of the English girl to whom he was about to say what he fully intended should only be a very temporary farewell. "Yes," he said mechanically. "Thanks awfully."

"Listen to me!" exclaimed M. Popeau imperiously. "You are to tell the manager of the Hôtel de Paris that our food has been—what do you say in England?—filthy for the last two days! Ask him to arrange that a lunch of surpassing excellence is ready in forty minutes from now. Can I trust you to do this, my friend?" He spoke so gravely that Lily began to laugh.

"You *are* greedy," she said reprovingly. "You make me feel quite sorry I didn't accept your offer!"

"There's still plenty of time to change your mind!" exclaimed both men simultaneously.

"My friends will have waited lunch for me." She did feel sorry that she could not go along with these kind people and have a good lunch before meeting Count and Countess Polda. But not for nothing had her Uncle Tom always called her, fondly, his dear old-fashioned girl.

She held out her hand to Captain Stuart. He took it in his big grasp, and held it perhaps a moment longer than she expected, but at last:

"Good-bye," he said abruptly. "Good-bye, Miss Fairfield. Let me see— today is Saturday. I wonder if I might call on you tomorrow, Sunday?"

"Yes, do," she said a little shyly. "You've got the address? La Solitude?"

It was nice to know that they would meet again tomorrow.

CHAPTER 2

As for M. Popeau, who was looking about him trying to find out if any changes had taken place in five very long years, he was telling himself, for perhaps the thousandth time in his life, what very odd people the British were!

He liked them, even better than he had done when, as a young man, he had met with a good deal of kindness in England. But still, how strange to think that a nice girl—a really nice girl—should permit such a stranger as was this Captain Stuart to call on her—without any kind of proper introduction. He hoped her Italian friends—or were they relations?—would not misunderstand. He feared they certainly would do so, unless she pretended—but somehow he did not think she would do that—that the young man was an old acquaintance, someone who had known her at home, in her uncle's house.

And then his quaint, practical French mind began to wonder whether Captain Stuart was well off—whether his affections were already engaged—whether, in a word, he would, or would not, make a suitable husband for this so charming girl?

Sad to say, M. Popeau's peculiar walk in life during the war-worn years had made him acquainted with the fact it sometimes happens that quite delightful-looking Englishmen are capable of behaving in a very peculiar manner when in a foreign country, and when in love!

He turned around abruptly. Captain Stuart was already some way off; and the Frenchman's eyes softened as they rested on the slender figure of the girl now standing by his side. She looked so fresh, so neat, too—in spite of the long, weary, dirty journey from Paris.

Lily, who, when she thought of her appearance at all, was rather disagreeably aware that she was clad in a pre-war coat and skirt, would have been surprised and pleased had she known how very well-dressed she appeared in this middle-aged Frenchman's eyes—how much he approved of the scrupulously plain black serge coat and skirt and neat little toque—how restful they seemed after the showy toilettes and extraordinary-looking hats worn by the fair, and generally eccentric, Parisiennes with whom fate brought him in constant contact.

A victoria drawn by two wiry-looking, raw-boned little steeds dashed down upon them. M. Popeau put up his hand, and the horses drew up on their haunches.

Giving the porter a very handsome tip, M. Popeau helped Lily into the carriage and then got in himself. "La Solitude!" he called out to the driver.

The man pointed with his whip to the mountain sky-line.

"Twenty-five francs," he exclaimed, "and that only because I wish to oblige monsieur and madame! I ought to ask fifty francs. It's a devil of a pull up there!" He rapped out the words with an extraordinary amount of gesticulation.

Lily had had some trouble in following what he said, but her experience with the Belgians stood her in good stead. A pound for what she believed must be a short drive? That seemed a great deal.

She turned in some distress to her companion. "Pray don't come with me," she exclaimed. "The man will take me there all right. I quite understood all he said."

"Of course I'm going to take you there," said M. Popeau. "My lunch will taste all the better for a little waiting. But you? Will you not change your mind and come and lunch at the Hôtel de Paris, mademoiselle?"

Poor Lily! She felt sorely tempted. But she shook her head.

And then something rather curious happened. A taxicab passed slowly by. M. Popeau stood up and hailed it. He took out of his pocket-book a dirty ten-franc note. "Here, my friend," he said, addressing their astonished driver, "it is too great a pull for your gallant little steeds, so we will take that taxi. Help me to transfer the young lady's luggage."

No sooner said than done, in spite of a very sulky protest from the taxi-driver, who had not the slightest wish to take on a new fare. He had brought a party out to Monte Carlo from Mentone, and was going back there.

"You should be glad, very glad indeed, my good boy," exclaimed M. Popeau, "to have the chance of earning twenty-five francs by a few moments' drive. Come, come, be amiable about it! You know perfectly well that you are bound to take me by the law."

"Not in Monaco," said the man sullenly. "The law is not the same in France as in Monaco."

"If you are a Monegasque," exclaimed M. Popeau, "then you must be well acquainted with my friend, M. Bouton."

The man's manner changed, and became suddenly cringing.

"Aha! I thought so!" M. Popeau turned to Lily. "My friend Bouton is Police Commissary here," he observed significantly.

"Where do you want me to go?" asked the man, in a resigned tone.

"To La Solitude."

Without anymore ado the taxicab turned round and started at a speed which seemed to Lily very dangerous. It was a whirlwind rather than a drive. But once they had left the beautiful gardens, and were through the curious network of town streets which lie behind the Casino grounds, the man slowed down, and soon they were breasting the hill up what was little more than a rough, dry, rutted way through orange groves and olive trees.

"Turn your head round," said M. Popeau suddenly, "and then you will see, my dear lady, one of the six most beautiful views in the world, and yet one which comparatively few of the visitors to Monte Carlo ever take the trouble to climb up here and enjoy."

Lily obeyed, and then she uttered an exclamation of delight at the marvellous panorama of sea, sky, and delicate vivid, green-blue vegetation which lay below and all about her. Monte Carlo, with its white palaces, looked like a town in fairyland.

Up and up they went, along winding ways cut in the mountain side. Even M. Popeau was impressed by the steepness of the gradient, and the distance traversed by them.

All at once the taxi took a sudden turn to the left and drew up on a rough clearing surrounded by old, grey olive trees. The atmosphere was strangely still, and though it was a hot day, Lily suddenly felt chilly—a touch, no doubt, of the mountain air. There crept over her, too, an eerie feeling of utter loneliness.

"Your friends have certainly well named their villa! Even I, who thought I knew the whole principality of Monaco more or less well, never came across this remote and lonely spot."

"This is the most convenient point by which a carriage can approach the villa," said the driver turning round. "The house is not far—just a few yards up through the trees."

"All right. Get down and help me carry the lady's luggage."

The man loaded himself up with Lily's small trunk, and M. Popeau took a big Gladstone bag she had had on the journey. "Please don't do that!" she exclaimed. "The man can come back presently for the bag. I'll give him a good tip in addition to the twenty-five francs."

"Nonsense!" said M. Popeau, quite sharply for him. "Of course this cab is my affair. It's going to take me back to the Hôtel de Paris. I intend to give the driver thirty francs—I had no idea it was as far."

At the top of a row of steps cut in the rocky bank was a wicket gate, on which were painted in fast-fading Roman letters the word "La Solitude."

The cabman opened the gate, and the three passed through into a grove of orange trees. Soon the steep path broadened into a way leading straight on to a lawn which fell sharply away from the stone terrace which formed the front of a long, low, whitewashed house.

In a sense, as M. Popeau's shrewd eyes quickly realised, La Solitude had an air of almost gay prosperity. It was clear that the bright green shutters, those of the six windows of the upper storey and those of the windows which opened on to the terrace, had but recently been painted.

Two blue earthenware jars, so large that they might well have formed part of the equipment of the Forty Thieves, stood at either end of the terrace, their comparatively narrow necks being filled with luxuriant red geranium plants, which fell in careless trails and patches of brilliant colour on the flag-stones.

Built out at a peculiar angle, to the left of the villa, was a windowless square building which looked like a studio.

Lily was surprised to see that every window on the ground floor of the house had its blind drawn down, and that above the ground floor every window was shuttered. But that, as any foreigner could have told her, had nothing strange about it. Most people living in Southern Europe have an instinct for shutting out the sun, even the delightful sun of a southern winter day. Still, to Lily's English eyes the drawn blinds and closed shutters gave a deserted, eerie, unlived-in look to La Solitude.

As they all three stood there, M. Popeau and the driver having put down the luggage for a moment on the hard, dry grass, the first sign of life at La Solitude suddenly appeared in the person of a huge black and white cat. It crept slowly, stealthily, round the left-hand corner of the house, intent on some business, or victim, of its own, and rubbed itself along the warm wall.

Lily felt a little tremor of surprise and discomfort. It was an odd coincidence that she should have seen in her dream-nightmare just such a cat as was this cat now moving so stealthily across her line of vision!

"The front door is to the right," said the driver.

They walked along the terrace, and Lily began to feel very much distressed and worried. Supposing the Count and Aunt Cosy had gone off on a weekend visit? Would their servants have left the house entirely alone? She feared the answer to this question might easily be "Yes."

The entrance to La Solitude was just a plain, green-painted door let into the bare house wall.

M. Popeau rang the old-fashioned iron bell-pull, and its strident tone seemed to tear across the intense stillness which enveloped them; and then they waited what seemed to all three a considerable time.

"I think," said M. Popeau, smiling suddenly all over his fat, pale, good-natured face, "that you will be compelled to come back with me and eat that good luncheon ordered by Captain Stuart, Miss Fairfield!"

But even as he said the words the door opened slowly, and an old woman, dressed very neatly in a faded blue print dress, with a yellow silk bandana handkerchief tightly wound round her head, stood, unsmiling, before them.

M. Popeau took command.

"This young lady has just arrived from England to stay with the Comte and Comtesse Polda," he said pleasantly.

"We did not expect the lady till the day after tomorrow. Please come this way."

She spoke quite civilly, but there was no glimmer of welcome on her thin, drawn-looking face. M. Popeau noticed that her intonation was pleasantly refined.

The driver put down, just inside the door, the luggage he had been carrying, and went off back to his taxi, while Lily and M. Popeau followed the old woman down the corridor. She opened a door to the left, and stood aside for the strangers to pass through into what seemed at first a completely darkened room. But with the words, "I will go and tell Madame la Comtesse you are here," she went and drew up one of the opaque yellow blinds.

Lily Fairfield, tired, hungry as she was, looked round with an eager sensation of curiosity, and, to tell the truth, she was exceedingly surprised and interested by what she saw.

The drawing-room of La Solitude was indeed strangely furnished and arranged—to English eyes. Considering the size of the villa, it was a large room, long, and in a sense lofty, with four French windows opening on to the stone terrace. As the windows were all shut there was a slightly muggy, disagreeable smell in the room. The old Italian furniture, arranged stiffly round the room, was upholstered in faded tapestry which had obviously been darned with skill and care.

The whitewashed walls were hung with faded Turkey-red cloth, a fact which, to Lily's eyes, added to the strangeness of the room, though, as a matter of fact, this material is a very usual, if old-fashioned, wall covering, in all French provincial towns and country houses. It formed a not unsuitable background to a number of mediæval and eighteenth-century portraits.

M. Popeau, who was looking round him with almost as much interest and curiosity as his young companion, realised, even in the poor light, that there was not what would be technically called a good—that is, a valuable—picture in the room. But he also told himself that they were genuine family portraits, proving that Count Polda—for he took the striking, sometimes sinister-looking, long-dead faces staring down at him to be the Count's ancestors—had a right to his title.

Between the windows hung two superb gilt mirrors in beautiful carved and gilt wood floreated frames. They, and an ebony and ivory cabinet, were the only things of real value in the room. A shabby card-table, on which there lay, face upwards, some not very clean patience cards, stood near the farthest window.

There came the sound of quick steps in the corridor. The door opened, and Lily Fairfield beheld, for the first time for over ten years, the woman who had produced such a brilliant, lasting impression on the quiet Epsom household.

"My dear child! What a surprise! We were not expecting you till—" and then Countess Polda stopped short, for she had suddenly realised that there was someone else in the room besides her young kinswoman.

M. Popeau advanced, and bowed in that strange, cut-in-half way which Lily thought so quaint and funny. "Forgive my intrusion, Madame," he said civilly. "I have been Mademoiselle's travelling companion from Paris, and as I am very well acquainted with Monte Carlo, while she is quite a stranger to this beautiful part of the world, I thought it best to escort her to your hospitable house."

While this colloquy was going on Lily was feeling more and more surprised, for somehow Aunt Cosy looked utterly different from what she remembered her as having looked twelve years ago. She had then appeared to Lily, a child of nine years of age, a very smart, fashionable-looking lady, wearing beautiful clothes. She now looked slightly absurd.

Meanwhile M. Popeau told himself that the Countess must once have been extremely handsome. He judged her to be about sixty, but she was tall, well built, and looked strong and active—in a word, younger than her years.

She wore a plaid skirt, one of those large patterns dear to the Parisienne's heart. Her plain white blouse was cut like a man's shirt and gave her, to a foreigner's eye, an English look—as did also the now old-fashioned tie-cravat which she wore pinned to the blouse with a large emerald pin. The pin attracted M. Popeau's attention, for it was set with an emerald which was, in his judgment, of considerable value. Doubtless it had belonged to the Count's father. It was the sort of tie-pin a foppish man of wealth and position might have worn in the early thirties of the last century.

But what in a very different way impressed both Lily Fairfield and M. Popeau was the Countess's singular-looking face and peculiar eyes. Her face, with its good, clearly-marked features and finely-drawn if narrow-lipped mouth, was of a most unbecoming colour, a kind of dusky red, which M. Popeau knew to mean some form of heart trouble. One of her eyes was green, the other blue.

She wore a curious and most elaborate "front," bright chestnut-auburn in tint, consisting of masses of tight little curls. It was evidently the sort of coiffure which had been worn when Countess Polda was a young woman. Now it gave a touch of the grotesque to her appearance, the more so that when she turned round to shut the door it became apparent that she also wore what used, many years ago, to be called a "bun."

Still, it was evident to M. Popeau that the person now standing before him was what is called, in common parlance, a woman of the world. She accepted his explanation of his presence with amiability, and expressed in well-chosen, voluble French her gratitude for his kindness to her young niece—he noticed she said "niece."

"It is still to be Aunt Cosy, is it not, dear child?" she drew the surprised Lily affectionately into her strong arms and kissed her on both cheeks. "It will be very pleasant, very delightful, to me and to my husband to have a young and charming girl about the house!" she exclaimed. "We are no longer young—and the war has made us very lonely—" She shook her head sadly. "No one would believe how it changed Monte Carlo for a while. But now our old friends—English, French, Italian—are beginning to return. Already the war is being forgotten like a nightmare, a bad dream."

They were all three still standing, and M. Popeau told himself that it was time he had his own good luncheon—and time for his young travelling companion to have hers. And then there came over the kind-hearted Frenchman a slight feeling of discomfort. Would Miss Fairfield be given a good luncheon, supposing the determined-looking lady who now stood before him had already had hers, in the foreign fashion, a couple of hours ago?

"I must be going," he began. "We have had no food, any of us. Mademoiselle, also, will be glad of her déjeuner."

As only answer the Countess went over to the window of which the yellow blind had already been drawn up, and with a vigorous movement she opened it. "Ah, that is better," she exclaimed. "*I* have all the English love of fresh air, but my husband—he fears for his pictures—for the furniture! Look at our view, my little one—and you, too, Monsieur. It is the most splendid view in Monaco!"

But M. Popeau was not bothering about the view. He was looking with some concern at Lily Fairfield. She seemed a rather pitiful, lonely little figure, standing there in this odd-looking room. Somehow he hated leaving her there!

But the Countess was still talking, in that full, hearty voice of hers. "My husband's family is of Monaco"—she smiled and showed her strong, good teeth. "In the fourteenth century they were almost as great people as the Grimaldis. Then the Poldas lived in Paris, in Rome, but when we lost our fortune, through unlucky speculations, it seemed simpler to come back to the Count's native place. Here we have lived—nay, here we have vegetated—ever since!"

When she stopped to take breath, M. Popeau managed to get in his goodbye. "I hope," he said pleasantly, "that you will allow me to come and pay my respects to you and to Mademoiselle? I will do myself that honour tomorrow, Sunday."

"We shall always be delighted to see you," replied the Countess heartily. "But it is a long climb. Still, kind friends sometimes take pity on my loneliness. As for my husband, he is like a goat, he can climb anywhere, he even disdains our good little Monaco carriages."

"That reminds me that the taxi we had the luck to find is waiting out there just below the orange grove. So I will go out this way," and M. Popeau walked out through the open window.

A few moments later there came the sound of the taxi turning round on the clearing below—and an acute feeling of loneliness and of depression stole over Lily Fairfield. She realised, suddenly, that she was tired out.

The Countess shut the window firmly, and she pulled down the thick yellow blind. Then she turned to her visitor. "Now," she said, "now, my little one, what is it you would like to do? I am for the moment very busy."

Her tone was still affectionate, still pleasant, but Lily felt a slight diminution of cordiality. "Perhaps I had better ask Cristina to show you your room. English ladies lie down a great deal, and you, my poor one, have been ill."

"What I should like," said Lily falteringly, "is something to eat, Aunt Cosy. I feel so hungry——" And as she saw a look of perplexity, almost of annoyance, pass over her hostess's face, she added hurriedly, "Anything would do—some bread-and-butter—a cup of milk—or perhaps an egg."

"I will see if there is any milk," said the Countess reluctantly. "Butter, I know we have none—there will be some, I hope, tomorrow morning. As for an egg—yes, I believe Cristina did secure two eggs the day before yesterday. Your uncle and I, dear child, follow the custom of the country; we have our lunch at eleven. I should have expected that you also would have had something to eat at eleven, even in the train—but no matter, I will see what can be done."

She went towards the door. "No, do not follow me"—her tone was peremptory. "Stay here for a moment. You can be looking at the pictures; they are of great interest and value—though, alas! the best were sold long ago to an American millionaire."

Then a most unlucky thing happened! Though the Countess closed the door behind her firmly, the catch did not act, and it swung ajar. That being so, Lily could not help overhearing the short conversation in French that took place between mistress and maid in the passage outside.

CHAPTER 3

"Come, come, Cristina, the young girl is hungry! It will not take you a moment to boil an egg."

"The fire is out."

"That does not matter; you may use my little English stove—it will not take many drops of wood spirit to boil an egg."

And then Lily heard the Countess add in a low, meaning tone: "Remember that we are receiving with her a hundred and twenty-five francs a week. If she is not satisfied she will go. Also, as the Count said only the other day, she may be useful to us in other ways."

The unwilling listener felt desperately uncomfortable. She began moving towards the door, but just at that moment the Countess, turning, saw that Lily must have overheard what had been said. Her already dusky face darkened. She looked excessively annoyed—a vindictive look came into her oddly coloured eyes. She evidently thought the English girl had been eavesdropping. But with an obvious effort she recovered her composure.

She motioned Lily farther into the darkened room and shut the door—this time making sure that it *was* shut.

"I desire to tell you one or two things," she said slowly. "You are going to be a member of our household for, I hope, a long time, dear child—so it is better to cross the *t*'s and to dot the *i*'s, as they say in France. Cristina is not only an old and faithful servant—she was my husband's foster-sister. You know what that means?"

Lily nodded.

"Thus we do not really regard her as a servant," went on the Countess. "We are both very fond of her. She is an excellent creature, but she is not very amiable. I had to tell her that you were coming as a paying guest"—the Countess made a slight grimace. "Cristina is an old woman, and I hope you will not be offended with me when I say that I shall be glad if you will help a little in the work of the house."

"I shall be delighted to do anything I can, Aunt Cosy," said Lily eagerly. "A home was started in Epsom for the Belgian refugees, and the ladies of the place took it in turns to go in and do the housework."

"You have relieved my mind! As I said just now to Cristina, I'm sure you will make yourself useful to us, as a dear, cherished little daughter might do. How sorry the Count will be that he was not at home to welcome you!"

Lily suddenly felt happier. It was nice of Aunt Cosy to have spoken to her so frankly.

"Do let me go into the kitchen and boil an egg for myself," she exclaimed.

"Very well," smiled the Countess. She preceded the girl till they came to a narrow passage, cut like a slit in the wall, to the right of the corridor. It led into the oddest little kitchen Lily had ever seen, and was not much bigger than an English bathroom. The stove—if you could call it a stove—was one for the exclusive use of charcoal. What light there was came from a far from clean skylight. On the distempered green walls hung various mysterious-looking copper pots and pans, the quaintest being a little roasting-machine in which could be cooked a tiny joint, or chicken. On the table was an old-fashioned methylated spirit lamp, on which there was now poised an enam-elled saucepan full of water in which was an egg.

"Unfortunately La Solitude was built against the side of the mountain," said the Countess, "so both the kitchen and the dining-room are lit from the sky. But from the front of the house we enjoy a view into three countries! We are not many yards from the frontier—the frontier which divides Monaco from France; and straight over the sea is Corsica, the cradle of the great Na-poleon! To the left, of course, is Italy, my beloved country, though I count myself English, as you know. And now," she concluded, "I will leave you in the good care of our excellent Cristina. I have some work to finish before tomorrow."

When the Countess had gone the old servant laid a clean, unbleached napkin across the end of the kitchen table. She put out a plate, an egg-cup, salt and pepper, and half a long loaf. Then she turned, with a look of apology, to Lily.

"The dining-room is already prepared for dinner," she said, in her soft, refined voice. "I fear I must ask you, Mademoiselle, to eat your egg here."

"Of course I will," exclaimed Lily. "And, Cristina, I hope you will allow me to help you a little in the housework?"

A curious look—was it of surprise or gratitude?—perhaps something of both—quivered for a moment over Cristina's pale face. "You are very good," she said quietly. "There is a good deal of work sometimes—when we have visitors."

The water was now boiling, and as she spoke she took the egg out of the saucepan, and put it deftly into the egg-cup. And then, after Lily had sat down, the old woman stood and watched her eat. Had not the girl been so very hungry she would have felt a little shy and awkward under that silent, tense scrutiny.

Cristina suddenly observed: "I suppose Mademoiselle is a Protestant?"

Lily looked up. "Yes, of course I am."

A sad look came over Cristina's face. "Mademoiselle looks so good, so pure," she murmured. "I thought perhaps that Mademoiselle was thinking of being a nun."

"Oh, no, indeed I'm not!" Lily laughed outright, for the first time in this strange house.

"I myself," said Cristina slowly, "at one time hoped to be a nun." And then, clasping her hands, and with an emotion which transformed her quietude into something which greatly startled Lily, so violent and unexpected was it, her pale face became convulsed. "The devil prevented my becoming a nun. But for the devil I should now be a good and perhaps even a holy woman!"

Her breast heaved—she seemed extraordinarily moved and distressed.

Lily jumped up—not perhaps quite so surprised as she would have been but for some of her experiences with the more emotional Belgians. "I'm quite sure that you are a very good woman," she said kindly.

But Cristina shook her head with an air of ineffable sadness and distress.

The kitchen door opened suddenly and Lily was astounded to see the change that came over the old waiting woman. She became coldly rigid; her look of agitation disappeared as if by magic.

She turned round: "Madame la Comtesse?" she said inquiringly, almost forbiddingly.

"Only to say, Cristina, that I'm going down the hill a little way to try and meet Monsieur le Comte. He will be loaded, as you know, with all manner of good things." The speaker smiled, showing a row of strong, white teeth. "Will you show Mademoiselle her room?" She turned to Lily. "And you, dear child? Have you had a nice fresh egg?"

Without waiting for an answer she turned and left the little dark kitchen.

Cristina waited, listening, and then, when she heard the front door, at the end of the corridor, close to: "Are you really her relation?" she asked slowly. "You are not at all like her."

"No: I'm not really related to the Countess." Had she been more at home in French she would have tried to explain the peculiar connection. Meanwhile a pleased look came over old Cristina's face. "I thought not!" she exclaimed.

There was a pause. Lily was telling herself with some amusement that, however fond the Countess might be of Cristina, Cristina was not over fond of the Countess. And yet how very nicely Aunt Cosy had spoken of the old woman!

Suddenly the huge cat, which had been the first living thing seen by Lily Fairfield at La Solitude, came noiselessly into the kitchen.

"Here is Mimi," exclaimed Cristina. "He is so faithful, so intelligent! He follows me about like a dog." She stooped and picked up Mimi. "Say good-day to Mademoiselle!" she said caressingly, but, as Lily drew near, the cat suddenly spat and swore.

Cristina put the creature down. "He is jealous," she said. "He perceives that I am going to love Mademoiselle." And sure enough, Mimi walked away with offended dignity.

"Before we go upstairs would Mademoiselle like to see the dining-room?" asked the old woman.

And then the girl had another of the surprises which seemed to be always meeting her in this curious French house—for she thought of Monaco as being part of France; which of course it is not. Turning the key in a door at the end of the corridor, Cristina stepped aside while Lily walked through into what struck her as a gloomy, and yet, in its way, a splendid room, and she realised suddenly that it was the windowless building she had seen from the lawn.

Through a circular skylight there fell a softened light on the beautiful old tapestry, moth-eaten in places, with which the walls were hung; and in the centre of the room was a round table, now spread with a lace tablecloth. It was set for three, a lace d'oyley marking each place, as did also three sets of exquisite old cut-glass goblets of varying sizes. In the middle of the table was a gold vase containing a bunch of brilliant coloured blossoms, such as may be bought anywhere along the Riviera for a few pence. They made a charming note of colour in the large room, and gave an air of festivity to the well-arranged dining-table.

The only other furniture in the apartment was a set of six tapestry-covered chairs, and a yellow marble sideboard with gilt legs.

On the sideboard were now set out three green and gold dessert plates, with Venetian glass finger-bowls on them, and two graceful, delicately-painted dessert dishes were placed ready for fruit.

Lily was rather surprised to see that there were no fewer than six cut-glass and coloured decanters filled with various wines and liqueurs, standing in a row behind the fruit plates.

Cristina stood by, looking at her expectantly.

"What beautiful tapestries, and—and what a lovely tablecloth," said Lily at last.

She felt bewildered. She had never seen anything quite like this before. It was the sort of dining-table that she would have expected to see laid out in a palace. "The glasses must be very valuable," she said admiringly. "I once saw a much less nice set, very like these, in a famous collection of cut glass."

"I suppose I must now lay a fourth place," said Cristina slowly. And then she added: "Mademoiselle was not expected till the day after tomorrow. Perhaps the Count will put off the visitor."

"Who is coming to dinner—a lady or a gentleman?" asked Lily pleasantly.

Cristina hesitated a moment—and then, "A gentleman," she answered.

The old woman led the English girl back into the corridor. A short, ladder-like staircase led to the upper floor of the villa. The storey above was divided like that below, by a corridor which ran right down the middle of the house.

Cristina took up the bunch of keys which hung at her girdle. "I sleep there," she said, pointing to the first door to the right, "and Mademoiselle here."

She unlocked the first door to their left, and ushered Lily into a room which impressed the girl as curiously dark and gloomy. But she soon saw the reason for that. The one window gave on to a stretch of deep, barren, heath-covered hill. Only by craning her head right out of the window could she see the sky. Below was a small, oblong yard, bounded by an outhouse.

Within the room, an old-fashioned mahogany bed of the low, curved Empire shape stood against the left wall. By the tiny fireplace was a shabby armchair upholstered in some kind of discoloured green material. There was no hanging cupboard; only a row of wooden pegs on the door. A pair of splendid brocaded silk and velvet curtains, looped up by the window, gave a touch of incongruous grandeur.

The room looked very unhomelike, and Lily suddenly felt sad and dispirited. "I think I will try and get a little sleep, so will you kindly call me, Cristina, when you think I ought to get up?" She hesitated a moment. "Does Aunt Cosy have afternoon tea?" she asked.

"Only when visitors are expected." And then Cristina added, "We have no tea in the house now."

"I have brought a little," said Lily quickly; "about two pounds."

Cristina went over to the window and drew the heavy curtains together, and then she slipped noiselessly from the room.

CHAPTER 4

When Lily awoke four hours later it took her a moment or two to realise where she was.

Jumping up, she drew back the curtains, and opened the window wide. Twilight was falling, and the stretch of heath-covered hillside looked dark, almost forbidding. She felt suddenly cold, and shivered as she drew back into the barely-furnished room.

Then she did her unpacking, quickly and methodically, and after a moment of hesitation put on a white gown. It was a white stockinette skirt and jumper, the sort of dress she would have changed into if she and Uncle Tom and Aunt Emmeline, in the old happy days, had been having some old friend to dinner. It was the first time she had worn anything but black since her aunt's death, and she felt a little pang of remorse as she took up a black ribbon and put it round her slender, rounded waist. She did not want the Countess to think that she had forgotten dear Aunt Emmeline.

And then Lily bethought herself that it was rather strange that Aunt Cosy had said nothing about either Uncle Tom or her own late step-sister. The girl could not help feeling that her unexpected arrival had put out both Aunt Cosy and old Cristina very much. But Cristina had quite got over it; somehow Lily felt that she and Cristina were going to be friends.

She was not quite so sure about Aunt Cosy! To tell the truth, the Countess was already a disappointment to the girl; she was so unlike Lily's recollection of her. She did not sufficiently allow for the great difference between her two selves—that between a shy, romantic child, and an observant, grownup girl.

With regard to the man she knew she would be expected to call Uncle Angelo, Lily was quite unprejudiced, for she had never seen him, and had no idea what he was like. She hoped deep in her heart that he would be quite unlike Aunt Cosy.

She glanced at herself in the plain, discoloured mirror above the empty fireplace. Yes, her hair was quite tidy, and the long sleep had done her good. Already the magic change of scene was beginning to work. After all, she was not going to be here for very long—three months would go by very quickly, and it was pleasant to feel that she had, at any rate, two friends near by, for so she could not help considering Hercules Popeau and Captain Stuart.

Captain Stuart had asked her if she played tennis. There were tennis-courts of sorts at Monte Carlo—so he had said with a very pleasant smile.

Like so many young Scots, he had a delightful smile. It quite transformed his keen, thoughtful, serious face.

At last she opened her door, and looked with some curiosity up and down the corridor. Four closed doors to her right evidently led into rooms which must have that wonderful view over which the Countess had waxed so enthusiastic. Lily was sorry Aunt Cosy hadn't given her one of those front rooms. It would have been nice to have had that beautiful view spread out before her, instead of only the bare mountain.

She walked lightly down the staircase, and then she waited a moment, wondering a little what she ought to do.

At last she opened a door which she knew led into the drawing-room. It was empty, and the blinds had all been drawn up, probably one of the windows had been left open, for the room no longer felt stuffy.

She walked over to one of the windows, and then she could not help giving a little gasp of surprise, for, walking so softly that she had not heard the cat-like footsteps, someone had followed her into the room and now stood, silent, by her side—

It was—it must be—Uncle Angelo!

Count Polda was a quaint, dried-up-looking little man. His body was very thin, and yet his pallid face was fat. He was looking at Lily with a fixed, considering look.

"Uncle Angelo?" she said shyly, and then held out her hand.

He took her little soft hand in both of his podgy ones.

"This is Lili?" he said in French. "Welcome to La Solitude." And then he dropped her hand, and with the words, "You play Patience—hein?" he turned to the card-table, and began moving the cards.

"No, I've never played yet."

"You will learn—you will learn." Uncle Angelo spoke in a preoccupied tone. "It passes the time away," he said, and, still standing, he played the Patience through. But he did not pull it off, and Lily had the uncomfortable sensation that he attributed his bad luck to her presence.

Suddenly he raised his voice: "Cosy! Cosy!" he called out fretfully.

The door was pushed open suddenly.

"Yes, my friend," said the Countess. She also had changed her dress, and now wore a purple tea-gown, and a handsome if old-fashioned-looking necklace composed of various large, coloured stones.

"Mr. Ponting will soon be here now," said Uncle Angelo. "Is not that so? Is everything prepared?"

"Certainly, my friend." Aunt Cosy spoke with a touch of impatience. "Cristina and I have got everything ready. I think you will have a good dinner. And so will our dear little Lily"—she drew near the girl, and put a big, powerful arm caressingly round Lily's shoulders. "There was nothing to eat in the house when this dear child arrived! But tonight there is a banquet. The friend who is coming to dinner is going a long journey," she said smilingly, "and so we want to give him what in England is called a good send-off."

Uncle Angelo looked round at his wife. "An excellent expression," he said slowly.

The Countess took her arm from Lily's neck. "Is it not a beautiful view?"

And Lily, in heartfelt tones, replied, "Indeed it is, Aunt Cosy!"

The vast expanse of evening sky was turquoise blue, the sea a deep aquamarine; and the trees, grass, and huge geranium blossoms just outside on the terrace had turned to soft greys and purples.

Suddenly Lily bethought herself that she had not yet asked after the son of the house. "I hope you have good news of Beppo?" she said a little timidly.

And then, to her surprise, there came over Aunt Cosy a curious transformation. It was as though she became again what Lily remembered her as having been in those far-away days at Epsom. She became cordial, affectionate—the touch of affectation which so disagreeably impressed her young companion slid off from her as if it were a cloak.

"How nice of you to remember him!" she exclaimed. "What talks you and I used to have about him, little Lily! My beloved Beppo! How I long for you to see him. But I fear he will not be here for some time. Perhaps after the New Year he will come and spend a week with his old father and mother. He is the best of sons!"

She turned round and said something very quickly in French to her husband, the purport of which was: "Lily has just asked me about our beloved son. I have been telling her what a good fellow he is."

Lily was touched to see how Uncle Angelo's fat, placid face altered.

"He is an excellent boy," he said quaintly. "The King of Italy thinks much of our Beppo. Some day Beppo will be what you call a—what?—a great man! He is already adding lustre to our name."

"How sorry he must be that he was not well enough to fight," said Lily shyly.

"He saw the Front," said the Countess quickly. "He was there for two whole weeks. I will show you his picture in uniform."

She left the room for a couple of minutes, and then came back with a photograph in her hand. "Is he not handsome?" she said eagerly.

Lily gazed at Beppo Polda's portrait with a good deal of interest. Yes, he had grown up into a very good-looking young man. He had his mother's good features, and he was evidently tall. Yet he was fairer than Lily supposed most Italians were.

"He is very English-looking, is he not?" said the Countess in a pleased voice.

"English-looking?" repeated Lily, surprised—to her eyes he looked singularly un-English-looking, but then perhaps that was owing to the way in which his hair was cut.

"My grandmother was an Englishwoman," went on the Countess, "that is why I am so fair, that is why Beppo himself is fair—fair and tall. Beppo is considered one of the handsomest men in Rome. Tomorrow I will show you a picture of Beppo on his horse. He is one of the great hunters, is my boy," said the Countess proudly. "He is quite in the English set. There is no body exercise in which he is not an adept—he can even play cricket."

Lily smiled. She liked Aunt Cosy much better than she did a quarter of an hour ago.

"Aunt Cosy?" she suddenly exclaimed. "Uncle Tom gave me fifty pounds in banknotes, and I think I had better ask you to keep the money for me. You can give me £5 from time to time."

"Fifty pounds! But how dangerous, dear child! There are many brigands about, especially since the war ended."

The Countess held out her hand, and Lily took the little leather case out of her bag.

"Angelo, where shall we keep this dear child's money?"

"In here," he said briefly, and going over to the ebony and ivory cabinet he unlocked it. Then he took the leather case and placed it in one of the drawers. Finally he shut the two folding doors of the cabinet and locked it up, putting the key back into a shabby purse which he had taken out of his pocket.

"I hope our friend Ponting has not elected to spend his last evening in the Rooms," he said uneasily. But his wife answered, "No, no! Were that so we should have heard. Ah, there he is!"

Lily looked out of the window, near which she was still standing, and in the now growing darkness she saw a tall figure come striding across the lawn.

The Countess opened the long French window, and Lily stepped back, instinctively, to allow her to greet her visitor.

He was a big, fair, loose-limbed man, and over his dress-clothes he wore a big, sporting-looking coat.

There was a quick interchange of words. She heard the stranger say, speaking with what seemed to her an American accent, "You'll have to be angry with me, Countess, for I've come to say that I can't stay to dinner."

And an exclamation of something like sharp displeasure did come from the Countess's lips.

"I know I've behaved badly—but there it is! Some fellows have persuaded me to spend my last evening with them. You've been so kind to me I felt as if I must come up and tell you myself. I've got a carriage waiting for me down there."

Both the Count and Countess expostulated more angrily than seemed quite civil. And then the Countess called out rather imperiously: "Lily, come and be introduced to our friend, Mr. George Ponting."

The girl came forward, smiling a little, as the visitor stepped over the threshold of the window.

He held out his hand, and Lily noticed that he was wearing a gold bangle. "Why, who are you?" he asked abruptly. "And where did *you* come from?"

Lily was amused. "My name is Lily Fairfield," she said. "I come from England. I arrived today. I'm going to stay at La Solitude for some time."

"We had promised her such a delightful evening in your pleasant, amusing company," said the Countess vexedly.

Mr. Ponting looked disturbed and sorry. "I didn't know you had asked a lady to meet me," he muttered.

He kept looking at Lily—it was rather a pathetic, hungry kind of a look. "It's a long time," he said, "since I've spoken to a young English lady. To my mind, foreigners don't count—I only care for the girls of the Old Country."

And then the Countess began to speak, kindly, persuasively. "Why not stop, Mr. Ponting? It will be better for you than having—what is the word?— a rowdy evening, and perhaps losing more of your good money."

"The path of true wisdom would probably be not to join those chaps tonight, eh, Countess?" He looked oddly undecided. "It does seem nice up here," he muttered.

"Dear friend, do me the pleasure of staying! Do not throw us over. See, my little Lily is longing for you to stay! My husband will go and pay off your driver."

And so it was settled, almost in a few moments, that Mr. Ponting would stay and dine at La Solitude.

The Count stepped out of the window, then he called out, "Shall I tell the man to come back for you at about half-past ten?"

"Yes. I'll be obliged if you will. There's a good train at eleven into Nice. I'm sleeping there tonight, and am off across the blue sea tomorrow."

Already the Count was disappearing down the path through the orange grove.

"Will you excuse me for a few moments?" said the Countess. "Lily, will you entertain Mr. Ponting?"

She shut the door, leaving the two young people alone together—not that Mr. Ponting was a young man in Lily's eyes. As a matter of fact he was rather under than over forty.

"They're awfully kind people," Mr. Ponting began at once in a confidential tone. "They've been ever so good to me the last few weeks! I'm a lonely chap, and the first time I came up to this cute little place, well, it was like heaven after the sort of gang I'd got in with down there."

"I suppose you're American," said Lily politely.

"American?" he coloured, slightly offended. "No—not I. I'm British, for all I come from Pernambuco."

He went on talking eagerly, evidently liking the sound of his own voice, and delighting in his attractive listener.

After a very few minutes Lily felt as if she knew all about Mr. George Ponting. How, though he had spent all his youth building up a good business in Pernambuco, he had started for the Old Country on August 6, 1914. How awfully lonely he had felt in England, not knowing a soul. But how he had been all right once he got out to Flanders. How, though three times badly wounded, he was now as sound as a bell. Finally, how he had come to the Riviera to see a little of the world before going home and starting work again, and how he had found a pal, a splendid chap, who was sailing with him from Marseilles tomorrow night!

It was a simple, usual little story, no doubt, yet it touched Lily, and made her manner very kind.

Suddenly Mr. Ponting took out of his pocket a shabby shagreen case. He opened it and held it out to her. On the worn black velvet lay a small gold box, exquisitely chased in different coloured golds.

"Pretty thing, isn't it?" he said complacently. "'Twould do for stamps—that's what I said to myself, though I believe it was what people used to keep snuff in—strange idea, wasn't it?"

"Yes," said Lily, smiling; "I think it is the prettiest little box I've ever seen!"

He opened it, and showed her engraved inside the lid the words, "Mon cœur à toi. Ma vie au Roi."

"Say!" he exclaimed. "Will you have it? Just as a souvenir, you know!"

Lily shook her head. She could not take so costly a gift from a complete stranger.

"I know it's good," went on her companion quickly, "for a chap who they say is a big Paris curiosity-dealer offered me five hundred francs for it this afternoon. I got it in a strange way. A poor old soul whom I noticed playing at the Rooms—the sort of woman who isn't up to Club form—came up to me last evening and asked if I'd give her a hundred francs for it. I'm sorry now that I only gave her that much! It must be worth a good bit more than five hundred francs if a dealer offered that for it."

He was still holding out the little shagreen case. "Look here," he exclaimed again, "you take it—do!"

Lily shook her head decidedly. "I shouldn't care to have anything so valuable, for I've no place to keep anything of that sort here," she said a little awkwardly. "I've even had to ask the Countess to keep the money I brought from England."

"Is that so?" he exclaimed. "But this little box isn't as valuable as all that! Do take it, Miss Fairfield."

But Lily shook her head again, even more decidedly than before. "Honestly, I'd rather not," she said firmly.

"All right! I'll just give it to the next pretty girl I meet." He looked hurt and angry.

"Please forgive me!" Lily was really sorry. Was she making a fuss about nothing? And yet—and yet she knew that the box was worth twenty pounds at least.

The door opened. "Supper is quite ready," said the Count, in his refined, rather mincing voice. "The Countess awaits you in the dining-room."

The curious, windowless apartment was lit by candles set in four cut-glass candlesticks on the table itself, and by two silver candelabra on the sideboard. Silver bowls full of delicious hot soup were standing ready on the round table, but the rest of the meal was cold.

The waiting was done deftly and quickly by Cristina; she had put on a lace cap and apron, and she looked a quaint and charming figure, in spite of her age. But Lily was concerned at her look of illness and fatigue. Cristina tonight was terribly, unnaturally pale.

Mr. Ponting, who sat opposite his host, did not need much entertaining, for he did all the talking, and ate but little of the delicious cold lobster souf-flé and big game pie which had followed the soup. But, as the meal went on, Lily could not help noticing uncomfortably that the visitor was drinking very freely the three kinds of wine.

Count Polda did not take any wine himself, but he often got up and helped his guest generously. The Countess also took wine, but in strict moderation. Once she offered her guest water, but he shook his head.

Lily grew more and more uncomfortable. She wished Mr. Ponting would eat more and drink less! She herself was dreadfully hungry, and she was the only one of the four there who made a really good meal. Rather to her surprise there was no sweet, only some fine fruit, and again she was the only one of the four who took any of it. And then, at last, Cristina brought in coffee. Lily refused to take any. She fancied it might keep her awake.

For perhaps the tenth time Mr. Ponting had begun a long, somewhat incoherent speech with the words: "And now I'll tell you a yarn," when Lily saw Aunt Cosy make her a little sign, and she got up.

The visitor looked up with a rather dazed look. "Why," he said thickly, "going already?"

"Only to the salon," said the Countess smoothly. "You and the Count, dear friend, will follow us presently."

She motioned Lily out in front of her rather mysteriously, and then she shut the door.

"Foolish fellow!" she exclaimed, and there was a touch of harsh contempt in her voice. "But still he is amiable, and the Count, who is a student of human nature, is amused by such a man as Mr. Ponting."

Lily said nothing, but she felt annoyed. It was horrid of Aunt Cosy to speak like that of kindly, grateful Mr. Ponting.

The Countess went on: "It is sad to see such a fine young man drink too much!"

Lily felt depressed, almost miserable. No man when in her company had ever become even slightly the worse for drink. A touch of resentment with the Count came over her; why had he gone on filling up Mr. Ponting's glass?

Almost as if Aunt Cosy could see into the girl's mind, she exclaimed: "The second time our friend dined here I said to Angelo, 'We will not let him have so much to drink.' But he actually got up, again and again, and went to the sideboard and helped himself. So Angelo, who is nervous about his beautiful decanters—they are very rare and could not be replaced under hundreds of francs each—Angelo made up his mind that he himself would pour out what our guest insisted on having!"

"It is indeed a pity," said Lily in a low voice.

She hated this talk about their guest, and she dreaded the thought of his reappearance in the drawing-room. It was therefore with relief that she heard the Countess suddenly exclaim: "And now you had better go upstairs and get a good long night's rest, dear child. Are you not sleepy?"

"Yes," said Lily. "I do feel sleepy. That's why I didn't take any coffee."

The Countess opened the dressing-room door. "Cristina?" She spoke for once in quite a low voice.

The old woman emerged at once from the little passage leading to the kitchen. "Yes," she said. "Does Madame la Comtesse want anything?"

And again Lily was struck by Cristina's deathly pallor.

"Bring a glass of water for Mademoiselle"—the words were uttered very curtly.

And then, rather to Lily's surprise, there came a touch of color in Cristina's pallid face. She turned away, then came back a few moments later with a glass of water in her hand.

"Thank you very much," said Lily gratefully. This was a kind thought of Aunt Cosy.

"I have got a candle already lighted in Mademoiselle's room," said Cristina.

Holding the glass of water, Lily turned to Aunt Cosy to say good-night.

"Take care!" cried the Countess sharply. "You might spill some of that water over my dress. I will not kiss you tonight, dear child, but I will make up for it tomorrow!"

It was clear she was anxious to get rid of the girl before the two men came out of the dining-room, and Lily went off, quickly, upstairs.

Her bedroom looked dreary and uncomfortable, very unlike her pretty, bright room at The Nest.

She walked over to the little table by the bed where stood a lighted candle, and began drinking the water. It had a slight taste, and holding it up to the light she saw that it was cloudy. She put it down without drinking any more. After all, she did not feel very thirsty.

She glanced round her—how dark and gloomy the room looked! It smelt stuffy and airless. She turned and pushed aside the heavy curtains and saw the window was closely shut. She opened it, top and bottom. Ah, that was better!

And then she looked at the little travelling clock Uncle Tom had given her the first time she had left The Nest on a visit, years ago. It was just after ten—later than she thought—still, she must unpack the rest of her things.

She had just finished doing so when she heard the noise of a door opening and shutting downstairs. That must be the Count and Mr. Ponting leaving the dining-room. How long they had stayed there!

There came the sound of another door opening and shutting—that of the drawing-room. And then Lily suddenly bethought herself with some dismay that she had no idea when the Count and Countess had breakfast, or at what time they would like her to be called. Surely she ought to ask Cristina?

She walked over and opened the door of her bedroom, and at once she heard a voice from below call out, "Is that you, Lily? Do you want anything?"

There was a note of apprehension and surprise in Aunt Cosy's accents.

"I only want to know what time breakfast is."

"If you will ring, Cristina will bring you a cup of coffee, English fashion."

The Countess actually came up the staircase. She looked flustered and ill at ease, and was gazing at the girl with a disturbed expression. "I hoped you would have been asleep by now, dear child," she said.

"I had to finish unpacking," Lily said. "I suppose Mr. Ponting is just going? Do remember me to him—I didn't say good-bye to him, you know."

"I will—I will!" said the Countess hurriedly. "Good-night, and sleep well."

Something—she could not have told you what—made Lily open the door after she had heard the Countess go down the steep, narrow stairs.

And then all at once there came Aunt Cosy's loud hearty voice: "Good-bye, Mr. Ponting, good-bye—and good luck!"

The words echoed through the quiet house. And Lily, now suddenly feeling very, very tired, after the many adventures of the day, undressed, said her prayers, and blew out the light. She was glad to feel that her first day at La Solitude was over, and that a long, quiet night lay in front of her.

CHAPTER 5

It may have been an hour later when suddenly Lily Fairfield sat up in bed. In a moment she knew where she was, and yet she did not really feel awake. She told herself with a feeling of fear that she was asleep—asleep, as she had been asleep that night ten days ago, when she had started walking in her sleep, so frightening greatly Uncle Tom.

Something now seemed to be impelling her, almost ordering her, to get up and to begin walking through the silent, sleeping house. She fought against the impulse, the almost command; but it was as if a stronger will than her own was forcing her to get out of the low, old-fashioned Empire bed.

She did so, slowly, reluctantly, and then she walked automatically across to the door of the room and opened it.

Surely she was asleep? Had she been awake she would have put on a wrapper before going into the passage. As it was, she felt impelled to open also the door opposite to that of her own room—the door which she had been told led into the room in which old Cristina, the friend-servant of the host and hostess, slept.

Lily walked blindly on, to the dim patch of light which was evidently the window of Cristina's room. The blind was up, but the window was closed. She stared out, but she could see nothing, for it was a very dark, moonless night, and the great arch of sky above the sea was only faintly perceptible. And then, suddenly, Lily knew that she was awake, not asleep, for there fell on her ear the sound of deadened footsteps floating up from below—that is, from the terrace. A moment later she heard the long French window of what the Countess called the *grand salon* open quietly.

And then it was that all at once, standing there behind the still closed window, Lily remembered her fifty pounds—the fifty pounds she had asked Aunt Cosy to keep for her, and which she had seen Uncle Angelo put in the ebony and ivory cabinet!

What should she do? Should she fling open the window and call out? No, for that would scare the burglars away, if burglars they were.

Lily listened again, intently, and after what seemed to her a long, long time, she heard the window below closing to, very quietly. Then came the sound of footsteps—it seemed to her more than one pair of footsteps—padding softly away across the lawn into the wood. Then followed a curious, long-drawn-out sound—so faint that she had to strain her ears to hear it at all.

She gave a stifled cry—something had suddenly loomed up on the broad ledge the other side of the closed window. It was the big cat Mimi—Mimi dragging herself along by the window-pane and purring, her green eyes gleaming coldly, wickedly, in the night air.

Frightened and unnerved, Lily turned and felt her way through the dark room to the bed. She might at least wake Cristina, and tell her what she had heard. She put out her hand, and felt the smooth, low pillow—then slowly her fingers travelled down, and to her intense surprise she realised that the bed was empty, and that it had not been slept in that night.

Then she had made a mistake in thinking this room was Cristina's room? She stood and listened—there was not a sound to be heard now, an eerie silence filled the house.

She suddenly made up her mind she would do nothing till the morning. It would annoy the Countess were she to make a fuss now. Already Lily was a little afraid of Aunt Cosy. If her money was indeed gone, then it was gone! Nothing they could do at this time of night would be of any use.

She walked gropingly across to the door, her eyes by now accustomed to the darkness, and so into the passage. Pushing open her own door, she quietly shut it. Then she went over to her window and, parting the curtains, took a deep draught of the delicious southern night air. It was extraordinarily and uncannily still and dark on that side of La Solitude.

She lay down and was soon in a deep, if troubled sleep.

When Lily Fairfield awoke the next morning she experienced the curious sensation of not knowing in the least where she was. What strange, bare, gloomy room was this? The very little she could see of it was illuminated by a shaft of dull morning light filtering through the top of the heavy velvet and silk curtains drawn across the window. To the left of the door was a long, low walnut-wood chest. With an inward tremor she told herself that it was like a coffin.

And then, all at once, she remembered everything! This was her bedroom at La Solitude—and yesterday had been the beginning of what ought to be quite an exciting and interesting experience.

All that had happened last evening came back to her with a rush. Her introduction to that rather rough Mr. George Ponting, who had yet been so kindly, so respectful, in his manner to her. She smiled and sighed a little as she thought of how hurt he had been at her refusing the beautiful little gold box. What sort of girl would get that box? she wondered.

Then she went over her strange experience of last night, or was it early this morning? It did not seem quite so real now as it had been then. Perhaps she had only fancied that one of the long drawing-room windows had been opened in the night?

She began to wonder at what time M. Popeau and Captain Stuart would come today. She did hope Countess Polda and her new friends would get on together. Somehow she doubted it—they were so very different!

She jumped up and pulled open the curtains. What a pity this room had only a view of the small courtyard below and of the bare hillside above! But she was not likely to spend much time in her bedroom.

During the last two years Lily had always got up extremely early because of her war work. She turned towards the travelling clock which she had put on the mantelpiece. Ten o'clock? Impossible! It must have stopped last night—but no, it was ticking away as usual. How dreadful that she should have so overslept herself! Dreadful, and yet, after all, natural, after all those days of travel.

And then she looked at the glass, the contents of which she had not drunk the night before. There was a white sediment at the bottom of the water. She told herself that perhaps the one thing in common between The Nest and La Solitude was that they were both built on chalk.

She wondered where the bathroom could be. Putting on her dressing-gown, she opened her bedroom door. The passage was full of sunlight—a curious contrast to her room.

The only open door besides her own was that just opposite. She peeped into it. It was a little empty slip of a room. It had seemed so big last night in the darkness.

She ran down to the kitchen. Cristina was sitting at a little table, drinking a cup of coffee.

As the door opened, the old woman jumped up with a curious look of apprehension and unease on her face. Then she smiled a rather wan smile. "Ah, Mademoiselle!" she exclaimed. "You startled me. Would you like a cup of coffee? If so, I will bring it up to you in a few minutes."

"I only want to know where the bathroom is," said Lily.

Cristina looked at her uncomfortably. "Does Mademoiselle really want a bath?" she asked. "Mademoiselle looks so clean!"

And then, for the first time since she had been at La Solitude, Lily laughed a hearty, ringing, girlish laugh, and Cristina put her fingers to her lips. "Take care," she murmured, "or you will wake *them*."

She opened the door of what Lily had supposed the day before to be that of the scullery. It led straight out on to the small walled courtyard into which the window of her bedroom looked down. She followed Cristina across the courtyard to what looked like a sort of outhouse. The old woman took up her bunch of keys and unlocked the large double door. Then she motioned the girl to go in.

Lily looked about her with considerable curiosity. Surely Cristina could not expect her to have her bath *here*? And yet—yet there *was* a long, narrow zinc bath in a corner of the whitewashed building.

Close to where they were now standing—not far, that is, from the door—was a peculiar-looking trolley, of which the four tyred bicycle wheels were so large that they came above the top of the quaint-looking vehicle.

Cristina gave a slight push to this odd-looking object, and it rolled back noiselessly.

"What a very droll-looking thing!" exclaimed Lily.

"It is droll but useful," said Cristina slowly. "It can be used for transporting anything. The Count uses it in the garden sometimes—it is very easy to move about."

The old woman walked across to the corner of the room where stood the narrow zinc bath, and then Lily saw that above one end of it was a cold-water tap.

"This is the only fixed bath in the villa," said Cristina apologetically. "It was installed on the occasion of Count Beppo's stay here two years ago. He was very angry that there was no bathroom on the English system. So the Countess had this put in to pacify him! But he never used it. He moved instead to an hotel."

Seeing Lily's look of surprise and dismay, she added quietly, "Perhaps Mademoiselle will not take a bath this morning?"

"Oh, yes, I must have a bath!" exclaimed Lily. "But tomorrow I'll ask you to let me make a good lot of boiling water in the kitchen."

"It would be possible to make water hot here," said Cristina hesitatingly.

And Lily saw that there was a little stove not far from the bath. She went up to the stove to look at it more closely, and then she put out her hand and touched it. "Why, it's hot!" she said in a startled voice. "There must have been a fire here this morning!"

Cristina grew faintly red. "No," she said, "not this morning—last night. But please do not mention it to Madame la Comtesse, Mademoiselle. I had a good deal of rubbish, and it is impossible to burn much in that tiny kitchen—" she was now speaking in a quick, agitated voice.

"Yes, I can well believe that," said Lily. The stove, unluckily for her, was only warm, the fire had gone quite out. "I will make a fire now," said Cristina, "and bring out a pot of water."

"No, don't trouble to do that. I'll manage all right this morning."

"Then I will bring Mademoiselle a towel." And bring one she did, but it had a big hole in it.

And then, after she had performed her toilet under somewhat difficult circumstances, Lily went into the kitchen and enjoyed a big bowl of *café-au-lait*.

"I suppose there is an English church in Monte Carlo?" she asked hesitatingly.

And Cristina said: "I hope Mademoiselle will not go out alone this morning—it would make Madame la Comtesse angry if she did so."

"Very well. I'll sit on the terrace in the sun and be lazy," said Lily.

Cristina came and unlocked the front door, and Lily walked round on to the terrace. The drawing-room doors were closely shut and the blinds were down. Surely she must have *dreamt* what had seemed to happen last night? But, alas! she had only been out there a very few moments when she heard loud exclamations of concern and surprise. It was the Countess talking rapidly and excitedly, by turns in French, English, and Italian. Mingling with her agitated accents were the more guttural tones of Uncle Angelo.

Lily sprang up from the basket chair on which she had been sitting and, turning round, through the now open long French window she saw the Count, the Countess, and Cristina all standing together in the drawing-room round the ebony and ivory cabinet.

As soon as she saw Lily the Countess called out: "A terrible thing has happened, my poor child! This room was entered in the night—the lock of the cabinet was forced—everything in it taken! Oh, why did Angelo put your fifty pounds there, instead of taking it up to his room, where it would have been so safe?"

The Countess was actually wringing her hands. She seemed almost beside herself with distress. As for Cristina, the tears were rolling down her cheeks; she looked the picture of utter woe. The Count appeared the least disturbed of the three—but he was rubbing his hands nervously, and muttering to himself.

Yes, it was only too true! One of the doors of the beautiful inlaid cabinet had been wrenched off its hinges; it lay on the floor. As for the drawer into which she had seen Uncle Angelo place her little bundle of five-pound notes, the thief, in his haste, had stuck it in again anyhow, wrong side up. Yes, another drawer lay on the floor with papers scattered round it.

"They took some of the family documents—not all; so far that is good," said Uncle Angelo at last.

"Would they had taken them all, precious as they are, and left our poor little Lily's money intact!"

"Of course, it's a misfortune," said Lily ruefully. "But never mind, Aunt Cosy. It can't be helped. I didn't even keep the numbers of the notes, so I'm afraid there's no hope of our ever being able to recover them. The police court at Epsom is always shut on Sundays, and I suppose it's the same here?"

No one answered this remark.

"I cannot understand when it happened!" exclaimed the Countess. She turned sternly to Cristina. "Did you oversleep yourself?" she asked accusingly.

"*I* know when it happened," said Lily. And then she told the Countess of her experience of the night before.

"Thank God you did nothing!" said the Count in French, and he really did look agitated at last. "The brigands might have shot you, had you given the alarm!"

As for Cristina, she sat down and, with a dreadful groan, threw her apron over her head and began rocking herself backwards and forwards.

"Be quiet, Cristina!" cried the Countess sharply. But the Count went up to his foster-sister, and patted her kindly on the head.

"You must come to me when you want a little money, dear child," said the Countess, turning to Lily. "Perhaps generous Tom Fairfield will send you another fifty pounds when he hears of your loss?"

"He won't hear of my loss for some time," said Lily, "for he is leaving England today for the West Indies. But never mind, Aunt Cosy. I've got a letter of credit on the bank here."

The face of the Countess cleared, and even Uncle Angelo looked round at her, quite an eager look on his fat face.

"I'm very glad to hear that," said the Countess heartily. "Tom is a very generous man. There is nothing low or mean about him."

"He is goodness itself!" said Lily. And then she added a little shyly: "But the money is really mine, Aunt Cosy. Since my twenty-first birthday, which was the tenth of last July, I've had my own banking account. As a matter of fact, Uncle Tom wanted to give me a present, but he didn't quite know what to get, so he gave me the fifty pounds."

"Angelo! See whether among your tools you cannot find something that will at any rate temporarily restore our poor cabinet," said Aunt Cosy briskly.

"As for you and I, dear child, we will go out for a little turn in the garden."

The little turn consisted in Lily and the Countess walking up and down the lawn for half an hour.

For the first time Aunt Cosy asked Lily all kinds of questions about poor Aunt Emmeline's illness and death—also as to whether she, Aunt Emmeline, had been a woman of means—whether she had left dear Lily a legacy—whether The Nest belonged to Uncle Tom, as also the furniture—and finally, whether Uncle Tom was likely to marry again? This last question shocked Lily, but it was evidently a very natural one from the speaker's point of view.

And then, all at once, the Countess exclaimed: "And how about Miss Rosa Fairfield? Is she still living?"

"Oh yes!" Lily laughed. "Cousin Rosa is very much alive, though she's over eighty. She leads that dull, quiet life so many very old people like to live. She much disapproved of my coming abroad; she wanted me to go and spend the winter with *her*."

"I wonder you did not do it," said the Countess thoughtfully. "Miss Rosa must be very rich."

"Yes," said Lily. "Cousin Rosa is certainly very rich. But I should have become melancholy mad—living that sort of life!"

There was a pause. "And who will get her money?" asked the Countess.

Lily hesitated a moment—then, "I believe—in fact I know, for she told Uncle Tom so three or four years ago—that I am to have most of it, Aunt Cosy."

"*You. Lily Fairfield?*"

There was an extraordinary accent of surprise, excitement, and gratification in Aunt Cosy's vibrant voice.

She stopped in her vigorous walk and turned and faced the girl. "Oh, you English?" she exclaimed. "How unemotional and cold you are! You do not show the slightest joy or excitement when telling this wonderful news. Why, Miss Rosa Fairfield must have—how much?" As Lily said nothing, the Countess went on: "A hundred thousand pounds—that is what poor Emmeline told me!"

"Yes, I believe she has quite that."

"And you do not feel excited?" The Countess Polda gazed searchingly at the now flushed girl.

"I suppose I should have felt excited if I'd suddenly learnt the fact," said Lily slowly; "But I've always known it—in a sort of way. I remember when I was quite a little girl hearing Aunt Rosa say to Uncle Tom that she thought she ought to be consulted about what school I was to be sent to, as I was to be her heiress. But I think Uncle Tom didn't feel quite sure about it till two or three years ago. She sent for him on purpose to read him her will."

"And what is your fortune apart from that, dear child?" asked the Countess abruptly.

It was rather an indiscreet thing to ask, but Lily had a straightforward nature, and, after all, she saw no reason for trying to parry the question. She had always heard that foreigners were very inquisitive.

"My father left me eight thousand pounds," she said quietly. "But Uncle Tom would never take any of the interest of it for my education. He paid for everything, just as if I had been his daughter. So I have got a little over ten thousand pounds now—you see, my parents died when I was such a little child and the money was very cleverly invested."

"Ah, yes, poor little thing!" exclaimed the Countess affectionately. "Well, even that is a pretty fortune for a young girl!"

She waited a moment as if making a calculation. "That would bring in— yes, if well invested—not far from fifteen thousand francs a year, if I am right. Then you have the enjoyment of that now, dear child?"

"Yes," said Lily, "I suppose I have."

"No wonder you took the disappearance of the fifty pounds in so philosophical a manner!" the Countess laughed rather harshly.

They walked on a few steps. And then Aunt Cosy said suddenly: "You should not tell people of this money, Lily. I hope you do not talk freely to strangers?"

And then the girl did feel a little offended. "I've never spoken of my money matters to any living soul till today," she said with some vehemence. "And I shouldn't have said anything to you, Aunt Cosy, if you hadn't asked me!"

"Ah, but it was right for me to know. I am your guardian for the moment. You have been entrusted to me. In Monte Carlo there are many—now what are they called in England? We have an expression of the kind in Italy, and there is yet another in France, but it is not so good as the English expression—"

"What expression is that?" asked Lily.

"*Fortune-hunters*," said Aunt Cosy grimly.

"Fortune-hunters are not likely to come across my path," the girl laughed gaily.

"No, not while you are at La Solitude."

The Countess smiled, showing her large, good teeth, which somehow looked false—so even, so strong, so well matched in colour were they. But they were all her own.

As at last they turned to go into the house, the Countess said suddenly: "Another Sunday, my dear Lily, I should like you to go to the English service. It is the proper thing to do."

Lily felt rather taken aback. "I thought of going this morning," she said frankly, "but Cristina seemed to think you would be annoyed if I went off alone to try and find the place by myself."

"I will see in the guide-book if there is an afternoon service," said the Countess hesitatingly. "Your Uncle Angelo might escort you as far as the door of the hotel where the English clergyman now officiates. I should not like you to walk about Monte Carlo alone."

There was a pause. "I think M. Popeau and Captain Stuart are coming today," said Lily at last. She could not keep herself from blushing a little.

"Captain Stuart?" echoed the Countess sharply. "And who, pray, is Captain Stuart?"

By this time Lily had become rather tired of Aunt Cosy's constant questions. "He is a friend of mine," she said quietly. "Perhaps he won't come, but M. Popeau said he meant to do so—don't you remember, Aunt Cosy?"

"Yes, I remember now. Well, he seems a very good sort of man—" She spoke with a touch of condescension in her voice. "And he must be rich, or he would not be staying at the Hôtel de Paris."

Lily could not help smiling a little satirically to herself. Aunt Cosy's love of money jarred upon her. It reminded her of the story of the man who, when his wife asked him to call on some people, giving as a reason that they were very rich, answered: "I would, my dear, if it were catching!"

Aunt Cosy, perhaps, thought that wealth *was* catching.

CHAPTER 6

Lily's first real luncheon at La Solitude consisted of the remains of last night's excellent, almost luxurious supper. But a rough-looking, unbleached tablecloth had taken the place of the beautiful lace one, and the fine cut-glass decanters had disappeared from the sideboard.

They all three drank out of coarse, thick glass tumblers, and they ate off heavy yellow plates. But the food was of the best, and they all made a good and hearty meal—once, indeed, Aunt Cosy, looking affectionately at the girl, exclaimed: "Yes, do not stint yourself, my little Lily, for we have to live as a rule exceedingly simply. It is a strange fact"—a hard tone came into her voice—"that Cristina has never learnt to cook. Even I can cook better than Cristina!"

She looked at her husband as she spoke, and he, glancing up, observed in French: "She does well enough. We have to buy cooked food, as fuel is so dear."

"Yes," said the Countess crossly, "but fuel was not always dear. And Cristina always cooked badly." She turned to Lily: "I had thought of asking you if you knew a little simple cooking—the delicious milk puddings that I used to have at The Nest long years ago even now make my mouth water, as you so funnily say in England. They are nutritious, and at the same time cheap. But they do not teach English girls to do such useful things."

"Indeed they do!" answered Lily, smiling. "I'll cook you a rice pudding tonight, if you like, Aunt Cosy, though I don't know if I shall be able to brown the top properly as you haven't got an oven!"

"No, no, I do not want you to roughen those pretty hands before Beppo arrives," observed the Countess. Then, all at once, she broke into rapid French: "I am explaining to our little friend that I want her to look her best when Beppo arrives."

"Beppo?" queried the Count. "But Beppo is not coming, that I know of, before the end of January?"

"Oh yes, he is! He is coming very soon. I heard from him today."

Lily felt surprised, for Cristina had told her that morning that there were no postal deliveries on Sunday at La Solitude.

They all three got up and went back into the drawing-room, and at once the Count walked over to the card-table and, sitting down, started on his Patience again.

"And now what will *you* do?" said the Countess hesitatingly, turning to Lily.

"I will go into the kitchen, Aunt Cosy, and help Cristina to wash up," said the girl.

"But take care of those pretty hands!" The warning was uttered very seriously.

Poor Lily! She could not help rather regretting her offer. At home there had been gallons of hot water, nice clean teacloths—everything, in a word, required for the tiresome process known as washing-up. But Cristina simply piled everything into a basin full of tepid water, then she rubbed each plate with a dirty-looking little mop, and finally handed each plate and dish to Lily to dry with what looked like a rather worn old towel!

Suddenly Lily realised that the towel she was using to wipe the plates was the very towel, with a hole in it, with which she had dried herself with such very mixed feelings in the outhouse this morning! It almost made the gently nurtured English girl feel sick; and yet what could she say or do? Cristina evidently saw nothing wrong in it. And it was a fact—to Lily rather a shocking fact—that the plates looked perfectly clean after having been submitted to this disgusting process.

All at once Cristina crept up close to her—it was such a quick, stealthy movement that it startled Lily.

"Listen," said the old woman. "Listen, Mademoiselle! You must insist on having enough to eat! You are paying one hundred and twenty-five francs a week. I know it; for the Countess had to tell me. So do not let her starve you!"

"Oh, I'm sure she wouldn't do that!" said Lily.

She smiled, but deep in her heart she was grateful to old Cristina. "What am I to say?" she whispered back.

"You are to say that you must have two eggs and two cutlets every day—also two large glassfuls of milk," said Cristina quickly.

"But surely there will be plenty of food when Count Beppo arrives?" said Lily.

Cristina shook her head. "The young Count is not coming till after New Year," she said.

"Oh yes, he is! The Countess told us at luncheon that she had heard from him today, and that he was coming very much sooner—perhaps in a week or ten days."

Cristina looked extremely surprised. Then she said suddenly: "Even so, speak today, Mademoiselle. Why be short of food for ten days?"

A dozen questions sprang to the girl's lips. But she did not wish to discuss her host and hostess with even the most trusted and best-liked servant. Even so, she made up her mind to take Cristina's advice, and to tell Aunt

Cosy courteously but firmly that she had been used at home to good plain food, and, further, that the doctor had said she required feeding up.

* * * *

Lily had only half-written her first letter to Uncle Tom when she heard the front-door bell echo through the house. She had not heard that bell ring since M. Popeau had pulled the rusty iron bell-pull on her first arrival at La Solitude, for their last night's visitor had come up through the orange grove and across the lawn. The front door seemed to be scarcely ever used.

She got up and opening her door, waited for quite a little while. No doubt it was M. Popeau and Captain Stuart? She was astonished at her own keen pleasure, and, yes, relief, at the idea of seeing her two kind friends again. And then, when there came another peal, she made up her mind to run downstairs. She could not help feeling that Aunt Cosy was not at all anxious to continue her slight acquaintance with M. Popeau. It would be dreadful, *dreadful*, if Cristina had been told to say "Not at home."

At the bottom of the staircase a door was open, giving access to a room Lily had not yet seen. It was evidently the Countess's own sitting-room. But there was a big writing-table near the window, and it looked more like a man's study than a lady's boudoir.

The Countess was standing not far from the door, with a very singular expression on her face. She appeared startled, even frightened, as also did Cristina, who was standing close to her. They both looked up when they heard the girl's light footsteps on the uncarpeted stairs. "Shall Mademoiselle answer the door?" Lily heard Cristina whisper.

"I think it must be M. Popeau and Captain Stuart," said Lily a little nervously.

"Of course! How foolish of me not to have thought of them!"

The Countess's face cleared, her look of anxiety was succeeded by one of relief. "Run, Cristina! Run and open the door to the two English gentlemen. What will they think of us keeping them waiting like this?" Then she turned to the girl: "I have no tea in the house, but you have some tea, I know, Lily. Will you give a little to Cristina?"

"It's so early—only three o'clock. I don't think they'll want tea now," said the girl smiling. She was feeling extraordinarily pleased at the thought of seeing her two travelling companions again.

But alas the visit was a disappointment to Lily.

They all five sat in a formal circle round the empty grate of the stuffy salon for some time, and Lily had no opportunity of exchanging a word alone with the visitors. M. Popeau talked a great deal, in fact at one moment he even out-talked the Countess. He answered her many questions as to life in war-time Paris with the utmost frankness and good humour; and he carelessly brought into his conversation the names of many well-known Parisians, all, it appeared, good friends of his. As he had intended should happen, his hostess's respect for him visibly grew.

But when the genial Frenchman threw out a suggestion that Miss Fairfield should come back with him and with Captain Stuart to spend an hour at the Casino, the Countess shook her head.

"No, no," she exclaimed. "Nice English people do not gamble on Sunday, M. Popeau! I should have thought that even you would have known that, speaking such beautiful English as you do. I seldom go down the hill. But soon my son will be here, and he will escort Miss Fairfield where I myself may not go. My son is an Italian, so he can do as he likes when he comes here; he can even go to the Club and play—to my regret. But his father cannot do so, being a native of the Principality!"

At last the Countess turned her attention to Captain Stuart, and it is not too much to say that she riddled her younger visitor with questions. How long had he been a soldier? In which of the battles of the war had he fought? Where exactly had he been wounded? How much money did a British captain earn? Was he an only child, or had he brothers and sisters? Were his parents still alive, and in what part of Scotland did they live?

All these somewhat indiscreet questions Captain Stuart answered with composure. But finally, when the Countess, looking at him searchingly, suddenly asked how long he had known Miss Fairfield, Lily was astonished to hear him answer thoughtfully: "It seems a lifetime to me since I first met Miss Fairfield." But after he had made this surprising answer, he looked across at Lily, and she saw a funny little twinkle in his eye.

A break occurred when Cristina opened the door noiselessly and announced that *gouter* was quite ready.

The whole party went off to the dining-room, where, Lily saw with amazement, the splendours of the night before had been restored. Once more the lace tablecloth was spread out on the round table, once more the fruit was piled on the beautiful high crystal dishes, and now there were five old painted china teacups set out in a semi-circle. The only incongruous touch was that the tea had been made in a fine old silver coffee-pot.

"Will you pour out the tea, dear child?" said the Countess suavely. "That is a task we always delegate to young ladies," she said, turning to M. Popeau. "In England the old wait upon the young. But that is not right."

Lily poured out some of the straw-coloured liquid into each of the cups. Both M. Popeau and Uncle Angelo took three lumps of sugar; Captain Stuart took none. As for the Countess, she declared she would not have any tea at all.

And then, at last, having spent altogether a little over an hour at La Solitude, the two visitors prepared to depart. Lily and the Count walked down with them through the garden, the Countess having decided that she would stay in the house. And then, for the first time, Lily and Captain Stuart were able to exchange a few words.

"Can't you give your aunt the slip and come off with us now, just as you are?" he asked in a low voice.

Lily shook her head. "Aunt Cosy would never forgive me! She'd be awfully shocked if I were to do that after what she said."

"I suppose she would," said the young man reluctantly. "Still, she can't keep you cooped up here all the time. Do make her understand that in England girls go about by themselves, Miss Fairfield."

"I'll try and make her understand it," said Lily, smiling, "but it won't be easy. She's *tremendously* determined."

"I can see that. I hope they're nice to you?" he added a little anxiously. And he looked at her with one of the quick, shrewd looks to which she had become accustomed during their long journey together.

But this time there was something added—a something which made Lily's heart beat. She asked herself inconsequently what exactly he had meant when he said that he felt as if he had known her a lifetime? But all she said was:

"They are very kind to me in their own way, and I think I'm going to be quite happy here."

Twice, while she and the young man had been talking apart together, she had seen Uncle Angelo look towards them uncomfortably, hesitatingly, almost as if he thought he ought to cut across their conversation.

"Can't you come down for a game of tennis early tomorrow morning? Do! I could come and fetch you any time you fix."

Perhaps M. Popeau heard the whispered invitation, for he said to Uncle Angelo: "By the way, it has suddenly occurred to me, could not you and Mademoiselle lunch with me tomorrow?"

The Count hesitated. It was clear that he was very much tempted to accept. "I'm not certain about my wife's plans," he said at last, "so I fear I must refuse your kind invitation this time."

"Captain Stuart has to go to Milan for a few days, and I am giving myself the pleasure of accompanying him. But we shall certainly be back by next Sunday," said M. Popeau amiably.

Lily felt curiously taken aback—indeed, sharply disappointed. The thought that her late fellow-travellers were going to be away for something like a week filled her with dismay.

She had known vaguely about this proposed trip of Captain Stuart's, for during their journey he had asked M. Popeau about the trains from Monte Carlo to Milan, explaining that he had a relation living there who had asked him to come over and see him. But at that time Captain Stuart had been a stranger to her—now she felt as if he was an old friend!

Perhaps something of what she was feeling showed in her face, for the Scotsman said suddenly: "I don't really want to go to Milan this week, Popeau. Why shouldn't I wire and say I will come later on?"

But M. Popeau shook his head decidedly.

"You forget, my friend, that all arrangements have been made. I do not think that we can make any change now."

"Well, well," said the Count easily. "I shall look forward to seeing you again, messieurs, in about ten days' time. Meanwhile, my young niece can have a real rest. She has been ill, and must not over-exert herself. There will be plenty of time to show her the sights of Monte Carlo after you return."

They were standing round the little gate which formed the boundary of the property of La Solitude, and after shaking hands, English fashion, with Captain Stuart and M. Popeau, the Count and Lily slowly made their way up to the house again.

The Countess was waiting for them, rather impatiently, in the salon. And then all at once Lily summoned up courage to say very quietly but very firmly: "I'm afraid, Aunt Cosy, you'll have to become accustomed to my going about by myself. You see, I'm not a French girl but an English girl. I simply couldn't stay in a house where I didn't feel free to come and go."

"But of course you're free!" exclaimed the Countess. "Absolutely free, dear child. I regret not having allowed you to go out this afternoon with M. Popeau and your old friend, Captain Stuart, but I did not think you would like to do what English people do at Monte Carlo on Sundays."

"I did not want to go to the Casino," said Lily, firmly. "But I do want to join the tennis club, and to have a good game now and again. I suppose you know some lady who would put me up, Aunt Cosy?"

The Countess hadn't the slightest idea of what Lily meant by being "put up," but she nodded amiably.

"Oh, yes," she said, "I will certainly find some lady. Meanwhile your Uncle Angelo will take you down to Monte Carlo tomorrow morning, just to show you the way. He has purchases to make, and he will be able to see about the tennis. It is, so I understand, quite a young girl's game."

"That Parisian asked me to lunch tomorrow; he desired Lily to come too," interposed the Count.

"Oh, I do not think you can do that, my friend," said the Countess decidedly. "I wish you to help with several important matters tomorrow. You can go some other day."

"He and the Englishman are going away to Italy for a few days."

"Are they indeed?" said the Countess, indifferently. She hesitated—"I would like to ask you what is perhaps a very indiscreet question, my sweet child," and she fixed her bright, differently-coloured eyes full on Lily.

"Yes, Aunt Cosy?" The girl looked up.

"I suppose you are not what is called in England 'engaged'?" asked Aunt Cosy, very deliberately.

The colour flamed up in Lily's cheeks. "No, I am not engaged, Aunt Cosy."

There was a curious pause, and then the Countess went on: "When you are writing to your uncle, dear girl, I hope you will tell him that we are doing our best to make you happy"—there was a pleading, almost an anxious, tone in her voice.

"Of course I will!" said Lily affectionately.

She felt, as she expressed it to herself, "rather a pig" for having stood up to the Countess. She was astonished too, at her easy victory. Aunt Emmeline had been so very different! *She* would never give in if she thought a thing wrong. Lily could not help reflecting that the five pounds a week must mean a great deal to Count and Countess Polda. She could see that they were both painfully anxious that she should stay on at La Solitude, and be happy and comfortable there.

* * * *

A week can pass like a flash, or it can seem an eternity. The first week of Lily Fairfield's stay at La Solitude was, truth to tell, more like a month, and a very long month, than a week. She did her best to feel happy and comfortable, though it was a strange kind of life for a girl used to all the cheerful comings and goings of an English country town. After she had helped Cristina with the housework each morning there was absolutely nothing left to do during the rest of the day.

Twice during that long week Lily accompanied the Count into Monte Carlo, or rather into that part of the Principality which lies in a hollow between Monaco and Monte Carlo, and which is called the Condamine. While there, they had spent the whole of their time shopping in the funny little native shops, the Count bargaining as if the question of a few sous was of the utmost moment to him.

The second time they went down the hill, she asked Uncle Angelo to show her where the English service was held each Sunday, and it was then that he offered to show her the English bank. Indeed, the only time she was allowed to go to Monte Carlo by herself was when she suggested that she should pay the Countess four weeks in advance.

It had seemed strange at first to be walking all alone in a foreign town, but she had managed quite well, and the famous bankers had been very courteous to their pretty new client. The gentleman to whom she had given her letter of credit had shaken his head when she had told him about the unfortunate theft of fifty pounds, but he had not been as surprised as she had been that the police had not been told about it.

"It would have been sheer waste of time, my dear young lady," he said smiling, "and would have only exposed your relations to a great deal of worry. A visit from the police always entails a great deal of fuss and unpleasantness on the Continent."

During the same little expedition Lily bought, at a very big price, six wicker chairs and a little outdoor table as a present to Aunt Cosy; and to her relief the Countess seemed delighted with the gift. As the days went on it became increasingly clear to Lily Fairfield that either the Count and Countess Polda were very poor, or very mean. They were always trying to save a sou here and a sou there; they were extraordinarily fond, too, of talking about money.

One rather surprising, and, yes, exciting, thing happened to Lily during that long, dull first week at La Solitude.

Captain Stuart wrote her three longish letters. They were simple, informal, pleasant letters, telling her something of how Milan had struck him, and how grateful he was to good-natured M. Popeau. But though they were in a sense quite ordinary epistles, they gave the girl pleasure, and made her feel less lonely.

But when the second letter came Lily could not help having an uncomfortable suspicion that it had been steamed open and then closed down again. She hated herself for suspecting such a thing, but she had already come to the conclusion that Aunt Cosy was sly and, when it suited her, very unscrupulous.

Now, it is an unfortunate fact that slyness always breeds slyness. Lily had a frank, open, straightforward nature; but, then, she had always been treated by Uncle Tom and Aunt Emmeline in a frank, open, straightforward way. Neither of them would have dreamt of opening one of her letters! Had they thought she was carrying on an unsuitable correspondence they would have taxed her with it at once, and Aunt Emmeline might have gone so far as to forbid her to receive letters from a correspondent of whom she did not approve. But it would all have been frank and above board.

Henceforth Lily took good care to be up when the postman came to the door, and so, when Captain Stuart's third letter arrived on the Saturday morning, it was handed to her direct. In this last letter the Scotsman told her that he hoped to see her at the English Church service on Sunday morning.

That was all. And yet it cast a glow of pleasure over the whole of that long, dull Saturday. It was hot and airless, even up at La Solitude, and in the night there was a terrific storm of thunder, wind, and rain.

CHAPTER 7

Lily got up the next morning feeling very happy and cheerful. Not only were kindly M. Popeau and her new friend Captain Stuart now back in Monte Carlo, but Beppo Polda's arrival was definitely fixed for the following Tuesday. His mother talked of him incessantly, and was evidently exceedingly anxious to make his visit a success.

Lily could not help feeling touched by Aunt Cosy's wonderful love of, and pride in, her son, and, as she got ready to start for church, the girl told herself that it would be amusing to see Beppo after having heard so much about him. And then, all at once, she asked herself, blushing a little, how Beppo Polda would get on with Angus Stuart! They were certain to be very different!

"When Beppo is here you will be very gay!" the Countess had exclaimed the night before. "I do not care for Monte Carlo. But you and Uncle Angelo will be there a great deal. Beppo knows all the smart set in London and in Paris as well as in Rome! I hope you have brought some pretty clothes with you, dear child. If not, perhaps it would be well to purchase one or two new dresses, eh?"

"Yes, perhaps I ought to get a few things," said Lily smiling. "I've hardly had anything new since the war. At first I felt it to be wrong; later on everything became so dear!"

"You will not find anything very cheap here," said Aunt Cosy, shaking her head.

And now, on this Sunday morning, she was sorry that she only had the plain black coat and skirt she had arrived in from London. Still, when she went into the kitchen, on her way out, Cristina looked up, and smiled at her very kindly. "Mademoiselle looks as fresh as a rose," she exclaimed.

"I'm going to church," said Lily. "Is there anything I can do for you in the town?"

And then Cristina said that she would be very grateful if Mademoiselle would do a little commission. Not in the town, but on the hill, at the cottage near the chapel where they sold her new-laid eggs. "Has Mademoiselle time to do this before going down to church?"

"Heaps of time," said Lily gaily, and then she added: "Now that my friends are back in Monte Carlo I hope I shall be able to join the tennis club, so you'll get rid of me sometimes, Cristina!"

And then Cristina said something which touched the English girl. "I shall miss you very much, my little lady. You are a ray of sunshine in this lonely house." And the old woman sighed, a long-drawn-out, mournful sigh.

* * * *

When Lily found herself on the rough path leading upwards towards the top of the great hill she was amazed at the destruction the storm had wrought. Even the sturdy olive trees had suffered, and the more delicate flowering bushes were beaten to the earth.

After doing her errand she walked on a few steps along the path across the mountain side. She felt tired of the road leading down past La Solitude, and so she made up her mind to go down by another way to the town. There was a rough, steep way cut into long, low steps—as is the fashion in those parts—which was bound to bring her not far from the hotel where the service was now held each Sunday morning.

After a while she realised that this new way of going down the hill would take her much longer than the old, familiar way. She glanced at her wrist watch. Though she had allowed herself plenty of time, she must hurry now, or she would be late.

She struck off to her left—intending to pick up the road which led straight down to Monte Carlo—into a beautiful, if obviously neglected, grove of orange trees. As she did so she realised that she had not got nearly so far down the hill as she had supposed, for she was only just below the little clearing where the taxi had stopped on her first arrival at La Solitude.

And then, while walking along a narrow path through a plantation of luxuriant bushes, Lily suddenly experienced what is sometimes described as one's heart stopping still.

Right in front of her, barring her way, there lay on the still wet earth an arm—stretching right across the path.

She stopped and stared, fearfully, at the stark, still, outstretched arm and hand lying just before her. The sleeve clothing the arm was sodden; the cuff which slightly protruded beyond the sleeve was now a pale, dirty grey; the hand was clenched.

All at once she saw the glint of gold just below the cuff, and she remembered, with a feeling of sick dread, the bangle which George Ponting had worn just a week and a night ago!

She did not turn and run away, as another kind of girl might have done. Instead she covered her face for a moment with her hands, and then forced herself to look again.

At last she stooped down, and then she saw that the arm belonging to a body which was mercifully half-concealed from her terror-stricken gaze by a large broken branch.

The deathly still, huddled-up figure had evidently rolled over forward during the storm from under the shelter of a big spreading bush.

She drew a little nearer, full of an awful feeling of repulsion, as well as of fear. And then she noticed that a small automatic pistol was lying on the coarse grass near the body.

Did that mean that the unhappy man had killed himself? Nay, it was far more likely, so the girl told herself, that he had been set on by the same gang who had broken into La Solitude the very night he had been there.

There was no sign of a struggle, but then the storm of the night before would have obliterated any traces of that sort. In the bright, clear sunlight the raindrops still glistened on the evergreen leaves; it was not only a beautiful but a very peaceful scene.

Again she forced herself to stoop down and look, and then tears welled up slowly into her eyes; it seemed so piteous that what was huddled up there should have once been a man—a man, too, who had seemed so full of life, even of a kind of bubbling vitality, only a few days ago.

She stood up, faced with a disagreeable personal problem. Ought she to go back to La Solitude and tell the Count and Countess Polda of her horrible discovery? Or would she be justified in going on straight down to the town, and first informing the two men who seemed so much more truly her friends than did Aunt Cosy and Uncle Angelo?

M. Popeau was always so helpful in an emergency. Surely he would know what to do far better than either the Count or Countess? They would probably be very glad to be relieved of whatever might be the necessary steps in such a case as this.

As she had been the first person to find the body, Lily naturally supposed that she would have to see the police, and she knew that it would be less unpleasant to do that with M. Popeau than with her nervous, fussy host, or her strange-tempered hostess.

She walked quickly upwards, to find herself, as she had expected to do, on the little clearing. From there she knew every step of the way down into Monte Carlo. So she hurried on, still feeling terribly shaken and upset, though much more at ease, now that she had made up her mind as to what she ought to do.

* * * *

As Lily approached the hotel where the English Church service was always held, she noticed that people were walking up to the door, reading a notice that had been pinned up on it, and then turning away. The notice explained that as the chaplain was ill there would be no service that morning.

A deep, low voice suddenly sounded in her ears, "Good morning, Miss Fairfield."

Such commonplace words! Yet as Captain Stuart held out his hand, for the second time today the tears welled up into Lily's eyes. But this time it was because there had come over her a sensation of such infinite relief. Somehow she felt as if the man before her was a bit of home, and she realised how dreadfully lonely and forlorn she had been since they had last met.

As for Angus Stuart, he was looking at Lily with concern. She looked ill—very ill! She was pale, and there was a look of terror on her face. What could have happened? A feeling of positive hatred for the Count and Countess Polda rose up in the young man's mind. What could they have done to make the girl look as she was looking this morning?

"Is anything the matter?" he asked abruptly.

Lily pulled herself together. "Forgive me!" she exclaimed. "It's stupid of me to be so upset. But something dreadful has happened to me this morning! I'll tell you about it, and then you will be able to advise me as to whether I ought to go to the police—now, at once. I also thought of asking M. Popeau what I had better do."

"Tell me what happened," he said quietly. "We will go and find Popeau presently. He's taking a little constitutional up and down outside the Hôtel de Paris."

And then Lily told him shortly and quietly of her awful discovery in the orange grove.

Angus Stewart was greatly surprised as well as concerned at her story. Then had done the Count and Countess Polda an injustice? They were in no way responsible for the way Lily Fairfield looked this morning.

"D'you mean that you've no doubt that the poor fellow you found today was the man who was dining at La Solitude the night you arrived?" he asked.

The fact struck him with fresh surprise. What odd people Count Polda must know! He had very little doubt in his own mind that the unfortunate Ponting had committed suicide after a big loss at the Casino.

"I think I can say that I am quite sure," she answered, in a troubled voice. "But I confess I didn't look at—at the face. In fact, I tried not to see it! Oh, Captain Stuart, I feel as if I shall never, never get that hand—that cuff—that bangle—out of my mind! I seem to see the poor fellow's arm lying across the path, as if barring my way—"

He saw that her eyes were fixed with a look of horror on the ground in front of her.

"Look here!" he exclaimed authoritatively. "That's quite wrong, Miss Fairfield—really wrong! Life is full of tragedy and unhappiness. I've seen some very terrible things in the last five years, and though I don't exactly want to forget them, I never allow my mind to dwell on them. It's morbid, as well as wrong! No doubt the poor man had lost heavily in the Rooms, and thought he would put an end to his troubles. But it was very selfish of him to go and do it there—in the garden of the people who seem to have been so kind to him."

"If he really did do it, he didn't do it exactly in their garden," she said in a low voice; "it was—oh, well, I should think quite thirty yards below the place where the grounds of La Solitude end. He chose the place so carefully that it might have been months before he would have been found, had it not been that I rather foolishly thought I should like to try and find a new way down into the town."

Somehow it was a comfort to Lily to find that Captain Stuart felt so sure Mr. Ponting had killed himself.

There was a pause. And then: "I feel better now that I've told you," said Lily in a low voice.

"That's right!" he exclaimed. "After all, we know that there are a certain number of suicides each year at Monte Carlo, though Popeau declares that there are much fewer than people believe."

They found the Frenchman walking up and down in front of the Hôtel de Paris, and Lily, troubled and upset though she was, told herself that she had never seen such a delightful scene! The palace-like white Casino, the brilliant-coloured flowers, the palms, the blue-green sea, made a delightful background to the groups of cheerful, prosperous-looking people who were walking about the big open space between the hotel and the Casino. It seemed like a scene on another planet compared to the hillside and the quiet, lonely house where she had spent the last week. But she could not help reminding herself that ten days ago poor George Ponting had probably formed part of this gay, carefree crowd.

"Welcome!" cried M. Popeau, in his hearty voice. "It seems a long time, Miss Fairfield, since I saw you. I hope that you are very well, and that all goes happily at La Solitude?"

"Miss Fairfield has just had a most painful experience," said Captain Stuart gravely. And then, in a few dry words, he told their French friend what had happened. But, perhaps because Lily again turned very pale, he made his story quite short.

Hearing the tale from another's lips, brought back what had happened with dreadful vividness to poor Lily. Her lips quivered.

"I suppose I ought to go straight to the police," she said nervously, "and I thought, M. Popeau, that perhaps you would not mind going with me?"

"Of course I will go with you." He spoke very feelingly and kindly. "Try not to think too much of this sad event, my dear young lady. There has always been that one black blot on this beautiful place."

He waved his hand towards the Casino. "Yonder is a monster which destroys the happiness of many while sometimes capriciously making the happiness of one. And now I suggest an early déjeuner. The Count and Countess cannot expect you back for another hour and a half at least. An English

Church service goes on for a long time. You will be more ready to face my old friend, the Commissioner of Police, after a good lunch!"

Lily knew that a very small luncheon was to have been kept for her, and she could not help looking forward to a good meal. Yet when it was put before her she felt suddenly as if she could not eat.

M. Popeau always sat at a delightful little table in one of the great windows of the famous restaurant, and all three were soon happily established there. But the kindly host saw with concern that poor Lily looked at the delicious *hors-d'oeuvres* with a kind of aversion.

He put out his hand and laid it lightly over hers. "Come, come," he said, and there was a touch of command in his voice, "this won't do! I should have starved to death a very long time ago if I had allowed the sad things I have seen and heard to stop my appetite!"

Lily could not help smiling at the funny way he said this, but, "What makes it so much worse," she said in a low voice, "is having actually known the poor man."

"What d'you say?" said M. Popeau in a startled voice. "Known the poor man? I didn't know that!"

"I forgot to tell you," interposed Captain Stuart, "that as a matter of fact, Miss Fairfield is convinced that the body she saw is that of an Englishman called Ponting who had dinner at La Solitude the evening of the day she arrived there, a week ago yesterday."

Lily turned her head away; the tears were now rolling down her cheeks.

"That certainly must have made the horrible discovery much worse for you," said M. Popeau sympathetically. "Did this Mr. Ponting seem at all worried or depressed, Mademoiselle?"

"No, I can't say that he did. We had a talk when he first arrived, for the Count and Countess left me alone with him for about ten minutes. Though he said he had lost a good bit of money, he didn't seem to mind. I remember his saying: 'I've done with Monte Carlo, and I've got off cheap, considering!'"

She felt it was too bad that she should spoil this pleasant lunch for her two kind friends. They all made a determined effort to talk of other things, and as the time went on, Lily unconsciously began to feel better.

"And how is my friend the Countess?" asked M. Popeau suddenly. "That woman interests me; I could not tell you why, but she seems to me a remarkable person—one with a tremendous amount of will power. I would not care to have been married to her! Hercules Popeau would have been a poor little bit of wax between her strong fingers."

The other two smiled, but he had meant what he said.

And then a feeling of loyalty to her hostess made Lily exclaim: "I think the Count is quite happy, M. Popeau. They seem devoted to one another, and just now they are extra happy—"

"Why that?" asked Captain Stuart drily.

"Because their son, who lives in Rome, is coming to pay them a visit. They simply worship him!" She added: "I'm quite looking forward to seeing him. According to the Countess, he's a most wonderful young man! He's a great athlete, and yet—" she hesitated, "though only twenty-seven, he did not fight. Is that not odd? His mother says he served Italy better by staying in Rome."

"Ah, an *embusqué*!" exclaimed M. Popeau.

"I hope not that!" said Lily.

"I should expect any child of hers to be exceptionally good-looking," went on the Frenchman reflectively.

"Would you?" Lily was rather surprised.

"Yes, for the Countess Polda must have been very handsome in her day."

"That's true!" exclaimed Lily. "When she came and stayed with us in England when I was a little girl, I remember thinking her the most beautiful person I had ever seen! But somehow—I don't know why—she looks very different now."

"It is a great art—that of knowing how to grow old gracefully," said M. Popeau sententiously. "The Countess does not possess that art. Only a very few women do possess it, my dear young lady. As you grow older do not forget the words of Hercules Popeau—every age has its own beauty. That is not an original remark; I believe it was first made by our great Napoleon when speaking of his mother, a very noble woman."

And then Lily, her new trouble for the moment out of her mind, went on: "The Countess says that she would like her son to marry an Englishwoman."

"Does she, indeed? and he is arriving here tomorrow?"

M. Popeau spoke with a touch of meaning in his voice, and the colour suddenly flamed up on Lily's face; yet she felt sure that Aunt Cosy had had no particular person in her mind when she had made that remark.

"What is the name of this prodigy?"

"Beppo Polda."

"Count Beppo Polda?" repeated the Frenchman. "I must try and find out something about this young gentleman, for I propose to do myself the honour of calling again on the Countess one day soon."

By this time they were drinking their coffee, and while the two men each enjoyed a liqueur, M. Popeau made Lily drink a second cup of coffee.

When she had finished he said; "Now, my dear young lady, we had better go and look up my friend Bouton. He will not like being disturbed on a Sunday, but I feel you will be more comfortable when you have seen him. I want you to forget this sad affair—to wipe it out of your mind completely."

He made a gesture in the air as if he was rubbing something out.

Lily felt as if she could never, never forget what had happened that morning. But she did not say so. She was asking herself, with some perplexity, where she had heard the name Bouton, and then, all at once, she remembered! It was the name which had produced such an extraordinary change in the taxicab-driver on the day of her arrival at Monte Carlo.

CHAPTER 8

As they walked along the broad road which leads steeply down from Monte Carlo to the quaintly named Condamine, M. Popeau began talking almost as much to himself as to his young companion.

"The man we're going to see," he said, "is an autocrat, Miss Fairfield—one of the last real autocrats left in Europe. He has absolute power in this little country—I mean in Monaco. From his ruling there is no appeal. I remember he once caused an Englishman to be what would now be called deported. A fearful fuss was made about it! The man—his name was Johnson—was a nasty, cantankerous fellow, and it seemed that he had some relation in your Foreign Office. The affair dragged on for months—frightful threats were uttered. The British Ambassador in Paris was brought in—in fact it is not too much to say that had Monaco been a real country, with a fleet and an army, war might have resulted. But friend Bouton stuck to his guns, as the British so cleverly and truly say, and poor Johnson never came back!"

They were now turning into a very quiet, shadowed street composed of small but prosperous-looking houses.

"Just one word, Miss Fairfield!" Lily's companion, guide, and mentor, stopped walking.

"Please do not volunteer any information unless you are asked a direct question," he said gravely. "Even then it is not necessary for you to answer a question unless you wish to do so. *I* will tell the Commissioner of Police what happened, and I hope—I am not sure, but I think I may say that that will be the end of the matter as far as you are concerned."

"I suppose I shall have to show the police where I found the body?" asked Lily in a low voice.

"I trust that will not be necessary."

A few moments later they were standing in a formal-looking sitting-room, on the ground floor of the house to which they had been admitted by a pleasant-looking *bonne à tout faire*.

After they had waited some minutes the door opened and a tall, thin man, with a napkin tucked in his collar, entered with hand outstretched.

"This is an unexpected pleasure, dear friend! What can I do for you?" he exclaimed. "You have come just too late to share our Sunday lunch. My married daughter, her husband, and her two children have come over from Nice and we have been having something of a festival. Sit down—sit down!"

As he spoke he was measuring Lily with what she felt to be a pair of very sharp eyes.

"I am ashamed to have come on a Sunday," began M. Popeau.

"Not at all—not at all! I am delighted to see you," said M. Bouton, "and there are certain things that will not wait. I hope Mademoiselle is not a new victim of the gang of thieves I mentioned to you yesterday? So far they have spared the Hôtel de Paris. But I have a clue—and it will not be long before they are laid by the heels."

"I am here," said M. Popeau quietly, "because a sad thing befell this lady, Miss Fairfield, today on her way to the English Church service. She is staying in a villa called La Solitude, some way above Monte Carlo, and, wandering a little way off the path, she suddenly came across a dead body! Of course, it gave her a terrible shock."

To Lily's astonishment, M. Bouton did not look surprised.

"Very sad," he murmured. "The matter will have my very earnest attention. If Mademoiselle will give me a few particulars as to the locality where she made this painful discovery I will see to the matter at once. Would you kindly come this way?"

He opened the door, and passed on, in front of them, into a room built out at the back of the house. It was obviously his own study.

"Here is the plan of our Principality," he observed, and Lily, glancing up, saw that a huge map covered one entire side of the room.

"Will you point out the exact spot where you made your sad discovery?" went on M. Bouton, handing her a long, light stick.

Lily stared anxiously up at the map, but she had no bump of locality on her pretty head.

M. Popeau took the thin stick from her hand. He laid the point lightly on the map, and pushed it up and up and up!

"Here is La Solitude," he said at last, "so now we shall be able to find the exact place."

"Ah, yes," said M. Bouton. "La Solitude belongs to Count Antonio Polda. He and the Countess are nice, quiet people, almost the only people in Monaco with whom I have never had any trouble! It is my impression that somewhere about the fourteenth century a Grimaldi married a Polda—so the Count is distantly related to our sovereign."

"Mademoiselle is a niece of the Countess Polda," said M. Popeau quietly. "She is staying at La Solitude for the winter."

M. Bouton looked at Lily with enhanced respect.

"Now take La Solitude as the point of departure, and try to concentrate your mind on where you found the body," said M. Popeau, handing Lily back the cane.

She moved the point slowly, hesitatingly, down the map.

"Surely you are going too far!" cried M. Popeau.

"Perhaps I am——"

She knitted her brow in some distress. "Do you remember the place where our taxicab stopped?" she asked.

"Of course I do—it's marked here."

He took the wand from her hand. "Here it is—this little white spot."

"It was just below there," said Lily.

"Was it? How very strange!" exclaimed M. Popeau. And then he looked at the other man. "Do you remember what happened just there, six years ago, the last time I was at Monte Carlo, Bouton?"

The other shook his head.

"The affair of the Mexican millionaire!" exclaimed M. Popeau.

The Commissioner of Police turned round quickly. "I remember all about it now! Why, you're right—it was just at that spot that he was found dead, too. What a strange coincidence! They mostly do it, as you know, within a very short distance of the Casino. You'd be astonished to know the number of poor devils who go and destroy themselves in that rather lonely place just beyond the station. They rush out of the Casino full of anguish and despair, and wander down the road. I always have a man stationed on point duty there—he has stopped more than one poor fellow from destroying himself. Ah, our beautiful, brilliant Monte Carlo has a very melancholy reverse side, has it not?" and he sighed.

But M. Popeau was still staring at the map. "It is indeed an amazing coincidence!" he muttered. "The more one thinks of it, the more amazing it is."

"Yes, it certainly is a very curious thing that the Mexican should have been found in that very plantation," said the Police Commissioner thoughtfully, "but life's full of odd coincidences."

"It will be quite easy for your people to find the body without further troubling Mademoiselle, will it not?"

"Certainly it will," said M. Bouton. "Mademoiselle must try to forget this painful incident; and if I may offer a word of advice——" he waited, and looked rather searchingly into Lily's candid, open face—"I counsel that Mademoiselle does not talk of what happened to any friends she may have in Monte Carlo. It naturally annoys the Casino Administration when these painful accidents are made the subject of gossip. Can we rely on Mademoiselle's discretion? Is it necessary that she should tell *anyone* about the matter?"

A troubled look came over Lily's face. "I feel I ought to tell the Count and Countess Polda," she said reluctantly. "For they knew the poor man quite well."

"Did they, indeed?" exclaimed the Commissioner of Police. "You did not tell me that, Mademoiselle." He looked surprised. "Then can you tell me the suicide's name?"

M. Popeau was standing behind M. Bouton, and Lily was astonished to see how upset he looked—he even made a sign to her to stop talking. She hesitated. But M. Bouton looked straight into her face and said sharply: "I don't understand! I thought Mademoiselle had come across the dead body of *an unknown man*. I had no idea that *she knew who the man was*."

He turned on M. Popeau. "You did not tell me that!" he exclaimed.

"There was nothing to tell," said M. Popeau quietly. "Mademoiselle did not see the dead man's face. She thinks it possible the body she saw was that of a man who dined at La Solitude about a fortnight ago. That is all."

"Only a week ago!" corrected Lily. "And I am *sure* it was the man I saw. He wore a peculiar kind of gold bangle or bracelet on his wrist, and there was a gold bangle on the wrist of—" she faltered, overcome with the vision her own words evoked of that stiff, stark arm lying across her path.

"What was his name and nationality?" asked M. Bouton, taking a writing-pad and pencil off the table.

"His name was Ponting," said Lily slowly, "P.O.N.T.I.N.G., and I think he said he came from Pernambuco."

M. Bouton suddenly uttered an exclamation of mingled surprise and relief. He rapidly unlocked a drawer in his writing-table, and took a packet out of it. "Your discovery, Mademoiselle, sets a mystery at rest! I was a fool not to think of it at once, for we have had urgent inquiries all this last week about this very man. But it never occurred to any of us that he had committed suicide—everything seemed against it! This is another proof that in a place like Monte Carlo you never can tell," he went on, addressing his French friend. "People come here when they are desperate—not only desperate with regard to money—though, of course, that is the most common case—but desperate with regard to other things; they come to drown disappointment and sorrow—they fail in doing so, and then they kill themselves! Perhaps that is what happened to this man Ponting."

"Yet he seemed quite happy," observed Lily thoughtfully.

M. Bouton hardly heard what she said. He was showing his friend and colleague the little packet of letters he held in his hand.

Lily waited a moment or two. "Then I may tell the Count and Countess Polda?" she asked.

"I think we shall save you that trouble, Mademoiselle. After the body is found we shall have to ask the Count and Countess to submit to a short interrogation. We should not dream of troubling them were it not that this Mr. Ponting had a friend who is much distressed at his disappearance. We shall be glad, therefore, to know exactly how he spent his last evening. Did you yourself see him leave La Solitude?"

"No," said Lily. "I had only arrived that day, and I went to bed early; but I heard the Countess say good-bye to him about a quarter of an hour after I had gone upstairs. As the house is not very substantially built, one hears everything."

"That is an important point," said M. Bouton. "You heard him leave the house, and then no more? You did not hear the shot fired, Mademoiselle?"

"I heard nothing at all. But I was very, very tired, and I went to sleep at once."

She wondered if she ought to say anything about the burglary which had taken place that night. Then she remembered what both the Countess and the banker had said: that bringing the police into the affair would only make a fuss and an unpleasantness for nothing. So she remained silent.

At last M. Bouton conducted them to his front door. He bowed to Lily, and shook hands warmly with M. Popeau.

"Without knowing it," he exclaimed, "you've done me a great service, my good friend! I confess I do not like being disturbed on Sunday—the weekdays are full enough of trouble and of perplexing affairs. But I am more glad than I can say that what I may call the Ponting mystery has been cleared up in so satisfactory a manner. We've had a great deal of worry over the matter. But the cleverest of my detectives—I call him the bloodhound—was convinced that M. Ponting was not only alive, but far from here engaged in having a very good time! The theory of suicide we had completely dismissed from our minds. Does not this show how wrong even the most experienced people may be when dealing with human life and human problems?"

After they had walked a little way in silence, Lily suddenly turned to her companion and exclaimed: "I'm afraid you did not approve of my telling M. Bouton that I knew about poor Mr. Ponting?"

"As a general rule, my dear young lady, the innocent cannot say too little to the police. But I confess that this time I was wrong; I'm very glad that you spoke with complete frankness, though I do not suppose the Count and Countess will be pleased—"

"I don't see why they should mind," but even as she uttered the words a slight feeling of discomfort came over Lily.

M. Popeau smiled rather mysteriously.

"People do not care to be mixed up with affairs of this kind, especially in Monte Carlo. You heard what our friend said? The Count and Countess, though they have lived here many years, have never troubled the police. They have never even had a row with one of their servants! Well, now that record is broken. A suicide has been found on their property."

"Not on their property," corrected Lily. "Near their property."

"That makes it all the harder for them to be brought into the matter," said M. Popeau good-humouredly. "Mr. Ponting ill-repaid their hospitality."

At that moment they both caught sight of Captain Stuart hurrying down towards them.

"Well?" he called out, "is it all right?" There was a note of anxiety in his voice.

"Yes," replied M. Popeau, "quite all right! And now we must think of something to distract and interest Miss Fairfield for at least two or three hours. By that time everything up there at La Solitude will be over, and I do not want her to be associated with it in any way."

Captain Stuart nodded. He thoroughly approved.

"I don't suppose you feel in the mood for the Casino?" He turned to the girl. "Besides, it's Sunday—and even I have an old-fashioned prejudice against gambling on Sunday!"

"Why shouldn't we go up to the Golf Club?" suggested the Frenchman. "It's quite a pleasant expedition, and from there it's an agreeable walk to La Solitude."

CHAPTER 9

The afternoon that Lily Fairfield spent on what is, perhaps, the most beautiful of all the golf courses in Europe will ever be remembered by her as a delightful interlude in a very troubled time.

For three hours she forgot the terrible thing which had happened to her that morning, or, if she could not entirely forget it, it receded into the background of her mind.

Everything is made easy—almost too easy—for the visitor to Monte Carlo. Thus Lily found an excellent set of clubs provided for her, and with M. Popeau looking on benevolently, she and Captain Stuart had a splendid game.

But when, at last, the three of them stood in front of the shabby front door of La Solitude a feeling of apprehension, almost of terror, came over the girl.

"I hope Aunt Cosy won't be angry with me for having gone to the Commissioner of Police," she said nervously.

"You were quite right to do so," said Captain Stuart shortly.

As for M. Popeau, he exclaimed, "Do let me come in with you, dear little lady! I can promise so to put the matter to the Countess that she will not be angry."

But Lily shook her head. "I'm not such a coward as that." She added, impatiently, "I do wish Cristina would come and open the door! I can't think why they keep it locked. It's literally the only way into the house, unless one of the drawing-room windows is open. In England there's always a nice back door to a house of this sort."

As she said the words, the door did open, and Cristina cautiously peered out to see who was there. The poor old waiting woman was very pale, and the two men, as well as Lily, were startled at her look of illness and of fear.

"Something terrible has happened!" Cristina muttered. "I fear I cannot ask the gentlemen to come in. We are in trouble here."

"I'm glad they know. That will save you a disagreeable moment," whispered M. Popeau, as he pressed Lily's hand.

Cristina cut short Lily's farewells, and shut the door almost rudely in the Frenchman's face.

"I'm sorry you have come back," she said to Lily, in a very low tone. "I wish you had stayed away till dinner-time! A fearful thing has happened!"

"I know," said Lily soothingly. "You mean about Mr. Ponting."

"You know?" echoed Cristina amazed, and she turned a startled look on the girl's face.

"It was I who found the body and told the police," the girl answered quietly. "But there is nothing to be frightened about, Cristina, though, of course, it is very, very sad."

She was speaking in her usual clear voice, when suddenly the drawing-room opened and the Countess peeped out. Her face was dusky red, and convulsed with anger.

"What is all this noise?" she exclaimed in French; "we cannot hear ourselves speak!"

Then, as she saw who it was, she went on, more quietly, in English, "Something very, very sad has occurred. You remember Mr. Ponting coming here to dinner? Well, after leaving the house that unhappy man, who had evidently been losing heavily at the tables, went out and killed himself. A cruel return for our hospitality! I desire you, Lily, to come in and tell this gentleman what you remember of that evening."

Lily looked at the speaker, astonished at her state of agitation. The Countess Polda's face looked terrible under the bright, auburn-brown hair on her "front." Her hands were trembling. Even her voice seemed changed—it was as if she had lost control over it.

"Come in! Come in!" she cried impatiently, and yet she herself had been blocking the door.

Lily walked through into the drawing-room, and she saw that the Count, who also looked disturbed, though much less so than his wife, was sitting at his green baize card-table, apparently affixing his name to some kind of paper.

Opposite to him stood a man of about forty. The stranger had a pleasant, keen face, and though he was not in uniform, Lily felt sure he had come from M. Bouton. Somehow, she could hardly have told why, the sight of him reassured her.

"Come, come," he said good-humouredly, "you must not allow this to disturb you so much, Madame la Comtesse. Desperate men are not likely to show much delicacy, even to those who have been kind to them. We are very glad indeed that the body has been found. My chief said to me only two hours ago that he owed a great debt to the young English lady."

"The young English lady?" repeated the Countess. "Whom do you mean?"

"It was this lady, was it not, who found the body?" he replied, looking at Lily.

"Yes, I found the body," Lily answered falteringly, for the Countess was now looking at her with a fearful expression of questioning anger on her face.

The man went on: "M. Bouton is most grateful to this young lady for having come and told him at once, today. But for Mademoiselle, the body of this man, Ponting, might have lain there a whole year! As you of course know, M. le Comte, that piece of property which lies just below your own orange grove belongs to that eccentric Sir John Cranion."

"I know," said the Count, looking up, "for I myself have tried to buy the property more than once. I wish more than ever now that I had done so, for we should have had it properly enclosed, and then this tragedy could not have happened there."

"It would have happened somewhere else," said the Frenchman philosophically. "And now, if Madame la Comtesse will also put her signature to this statement, I shall not trouble you anymore, ladies and gentlemen."

He waited a moment. "By great good luck, Mr. Ponting's partner happened to be in Monte Carlo this afternoon. One of my men came across him in front of the Casino—they have all grown only too familiar with his appearance. He is, of course, very much distressed, and, what is more, foolishly convinced that his friend did not kill himself!"

"How can anyone feel any doubt about it?" cried Count Polda. "Everything points to the fact that the unhappy man, after leaving us, went off and shot himself. We all thought him very excited, and in a strange kind of mood—did we not?" he glanced at his wife, and at Lily.

"The funeral will take place tomorrow morning at the English cemetery," went on the police-agent. "And that ends the story."

"Would you like to interrogate my English niece?" asked the Countess suavely. She was beginning to recover her composure.

"No, I do not think it will be necessary. My chief himself saw the young lady, and heard what she had to say."

He took his hat from one of the chairs. "And now," he said politely, "I must bid you *au revoir*, and I hope it will be a long time before we have occasion to meet again!"

"Would you like to go out by this short way?" asked the Count obligingly. He opened a window, and the man, who Lily now felt sure was "the bloodhound," passed rapidly through it, with a bow and a smile, and began walking across the lawn.

The Countess suddenly touched her husband's arm. "Run after him," she exclaimed, "and ask at what time the funeral will take place. I think it would be a mark of respect on your part to attend."

He hesitated perceptibly.

"Do what I suggest!" she said urgently. "I am *sure*, Angelo, that I am right—quite, quite sure!"

The Count looked at his wife, and, after that look, he too went through the window, and began running after their late unwelcome guest.

And then all at once there crept over Lily Fairfield an acute, unreasoning sensation of acute, unreasoning fear. She told herself that her nerves were all upset; that everything was all right *now*. But—

The Countess shut the window; she turned round and put her arms akimbo; and Lily had never thought such anger and venomous rage could fill a human countenance. Instinctively she moved back, till a chair stood between herself and the woman who was now looking at her with such a terrible expression on her face.

"I do not at all understand what happened," said the Countess at last, and though she did not raise her voice there was something very menacing in the tone in which she uttered these commonplace words. "Tell me exactly what took place this morning. How was it that you were away from the road? Why were you wandering in that deserted garden? Were you alone, or in company?"

Lily looked at her straight in the eyes.

"Of course I was alone, Aunt Cosy. I was on my way to church. As it was still early, I thought I would go down to the town by a new way."

Her voice faltered and broke, and she burst into bitter tears.

The Countess pointed imperiously to one of the moth-eaten armchairs, and the trembling girl sat down on it, and buried her face in her hands.

"What I really want to discover"—the words were uttered with slow, terrible emphasis—"is why you went to the police without consulting us? Surely it would have been easy to come back to the house and tell your Uncle Angelo of your discovery?"

And then, perhaps fortunately, for Lily would have been hard put to it to give a truthful answer to that question, the Countess, carried away by her feelings of indignation and outraged wrath, hurried on, without waiting for the weeping girl's reply:

"But no! It seemed simpler to go down and let all Monte Carlo know what had happened! I suppose it was your friend, Captain Stuart, who advised you to do that foolish thing—to go to the police?"

Lily raised her tear-stained face.

"No, it was not Captain Stuart," she said dully. "I thought of it myself, Aunt Cosy. It was the first thing one would have done in England."

"England is not Monte Carlo!" exclaimed the Countess harshly. "How often have I to tell you that? I shall never forget this afternoon—never! Thank God, my Beppo was not here!"

And then a most fortunate inspiration came to Lily Fairfield.

"The Commissioner of Police spoke very highly of you and of Uncle Angelo," she said falteringly. "He seemed very sorry that such a thing should have happened so near La Solitude. He said you were related to the Prince of Monaco—I never knew that, Aunt Cosy."

"It is not a relationship which we have ever presumed upon," said the Countess rather stiffly, but her face cleared somewhat, "though it is true that hundreds of years ago a Grimaldi married a Polda. Still, I am glad of what you tell me, Lily, and it will console your uncle for the painful ordeal he had to go through. You will understand why I feel so angry and, yes, so hurt, that you have brought this trouble upon us, when I tell you that your Uncle Angelo had the awful task of identifying the body!"

An exclamation of regret and concern came from Lily's lips. She did indeed feel very sorry for the Count.

"And then," went on the Countess, "the affair has so upset Cristina! I really thought at one moment she would drop dead. But now"—she tried to smile, but it was much more like a grimace—"now we must all try and forget that it happened!" She took a turn about the room. "And I beg of you most earnestly, dear child, not to say a word about it to my son."

"I promise that I will not do so," said Lily eagerly.

"I am glad for your sake that that odious man did not ask for a statement from you. Had you to sign anything at the police station?" To Lily's intense relief, she now spoke quite amiably, and her face was again set in its usual grim, handsome immobility.

"No, I was not asked to sign anything," said the girl. "In fact, the Commissioner did not ask me many questions. He only wanted to know at what time poor Mr. Ponting left La Solitude, and I told him that as I was going up to bed I had heard you say good-night to him. And, of course, of course, Aunt Cosy—" she blushed, and looked distressed.

"Yes?" said the Countess uneasily, "yes? What is it Lily? Is there anything that you've not yet told me?" A look of apprehension came into her eyes.

"I did not think it necessary to say that I thought poor Mr. Ponting had had too much to drink."

"I'm glad you kept that to yourself!" There was great relief in the Countess's voice. "I did not like to ask you, dear child, but, of course, I have had that painful memory in my mind all the time. To people like us there is something so strange in the love of strong drink. The first time that poor man came here he took a little too much, and I remonstrated with the Count—I begged him not to bring him again. But alas! Angelo has so kind a heart, and the poor fellow seemed so lonely."

"I suppose one cannot help a guest having too much wine?" said Lily hesitatingly. There had come back to her mind the way the Count had filled up his guest's glass again and again.

"It is difficult—very difficult! But you may have noticed that I offered him water?"

"Yes, I did notice that," said Lily.

"Can you remember any of the questions asked you by that M. Bouton?"

Lily shook her head. "He asked me hardly any questions. He seemed exceedingly glad that I felt so sure it was Mr. Ponting's body, for he had been having a lot of trouble over the poor man's disappearance."

Lily got up from the chair on which she was sitting.

"Please forgive me," she said pleadingly. "I am very, very sorry that I've brought all this trouble and worry on you and on Uncle Angelo. It wasn't my fault."

"No, it was not your fault," said the Countess graciously, "and I must ask you, dear child, to accept my own apology. I fear you thought me rather unkind. But you do not know—English people never can understand—how very disagreeable any *fracas* with the police can be, in either France or Italy. It means such endless trouble!"

The Countess walked to the window, she opened it and looked out into the semi-darkness.

"I suppose Angelo walked on down the hill with that man—perhaps to find out for himself the hour of the funeral. Do you mean to go to it, dear child?"

The question surprised Lily. "Would you like me to do so, Aunt Cosy?"

The Countess remained silent for a few moments.

"Yes," she said decidedly. "It would be a mark of respect. I will not offer to go myself. There are things I must do before the arrival of my beloved Beppo. And then I could not walk up the hill again. I should have to have a carriage. You and Uncle Angelo do not mind walking." She lowered her voice: "With regard to Cristina, encourage her to think of other things. Fortunately, she is fond of Beppo. His coming will be a distraction and pleasure to us all. Oh, my dear Lily, I do hope that my son and you will be good pals—as you so funnily say in England!"

* * * *

It was past the hour at which they generally sat down to their simple evening meal. And Lily and the Countess were already in the dining-room when Count Polda walked in and sat down.

His wife was looking at him anxiously. "Is it all right?" she said in English. And he replied in French: "Yes—quite all right. The funeral is at ten o'clock tomorrow morning." He sighed. "I am hungry!" he exclaimed plaintively.

The Countess got up and went to the sideboard. From there she brought back a beautiful liqueur decanter which Lily knew contained brandy.

"Have a little of this. It will do you good," she said solicitously.

There was a pause. "Lily is very sorry that she brought all this trouble upon us, Angelo. But it was not her fault, poor child. She did not know any better. We must try and forget this tragedy—and nothing must be said of all this to Beppo, or in front of Beppo."

"No, indeed!" said the Count.

And then his wife remarked rather suddenly: "I hope you remembered to order a wreath, Angelo?"

"Yes, I did remember."

"Ah, that is right! I have told Lily that I should like her to go with you to Mr. Ponting's funeral."

"That is an excellent idea, Cosy!" The Count smiled. For once he looked really pleased, and Lily told herself, not for the first time, that he was a very odd sort of man.

CHAPTER X

As she got up the next morning Lily began to shrink inexpressibly from the thought of going to poor Mr. Ponting's funeral. She longed to summon up courage and tell Aunt Cosy that she really felt too ill. As so often happens after a shock, she felt far worse today than she had done even immediately after her fearful discovery.

She went downstairs with laggard steps, to be met in the corridor below by the Countess.

"There is a quarter of an hour before you and Uncle Angelo must start," she exclaimed, "and I have told Cristina to boil you an egg. Coffee is not sufficiently substantial."

She shepherded the unresisting girl into the kitchen. Cristina's eyes were swollen; she looked as if she had been crying all night.

"Now sit down," commanded the Countess, "and eat what you call in England a good breakfast. It is right to show sorrow when something sad has happened, but do not look as if you yourself were dying! I do not want people to think that you, Lily, were in love with Mr. Ponting."

Lily felt a shock of disgust. What a vulgar, heartless thing to say! She grew very red, and Aunt Cosy laughed harshly.

And yet the Countess Polda was feeling far better disposed to the girl than was usual with her. As she watched Lily daintily eating her egg, she was telling herself that her guest was certainly a very pretty girl. The type, too, that Beppo admired—that fair, rather delicate. English type dowered with an exquisitely clear complexion and what the French call *blond cendré* hair.

The pleasant thought that her beloved son would certainly approve of Lily cheered up the Countess mightily, and when Lily stood up she patted the girl's hand. "You look very nice," she said. "That black coat and skirt and the little toque compose just the right costume to wear on such a sad occasion as this."

The Count's voice was heard in the passage. "Cosy! Cosy!" he called out impatiently.

The Countess hurried out of the kitchen. And then Cristina seized Lily by the arm; "You will say a prayer for me," she said in a trembling voice, "will you not, Mademoiselle?"

Lily was touched. "Yes," she said, a little shyly, "I will certainly do so, Cristina."

"I shall never forget yesterday—never—never—never!" Cristina uttered the words in a low voice, but with a terrible intensity.

"But you must try and forget yesterday," said Lily firmly. "I mean to force myself to put out of my mind what happened yesterday morning. That, honestly, was much worse than anything that can have happened to you afterwards."

"Yes, indeed! Had I been you I should have fainted!"

At that moment, "Lily! Lily!" came from the passage. "Come, my child, come! Your Uncle Angelo is quite ready."

Lily ran into the corridor, and then, had it not been such a sad occasion, she would have burst out laughing! For the Count was dressed in an extraordinary costume. He wore a seedy old black dress suit, and on his head was a dirty white Panama hat with a deep black crape band. But Uncle Angelo was obviously quite unaware of the ludicrous effect he produced in the English girl's eyes.

"Come, come," he said impatiently. "I want to be in good time at the cemetery, for I shall have to leave at once after the funeral. There are several things I have to do in the town."

"Do not forget to order the carriage for Beppo tomorrow," called out the Countess.

"Is it likely that I should forget that?" There was a touch of scornful ill-temper in the Count's usually placid tone.

The two curiously unlike companions walked down the hill in almost absolute silence. Lily often felt consciously glad that Uncle Angelo was such a very quiet, reserved person. Aunt Cosy's constant torrent of talk tired and bewildered the girl.

"The cemetery is on the Nice road," said Count Polda at last; "this is the shortest way to it." They were now going down a rough stairway cut in the hillside.

It was still so early that there were only a few country folk laden with country produce trudging towards Monte Carlo. A delicious breeze blew up from the sea on to the broad, exquisitely-kept carriage-road which links Monaco with Beaulieu.

They had been walking along that road for only a few minutes when they were joined by M. Popeau. Lily was secretly very glad to see him, yet she was also surprised—not so surprised however, as he was to see her.

He turned courteously to Count Polda. "I have been wondering if you and Mademoiselle would care to go with me to the Prince of Monaco's beautiful aquarium—I mean, of course, after the sad ceremony is over?"

"I fear I cannot have the pleasure you so amiably propose," muttered the Count. "But I do not see why my niece should not avail herself of your kind thought. It would, as you say, distract her mind." He spoke in a weary, preoccupied tone, as if hardly thinking of what he was saying.

They turned into the gate of the cemetery, and made their way to that portion of it where those English folk who die at Monte Carlo are reverently laid to rest. They soon came to the place they were looking for, and found a tiny gathering round the open grave. Lily was the only woman there, and her eyes filled with tears as she listened to the beautiful, solemn words of the English Burial Service being read over poor Mr. Ponting's coffin.

Short as was the ceremony, it was scarcely over before Count Polda detached himself unobtrusively from the group of mourners, and disappeared in the direction of the gate.

As, slowly, Lily and M. Popeau walked away together, she suddenly heard herself addressed in a voice unknown to her.

"Are you Miss Fairfield? If so, may I have a word with you, madam?"

She looked round, startled. A tall man, obviously an Englishman, stood before her.

"Yes," she said falteringly, "I am Miss Fairfield."

"My name is Sharrow. I was Mr. Ponting's friend and partner. I understand that you found the body?"

Then M. Popeau intervened. "Perhaps you will pardon me, sir, for saying that the police have all the particulars of that painful occurrence."

"I have heard all they have to say; but I hope Miss Fairfield will not mind my asking her a few questions?"

M. Popeau looked very much annoyed and disturbed, perhaps unreasonably so, and Lily was thankful indeed that Count Polda was no longer there. After all, it was natural that this Mr.—what was his name?—Sharrow should wish to speak to her. She nerved herself for what must be, at best, a rather painful little conversation.

Mr. Sharrow's next words took her by surprise.

"I think you will agree with me," he said, slowly and impressively, "that Mr. Ponting was the very last man in the world to take his own life."

Lily hesitated. She really did not know what to answer. And then M. Popeau again intervened.

"You forget, sir, that this young lady hardly knew your unfortunate friend."

"Nonsense!" said Mr. Sharrow rudely. "She knew him quite well. He had been, to my knowledge, at least six or seven times to La Solitude. More than once I wanted him to take me up there, but no—he seemed to think that it would be indiscreet—that the Poldas were quiet people who would prefer to entertain one rather than two."

"But I had only arrived at Monte Carlo on the day he came to dinner there for the last time," exclaimed Lily. "I did have a few minutes' talk with him alone, just before we went into the dining-room—but that was all."

"I beg your pardon," said Mr. Sharrow. "I did not know what you have just told me."

"He seemed very happy," she said slowly, "and yes, I must say that he did not seem to me in the least the sort of man to kill himself."

Her evident sincerity touched the stranger, as did, too, her young, girlish charm of manner.

"I wish you would tell me exactly what *did* happen on that fatal evening," he said earnestly. "The whole thing is so mysterious to me! Ponting had promised some friends of ours to dine with them and then to spend the evening at the Club. Unluckily I had an engagement at Nice, or I should have been there too. As it was, they waited on and on for him, but he neither came nor sent a message."

"That's very strange," said Lily, "for I know that his cabman was told to take them a message."

"That doesn't surprise me," said M. Popeau drily. "Cabmen are the most untrustworthy of messengers!"

"Oh, so he gave a message to the cabman?" said Mr. Sharrow slowly. "Of course, I didn't know that. But what made him change his mind, Miss Fairfield? Surely he went up to La Solitude in order to tell the Count and Countess Polda that he couldn't have the pleasure of dining with them?"

"I expect," said Lily reluctantly, "that he saw how annoyed they were at his change of plan. They're old-fashioned people, the sort of people who make rather a fuss about having anyone to a meal, even to tea"—a slight smile quivered over her face, and M. Popeau nodded—"and the Countess was rather disagreeable in her manner, when Mr. Ponting said he could not stay. I think they were really hurt," she added. "They had got fond of him, and they had set their hearts on his spending his last evening with them; so, suddenly, he made up his mind that he would do so."

"You've relieved my mind very much," Mr. Sharrow was speaking quite politely now. "There seemed such an extraordinary mystery about the whole thing! But what you tell me clears it up. I should like to ask you one other question. About what time did Ponting leave La Solitude?"

"I had a very long, tiring journey," said Lily frankly, "and I went up to bed quite early, before he left. Still, I heard the Countess Polda say good-bye to him—I should think a little before ten."

"That fits in with my theory." Mr. Sharrow nodded. "I think he left La Solitude with the idea of catching the ten-thirty train, and that then, on his way down to the station, he was waylaid and murdered."

"Perhaps that was what did happen."

But Mr. Sharrow was going on, as if speaking to himself, though addressing her.

"In this cursed place," he said, "the police are so used to coming across suicides that they won't admit the probability of murder—that must be very convenient for the kind of bandits who infest Monte Carlo! Why, they've had the most awful gang of thieves here during this last fortnight. The Commissioner of Police told me himself that they were desperate men who stuck at nothing. One of them when caught yesterday made a slash at his captor with a razor, and hurt him most awfully."

"But is it likely that any of that gang would have been in that lonely place? It's a sort of deserted garden, with boards up, warning people that it's private property."

"I know—I know! Of course I've been there—" He spoke with a touch of impatience.

"And then," said Lily, "surely a thief would have taken away that curious kind of gold bangle poor Mr. Ponting wore? It was by that bangle," she went on in a low voice, "that I identified him—I didn't see his face."

The words she uttered brought back very vividly her terrible experience, and her lips quivered.

Mr. Sharrow looked at her with concern.

"Forgive me," he said impulsively, "for asking you all these questions; but Ponting has a mother out there, and you know she'll want to hear everything."

"There isn't much to tell," said Lily. "I was going down to church yesterday morning, and I rather foolishly tried to find a short cut, and—and— quite suddenly I saw an arm stretched across my path"—she stopped, overwhelmed with the recollection. "I saw something gleaming—it was Mr. Ponting's bangle!"

"Yes," interjected M. Popeau. "If your theory is correct, sir, why did the thieves leave this bracelet?"

"They took everything else," said Mr. Sharrow shortly. "Luckily, he hadn't much on him—perhaps thirty or forty pounds. But he had certain identification papers—a passport, and so on. They also disappeared. All that was left was the bangle, and his watch and chain. I don't suppose altogether they were worth five pounds. The watch was only a plain silver watch, but he had worn it through all his fighting, and he was fond of it. He told me once he wouldn't exchange it for the finest gold chronometer that was ever made."

Mr. Sharrow's voice became charged with emotion. "I dare say you gathered that he was a rough diamond, Miss Fairfield? But he was a thoroughly good chap, a splendid man, straight as a die, and generous—one of the most generous chaps I ever met!"

"Yes," said Lily slowly, "I know that. He tried to make me accept a beautiful little gold snuff-box he had bought, out of kindness, from a poor old lady who had lost her money at the tables."

"You never told me that," said M. Popeau, surprised. "Have you got the box?"

Lily shook her head. "Oh, no. I couldn't take such a valuable present from a stranger."

"Then that was also included in the haul the thieves made?" exclaimed Mr. Sharrow. "But I'm very glad I've heard about that box, for it might help to catch Ponting's murderers. It's just a chance, to tell you the truth, that they didn't make a much bigger haul. Ponting was an eccentric chap in some ways—the sort of man who doesn't trust banks. As a rule he carried about with him a very big sum. But on that very day—the day, I mean, that he was killed—I got him to deposit the kind of satchel thing in which he kept his money in the safe of the hotel where he and I were staying at Nice. The manager there has hit on the rather clever idea of having a number of little safes, which he lets out at five francs a day. I persuaded Ponting that it would be very much safer to leave his securities—for part of the money was in what they call 'bonds to bearer'—there. It was insane to come every day, as he used to do, to a place like Monte Carlo with all that money on him."

"What you tell me," observed M. Popeau musingly, "alters everything, Mr. Sharrow. Of course, the fact that he might have had what was practically a fortune on him would give a very strong motive for his murder!"

"And yet," exclaimed Mr. Sharrow impatiently, "I told all that to the Commissioner of Police, and it made no impression on him at all."

"The truth is"—the Frenchman spoke with some heat—"the authorities here at Monaco don't want to believe that a murder is ever committed. In such a garden of paradise"—there came a note of deep sarcasm in his vibrant voice—"they never look for the snake!"

"The police are convinced that during the eight days that the body lay in that orange grove some passer-by, probably a peasant, came across the body, took everything from it, and naturally said nothing of his discovery," observed Mr. Sharrow.

"I confess that that has been my own theory up to now," said M. Popeau. "And it would take even more than your curious revelations as to poor Mr. Ponting's peculiar habit of carrying about his money to destroy that theory entirely. I think another thing. I can't help suspecting that a professional thief, or gang of thieves, would have left the little gold snuff-box as well as the watch and the bracelet. They would naturally not care to take away something that could be identified positively as having belonged to their victim."

"On the other hand," said Mr. Sharrow thoughtfully, "one would never have thought they would have left anything made of gold."

"You're wrong there!" cried M. Popeau quickly. "Such folk are sometimes very superstitious. They probably thought that bracelet was the dead man's mascot, and might bring *them* ill-luck! Besides, even a peasant would know that a thin gold band was not really valuable. Forty francs—fifty francs—even thirty francs might have bought it from what I hear."

And then something which seemed to the Frenchman very dramatic occurred. Mr. Sharrow suddenly put his hand in his pocket and held out a thin gold hoop. "Here it is!" he exclaimed.

Lily gave a little cry and gasp.

"I beg your pardon," he said remorsefully. "I didn't mean to startle you, Miss Fairfield. I am keeping it for the poor chap's mother. This little bangle and the silver watch are the only two things I shall have to take back to her. It's so pitiful! She was expecting him home after four years."

"Yes, indeed," said Lily, and she turned away. The tears had welled up into her eyes.

"Well," said Mr. Sharrow, "there's nothing more to say, I suppose. Thank you very much for having answered my questions so clearly. I wanted to go up and see the Count and Countess Polda, but I shan't do so now. The Commissioner of Police begged me not to do it. He said they'd been terribly upset about the whole thing. After all, they were very kind to poor Ponting. It's rather too bad they should have had all this worry through him, even if they did lead indirectly to his death."

"Oh, don't say that!" said Lily, distressed.

Deep in her heart she could not help knowing that it was because of *her* presence at La Solitude that the unfortunate man had stayed on, and this secret knowledge was a bitter trouble to her—one, too, which she felt she could never confide to anybody as long as she lived.

"Well, but it's true!" persisted Mr. Sharrow. "If he hadn't stayed on there that evening he would be alive today. He and I would be on our way home by now." He sighed and held out his hand. "Good-bye, and forgive me for the trouble I've put you to."

"Good-bye," said Lily mechanically.

M. Popeau lead the now weeping girl into a side path where there was a bench.

"You must not take this sad affair too much to heart," he said soothingly. "You must try and forget it."

"I can't forget it! I shall never forget it!" sobbed Lily. "I've had such a terrible time since I last saw you, M. Popeau. The Countess was terribly angry that I had gone to the police!"

"I told you she would be," interjected the Frenchman.

"Yes, I know you told me so. But that didn't seem to make it any better!" Lily smiled, and tried to regain her composure. "Luckily, her son comes tomorrow, and I hope that will make her forget this dreadful, dreadful thing! But *I* shall never forget it."

"Indeed you will, and must," said M. Popeau, and there came a very authoritative tone into his kind voice. "It is your duty to do so, Miss Fairfield. English people have a great sense of duty—I appeal to that sense now! You must put this poor man out of your mind"—he hesitated—"forever. Now promise me? You know I am your friend—I hope I shall always be your friend, Miss Fairfield."

"I hope so too," said Lily gratefully; "you've been wonderfully good to me! I don't know how I should have got through the last fortnight if it hadn't been for you—"

"If you are really grateful to me," said M. Popeau gravely, "then there is one mark of your gratitude which I should very much appreciate."

Lily looked round at him rather surprised. "Yes?" she said.

"That mark of gratitude," he said deliberately, "is to trust me, Mademoiselle—always come to me when you are in any trouble. I do not only mean now at Monte Carlo. I mean afterwards. When in trouble, real trouble, come to Papa Popeau! Although I do not often talk of it—for, though you may be surprised to hear it, I am what you in England call a modest fellow, Miss Fairfield—Papa Popeau has a great deal of power. Papa Popeau can do all sorts of strange and wonderful things to help his friends."

"I know he can," said Lily gratefully. "I think that only Papa Popeau could have secured me such a comfortable journey."

"That is true," he said gravely.

He got up from the bench, and they began walking slowly down a cypress alley. "I think Captain Stuart is waiting for us in the road," he observed.

And then Lily—she could not have told you why—blushed very deeply.

"You like Captain Stuart, eh?" said M. Popeau.

He was looking straight before him and he spoke quite lightly, yet Lily felt a little confused. She knew that he had seen her blush.

"Yes," she said at last, "I do like him. He seems to me so—so—"

"I know," said M. Popeau, "'straight.' That's a fine English word. You are right, Miss Fairfield. Captain Stuart is a 'white' man—another of your English expressions that I like, that I have adopted for my own. But, Mademoiselle, he is also a jealous man. I would not like to make Captain Stuart jealous."

And then all at once Lily remembered something the young Scotchman had said to her, something of which he had had the grace to be ashamed a moment later. "Foreign fellows are so infernally familiar!"—that was what Captain Stuart had said to Lily Fairfield after there had come a laughing interchange of words between herself and M. Popeau. It was impossible that the Frenchman could have heard those words. And yet—and yet—Lily felt a little uncomfortable.

"It is lucky that I am an old man," went on her companion quietly. "Were I not an old man, I feel that our friend might possibly become jealous even of me. That would be most cruel, most unfair, and very hard on poor Papa Popeau! *Hein?*"

He pirouetted round on his heel for a moment, and then bowed.

"Mademoiselle," he said, "of all your servants I am the humblest and the most devoted, and I regret very much now that I did not compel you to allow me to go into the villa with you yesterday afternoon!"

"I am sorry too," said Lily in a low voice. "But I don't know—I think Aunt Cosy would have had it out with me just the same after you had gone. She didn't say much till the Count and the man from the police had left the house, and then—oh, then, M. Popeau, I've never seen anybody so angry!"

As they came through the gate to the cemetery they saw Captain Stuart's lithe figure striding impatiently up and down the road. He took Lily's hand—she had taken off her glove—and held it tightly for a moment, then he dropped it.

"I had no idea the funeral would take so long. Where are the other people?" he asked.

"There is another gate, they all went out by that, but I expected that you would be waiting here, my friend," said M. Popeau smoothly. "And now we are going off to a little restaurant in the Condamine to have a good lunch."

"I thought we were going to the Prince of Monaco's aquarium," said Lily smiling.

"All in good time." M. Popeau looked as happy as a boy. "We must make the best of today," he said, "even if it has begun badly, for from tomorrow, Mademoiselle will probably be much occupied."

Captain Stuart looked quickly round at Lily. "Why that?" he asked shortly.

And even Lily felt surprised. What could M. Popeau mean?

"I think you will find that the arrival of the Countess Polda's son will mean that you will be very much occupied," said the Frenchman quietly.

Captain Stuart looked disturbed. "But you don't even know this fellow?" he said, turning to Lily. "You've never seen him, have you?"

"No, that's quite true. But all the same, I'm afraid M. Popeau is right. Only this morning the Countess told me that she hoped—" She waited a moment.

"Yes?" said Stuart impatiently. "She hoped what, Miss Fairfield?"

"She hoped that Beppo and I would be great friends."

Lily felt a little ashamed of having said that. But, after all, it was quite true, and she did so want to know if Captain Stuart would—mind. Rather to her disappointment he remained silent.

CHAPTER 11

After a delicious fish lunch, which included the celebrated bouillabaisse so delightfully sung by Thackeray, none of the three felt in the mood for a visit to the Prince's famous aquarium. Instead, they slowly went up to old Monaco and lazed about in the terraced gardens which overhang the sea.

After a while M. Popeau exclaimed: "I'm afraid I ought to go back now to the Hôtel de Paris, for I'm expecting a message from Paris."

He looked at Captain Stuart and at Lily Fairfield in an odd, undecided way, and Captain Stuart reddened slightly under his tan. "I'll take Miss Fairfield up to La Solitude," he said shortly.

"I suppose that will be all right," but the Frenchman still looked as if uncertain what to do.

"I can walk back to La Solitude quite well by myself," said Lily smiling.

It always amused her to notice that M. Popeau seemed to regard her as something fragile and delicate, that required a great deal of looking after.

"I do not think that will be necessary, Mademoiselle," the Frenchman said in a rather dry voice. "I can trust our friend here to see that you are provided with an escort." And then he took the girl's hand and held it in his powerful, cool grasp for a moment or two.

"I am sorry you have had all this trouble," he said feelingly. "You must forget that poor Mr. Ponting ever existed."

"I don't think I shall ever forget that, M. Popeau," said Lily slowly, "or your kindness to me about it all."

He ambled off, swaying a little as he walked. Lily looked after the peculiar and rather ungainly figure with a touch of affectionate regret.

"What a pity M. Popeau doesn't take more exercise—just to keep himself in condition," she said. It was strange to feel, as she did feel, that this foreigner, whom she had only known a fortnight, had already a very secure niche in her heart—in fact, a niche next to her dear Uncle Tom. "What a dear he is!" she exclaimed.

And then, for her companion remained silent and began tracing imaginary patterns on the sandy path with his stick, Lily suddenly felt overwhelmed with a sensation very new to her—that of intense shyness.

Strange to say—it really was strange when she came to think of it—this was the very first time she had ever been alone with a man who sat so curiously silent by her side, for she did not count the few moments they had spent together yesterday morning. She remembered a funny little interchange of words they had had yesterday on the golf course, when Captain Stuart had said in such a whimsical way that he wished they two could walk on and on "beyond the mountains' purple rim." It had been said lightly, as if in fun, and yet—though Lily's mind and thoughts were then still full of her dreadful discovery—she had felt somehow that Captain Stuart's fanciful suggestion had come from his heart.

He turned towards her, and, as if echoing her thought: "I wonder if you realise that this is the very first time, if we except yesterday morning, I've ever had an opportunity of saying a word to you alone!" he exclaimed.

And Lily answered with that touch of unconscious hypocrisy which even the most truthful girl may show in such a circumstance, "I suppose it is."

"Our good friend, M. Popeau," Angus Stuart spoke with a touch of irony, "shows himself a most efficient chaperon, Miss Fairfield—"

"He has very old-fashioned ideas," said Lily a little awkwardly, "but I like him all the better for that."

"So do I," her companion's voice altered, the irony died out of it. "Most nice Frenchmen have old-fashioned ideas—I mean about young ladies. I found that out during the war. But all the same—well, I often feel envious of M. Popeau, for he seems to be always doing things for you." He turned round on the bench on which they were both sitting, and looked at her very earnestly. "I'm a lazy chap, but I'd like to—to be able to prove—"

Then he stopped dead, and Lily's heart began to beat unaccountably.

What a pity it is sometimes that two human beings cannot see what is passing through each other's minds and hearts. What a lot of trouble, pain—aye, and danger—their doing so would often save.

Angus Stuart was feeling exasperated with himself, and yet—and yet how could he take advantage of this unlooked-for opportunity? Deep in his heart he knew that he had fallen in love, practically at first sight, with Lily Fairfield, and that he was falling deeper and deeper into love each day. And yet, in a conventional sense, he hardly knew her, for they never could escape from M. Popeau. This was really the first time they had ever had a chance of a real talk together!

M. Popeau, well as he knew English, did not always express himself very happily. "Take advantage of her today, my friend," was what he had said this very morning. But that was the very last thing he, Angus Stuart, would care to do with regard to any human being, least of all with a girl whom he was almost angry with himself to find he loved.

There had been a hint, too, about her having money. If there was anything in that, it also put him off. He was, as are so many young Scottish soldiers, "a penniless lad with a long pedigree." Yet he didn't want to marry what M. Popeau had called "a 'airess." Still, deep in his heart he knew that all that really mattered to him was that he loved Lily Fairfield. During those long, dreary days at Milan he had thought of her the whole time—of her and of nothing else.

Stuart realised that he loved everything about Lily—from every shining hair on her well-set head, down to the unpractical buckled shoes on her pretty little feet. He had supposed, in his simplicity, that when one fell in love the right words always came. But they did not come to him today, sitting there by her side in that solitary garden full of brilliant bloom and colour, with the marvellous blue sea spread out before and below them, as far as the eye could see.

There are men, many men, who are in love with love. They delight in falling in love; the fact that they fall out of love almost as easily as they fall into love makes no odds at all.

But Angus Stuart was not that sort of man. Love was still to him an unfamiliar, rather menacing shape. He was ashamed of the strength of his feeling for Lily Fairfield. Now, at this moment, he felt he would give years of his life to have the right to turn round, take her in his arms and kiss her. What madness was this that was working in his brain?

He got up, and in a voice which shook a little, he said, "Shall we walk about a bit? You've never been up here in Monaco before, have you?"

"No," said Lily. "And in some ways I like it even better than Monte Carlo. It's as if one stepped right back into history, isn't it?"

But she felt chilled, and somehow disappointed. She would have been quite content to sit on there in the lovely, deserted garden. She had thoughts that her acquaintance with Captain Stuart would make great strides once they were really alone together—that he would tell something about himself and his people. Why, she didn't even know if he had a sister!

And yet in a way she did feel as if she already knew the young Scots soldier very well. It was as if they were bound by a strong invisible link the one to the other. She remembered the wonderful gentleness and kindness of his manner when she had come up breathless to the hotel door yesterday morning, her face blurred with crying. He had seemed to understand exactly what she was feeling, and he had soothed and comforted her. But now, this afternoon, he seemed quite unlike the man whom she had first told of her hideous discovery.

"I think I must be going up to La Solitude soon," she said rather nervously. "Beppo Polda is arriving tomorrow, and they're having a kind of spring cleaning in his honour;" she smiled a little. "I said I'd help Cristina with it."

"Surely you needn't go yet? It's quite early,"—there was an urgent note in Captain Stuart's voice.

"I ought to have been back by four. It's that now," she said.

As they walked through the narrow, mediæval street which leads to the great square in front of the Palace of Monaco, and as they made their way across the square to the kind of mall where stand the ancient iron cannons pointing their toy-like muzzles towards France, the barrier, the impalpable, yet very real barrier, which each felt had arisen between them seemed to melt gradually away.

It was Lily who first broke the barrier down. He had just told her that early in the war he had been given a special training job and had been stationed, though only for five weeks, near Epsom.

"I wish we had met then," she said quickly, regretfully.

He answered eagerly. "I wish we had! Those were the loneliest five weeks of my life!" And then he said something implying that though there had been a great deal in the papers early in the war about showing soldiers hospitality, not much of it had come his way.

"That was perhaps a little bit of your own fault." Lily wondered at her own daring, but he took it in good part.

"I daresay it was," he said gravely. "I—I don't make friends easily, Miss Fairfield." Something outside himself prompted him to add: "I've never had what so many chaps seem to have now—a woman pal." He added, honestly enough, "I never felt I wanted one till now." And then, more lightly, "I wish you'd think of me as you do of—of M. Popeau."

And then for the first time with him, there came a touch of coquetry into Lily Fairfield's manner—that touch of coquetry which nature teaches every normal, happy-natured girl when the ball lies at her feet.

"He asked me to call him 'Papa Popeau' today," she said demurely. "Somehow I can't imagine your asking anyone to call you 'Papa Stuart!'"

They both laughed, a mirthful, youthful peal of joint laughter. "And are you going to call him 'Papa Popeau?'" asked Captain Stuart, smiling broadly.

She shook her head. "No, I really can't do that—though I do like him—most awfully!"

"I won't ask you to call me anything yet," he said seriously.

He stopped speaking abruptly, and Lily, almost as if she was being "willed" to do it, turned and looked up into his face. She told herself that it was a fine, honest, strong face—not perhaps that of an always good-tempered man, but a face one would like to be looking up into if one were suddenly caught in a tight corner.

"I want to feel that we're friends—really friends," he said slowly. "If anything else disagreeable or painful should happen to you—which God forbid!" he added hastily, for he saw her face quiver and change a little—"then I hope you'll come to me as readily as you would to—Papa Popeau!"

"I did come to you," she said in a low voice. "I thought of you at once, yesterday morning. Aunt Cosy was furious with me because I didn't go back to the house. But somehow I felt I would much rather come and tell you the dreadful thing which had happened to me."

"I'm awfully grateful to you for saying that!" Angus Stuart's measured voice became charged with emotion. He went on, speaking a little quickly: "I longed to take you to that police chap myself, but I knew that Popeau would do the job much better than I could do it. I suppose you know what Popeau really is?"

"I haven't the slightest idea!" she exclaimed.

"He's the head of a very important branch of the French Secret Service. Since the war he's been worked to death; and though he's on holiday now, they keep in very close touch with him."

Lily was extremely surprised, and rather thrilled. "I wonder why he didn't tell me?" she exclaimed.

"He's an odd sort of man," said Angus Stuart thoughtfully. "I don't think he's exactly proud of his job, Miss Fairfield. Perhaps he'd rather you didn't know. You'll keep the fact to yourself, eh?"

"Of course I will!" said Lily.

She was beginning to feel very tired, and her companion looked at her solicitously.

The last few minutes had made a great difference to him. He felt a curious sense of peace come over him. How angelic of her to want to come to *him* when that dreadful thing happened to her! He would never, never forget her saying that to him. It was the first mile-stone in their friendship—a golden moment in his life. He had always felt that a woman worth the winning must be wooed before she is won. He told himself, as they walked side by side across the great sunlit space, that he had made a very good beginning.

"Now I'm going to drive you up to La Solitude," he exclaimed, with a touch of that masterfulness which somehow Lily liked—when it came from him.

He hailed the solitary open cab which stood in the shadow of the building, now a barrack, where gambling was first started in the Principality fifty years ago.

To Lily's distress, he did not bargain with the man—he simply threw him the name, "La Solitude," in rather indifferent French.

The cabman whipped up his little horses, and a moment later they were rattling down the winding road cut in the side of the rock at a breakneck pace.

All too soon—or so it seemed to them both—they had reached the clearing below the Lonely House. Angus Stuart gripped Lily's hand. "Then from today we're pals—real pals?" he said, and Lily answered very seriously, "Yes."

To Lily's relief, the Countess was far too full of Beppo's coming arrival on the morrow to trouble as to how the girl had spent her time after the funeral of George Ponting: and the rest of the afternoon was devoted to preparing a large front room, which was apparently always kept for Beppo.

There was not very much to be done, but certain pieces of furniture were moved in from the other rooms in order to make it more comfortable for the apparently luxurious young man's occupation.

When, at last, tired out by the varied emotions of the day, Lily was going off to bed, the Countess said briskly: "We must be off early tomorrow morning to choose your pretty frocks before Beppo's arrival! I shall be ready to start at nine o'clock. Your Uncle Angelo has ordered a carriage for us."

Lily felt taken aback, and disappointed, too. She would so infinitely rather have chosen her new clothes herself! But there was nothing to be done, and as events turned out she was wrong to be disappointed, for she could not have done as well as she and Aunt Cosy did together.

CHAPTER 12

Monte Carlo in the morning is very unlike Monte Carlo in the afternoon or evening.

Though the sun poured down on the beautiful gardens, there was a sleepy, unawakened look about the place—an air of *déshabille*. The majority of the windows of the Hôtel de Paris were still closely shuttered, and the Paradise of Pleasure Seekers, as it has been somewhat cynically called, was now given over to the toilers whose lifework is to provide life-ease for others.

Dozens of gardeners were busily engaged in sweeping the paths of the embowered gardens, and in watering the brilliant, many-hued blossoms which compose the vast, carpet-like parterre in front of the Casino. Ant-like convoys of country folk, laden with vegetables, flowers, eggs, cheese, and so on, were moving slowly across the Grande Place.

Lily looked about her with curiosity and interest. The Monte Carlo of the foreigner and the gambler was still fast asleep. Was it likely that any of the smart shops would be open?

The Countess called out to the driver and the carriage stopped. Then, turning to Lily, she observed: "We will walk to the Galerie Charles Trois. I know a very good dressmaker there—as a matter of fact, she is connected with the Polda family, for her grandfather was steward to your Uncle Angelo's grandfather. Her sister keeps an hotel in the Condamine."

The Galerie Charles Trois, with its luxurious-looking, magnificent restaurants and elegant shops, also looked strangely deserted, though it was occupied by an army of dusters, sweepers, and window-washers. Several of the shops were shut, but still, many were open, and the two ladies walked slowly along, admiring the pretty things on view. What specially fascinated Aunt Cosy were the jewellers' windows, and Lily had never seen such splendid gems or such gorgeous ornaments even in Bond Street or Regent Street.

All that makes of Monte Carlo a place absolutely apart seemed this morning more vividly real to the English girl than anything she had seen yet. Those for whom all these preparations were being made, and all these luxuries laid out, were still heavily asleep for the most part. But the army of men and women who ministered to their pleasure were all hard at work, for the most part with an air of anxiety and fatigue on their faces. Even the working folk of Monte Carlo do not go early to bed.

At last, when they were close to the end of the Galerie, the Countess exclaimed: "Here we are!" And Lily, looking up, saw a modest little shop, inscribed in gold letters, "Madame Jeanne." In the window were displayed three simple-looking hats and a muslin gown, also a plain grey and white silk jumper, with regard to which, nevertheless, Lily told herself that it was one of the prettiest jumpers she had ever seen.

"Now, Lily," said the Countess earnestly, "you may absolutely trust the taste of Madame Jeanne. She was *première* in a great Paris house before she started for herself; and though there may not seem to be much in the shop, what there is will be of the very finest quality; also, she will know what young girls are now wearing in Rome and Paris." As she said those last words she walked into the shop, and a pleasant-looking, middle-aged woman came forward.

"Madame la Comtesse? This is indeed a pleasure!" she exclaimed effusively. "Why, it is more like years than months since last I had the pleasure of seeing Madame la Comtesse!"

"Yes, my good Jeanne," said the Countess graciously. "It is indeed a long time since we met. But the Count went to your sister's hotel only yesterday, and was able, I am glad to say, to do one of her clients a little service. I am bringing you today a good new customer! We want two or three pretty dresses, and we want them at once. As you see, Mademoiselle is in half-mourning, so we must only choose white and grey gowns, for mauve is not a young girl's colour."

"I can make Mademoiselle something very pretty," began the woman, but the Countess cut her short: "We want today a simple, yet smart, coat and skirt, an afternoon Casino and restaurant gown, and a simple, girlish evening dress. We want to take them away now, this morning."

Mme. Jeanne looked a little uncomfortable, and also a little surprised.

"Everything is very dear—" she began, hesitatingly, "though of course I should always make a very special price for Madame la Comtesse."

"I count on that, my good Jeanne, for Mademoiselle will pay ready money."

The woman's face cleared as if by magic. "If I have not got exactly what Mademoiselle requires, I can borrow something from one or two of my rivals," she said smiling.

The two ladies were shown into an inner room panelled with looking-glass. There they waited for a very few minutes—though the Countess was fidgety, and kept saying that she thought Jeanne might hurry herself a little more—before two neatly-dressed girls with beautifully-done hair, brought in, the one a selection of delightful-looking pale-grey and cream coats and skirts, and the other an armful of filmy white blouses.

Lily tried on all the coats and skirts, but the second one she had put on obviously suited her the best. It was of a delicate, pale brownish-grey tint, and though it was very simply made, she was at once agreeably aware, as she gazed this way and that, seeing reflections of herself wherever she turned, that she had never looked so well-dressed in her life as she looked in this little coat and skirt.

As for the blouses to be worn with the frock, they were all so pretty that she could not make up her mind between them, and she ended by choosing five.

Before she took off the coat and skirt, Mme. Jeanne suddenly exclaimed: "Surely Mademoiselle will want a hat to match the costume?" And before Lily could answer a delightful little grey toque, trimmed with Mercury wings, was produced.

The selection of a muslin gown and of a silk coatee to wear with it was a very quick affair. In spite of the Countess's objection to mauve, Mme. Jeanne persuaded her that Mademoiselle would look well in deep violet. The collar and cuffs of the coatee were of dark fur, and the same note of colour was repeated in a tiny round purple hat trimmed with some pompoms of fur which Lily felt she must certainly buy too!

Then came the important question of the evening dress. Over that business the two ladies spent a long time. Gown after gown was rejected by the Countess as too elaborate, and not young enough for her niece, and at last Lily felt quite tired out of standing like a doll to be dressed, redressed and undressed.

Mme. Jeanne, on her side, began to wonder if she would ever please her difficult client, the Countess Polda, when suddenly a simple pale grey chiffon gown was produced and slipped over Lily's head. It was what is called in England a picture dress. It belonged, that is, to no special time or fashion, and it was extremely becoming to the wearer's delicate, brilliant complexion, and beautiful fair hair.

"Even if Mademoiselle is in mourning, could she not wear with this gown a turquoise-blue velvet belt?" Without waiting for an answer, Mme. Jeanne fetched a bit of turquoise ribbon and put it around the girl's slender, rounded waist. The effect was enchanting!

But the sight of the velvet ribbon made Lily feel guilty. Though she often felt now as if she were living in another world, she did not forget The Nest at Epsom, and Aunt Emmeline's long, loving kindness to her. She grew very red, and said quickly: "I would rather have a black belt."

"No, no, not black!" exclaimed Mme. Jeanne decidedly, "but grey if you like, to tone in with the gown, Mademoiselle. That will be quite pretty. And here is something else—a real bargain this time!" As she spoke she went to a cupboard and took out a black and white striped evening cloak. It was a very attractive garment, though perhaps a little old for a girl.

"This was ordered by a war widow; but between ordering this cloak and its completion, which was only three days, the lady became engaged! So she made up her mind she need not wear mourning for her departed hero anymore. Only three hundred francs?"

She threw it over Lily's shoulders, and the girl realised that it gave a touch of elegant finish to her appearance.

"The cloak goes so well with this dress," went on Madame Jeanne, "because it, also, was copied from an old picture—a picture which hangs in the Palace of Monaco. If I may venture to advise Mademoiselle, I should have this beautiful cloak repeated when Mademoiselle goes back to colours. It would look exquisite in pale lemon yellow and turquoise blue."

And as Lily was still hesitating, Mme. Jeanne exclaimed: "Oh, but I forgot—there is a bag that goes with the cloak. That alone was to have been a hundred francs, but I shall give it to Mademoiselle—it shall be thrown in!"

She pulled out a drawer, and took from it a quaint little silk bag. The clasp was of light tortoiseshell, and it really was a charming little object.

"Thank you so much, Jeanne! I knew I could count both on your kindness and on your beautiful taste," said the Countess very cordially. "And now," she turned to Lily, "we must go off to the bank and get the money for Mme. Jeanne! Make out the bill Jeanne, and remember that we are paying cash!"

Madame retired into an inner room for a few minutes, then came back and handed the account to the Countess.

"I hope Madame la Comtesse will consider that I have been more than reasonable," she said a little nervously.

The Countess frowned as she looked over the bill. Then she sighed. "Yes, my good Jeanne, I suppose that these monstrous prices *are* being given nowadays! But still, three hundred and fifty francs for a muslin gown—and two hundred for the silk coatee! The sort of gown which as a young girl I should have had for a hundred francs—or less, indeed, had it been made at home! And the hats? Jeanne, Jeanne—the hats are surely very costly for a young girl?"

Madame looked over the bill as if she had forgotten what she had put down for the hats; then she observed with a virtuous air: "I will take ten francs off each of the hats to please Madame la Comtesse."

All this time Lily stood by, not being consulted, not even knowing the amount which she was going to pay. The only time she herself had interfered had been in connection with the grey gown. The Countess had seemed to think that the price of the very simple chiffon frock—five hundred francs—was really too much. But Lily had suddenly felt she *must* have *this* dress! It was the prettiest evening gown, so she told herself secretly, that she had ever had the chance of wearing, and she did not want to lose it.

"Get everything packed as quickly as possible," exclaimed the Countess, "for the Count and I have a great deal to do before the arrival of Count Beppo."

"Is Count Beppo coming to Monte Carlo?" exclaimed Madame Jeanne, evidently much interested by this little item of news.

"Yes," said the Countess. "He was not coming till the spring, but now, to my great joy and satisfaction, he has been able to leave Rome, and we hope he will be with us for some time."

"And is Mademoiselle also staying at La Solitude?" asked the woman. There was a touch of eager, but kindly, inquisitiveness in her voice.

"Yes, my good Jeanne," said the Countess. "We hope to keep my niece all the winter."

"I hope it will not be long before I see Madame la Comtesse again," said the woman.

"As you know, I cannot walk uphill, and carriages are now so expensive—" the Countess sighed. "But still, while my son is here I hope to come down to the town now and again, and I will certainly look in."

She went out of the shop, followed by Lily. "Now, my dear, we must go to the bank, come back here, and then return as quickly as possible to La Solitude. You will not mind lunching by yourself? Uncle Angelo and I have several things to do in view of our beloved Beppo's visit—and his train arrives at two o'clock."

Not for the first time the girl was struck by Aunt Cosy's air of fierce determination. She looked, in spite of her weak heart, energy personified.

But, determined as was the Countess Polda, there was a strain of obstinacy in Lily Fairfield, too, as the older lady sometimes found to her cost.

When they got back to La Solitude, before the Count and Countess started for Monte Carlo, quite a passage of arms took place between them. The Countess was not satisfied with the simple frock in which Lily had come down that morning, and, to please her, Lily changed into a white serge skirt and put on one of her new blouses. But, even so, the Countess was still dissatisfied.

Then it was that Lily made a stand. "No, Aunt Cosy, I really can't put on one of the smart dresses we bought this morning—I should feel so odd and uncomfortable!"

Aunt Cosy had given in, but there came a gleam of anger in her bright blue eyes. "I asked you to do so in your own interest," she said coldly. "Beppo is very observant. He is an expert as to ladies' dress. I have heard him make very scathing remarks about the clothes worn by certain pretty ladies!"

A very scathing reply trembled on Lily's lips—but she forced it back; and, at last, to her secret relief, she saw the Count and Countess disappear together on their way down to the town. What a singular young man Beppo Polda must be! Lily made up her mind that she was not going to like him.

CHAPTER 13

Lily got up from her simple luncheon with the agreeable knowledge that she was free to do exactly what she liked for the next three hours.

Aunt Cosy had a way of continually asking her what she was going to do next, which was annoying to a girl who had always planned out her day very much as she thought best. Now she remembered that Uncle Tom had ordered a number of picture papers to be sent out from England each week, and that the first big batch had arrived this morning.

Gathering the heavy, rolled-up parcels together, she went out of doors, and sat down in one of the comfortable wicker chairs which had been her first gift to the Count and Countess.

How still, how beautiful, how exquisitely peaceful was the scene round, above, and below, the terrace of La Solitude! No wonder she was beginning to feel marvellously better....

She had been reading for rather over an hour when there broke across the intense, brooding quietude of the early afternoon the hoot of a motor. She glanced at her wrist watch. It was only one o'clock—Beppo's train would not be in for a long time. But Captain Stuart had said something—when they had bidden each other good-bye yesterday—about their meeting again today. Perhaps he had come up to make some suggestion about tennis or golf? If so, how fortunate it was that Aunt Cosy was out!

Lily stood up and stepped down on to the lawn, quite unconscious of the eager, welcoming, happy look on her face.

All at once there emerged from the path leading up through the orange grove a tall, dark young man, wearing white flannels and a straw hat. For a moment she felt a shock of deep disappointment, for it was not Captain Stuart—a moment later she told herself that it was, it must be, Beppo Polda!

Lily Fairfield made a delightful picture as she stood on the grass below the terrace, a delicate yet vivid colour coming and going in her cheeks, her lovely, fair hair uncovered, for she had not troubled to put on a hat. Thus, even apart from a very special reason he had for feeling interested in her— and he had such a very special reason—Count Beppo Polda felt extremely attracted to the pretty stranger.

He took off his smart straw hat with a graceful gesture, and, speaking in remarkably good English, though with a strong foreign accent, he exclaimed: "Have I the honour to greet Miss Fairfield?"

He held out his hand and fixed on her a pair of brilliant penetrating eyes.

As he came close up to her, Lily felt a most curious sensation creep over her, a mingling—if it be not a contradiction in terms—of attraction and repulsion. Of attraction, because, though she was not the kind of girl to set much store by looks, Count Beppo was so extraordinarily handsome: of repulsion, because he was so very like his mother! Lily though hardly conscious that it was so, was beginning strongly to dislike, as well as fear, the woman whom she called "Aunt Cosy," and that, though she often tried to feel grateful for the Countess's undoubted, if often fussy, kindness to her.

Count Beppo had all his mother's good points; her tall, upright figure, her clear-cut features, and her one-time thick, curling hair. From his plain, short father, he had inherited that indefinable look of race which generally, though not always by any means, implies in its possessor a long pedigree. He also possessed what is, in most countries a rare gift—that is, a most beautiful speaking voice. Just now he was in the pink of physical condition, very unlike the still war-weary young Frenchmen Lily sometimes saw walking about Monte Carlo, or playing on the wind-swept golf course.

Taking the hand the girl held out to him, the young man respectfully lifted it to his lips. Now this was the first time Lily's hand had ever been kissed by a man, and she thought it a pretty, if rather a singular, custom.

They stood talking together for a few moments while Count Beppo explained in his full, caressing voice how he had always longed to meet Miss Fairfield, ever since his mother had told him of her many delightful qualities, when he was still a boy, years ago, after the Countess had paid her memorable visit to England!

Lily felt just a little embarrassed, as well as rather thrilled. She had never met anyone in the least like this young man before! Then she bethought herself of the Count and Countess. And how about Count Beppo's luggage? He had nothing in his hand but a Malacca cane set with one large, pale-green turquoise. Held by a young Englishman, the cane would have looked foppish, and a trifle absurd: but, somehow, it seemed in perfect harmony with the rest of Count Beppo's smart, rather dandified appearance.

"And now," he said at last, "I suppose I must go in and greet my papa and mamma—or are they having a siesta? If yes, perhaps I may linger in Capua yet a little longer," and he smiled down, very delightfully, into Lily's pretty face.

"Didn't they meet you?" she exclaimed. "They were expecting you by the two o'clock train!"

Her companion laughed. "I gave them what you in England call 'the slip'! I arrived at Monte yesterday!"

"Yesterday?" Lily was much surprised.

"I have put up at the Hidalgo Hotel," he went on. "It is very select and comfortable."

Lily remembered the hours she and Cristina had spent in making what was evidently the real spare room of La Solitude pleasant and habitable from the point of view of a highly civilised young man. Also, it must be confessed that she felt a little disappointed. Life at La Solitude was sometimes very dull!

"I suppose some letter you wrote was lost in the post. I know that your mother thought you were going to stay here."

Beppo looked at her with a rather funny look, and then lowering his voice slightly, he exclaimed: "La Solitude is a delightful place—but the last time I stayed here I said to myself, 'Never again!' You see, I'm used to being able to take a hot bath whenever I feel like it! Then there's another reason. If I stay at La Solitude it becomes a delicate matter for me to join the Club! The rule is absolute with regard to land owners in Monaco; none of them may play either in the Casino or at the Club."

"You know what mamma is like," he went on confidentially. "If I had told her that I was going to an hotel, there would have been endless discussions and long letters—for my dear mamma is a great letter-writer! I intended to send up a note this morning, but I was having such a splendid game of tennis;" he smiled a little self-consciously. "I was playing a single with the Spanish champion! So I really could not tear myself away!"

Lily felt suddenly revolted by Beppo's callous indifference to the disappointment he had inflicted on his devoted father and mother.

"I think you ought to go down into the town now," she said firmly, "and try to find them. It'll be a dreadful blow to them if they go to the station and find that you are not there."

"I'll tell you what I'll do—I'll send down Cristina!" She asked herself why the deep caressing voice had such a curiously attractive lure about it.

And even as he spoke her name the old waiting woman appeared at the open drawing-room window. Joy flashed into her face, and a moment later his arms were round her neck, and he was kissing her affectionately.

A few seconds ago Lily had felt as if she hated Beppo for his selfishness, and utter lack of consideration for his parents. But now she saw that there was, after all, a very kindly side to his nature.

With one arm still round Cristina's shoulders, he turned to the girl and smiled, not a trace of embarrassment on his handsome face.

"Cristina is my second mamma!" he exclaimed. "She was my darling, kind nurse—as kind to me as the nurse in your Shakespeare's beautiful tragedy, 'Romeo and Juliet' was to her sweet girl."

He turned, and repeated what he had said in Italian, and a little colour came into Cristina's pale, sensitive face.

"Mademoiselle does not know our language," she said in French, and then she added something in Italian.

He turned laughingly to Lily. "She tells me that I have a rival in her heart! You have made a conquest, Miss Lily! Cristina is hard to please where young ladies are concerned."

There was no contradiction from Cristina, and he went on, shaking his finger at the old woman: "Never shall I forget bringing a beautiful lady to call on my mother! She was beautiful, but alas! her cheeks were too pink, her lips too red, her hair too yellow, to please the holy Cristina. So Cristina was very, very cold to the charming creature!"

Though Cristina knew no English, she evidently guessed what he was saying, for she shook her head and again said something in Italian.

"She says that you are not at all like the naughty ladies of today—that everything about you is real, and that you are more like one of the beautiful saints of old. And now,"—turning to Cristina and speaking in French—"Miss Lily and I wish you to do something for us, dear friend. We want you to go down into Monte Carlo and find papa and mamma. Just say that I have arrived—you need not say anything more. Let them think that I came by one of those de luxe trains that arrive in the morning."

To Lily's surprise Cristina made no objection. "In a few moments I will be gone," she said.

As she turned away Beppo called out after her: "Cristina! You might go to the Hidalgo Hotel before finding my parents. Get the first-floor valet—he's a very decent fellow, an Italian—to give you my dress clothes. I'll dress up here, in the delightful room which mamma has had prepared for me, and which I am not going to occupy—or at any rate not yet! And Cristina? Tell the valet to order a motor to come up for me at—let me see, you're early folk, aren't you, and the Club's open late—well, let's say half-past ten, and then I can spend a pleasant hour at the Club before turning in."

He took a bundle of notes out of his pocket and put them in Cristina's hand. "I'm very poor just now! But you must see that we have a good dinner tonight. And buy a pretty bouquet for Mademoiselle!"

Cristina smiled more joyously than Lily had ever seen her smile, as she nodded her head wisely.

When she had gone: "I wish mamma was more like Cristina!" he exclaimed, with a funny kind of look. Lily could not help smiling. There was certainly something attractive about Beppo Polda!

The hour that followed seemed to go by very quickly—more quickly than any hour the girl had spent since her arrival at Monte Carlo.

The young Count had plenty to say for himself; also he managed to convey how much he admired her—Lily. At once he had claimed relationship. Soon he called her "my pretty cousin," and instructed her to call him "Beppo." He also told her, which amused her, that he and his mother always talked English when they were 'talking secrets.' "We shan't be able to do that now," he said, laughing.

Perhaps one reason why Lily liked Beppo so much was that he was such a pleasant surprise! Somehow, while looking forward to seeing him, she had felt sure he would be a disagreeable, supercilious young man. She was astonished to find how quickly she felt at ease with him. More than once during that first hour of their acquaintance the thought of Angus Stuart flashed into her mind. How would those two get on, she wondered—perhaps not so badly, after all?

Beppo, in spite of his appearance, was more like a child than a man, so Lily decided within herself. He had a happy child's self-confidence and belief that everyone was going to be kind to him. But he was like a spoilt child; though that, she decided, was his mother's fault.

Just as she was thinking this, they heard the sound of wheels on the little clearing below. Lily got up from her wicker chair and, to her surprise, Beppo took her hand as if to help her, and then kept her hand within his and looked down ardently into her eyes. With a sensation of surprise, she told herself that he was not a child at all, but a very determined man! There was a look on his face which made her feel suddenly uncomfortable.

She freed her hand from his rather quickly, and he said: "Forgive me! But I cannot help remembering that we shall not be alone together again for a long time. Do you realise, Cousin Lily, that we have been alone—quite alone—up here, in this lonely place, for sixty full minutes?"

"Of course I do," she answered, blushing a little. "But I never thought about it."

"I remembered it," he exclaimed, "every minute of the time! And I couldn't help being sorry we were not greater friends than we are—yet."

He said those words in a low, meaning tone, and somehow that little interchange of words spoilt the girl's pleasant feeling of being at ease in his company. Why had he said that? She hoped he was not going to try to flirt with her! Lily would have been very much surprised, and even indignant, had someone told her that Count Beppo Polda had been doing nothing else since they had first met one another an hour ago.

Even so, she felt just a little nervous as she saw the three figures emerging slowly from the orange grove; but the Countess said not a word as to her son's having disappointed her with regard to the time of his arrival; and she pretended to think it quite natural that he should be staying at an hotel. With regard to that, however, Beppo had the grace to say a few apologetic words, explaining, what he had not told Lily, that some friends of his were staying at the Hidalgo, and that he had promised long ago that when these people came to Monte Carlo he would be one of their party.

Lily made more than one effort on that afternoon to leave Beppo alone with his parents. Surely they must have things to say to one another, after their long separation? But both the young man and his mother seemed determined that she should stay with them all the time.

At last she went up to dress for dinner, and she had put on the pretty muslin dress Aunt Cosy so much admired, and had wished her to put on that morning—when, opening the door of her room, she suddenly heard Beppo's voice coming from below.

He was speaking, very sternly and decidedly, in English.

"A promise is a promise, mamma! I absolutely counted on that money. I had hoped to stay with you till the New Year. As it is, I must go back to Rome in a very few days."

Lily heard the murmured answer: "If you should receive the money within, say, a week, could you then stay on?"

"Certainly I could."

And then someone—probably the Countess—walked quickly across to the door of the small sitting-room at the bottom of the staircase, and shut the door. Lily felt sorry she had heard so much, or so little.

Now, for the first time, it did strike her as very strange that Beppo should look so well-to-do, so entirely the idle man of fashion, while she knew the money his parents received from her as their paying guest meant so much to them. Once or twice the Countess had spoken to her as though Beppo was concerned with big business affairs; but if that were so, how could the small amount of money his mother might, or might not, send him, make the slightest difference to his movements?

On going downstairs, Lily went into the kitchen to see if she could help Cristina. The old woman was standing there, a smile on her face. She looked extraordinarily happy. She took hold of the girl's hand.

"How do you like our Beppo?" she said eagerly. "He is so kind, so generous, and so very, very handsome—do you not think so?"

Lily laughed. "Yes, I think he is very handsome," she said frankly. "And very like his mother."

"No, no!" Cristina frowned. "He is like his grandfather, the Count's father. He was a beautiful man, and a friend of the first King of Italy."

Beppo's coming had quite changed Cristina: she looked much more alive, and talked in an eager, decided way.

"Can I help you at all?" asked Lily.

"Everything is ready! I did not use any of the child's money. I gave it him all back. The Count and Countess had already bought everything. We shall have a feast tonight!"

"I'm sorry he's not staying here," said Lily slowly.

Cristina gave her a curious look. "*You* ask him to come!" she exclaimed. She evidently thought that Lily was sorry for her own sake. As a matter of fact, Lily was now only sorry for Aunt Cosy's sake.

"I think," she said quietly, "that Count Beppo ought to have arranged to stay here, as his parents wished him to do."

But Cristina shook her head decidedly. "No, no," she answered, "he would not be happy here. He likes what we call 'the English comfort,' my little lady."

CHAPTER 14

But next day all was radiant happiness and good humour—indeed, the whole atmosphere of the Lonely House seemed transformed. Even Mimi looked as if it knew of Beppo's arrival, for the cat walked about purring, and for once left the birds alone.

The night before, during dinner, Beppo had overcome his mother's dislike to leaving La Solitude.

"I won't ask you to come often," he said coaxingly. "But tomorrow we'll just have a nice little luncheon—you, and papa, and our charming English cousin! The Pescobaldis are going out to lunch."

As Beppo uttered the long, peculiar Italian name the Countess frowned for the first time since her son's arrival. "Have *they* come with you?" she exclaimed, in a surprised, annoyed tone. "You did not say that they were the friends who are staying with you at the Hidalgo Hotel!"

"Surely I did, mamma?" said the young man uncomfortably. "That is the reason why I am at the Hidalgo instead of here."

There was a pause, and then Aunt Cosy turned to Lily.

"It will interest you to meet the Marchesa Pescobaldi," she observed. "She is a very charming and clever woman. It would, perhaps, be unkind to add that the Marchesa has the unfortunate reputation of possessing the evil eye."

Now it was Beppo's turn to frown, and a very angry look came over his good-looking face and brilliant, piercing blue eyes.

"It is very wrong of you to say that to Lily!" he exclaimed. "You must understand"—he turned rather quickly to the girl—"that in Italy any person is said to have the evil eye who even for a moment is disliked by the speaker. It is a malicious thing to say! Let us be frank, as you say in England. Mamma does not like my friend; therefore she attributes to her the evil eye—that is all!"

Poor Lily felt desperately uncomfortable, so she wisely said nothing. As for the Countess, she burst out into somewhat bitter laughter.

"Beppo does right to defend the Marchesa," she said sarcastically, "for the lady's husband is his greatest friend."

"Cosy, Cosy!" interposed Count Polda, "you forget that the Pescobaldis are connections of ours."

* * * *

By eleven o'clock they were all three ready, Lily wearing her new coat and skirt and becoming little hat. The Countess called Cristina to see how pretty the girl looked, and Lily could not help feeling grateful and touched. What a strange mixture Aunt Cosy was! A mixture of generosity and meanness, of good humour and frightful temper, of kindliness and spitefulness.

When Beppo arrived they were taken by surprise, for, according to his mother, he was most unpunctual.

"Come quick!" he called out. "The Pescobaldis are waiting for us in the car. We shall all drive together to Eze, where they are going to lunch with some friends who have a villa there, and then we four will go for a delightful little drive, and end up at the restaurant of the Hôtel de Paris."

It was a perfect day. The sun was shining, the air was full of an exquisite limpidity, and Lily, as she walked out of the drawing-room and joined Beppo on the lawn, feeling perhaps a little self-conscious in her new coat and skirt and smart hat, told herself that "all this" was great fun!

She could not but be aware that Beppo was looking at her with a bolder, franker admiration in his eyes than any Englishman or even Frenchman would have done.

They hurried down through the orange grove, to see on the clearing, which always recalled to the girl the dreadful morning when she had found George Ponting's body, a large open touring-car, in which were seated a lady and a gentleman.

As they emerged from the wood, the lady stood up—and Lily gazed at the most beautiful woman she had ever seen.

The Marchesa Pescobaldi was tall and slender, her face was a perfect oval, and her complexion had a delicate, camelia-like bloom, while her silvery grey hair was abundant, and beautifully dressed.

She looked neither old nor young. Her glorious beauty might almost have been described as of an ageless type. As for her grey hair, it set off her flawless complexion, and intensified the dark fire of her large eyes. She made Lily feel curiously young and unimportant.

As the Count and Countess appeared she called out the English word "Welcome!" and then she threw a long, intense, critical glance at Lily Fairfield.

The English girl made a very dainty and delightful picture against the dark-green, glossy leaves, and the Marchesa Pescobaldi noticed that she walked with a graceful, assured carriage. For a long flashing moment Lily's hazel eyes and the full, dark, brilliant orbs of the older woman crossed like swords, and Lily felt a thrill go through her as she remembered what Aunt Cosy had said. Had the Marchesa really the evil eye?

Lily looked shyly at the man who was evidently the owner of the car. The Marchese Pescobaldi was very thin and very yellow—much, indeed, Lily's idea of what an Italian nobleman would look like. He seemed in a great hurry to be off, and they all settled down into the car very quickly, the three ladies behind, the three men in front. The Marchesa sat between the Countess and Lily, and soon they were whirling on, sometimes zig-zagging along rather rough roads, Beppo driving with great skill and judgment.

Lily sat well back, enjoying the drive, while her two companions talked together, speaking very quickly in French. Now and again she caught a word or two of what they were saying in the rushing wind.

But she was not thinking of the Countess Polda and of the Italian lady who now sat next to her. She was wondering, with a touch of discomfort how she could manage, now that Beppo was here, to communicate with M. Popeau and Captain Stuart. Somehow she felt that it would not be as easy as it had been hitherto. Perhaps she might write M. Popeau a little note, saying how very grateful she was for all his kindness over the sad business in which they had been so curiously associated, and explaining that, owing to Count Beppo's arrival, she was likely to be a good deal engaged the next few days.

Suddenly they came to a yellow marshy piece of ground, and the motor sank in the quaking mud. Beppo stopped the motor dead for a few moments. Then it was that Lily heard the following little snatch of conversation between the two who were sitting next to her.

"All I ask is, are you really satisfied about the only thing that matters—the money?" asked the Marchesa in French. "Can you swear this on the head of the person in whom we both take an interest? If yes, then instead of hindering you, I shall try in every way to further the affair."

The question, or series of questions, were uttered in a low and quick but very clear voice.

There was a pause, and then came the answer, uttered solemnly, "I swear to you that the money is assured, Livia."

It was the first time Lily Fairfield had ever heard the woman she called Aunt Cosy give a short, direct reply to any question, but it was not the first time by any means that she had been as if compelled to note the extraordinary importance foreigners seemed to attach to the possession of money! Lily could never get accustomed to this peculiarity in either Aunt Cosy or Uncle Angelo. And how this haughty and evidently very rich Italian lady was talking in just the same way—as if money was the only thing that mattered in life.

The motor started off again, and after a few more minutes' delicious rush through the scented air it drew up before the gates of a large villa.

Everyone stood up: the Countess Polda, indeed, stepped out of the car in order that the Marchesa might get down more comfortably.

And then once more Lily told herself that she had never seen such a beautiful woman as was this Marchesa Pescobaldi! She was dressed in a severely simple black cloth coat and skirt, but that only emphasised the graceful, supple lines of her tall figure. There was also a wonderful look of health and of power about her whole appearance. Yet she did not look happy, or at ease. She looked bored and cross, and while she waited for the two men she tapped her arched right foot impatiently.

Beppo Polda accompanied his friends a few yards up the path which led to the villa, and Lily, as she gazed at the group, could not help thinking what a fine, strong young man he looked compared with his thin, dried-up-looking Italian friend.

At last he stayed his steps, and, turning, said something to the Marchesa. She held out her hand, and he lifted it up to his lips, and respectfully kissed it.

Then he hurried back to the car.

Waiting till the Pescobaldis were well out of earshot: "Now, Lily," he cried out gaily, "come and sit by me, pretty cousin! I'm going to take you all just a little round before we go to the Hôtel de Paris for luncheon. Papa, do you mind sitting by mamma?"

The Count got into the back of the car by his wife, and Lily took the place in front. Somehow she now felt exhilarated and pleasantly at ease. The Marchesa's personality had affected her disagreeably.

As they drove along, Beppo talked to her with eager animation, telling her all sorts of curious, interesting, and yet, amusing things, about the places they passed. She learnt more from him in half an hour about this quaint and beautiful part of the Riviera than she had learnt from his father and mother all the time she had been at La Solitude.

At last they turned round, and swept down into Monte Carlo. "The Marchesa's chauffeur will take over the car and then come back for us in an hour," said Beppo.

"Have you ordered luncheon?" his mother inquired.

"Mamma! Of course I've ordered a very nice luncheon, including the lobster à la sauce verte of which you are so fond! Neither have I forgotten papa's spaghetti. But as something tells me that cousin Lily and I have the same tastes, we are going to share a delicious *sole à la Monte Carlo*."

When the little party walked through into what has become one of the most famous restaurants in the world, it was clear that Count Beppo Polda enjoyed there a high reputation as host. The head waiter himself marshalled them to a light, well-placed table, where they could see everything without being themselves overlooked or overheard.

There were comparatively few people lunching, for Monte Carlo, like the rest of the Continent, gets later and later each year as to its hours and habits. But all at once Lily's heart gave a leap, for she saw some way off, seated at a little table for two, the man whom she by now always affectionately called in her own mind "Papa Popeau." He was with a stranger, and she felt just a little disappointed.

Yet Lily was not particularly anxious that Count Beppo and Captain Stuart should meet. They were so very different—something seemed to tell her that they would not get on together, and, after all, Beppo's visit to Monte Carlo was to be only for a few days.

Little by little the great room began to fill, and the Countess was soon making shrewd and not over-kindly remarks about some of the people coming in.

Lily was amused to notice how interested Aunt Cosy was in everybody—their appearance, their jewels, their clothes, their manners! She was evidently much enjoying her little outing, and Beppo's knowledge of her taste was well shown by the eager satisfaction with which she ate the lobster he had thoughtfully ordered for her.

But though the Countess ate heartily, she also talked a great deal—indeed, most of the conversation was carried on by her and by her son.

Count Polda remained quite silent, though his observant eyes often became closely fixed on some individual who in Lily's eyes looked particularly uninteresting, for almost always the person in question was a man. Once he stared with a strange intentness at a rather curious-looking individual.

"Look," he exclaimed, and it was the first time he had broken silence— "Look, Cosy! There is the great Chicago Sausage King! He is one of the richest men in the world!"

Aunt Cosy glanced sharply at the individual in question. Then she looked away, and began talking of something else.

As for Lily, she was now feeling quite gay and quite cheerful. Her share of the luncheon was proving delicious, and the brilliance and lightsome charm of the scene about her delighted all her senses. Also, she could not help feeling just a little happier for the proximity of good Papa Popeau. Now and again she would find his eyes fixed on their little party, always with a benevolent, inquiring, kindly, interested glance. She hoped, with all her heart, that he would come up and speak to them.

At last they reached the coffee stage of their déjeuner and at the same moment the man who had been Hercules Popeau's guest got up and, shaking hands with his host, left the restaurant. M. Popeau signed his bill, and then he threaded his way slowly between the now very crowded tables to where Count Beppo's party were seated.

The Countess greeted him effusively. "Let me present my son to you," she cried. "Beppo! This is a gentleman who was remarkably kind to Lily on her long and disagreeable journey from Paris."

Count Polda and Count Beppo, who had both risen courteously from their seats, exclaimed almost together: "Do have your coffee with us—or have you already had it?"

"I have had my coffee," said M. Popeau amiably. "But I will, with your permission, sit down for a few minutes. It is a pleasure to see Miss Fairfield again. We met last under such very different circumstances!"

Lily saw a look of apprehension and unease come over both the Count and Countess's faces, and she thought it a little tactless of her French friend to remind them all at such a pleasant moment as this of poor George Ponting and his piteous fate.

All? No, of course, Beppo knew nothing about that tragic Ponting affair.

"I suppose Mademoiselle is the first lady who has ever stayed for as long as a fortnight at Monte Carlo without going into the Casino," said M. Popeau, smiling.

"Have you never been to the Rooms?" exclaimed Beppo. He seemed quite shocked. "What a pity it is that I cannot take you in there this afternoon. But, alas! I have to go back to Eze. I promised my friends that I would do so."

"I can go to the Casino any time," said Lily, laughing. "There's no hurry at all—though, of course, I should be sorry to leave Monte Carlo without having seen anything of the famous gambling-rooms."

"I was going to propose," said M. Popeau, quietly, "that *I* escort Mademoiselle to the Casino this afternoon. I know that the Count and Countess, being residents, cannot have the privilege."

Lily looked eagerly at Aunt Cosy, and, to her secret astonishment, the later nodded quite amiably. M. Popeau offered Count Polda a cigar, and then Beppo took something out of his pocket and held it out, smiling, to Lily. "Even a baby," he said, "could smoke one of these cigarettes!"

Lily bent forward eagerly, and then her face changed utterly, and, with a gasp of amazement, she uttered a low, involuntary "Oh!"

Yes, she could not be mistaken. What lay on the white tablecloth before her was surely the exquisitely-chased little gold box which she had last seen held out to her by George Ponting?

She bent down, lower and lower, regardless of the people about her. Yes, there was now no doubt at all, for inside the pale gold lid were engraved the words: "Mon cœur à toi. Ma vie au Roi."

But so little do those about us realise of what we are thinking that only Hercules Popeau noticed the girl's agitation. As for Beppo, he laughed and said: "Yes, these are what would be called in England midget cigarettes, are they not?"

It was clear that he had taken Lily's exclamation of surprise as an involuntary tribute to the daintiness of the quaint little cigarettes which filled the one-time snuff-box. Lily was too surprised and disturbed to speak: the sight of the gold box had brought with it a rush of painful, distressing memories.

Hercules Popeau leant forward.

"You have there, my dear Count, a most delightful and valuable cigarette-case," he observed suavely. "If I mistake not, it is an exquisite specimen of late eighteenth-century work. I remember once seeing a curio extremely like this in a collection of pathetic little objects which had belonged to Mme.

du Barry. The snuff-box in question had been given to her by King Louis the Fifteenth. May I look at it for a moment?"

"Of course!" said Count Beppo courteously.

He pushed the box across the table, and M. Popeau took it up and examined it closely.

"I see," he said at last, "that it is not as I first thought! This box is of rather later workmanship than I supposed. It was probably made during the Revolution. Is it not strange to think that these costly and exquisite objects were being fashioned even at such a time as that?"

He was obviously talking to give Lily time to recover her composure.

And then the Countess broke in: "My son is very clever at picking up pretty things," she said, smiling. "He bought that little box at an old curiosity shop for a mere song—not that one gets very much nowadays anywhere for a mere song! Is it not true," she said, turning to Beppo, "that the man who sold it to you said it was but silver gilt?"

Beppo looked surprised. "If I told you so, it is so, mamma. I cannot remember," he replied.

"I congratulate the Count on his find," said M. Popeau gravely. "I should like him to tell me in what shop in Monte Carlo he found such a great bargain?"

The Countess answered for Beppo. "My son did not buy the box in Monte Carlo," she said quickly. "He got it—was it at Milan, Beppo?—last time he was on his way to Monte Carlo."

Lily felt bewildered but relieved. She had made a mistake, and so obviously also had Papa Popeau. She felt sure that, like herself, he had at first supposed this little gold box to have been the one belonging to the unfortunate Ponting. If Beppo had bought what was now a cigarette-case in Milan some time ago, its being exactly like Mr. Ponting's gold box was simply an amazing coincidence.

"While we are talking about the box we are forgetting the cigarettes," said Beppo. "Do allow me to tempt you, Cousin Lily!"

And Lily laughingly consented to be tempted. They were very mild little cigarettes, far milder than those which she had occasionally smoked with Uncle Tom—to Aunt Emmeline's disapproval.

At last they all got up and began walking out of the restaurant, Beppo leaving what seemed to Lily an enormous tip on the table. He explained, smiling, that he had a bill, and so only paid once a week.

"That," said M. Popeau civilly, "shows, M. le Comte, that your reputation must indeed be high, for they have to be very careful here, even with quite well-known people. Without being in the least dishonest, it is so easy to find oneself cleared out at the tables, and then to forget all about such an account as that of a restaurant."

"They all know that my father is a native of Monaco," said the young man, rather shortly.

When they joined the others, M. Popeau said firmly: "I will now take charge of Mademoiselle, and I promise to bring her back to La Solitude at— shall I say—half-past four, Madame la Comtesse?"

"Yes," said the Countess graciously, "that will do quite well. It is very good of you to take my niece to the Rooms. I am sure that you, Monsieur, will be quite as effective a guardian as I should be myself! There are often very strange people in the gambling-rooms."

"There are indeed," said M. Popeau gravely, and there was no twinkle in his eye. Frenchmen of his type are, as Captain Stuart had truly said, extremely particular in this matter of a young girl's surroundings and reputation.

The big car was waiting for Count Beppo, and he put his parents into it with great care and affection. "Now, I will drive you home," he exclaimed. Turning, he held out his hand to Lily. "I wish you and I could meet later in the afternoon, after I have come back from Eze," he said hesitatingly. "About what time will you be leaving the Casino?"

But M. Popeau intervened. "I don't think we can make any plan of that sort," he said; "we should only miss one another. I will take great care of Miss Fairfield, and bring her up to La Solitude in good time."

CHAPTER 15

The moment Lily found herself alone with M. Popeau, forming part of the crowd of walkers who were all on their way to the Casino, she exclaimed, a little nervously. "Wasn't it an extraordinary coincidence that Beppo Polda should have *exactly* the same gold snuff-box as that which poor Mr. Ponting bought from an old woman gambler?"

"Extraordinary indeed," answered the Frenchman drily. "I wish you'd ask him the exact date of his purchase of it, Mademoiselle."

"I will," said Lily. Then something prompted her to add, "I hope you like Beppo Polda? I can't quite make him out, yet he seems so very much nicer than I expected him to be."

M. Popeau evaded her question. "I agree with you," he said; "he is very much nicer than one would expect the son of either his father or his mother to be. Also, Mademoiselle, he is extremely, quite exceptionally, handsome."

He looked down at her thoughtfully. "No man can ever tell," he said; "not even the extremely foolish man who prides himself on his knowledge of the feminine heart, how far good looks influence—or don't influence—a woman when she is considering a member of my sex!"

Lily laughed, and blushed. The problem had never been put to her before.

"I suppose one can't help being rather affected by a human being's outward appearance," she answered; then added, with a little smile on her pretty face: "At any rate, *men* are very much influenced by appearance, aren't they, M. Popeau?"

"I'm afraid that can't be denied! But tell me—if you don't think the question indiscreet—does a young lady ever look at a good-looking man, and long to know him? That, I need hardly tell you, is what many a man—nay, almost every man—does do at times with regard to a beautiful woman!"

"I can't imagine any nice girl feeling like that about an entire stranger," began Lily hesitatingly.

"What a wonderful word is that English word 'nice'!" said M. Popeau reflectively. "It may mean such a very great deal, or nothing at all. It is—it is—"

"I know exactly what you mean," exclaimed Lily. "The word 'nice' is certainly a *camouflage* word!"

"That's it!" cried M. Popeau, delighted. "You've put it exactly, Mademoiselle! But supposing I were to tell you—to return to what we were talking about—that there are very, very few *nice* girls in the world?"

"I shouldn't believe you!" cried Lily stoutly.

"Supposing I were also to tell you," went on M. Popeau gravely, "that a great many women you would probably describe as nice do not only pick out a handsome man and feel that they would like to know him, but that they go further—that sometimes they actually make the first advances, and *do* strike up some kind of acquaintance with him? Supposing I were to *prove* that to you?"

Lily looked and felt uncomfortable. She did not quite know what to say.

"Take your cousin, Count Beppo Polda," went on M. Popeau meditatively. "I should think that ever since he reached man's estate he has been—shall we say pursued?—by pretty ladies desiring his friendship. Any girl who marries Beppo Polda must make up her mind to endure the torments of jealousy. I suspect," said M. Popeau, looking down into Lily's open, flushed, ingenuous, and, yes, exceedingly pretty face, "that you, Mademoiselle, are among the few happy human beings in Monte Carlo who really do not know what jealousy is?"

Lily hesitated. "It's quite true," she said slowly; "I don't remember ever feeling jealous—not really jealous!"

M. Popeau drew a long breath. "That shows you have never been in love," he said quietly. "But to return to Count Beppo. I happen to know that he is acquainted with one lady who very often does him the honour of being jealous of him."

"Poor Beppo!" said Lily. "How horrid for him!" Then—for this little bit of gossip interested her very much—"Is Beppo in love, M. Popeau?"

"He has been in love for a very long time," answered her companion gravely.

Lily felt thrilled, and yes, just a trifle disappointed.

"Do you mean," she said, "that Beppo is engaged? If so, I'm sure his parents don't know it."

"Engaged? Oh no"; the Frenchman looked curiously surprised. "When I said that Count Beppo Polda is in love, I mean the phrase in a general sense. He is in love with love—"

"Oh! Is that all?" Lily felt relieved.

M. Popeau went on: "The Count, for the moment, is what you call in England fancy free. Still, he is now absorbed in a very important quest—that of finding for himself a rich wife. Meanwhile he, of course, amuses himself—" he said the words in a very significant tone, and Lily blushed a deep, unbecoming blush. She felt a little indignant. She realised that M. Popeau thought that Beppo would flirt with her, and that she, Lily, would not be able to help falling in love with him!

They walked on in silence.

Hercules Popeau was a shrewd student of human nature, but this simple English girl was to him a real enigma. Was she aware, for instance, that Angus Stuart was deeply in love with her? And if the answer to this was "yes," how did she, on her side, regard the young soldier?

He had made it his business during the last few days to find out whatever there was to be found out about Count Beppo Polda. Among his best secret agents during the war had been a Frenchwoman living in Rome. He had got in touch with her yesterday afternoon, and she had at once told him the little there was to tell about the young man. Hercules Popeau had been almost disappointed to find that, as reputations go, in that curious cosmopolitan world which has its social centre in Rome, Count Beppo Polda had by no means a bad reputation. In fact, he was popular both with men—for he was a good sportsman—and with women.

But there was a certain mystery as to how he lived. He had been brought up as an entirely idle man of pleasure. At times he spent money recklessly, and then would come an obvious period of penury, when he more or less lived with, and on, his bosom friends the Marchese and Marchesa Pescobaldi.

More than once he had been associated in some big business enterprise, but real, regular work bored him. It was now well known in Roman society that he was looking out for a rich wife. M. Popeau's informant had added that had the Count been indifferent to the appearance of the lady, he could have made more than one very wealthy marriage. But he was fastidious and over-particular. Not long ago he had very nearly become engaged to a great American-Irish heiress. But the young lady, unlike most Irish girls, had been unattractive, and at the last moment Count Beppo had drawn back.

This had been the more foolish of him because money was to Count Beppo like the air which we human beings breathe—it was a thing which he could not do without.

M. Popeau, who naturally regarded Lily as being only the niece of a fairly well-to-do British ex-civil servant, felt very uneasy.

He was seriously afraid that the good-looking Italian, taken as he obviously was with the girl's innocent charm and beauty, would make violent love to her and then ride away—as men of his type are doing every day all the world over.

To a Frenchman there could be no comparison between Angus Stuart and Beppo Polda. Polda was a fascinating man knowing all the turns of the great game of love, Stuart simply an honest, straightforward, fine-natured young soldier. He longed to warn the girl more explicitly of the danger she was running. He told himself that perhaps it would be wiser to do so a little later on.

"I understand," he said, "that Count Beppo is staying in Monte Carlo for some time?"

"That is what the Countess hoped," answered Lily, a little coldly. "But he spoke last night as if he could only stay a few days."

She still felt very ruffled. Fond though she was of M. Popeau, she did not intend to allow him to give her hints as to how to behave herself with a young man.

"I'm glad to hear that," exclaimed the Frenchman, and there was indeed a tone of hearty relief and surprise in his voice.

"As for me, I'm sorry he's going so soon!" Lily exclaimed. "*I* like Beppo! I think he and I are going to be great friends."

They were now close to the steps of the Casino. Angus Stuart came up to them, an eager look on his face:

"May I join you?" he asked, with the touch of old-fashioned courtesy which M. Popeau found so pleasant in the young man.

"Of course, of course, dear friend! You shall come and assist me in initiating Mademoiselle in the joys of play!" He turned to Lily. "How much money have you got with you?"

Lily opened her bag and counted. "Forty francs," she said.

"Well, that is exactly right. It will not ruin you to offer up that tribute to the Goddess of Chance. On the other hand, it will be pleasant if the forty francs become a hundred or two hundred francs!"

"That would be very nice indeed," confessed the girl, smiling.

She was astonished to find how intensely conscious she was of Angus Stuart's quiet presence by her side. She longed—which was not very grateful of her—for M. Popeau to move away, and leave them alone together. They hadn't met for two whole days, and she suddenly felt what a long time it had seemed.

The pillared hall or atrium of the Casino was full of a motley crowd of people, and Lily began to take eager notice of the amusing scene before her. Beppo had been quite right—all colours and all types of humanity were represented in the moving mass of men and women now gathered together in this, the splendid palace of the Goddess of Chance.

"I will see to your admission card. Have you anything you desire to leave in the way of a cloak or a parasol?"

She hesitated. "Yes, I think I will leave my parasol," she said.

Angus Stuart accompanied her to the counter, where a gorgeous-looking flunkey took her parasol and gave her a voucher.

"I feel so excited!" she exclaimed, looking up at her companion.

He said in a low tone, "Have you had—" and then checked himself sharply, for M. Popeau had come up to them.

"Come along!" cried the Frenchman. "This is a great moment in your life!"

He spoke half-seriously, half with a touch of good-natured banter in his voice.

Drawing a deep breath of excited anticipation, the girl passed through into the historic rooms which have seen so many dramas silently enacted—

for not once in a thousand days is there anything in the shape of a "scene" in the still, golden-haze atmosphere of the Temple of Chance.

Though it was early, there was a crowd round each of the roulette tables, and for a moment Lily only noticed the curious-looking people composing the crowd. Then, gradually, she began to see the table, the more so that her two companions were quietly shepherding her to a good place, close behind one of the croupiers.

At first the girl felt as if she would never understand the complicated game; and then gradually she began to see the relation between the plan or tableau, divided off with yellow lines into squares, and the complicated giant yet toy-like wheel which was sunk in the centre of the long, comparatively narrow table.

"And now," said M. Popeau, "would you like to stake what is equivalent to a five-franc piece on a number? What number will you choose?"

"If I were you," said Angus Stuart, "I should back twelve numbers. If you put your money on only one number you've thirty-five chances against you."

Lily hesitated. "Yes, do as he advises," said M. Popeau good-naturedly.

And so Lily, guided by the Frenchman, put her small coloured counters on the middle dozen; thus she covered the numbers 13 to 24.

The croupier behind whom Lily was standing gave the huge wheel a powerful twist, then he flung a little ball into the revolving disc. It spun round and round, jumping about as if possessed by the spirit of motion. Then, at last, the great disc began to slow down. A croupier called out, "Rien ne va plus!" The ball leapt into one of the red and black pockets (each of which bears a corresponding number to one marked on the plan), and the wheel ceased to revolve. Something was shouted out, and then Lily saw with surprise and joy two other five-franc counters joined to her stake. She looked round at her two companions.

"Pick your money up," said Angus Stuart quickly, "or someone else will get it!"

Sure enough, as she put out her hand hesitatingly, another hand—a big, rather dirty-looking man's hand—took up her three counters.

"That money belongs to Mademoiselle!" called out M. Popeau angrily.

There came a murmured "I beg your pardon; I made a mistake!" and the counters were dropped.

Lily picked them up, feeling happy, and a little confused.

"You might let her put on an *en plein* now," pleaded M. Popeau with Captain Stuart.

"Very well." The Scotsman's voice was reluctant and hesitating. "Put a five-franc counter on any number you like. You're sure to lose it!"

In spite of his discouraging remark, Lily put her counter on number twenty-one.

"If I were you," said Captain Stuart suddenly, "I should also put one on zero. That will give you two chances out of thirty-five."

She obeyed him.

Once more the ball was flung into the middle of the revolving disc, once more it leapt about this way and that. And then, at last, after an extraordinary number of revolutions, it settled down into a pocket, and Lily heard a murmur of sharp disappointment run round the table.

"You've won!" exclaimed Captain Stuart in an excited voice. "Zero has turned up! You've won—let me see—seven pounds, Miss Fairfield! Isn't that splendid?"

Lily felt very much pleased. She had been the only person to put anything on zero; accordingly, envious, congratulatory glances were cast on her from all parts of the table.

"I wouldn't play any more today if I were you," whispered Captain Stuart. And again she obeyed him, stuffing all the money she had won anyhow into her pretty little bag.

And now M. Popeau began to play. The other two watched him—Angus Stuart with amusement, Lily with great curiosity.

"He always plays the same cautious game, for all he's so fond of advising other people to put on full on one number!" whispered the young man in the girl's little ear.

For a while Lily could not imagine what game M. Popeau was playing. He put the equivalent of thirty francs on the space marked *passe* and that of twenty francs on the first dozen. It looked to Lily as if he won every time—won, that is, something, somewhere. She couldn't make it out!

"How does he do it?" she asked, puzzled. It was to her so strange that everybody didn't play like Papa Popeau if he won every time.

"You see, he covers nearly the whole of the board," muttered Captain Stuart. "He only loses right out when six numbers turn up out of the thirty-five. Even when zero comes he doesn't lose everything, for the money he has on *passe* is only 'put into prison,' as they call it. Yes, it's an ingenious system, and I often wonder more people don't play it. Of course, if you go on long enough, you're bound to lose—even at Popeau's game."

By this time the Frenchman was absorbed in his system, and the two young people moved just a little way away from the table. Their friend glanced up to see where they were, and then went on playing.

Lily was looking about her now with great amusement and curiosity. She felt in a happy mood. It was delightful to have won all that money—and so easily! It was very pleasant also to be with Angus Stuart. It seemed a long time since they had parted two days ago, he gripping her hand hard under the smiling eyes of the cab-driver.

"I should so like to come here in the evenings," she exclaimed.

"The Club's the place to see in the evening," he answered quickly.

Anyone watching the two would have seen that they were in very different moods. Lily looked radiant. She was certainly the prettiest, as well as the best-dressed, girl in the rooms at that particular moment. As for her companion, a look of doubt, of discomfort, of suspense was on his face. But she was quite unaware of it. She prattled gaily on, excited and interested by all she saw. Even when two stout women pushed so roughly past her as almost to make her lose her balance she only laughed.

At last, as they saw M. Popeau detach himself from the table and began his ambling walk towards them, a satisfied air on his fat, placid face, Angus Stuart suddenly whispered, "I suppose you got my letter all right, Miss Fairfield?"

"Your letter? No! I've had no letter from you since the last one you wrote to me from Milan."

"I wrote to you the day before yesterday evening!" he exclaimed under his breath. And then, straightening himself, remarked with an air of rather elaborate unconcern, "Well, Popeau, how goes it? Have you broken the bank?"

"I have not broken the bank, but I have made two hundred francs!" replied the Frenchman gaily. "And that, after all, is not bad! At one moment I had made a good deal more, but alas! twice number fifteen turned up and swept away a hundred francs of my winnings. I was very foolish not to leave off—as Mademoiselle so wisely did."

And then something very untoward happened. Lily suddenly discovered that her charming little bag and its contents had disappeared. The silk cords by which it had hung loosely on her right arm were still there, dangling helplessly.

She looked about her, bewildered and chagrined.

"It must have been taken by one of the women who pushed past you just now," exclaimed Captain Stuart.

"I'll try and not think any more about it. After all, I've only really lost forty francs," said Lily vexedly.

CHAPTER 16

They strolled about the Rooms for a while, and finally spent an amusing half-hour watching the "trente-et-quarante" players. But all the time Lily was asking herself what there could have been in the letter which Captain Stuart had written to her, and which had not yet reached her? As for the loss of her money, she really did manage to forget it.

Angus Stuart put a pink counter, that is, twenty francs, on the board three separate times, and each time he lost.

"Unhappy in play, happy in love, my friend!" quoted M. Popeau chaffingly. "I think I shall have to give you a mascot."

And then Lily bethought herself of what Aunt Cosy had said concerning the Marchesa Pescobaldi. "Do you believe in the Evil Eye?" she asked eagerly.

Somewhat to her surprise, M. Popeau hesitated.

"That is a curious question," he said, "but I will answer you truly. I have long thought that there are in this strange world both men and women who can bring misfortune on those whom they do not like—just as there are human beings who radiate happiness and goodness."

Captain Stuart broke in: "Surely persons may have the Evil Eye and so injure what they love best in the world, without being able to help it?"

"Yes," said M. Popeau gravely, "that is the true Evil Eye. I hope you have not met anyone with the Evil Eye lately, Mademoiselle? That would certainly account for the theft of your winnings this afternoon!"

"Yes, I'm afraid I have." She laughed gaily.

"Has Count Beppo the Evil Eye?" asked M. Popeau.

"Oh, no! Whatever made you think such a thing? The person who is supposed to have the Evil Eye is a woman. Beppo Polda is staying here with a certain Marchese and Marchesa Pescobaldi. According to my aunt"—Lily had now quite slipped into the way of calling the Countess Polda her aunt—"this Italian lady has the Evil Eye."

"I don't know that I would believe everything the Countess Polda would say about another lady," said M. Popeau reflectively. Then he added, almost as if speaking to himself: "I did not realise that Count Beppo was with the Pescobaldis."

"They all came together, and they are all going away together, very soon," said Lily.

"And what do you think of the Marchesa?" asked the Frenchman. "She was a very beautiful woman when I last saw her—before the war."

"She is very, very beautiful still!" exclaimed Lily. "Her eyes are lovely—like large sparkling jewels. I looked well into them, but, of course, I could not see which was the Evil Eye!"

"Do not laugh at the Evil Eye," said M. Popeau warningly. "I could tell you some curious stories about those who are supposed to possess it. The most dramatic of all my tales concerned the terrible fire which took place in Paris years ago, at what was called the Charity Bazaar. There were people who were so unkind as to suggest that the tragedy occurred owing to the presence of a very high Italian personage who was known to have the Evil Eye. He had just left the building when the fire broke out."

They wandered about, all over the Casino, and then they went across to the Hôtel de Paris and M. Popeau ordered tea. Both the young Scotsman and the elderly Frenchman vied with one another in "fussing" over their guest, and Lily felt happy and exhilarated—what a delightful day she was having!

"And now," said M. Popeau at last, "I fear it is time that I fulfilled my promise of escorting you back to La Solitude, Mademoiselle."

"I hope you will allow me—" began Captain Stuart, but before he could finish his sentence, Lily exclaimed, "Why, there's Beppo Polda!"

Hurrying towards them was a tall, dark man to whom Angus Stuart took an instant, instinctive, violent dislike. He told himself that Beppo Polda looked a foppish, theatrical fellow. That, however, was very unfair—it only meant that Beppo looked exceptionally well-dressed, what some people call "smart."

"I was so afraid that I should miss you!" he exclaimed, taking very little notice of Lily's companions. "Are you ready, Lily? I've got the car outside. We ought to start pretty soon, as I have to get back to the Hidalgo by five o'clock."

"You will do that very easily," interposed M. Popeau. "It's only a quarter-past four now."

Stuart felt annoyed that the Frenchman seemed to take it for granted that Lily would go off with this dandified-looking foreigner.

"I propose taking Miss Fairfield for a short drive first." There was a touch of haughty decision in the young Count's voice. It was not that he resented M. Popeau's apparent friendship with Lily, but already he reciprocated Angus Stuart's sudden, unreasoning dislike. He pretended not to know that the Scotsman belonged to the little party.

"Beppo," said Lily, rather awkwardly, "this is Captain Stuart. Captain Stuart, may I introduce my cousin, Count Beppo Polda?"

The two men looked at one another with a long, measuring glance, then they shook hands frigidly.

As they were making their way to the door, Lily fell behind for a moment by Angus Stuart's side. "Perhaps I shall find your letter at La Solitude," she whispered. She added: "I hope I shall."

His thin, keen face lit up. "D'you really mean that, Miss Fairfield?"

"Of course I do!"

She shook hands with him and with M. Popeau; and a few moments later the car was going at a good pace past the Casino, in the opposite direction to that which would have taken them up to La Solitude.

"Is Captain Stuart an old friend of yours?" asked Beppo abruptly.

Lily hesitated. To her secret relief, he went on at once, without waiting for an answer: "The word friendship may mean so much or so little, my little cousin!"

"That is very true!" said Lily demurely.

"But there can be no such doubt about the word *love*!"

Her eyes dropped before her companion's eager, searching, ardent gaze. Was this what M. Popeau had meant to warn her against?

The motor slowed down. They were now looking across the great green promontory which juts out of the blue sea to the left of Monte Carlo.

"I wish I could stay on a little longer," said Beppo in a low voice. "What a cursed thing is money! Still, we poor mortals can't do without it. So I shall go back to Rome and try to make what we call a lucky hit, eh? Then I shall come back, and perhaps stay up at La Solitude. Shall I be welcome, Lily?"

She looked up at him. "Yes," she said slowly. "Of course you will be welcome, Beppo!"

As is almost invariably the case with a certain type of girl, Lily liked to mix the jam of flirtation with the powder of good advice, and she did feel that Beppo, with regard to his father and mother, was indeed very thoughtless and selfish. So she added, deliberately: "Your return will be welcome to me, and also—"

"Also?" he repeated eagerly. He tried to guess what she was going to say, but failed.

"Also to your father and mother," she said gravely. "I wonder if you know how much they care for you? They really live for you, and for nothing else, Beppo!"

To her surprise he looked disturbed and troubled. "I'm afraid that's true," he said ruefully. "And yet, Lily, seriously, I feel I really know very little about them! I know they love me, Lily—nay, that there is nothing that they would not do for me—and yet they seem to me almost like strangers."

Lily was indeed astonished. "I don't understand," she exclaimed. "What exactly do you mean, Beppo?"

Somehow they seemed to have come much nearer to one another in the last two or three minutes, for Beppo Polda's deep, vibrant voice had in it a note of sincerity which surprised the girl, and made her feel far more really kindly to him than she had done yet.

"They never tell me anything about their private affairs," he went on slowly. "I need not tell you—for, of course, you must have seen it for yourself—that mamma's is the master mind. She is a very clever woman. Sometimes"—his voice dropped—"I wonder if she is not too clever! I speak to you thus frankly because I feel that you are already one of the family."

Lily felt touched by his words—though she thought it an odd thing to say, for, of course, she was not really related to them at all. She wondered, uncomfortably, if Beppo knew that she was his parents' paying guest.

"Ought we not to be turning now?" she suggested. "I'm afraid Aunt Cosy will be getting anxious about me. She is very particular."

"One can never be too particular about a young girl," observed Beppo sententiously. "But still, it won't hurt mamma to be anxious for another twenty minutes or so."

They drove on, and Lily told herself that it was very pleasant to be motoring through this beautiful country, while listening to Beppo's full, caressing voice. She found herself answering all kinds of questions about her own childhood and girlhood, and she could not help feeling flattered that Beppo was so obviously interested in all that concerned her. In that he was very unlike Captain Stuart. *He* seemed to take everything for granted. Beppo was even anxious to know of what illnesses her father and mother had died!

In some ways this fine, strong-looking young fellow seemed to the English girl more like a woman than a man. He was so interested in the sort of things which are supposed, perhaps erroneously, only to interest women. He spoke admiringly of her frock and her hat, and she gave him a lively account of her expedition to Mme. Jeanne.

"Excellent Jeanne!" he at once exclaimed. "I must manage to find time to go and see her." He added: "She has a sister who keeps an hotel in the Condamine. My father was saying only today that Jeanne's sister had written to him about some man in her hotel who desired a card of admission to the Club. Papa is so good-natured!"

Lily made no answer to that remark. She did not think the Count at all good-natured. He was entirely absorbed in himself, and in his own concerns. But, of course, there could be no doubt at all about his great love for his son.

They were nearing La Solitude when Lily bethought herself of what had happened in the restaurant about the gold snuff-box. "I want to ask you something," she said suddenly.

Beppo turned his face down on his pretty companion. "Ask me anything you like," he exclaimed gaily. "And I promise that you shall have a true answer!"

"It's only," she said, rather nervously, "that I wish you would show me that lovely little cigarette-box again, Beppo. Is it really true that you bought it in Milan? Somehow I don't think it is—"

"Well, no," Beppo answered smiling. "It is not true. But you are a clever little witch to have discovered the fact!"

He stopped the car. They were on a lonely cross-road, and Lily will always remember the exact spot, and what was said there, though at the time it did not make very much impression on her.

He took the gold box out of his pocket and handed it to her.

"Look here!" he exclaimed. "If you've taken such a fancy to it, allow me to present it to you, my fair cousin—just as a souvenir?"

How strange that he should say that—it was almost exactly what poor George Ponting had said!

"I don't want it, thank you, Beppo. I only wanted to look at it again. Then if you did not buy it at Milan, how did you get it?"

The more she looked at it, the more she felt certain that it was the box she had seen on the evening of her arrival at La Solitude.

"I don't see why I shouldn't tell you"; he hesitated a moment, then said frankly: "This box was a present from mamma. As a matter of fact, she gave it me yesterday, when you went off to see Cristina in the kitchen. Do you remember?"

"Yes," said Lily in a low voice. "I remember when you mean." And she handed the box back to him.

"I confess," went on Beppo, "that I did not in the least understand why there should be any mystery about it! But, of course, I could not contradict mamma when she came out with that absurd tale of my having bought the box in Milan last year."

At last they reached La Solitude. "No, I won't come in," said Beppo, shaking his head. "I've got to go back to the Hidalgo Hotel, and take the Marchesa for a drive before it gets pitch dark."

"I hope I haven't made you late!" exclaimed Lily, for as a matter of fact it was now after five o'clock.

"Oh, no. I shall say that something went wrong—things are always going wrong with this old car! It's high time the Marchese had a new one. But he is careful! Carefulness is an Italian virtue—*I* call it an Italian vice!"

"Aunt Cosy will be dreadfully disappointed," said the girl.

And there Beppo suddenly changed his mind. The thought of spending even a few more minutes in Lily Fairfield's company was pleasant to him. He would tell the Marchesa that he had had a bad puncture.

"To please you I will just go up and say how-d'you-do to Mamma!" he exclaimed, looking at her tenderly.

Together they walked up through the wood, and so on to the lawn, whence Lily noticed Aunt Cosy's ample form behind one of the drawing-room windows.

The Countess waved her hand gaily to the young couple. She opened the window. "I was getting quite anxious about you, Lily," she exclaimed. "But all's well that ends well."

"Lily and I have had a delightful drive," said Beppo. "And I've just come up to say how-d'you-do and good-bye!" And then, to Lily's discomfiture, he suddenly asked:

"By the way, Mamma, why did you tell that story—they call it a tarra-diddle in England—about the snuff-box you so kindly gave to me?"

The Countess looked disturbed and surprised at the question.

"I will tell you why, my son," she said slowly. "That beautiful box was given to me by a friend who is now dead. I did not wish to speak of him. That is why, my dear child, I made up that little tale."

"You made me look like a fool!" said Beppo crossly. "You need not have said anything at all—and I would not have said anything either! After all, it is no one's business what you give me or what I give you."

Still, he kissed her very affectionately and then went off, leaving them standing together.

Lily turned impulsively to the Countess.

"Then poor Mr. Ponting gave you that box when he said good-bye?" She spoke in a very low voice. "He offered to give it to me. But I wouldn't take it. He was grateful to you, Aunt Cosy, for all your kindness, so I quite under-stand his having given it to you."

The Countess was now looking at Lily with a long, measuring, rather anxious look.

"Yes," she said at last. "You have guessed the truth! That charming little object belonged to poor Mr. Ponting. He asked me to take it as a last gift; and though I, too, hesitated, feeling the delicacy that you so rightly felt, I did end by taking it, for I thought of Beppo. I knew he would like it. But I did not want to recall that sad affair today, when you were all so happy."

"I wish you would let me tell M. Popeau," said Lily. "I know the description of that snuff-box has been circulated all over Nice and Mentone—"

"Let me beg you," cried the Countess hurriedly, "to say nothing about it, Lily! We have suffered enough over that business. They would probably send up again from the police, and it would be odious."

As the girl, surprised, remained silent, the other went on urgently: "May I trust you? Will you give me your word of honour you will say nothing about the gold box, dear child?"

"I certainly will say nothing if you would rather I did not do so," said Lily. Still, she was sorry to know that she had unwittingly deceived both Mr.

Ponting's friend and the police. She knew that they had attached considerable importance to the disappearance of the gold box.

Before going upstairs Lily went into the kitchen, and there, lying on the table was the letter which had been posted by Angus Stuart something like thirty-six hours ago. She took it up, Cristina watching her the while.

"Did this letter arrive yesterday morning?" she asked.

Cristina hesitated. "The Countess brought it in about an hour ago; I do not know when it arrived," she said at last.

Lily took up her letter and turned away. She went up to her room, and walked right across to the window. Then she saw that the letter had been steamed open, and fastened down again rather clumsily. It was too bad of Aunt Cosy! It was hateful of her!

The letter ran as follows:

Dear Miss Fairfield,

This is to tell you that I am very, very glad you and I are friends as well as pals—pals as well as friends. I feel awfully distressed that such a fearful thing happened to you on Sunday. Remember your promise to your friend,

Angus Stuart.

CHAPTER 17

"There is nothing else to be done, Angelo. I regret the necessity as much as you do."

It was the day after Lily's delightful drive with Beppo, and the words floated out to where she was sitting in the late morning sunshine. They were uttered by the Countess, whose sitting-room window was open.

The Count's low answer to his wife's observation took Lily somewhat by surprise, for he spoke with much more feeling than she had yet heard him display.

"I will not sully my lips by telling you the kind of information about Monte Carlo the old brute expected me to give him."

"All the more do I ask you to do this for the sake of our Beppo. His whole future depends on it."

"If I do as you wish, Lily will have to accompany me."

The Count uttered these words in a slow, hesitating voice.

The girl had no wish to act as eavesdropper, so she called out: "Is there anything I can do for you, Uncle Angelo?"

The Countess appeared at the window. She was flustered and looked annoyed.

"The truth is," she exclaimed volubly, "that Beppo is in business relations with a Dutch gentleman. The matter concerns a British affair in which they are both interested, and we think you may be useful in assuring the Dutchman that things in England are going on quite well. You came so lately from London, and we think this person will take your word, when he would not take ours—" she waited a few moments, then said firmly, "I should like you to go now, so will you put on that pretty new coat and skirt? Then you can accompany Uncle Angelo to the Condamine."

Lily hurried into the house, and a few minutes later the Countess was walking across the lawn to see them off.

"Do not say anything of this matter to Beppo," she said anxiously.

And Lily answered: "Of course I won't, Aunt Cosy." But she spoke very coldly. She could not forgive the Countess Polda for having opened her letter.

The two ill-assorted companions went down the hill together in absolute silence. Count Polda was always a man of few words. But at last:

"I shall be asking my friend, Mr. Vissering, to supper tonight," he said suddenly. "I shall be obliged, Lily, if you would refrain from mentioning the fact that you will be out this evening. He is very fond of English people, and

I do not know that he would come if he thought that he was only to be alone with your Aunt Cosy and myself."

Lily felt just a little uncomfortable. Not for the first time she told herself that foreigners seem to have a curious dislike to telling the truth.

But the girl had many things to fill her mind just now. In a sense she was sorry that Beppo Polda was going back to Rome in two days, for she had enjoyed seeing even a little glimpse of the brilliant, amusing world of Monte Carlo in his company. Also she felt flattered at his obvious admiration and liking for herself. Nothing could be nicer than the way Beppo had behaved to her yesterday, and she resented M. Popeau's hints and insinuations very much indeed.

These desultory thoughts passed to and fro through Lily Fairfield's mind during the longish walk, and she was suddenly surprised to find herself and the Count in a part of the Condamine where she had never been before.

Was it here that Uncle Angelo's business friend lived? Yes, for at last they stopped in front of a large, old-fashioned house, across which was written in large, black letters, "Utrecht Hotel."

Walking through the open door into a small hall lit by a skylight, Count Polda shook hands in a friendly way with a respectable-looking woman who sat at a desk making out an account.

"Is Mr. Vissering in, Madame Sansot?" he asked. And the woman said, "Yes, I believe so, Monsieur le Comte. But I will go and see."

The woman came back after a few moments. "Mr. Vissering is very busy writing in his room," she said. "He begs Monsieur le Comte to call another time."

"Will you please take him up this card?" said Count Polda.

He went up to the desk where the woman had been sitting and dipped a pen in the ink. Lily could not help seeing that on the card, on which was engraved, above "Count Polda," an elegant little coronet, he wrote the words: "I have brought with me Miss Lily Fairfield, my young English niece, whom you will perhaps be pleased to meet."

Again the woman went off, and when she came back she exclaimed, "He will be down in two or three minutes. Please come this way!"

She showed the visitors into a dingy little back room, where there were three deep armchairs and a number of cane-bottomed chairs. On two marble-topped tables were ashtrays and match-boxes. The windows were shut, and the room smelt musty. What a strange place in which to receive visitors!

Before leaving the room the woman came close up to the Count and said in a low voice:

"Does Monsieur le Comte know anything about Mr. Vissering? We find him a very curious kind of gentleman! He insists on paying every day, and he is so mean—he scrutinises every sou in the account! Yet we know that he has a very large sum of money always on his person. That is not safe in a place like Monte Carlo, and my husband has begged him again and again to leave his money in our safe. But he is very suspicious."

"I know even less about him than you do," answered the Count amiably. "But I am not surprised at what you tell me. A certain type of *nouveau riche* either spends too much or too little. I know very little of your client. You will remember that you yourself introduced him to me."

"Yes, and I'm very grateful to Monsieur le Comte for the trouble he took. But as a client Mr. Vissering has disappointed us very much!" She waited a moment. "Was Monsieur le Comte able to get the card of admission he desired so much to possess? Fancy a man of that wealth not being able to get into the Club!"

"That was simply because Mr. Vissering did not already belong to a club in his own country. He is very old-fashioned, as you know, but there is no harm in him."

The woman looked dubiously at Lily. "Ah, Monsieur le Comte, you do not know the things that I know! But there—I will say nothing."

After Madame Sansot had left them the Count turned to Lily: "This fellow Vissering is truly an odd kind of man," he muttered. "He was one of the war profiteers of Holland. That makes him feel he has the right to be insolent. You must not notice his odd manner."

Lily smiled.

"Of course I won't, Uncle Angelo!"

Those who love Lily Fairfield hope that she will live to a good old age, but however long she lives she will never, never forget that shabby little smoking-room of the Utrecht Hotel. And yet what happened there did not seem at the time so very remarkable, memorable, or strange—it was simply very disagreeable and unexpected.

After they had been waiting there perhaps in all five minutes, the door opened, and a huge old man walked into the room. Lily told herself that he looked like a big, shaggy Newfoundland dog—only not so nice! What was impressive about the stranger was a look of age wedded to that of great vitality. His ugly, powerful face bore a strange expression of hesitancy and expectation.

Count Polda bowed, coldly and distantly.

"As I was passing by, I thought, Mr. Vissering, that I would come in and convey to you an invitation from my wife. The Countess will be very pleased if you will come and spend this evening with us."

There was a pause. By way of answer the old man came close up to where his visitors were standing. He did not even glance at the Count, but he stared at Lily, and there was something so searching in that bold, hard, measuring look that the girl's own eyes fell before it.

"So this is your niece, Monsieur le Comte?" he said at last, speaking French with a strong, guttural accent.

"Yes," replied the Count, rather nervously. "This is Miss Lily Fairfield, my English niece."

Then the old Dutchman broke into English.

"Is it true," he asked the girl abruptly, "that the Count is your uncle?"

If it came to the point, it was, of course, not true. But Lily told herself quickly that what she was or was not did not concern this odious old man.

"I am on a visit to my aunt, the Countess Polda," she said quietly.

"Then Madame la Comtesse is English?" asked Mr. Vissering.

That question Lily did not feel called upon to answer. And the Count interposed: "I shall be grateful if you will speak French. I learnt English as a young man, but it is not a language with which I am familiar."

And then the old Dutchman turned again to Lily, and, speaking this time in French, and with a kind of ogreish look and familiar intonation, which she found very unpleasant and disconcerting, he exclaimed:

"I asked you that question, Mademoiselle, because, as a matter of fact, I inquired of my good new friend here, Count Polda, whether he knew any charming young ladies in Monte Carlo with whom I might make acquaintance. I am on the look-out for a little wife."

Lily stared at him. What an extraordinarily disagreeable, ridiculous old man! And what a very odd kind of joke to make to a girl he had only met a few moments ago!

"I have always admired young English ladies very much," went on the strange old fellow, "and I have here before me a perfect specimen." He bowed.

It was an ungainly bow, a kind of imitation of the Count's elegant and graceful salute.

"My niece," interposed Count Polda quickly, "has just come from London, and she has much that is interesting to say about her happy, prosperous country."

"There are not many Dutchmen in London," said Mr. Vissering grimly. "Before the war Germans were preferred." He laughed harshly. "As for us, we have always preferred France to England."

And then Lily, feeling that the time had come when she must say something to help Uncle Angelo, suddenly remarked, a little timidly, and yet firmly too:

"I wonder, Monsieur, if you are acquainted with a Dutch gentleman named Baron van Voorst? He is the only Dutchman I have ever met."

And then, to her surprise, and to the Count's relief, there came a distinct change over the old man. He drew a long breath.

"I have not met him," he said, again speaking in English, but in a very different and a far more courteous tone. "The Baron is certainly a very distinguished man; one of our best-known statesmen. Do I understand you to say that you are personally acquainted with him?"

"Yes," said Lily, feeling—she could not have told you why—a little less uncomfortable. "I know him and his family quite well. He had his daughter with him—a girl about my own age—and they both said they hoped I would go some day to Holland; in fact, they asked me to go and stay with them there next spring to see the tulips in flower."

Here Count Polda intervened with what Lily could not help feeling was a rather uncalled-for, and snobbish, interruption:

"My niece, Miss Fairfield, comes of a very good English family," he observed pompously.

"People of good family are but human after all," said the old man disagreeably. "Does Mademoiselle frequent the Casino?"

He was certainly speaking more pleasantly, but, still, there was a curious note in his voice—a note to which Lily was very unaccustomed, that of a certain contemptuous familiarity.

"I've only been in the Rooms once," she said quietly.

"And did Mademoiselle play?"

Lily laughed. "Oh yes," she exclaimed. "Of course I played—and I won too! But my bag was stolen."

There was a long pause, and then all at once Mr. Vissering exclaimed: "I beg of you to sit down! Forgive my rudeness for not having invited you to do so before."

Count Polda hesitated. He looked at Lily, as if wishing to discover how she felt. But she, on her side, was only anxious to do what would best further Uncle Angelo's and Beppo's business relations with this unpleasant, eccentric old man. So she sat down on one of the cane-bottomed chairs, and Mr. Vissering let himself fall heavily into one of the armchairs.

"Well," he said, "is it a bargain? Am I to have the company of Miss Fairfield this afternoon in the Rooms? If so, I will bring with me a pretty gold purse containing a thousand francs, and I will give her a lesson in gambling."

The Count answered for the now astonished and indignant Lily.

"I am sorry, but that is impossible! My niece has an engagement this afternoon. Meanwhile, I recall to your memory my wife's invitation. We hope you will do us the pleasure of coming up to La Solitude for supper. We are simple people, but I think you would enjoy an evening in the pure air."

The old man seemed to be hesitating. "I do not know how I should find your house," he said at last. "I should not care to take a taxi. Once you are in a taxi you are no longer your own master! I am one of those men who believe in their own good right arm, as our friends the Germans used to say. I like to carry my fortune—or as much of it as I have with me—on my person."

"There need be no question of a taxi," said the Count quickly. "I've been offered the loan of a motor by a friend. I will call at the garage on my way home and arrange to fetch you. The same motor will, of course, bring you back. You will be put to no expense."

"Ah, that is better! And you will bring our charming young friend here to fetch me?"

The Count shook his head. "*I* will fetch you, Mr. Vissering. Mademoiselle will be with my wife, waiting to greet you at La Solitude."

"Did you say dinner would be at seven o'clock?" asked the old man. "It is my habit to lunch early, therefore I am hungry by seven."

"It shall certainly be seven—or even half-past six, if you prefer it," said the Count courteously.

"No, seven will do. I shall expect you here at half-past six. Oh—and a word more. I was much gratified the other day by your kindly giving me a card of admission to the Club. But I have not cared to use it, being alone. Would you mind coming down with me there tonight, and acting as my introducer?"

"I, being a Monegasque, have no right to enter the Club," said the Count. "But I have many friends, any one of whom would be charmed to introduce you. I will see one of them, the Marchese Pescobaldi, about the matter at once on leaving here."

"I thank you," said Mr. Vissering slowly.

"And now we must be going home, Lily," said the Count in a relieved tone. "Your aunt will be expecting us."

The girl got up. Somehow she felt she did not want that strange old man even to touch her hand. She bowed distantly.

He accompanied them into the hall. "Till tonight, then," he said in French. Then, breaking into English, he exclaimed, "And do not forget—do not forget what I told you just now, my fair young lady!"

"What you told me just now?" repeated Lily uncomfortably. Did he mean that ridiculous proposal that he should take her to the Casino and give her money to gamble with?

"That I am on the look-out for a dear little wife!"

Lily made no answer to this peculiar remark. She tried to smile, but when she got out in the street she took a deep breath. She had felt as if stifled in that frowsy little smoking-room.

"What a brute, eh?" exclaimed the Count, after they had walked a few yards in silence. "You must forgive me, my dear Lily, for having exposed you to that low fellow's vulgar joking!"

"I've never met such an extraordinary man," said the girl hesitatingly. "His manner was so odd. Do you think that he is a little mad?"

"He is an eccentric," said the Count shortly.

"I can't imagine why he wants to belong to the Club."

"He is, as you say in England, a snob," observed the Count drily.

"And do you really think he will be useful to Beppo?" asked Lily.

"I know he will be," replied the Count grimly.

Then he fell into one of his long silences.

"Have you not forgotten, Uncle Angelo, the message to the Marchese?" asked Lily at last. "I mean about Mr. Vissering and the Club."

"I have thought the matter over," said the Count gravely, "and I do not feel I can propose such a plan to the Marchese. Mr. Vissering would be out of place in the Club."

"You also said something about a car for tonight," said Lily.

"I have changed my mind about that too. I do not care to ask favours of people. I shall take one of those nice taxis that look like a private car, from one of the hotels."

When they were within sight of La Solitude, he asked suddenly: "Are you going out with Beppo and the Pescobaldis this afternoon?"

"No," said Lily. "There would not be room for me in the car. The Marchesa has asked some people they know in the hotel to go with them. Beppo said they meant to start early this morning, but they will be back in ample time for dinner, of course. I am to be at the Hidalgo Hotel at a quarter to seven."

"And what time will you be home?" asked the Count. He turned and looked at Lily as he spoke. She was surprised, for he never seemed to take the slightest interest in her comings or goings.

"Beppo wants me to have supper with him and his friends after the performance. They kindly suggest bringing me back, as Aunt Cosy would not like me to return alone so late."

"Then we cannot expect you home till after eleven?"

"I fear it will be twelve o'clock, Uncle Angelo. But Cristina is going to sit up for me. It is very kind of her to do so."

She waited, and then added, a little shyly: "I am so very fond of Cristina, Uncle Angelo!"

"You are right to be that," he said feelingly. "She is a most excellent woman."

"She is so fond of Beppo," said Lily.

"Yes—yes, indeed; she could not love him more if she were his own mother! There is nothing—nothing that Cristina would not do for my Beppo—"

There came a tone of real emotion into the Count's voice, and the girl, looking round at him, told herself how very strange it was that the same man could be so frank and so deceitful, so cold in manner and at the same time such a devoted father. He now looked curiously pale and puffy, as well as very, very tired.

"I wish Beppo could have stayed on in Monte Carlo a little longer," she said kindly.

The Count looked at her fixedly. "I hope," he said slowly, "that Beppo will stay in Monte Carlo for a considerable time."

Lily was surprised to hear him say this. Surely Beppo was going back to Rome at once? His own and his friends' rooms at the Hotel Hidalgo were already let to another set of people from two days hence.

Lily was surprised to hear her . . . Swiftly Beppo was going back to . . . . His . . . as just as . . . of the steel lighting . . . by . . . to the . . .

CHAPTER 18

Lily sat waiting in the brilliantly lighted vestibule of the Hotel Hidalgo. In her grey chiffon evening gown, and charming black and white cloak, she looked a sufficiently arresting figure to cause many admiring eyes to turn towards her as people passed through on their way to the dining-room.

The party were to dine at seven sharp in order to be in good time for the gala performance at the Casino, and Lily had arrived about five minutes before the hour fixed; but now it was nearly half-past seven, and they were not yet back from their drive. She began to grow impatient.

Poor Lily! She did not feel particularly happy this evening. After the amusing and exciting days she had just gone through, today had dragged by dully and wearily, the only interlude being that unpleasant visit to Uncle Angelo's odious acquaintance. She was glad indeed not to be dining at La Solitude tonight. The Dutchman's manner had been so insultingly familiar till she had mentioned Uncle Tom's nice friend, the Baron Van Voorst. Mr. Vissering was evidently an awful snob!

During the whole of the afternoon there had seemed to rest a heavy load of depression on the Lonely House. Aunt Cosy was impatient and restless, while Cristina, obviously ill at ease, kept sighing long, sad sighs. As for Count Polda, he had disappeared about four o'clock, to return a little before six laden with the costly makings of a luxurious cold supper. She, Lily, had helped Cristina to prepare the dining-room; then she had dressed, putting on for the first time her beautiful grey chiffon evening gown, and magpie cloak. But, alas! with no delightful little bag to match.

While waiting for the car which was to take her to the Hotel Hidalgo there had again been some discussion as to what time she would return that night.

"Understand, my little Lily, that I desire you to stay to the supper after the play. Beppo would be terribly disappointed if you did not do so!" So had said the Countess firmly, and Lily had answered, truthfully enough, that she would like very much to stay to supper. She had never been out to supper after a play, but many of her friends in England had sometimes talked as if the supper rather than the play was the most amusing part of an evening's entertainment—and if amusing in London, how much more amusing at Monte Carlo!

* * * *

At last a quaint-looking little man approached her, and, bowing low, observed: "Do I speak to Miss Fairfield?" And then he went on: "I have to tell you, Mademoiselle, that Count Beppo Polda and his party have had a breakdown in the mountains, forty miles away! The Count found a house where they allowed him to telephone, and the message has just come through. He is greatly distressed, and suggests that Mademoiselle should have a little dinner here, and that then we should arrange to send Mademoiselle home with one of our chambermaids. There is no hope of Count Beppo being in time for the gala performance tonight. I can dispose of the tickets, if you approve that I do so."

Lily felt sharply disappointed. But she blessed Beppo for his kind thought. She was hungry as well as tired, and it would be such a comfort to have dinner here, at the Hotel Hidalgo, and then go back to La Solitude. If that odious Dutchman was still there she could slip up to her bedroom without going into the drawing-room, leaving Cristina to explain later to the Countess what had happened.

Conducted with ceremony by the manager to a little table in the dining-room, Lily enjoyed a most excellent meal. If only Papa Popeau and Angus Stuart had chosen the Hotel Hidalgo to come to this evening how delightful it would have been! She longed to tell Captain Stuart that she had had his letter....

By the time Lily had finished her meal most of the other diners had left. Again the manager himself escorted her to a car, in which she found a respectable-looking, elderly Frenchwoman already seated.

"I should like to pay for my dinner," she said a little awkwardly.

The man shook his head. "If I allowed Mademoiselle to do that, Count Beppo Polda would indeed be angry with me!" he exclaimed.

As they rolled quickly along, the woman by Lily's side began talking in a pleasant, easy way. She explained that she was the head chambermaid of the Hotel Hidalgo, and as such had special charge of the Marchesa Pescobaldi's apartments. She spoke admiringly of Count Beppo. And then she startled Lily by saying something which made it clear that the good woman believed that the young lady by her side was his *fiancée*.

Lily felt annoyed, and very much taken aback. But as the actual word had not been spoken, she did not feel that she could put the woman right. Still, she did rather go out of her way to say that she was related to Count Beppo's mother, and that she was only here, at Monte Carlo, on a visit.

When they reached the clearing among the olive trees which, to Lily, always recalled that terrible morning when she found poor George Ponting's body—she pulled five francs out of her purse, and put it into the chambermaid's hand.

"I will be sure and tell Count Beppo that I brought Mademoiselle quite safely home," said the woman meaningly.

Lily made her way slowly up the broad path through the little wood. There was a brilliant moon, and as she emerged on to the lawn she saw the long, two-storeyed house almost as clearly as if it was daylight. So absolute was the stillness that Lily, with a sense of relief, told herself that the eccentric guest had surely gone.

All the windows opening on to the terrace, as was always the case in the evening, were tightly closed, and shuttered too. That meant that she must go round to the front door.

She rather dreaded what she believed was certain to happen—the Count's quiet surprise at her early return, Aunt Cosy's vociferous lamentations and expressions of regret at Beppo's accident among the mountains, and Cristina's sympathy with her, Lily's, disappointment. There was a chance that the Count and Countess, who were fond of going early to bed, had already retired. If so, she might postpone the story of what had happened till the next morning.

While these thought were passing quickly through her mind, one of the drawing-room windows opened very quietly, and Cristina walked out of it. She looked curiously ethereal and ghostly in the moonlight, and her small face was white and drawn. She put her finger on her lips.

"Hush!" she whispered. "I thought I heard footsteps, so I peeped out and saw that it was only you, Mademoiselle."

"Yes," whispered back Lily. "Count Beppo had a breakdown, and couldn't return in time for the play, so I've come home. Are the Count and Countess upstairs yet?"

The question seemed superfluous, as otherwise they would have been in the room whence Cristina had just come. But the old woman shook her head.

"Sh—sh!" she murmured under her breath. And then she uttered the words, "*Il y a du monde.*" It is an untranslatable expression, which may be roughly rendered as, "We have company tonight," the words being applicable to one visitor or to a dozen.

"Hasn't Mr. Vissering gone yet?" asked Lily. "How very strange, Cristina—he said he must go quite early. I'd better go straight up to my room," went on the girl in a low voice. She stepped into the dark drawing-room. Where were the Count and Countess and their guest?

"The visitor came late," murmured the old servant. "They are still in the dining-room."

In a darkness made more dense by the moonlight outside, Cristina took Lily's hand, and together they crept very quietly into the corridor.

And then something curious happened. When they were about to go past the aperture which led into the dining-room, of which the door was wide open, the old woman stepped back and turned down the little oil lamp which lighted the corridor. Thus, for a moment, Lily was in darkness, while able to see clearly into the large, windowless room.

The Count and Countess were sitting one on each side of their guest. He, alone, had his broad, bent, high back to the door.

Coffee had evidently just been served. But what astonished Lily was the silence—not one of the three was speaking to the other. The Count and Countess, their heads bent forward, seemed to be listening intently—they had probably heard the sound of the drawing-room window, and of the door into the passage, opening and shutting.

Suddenly, as if moved by a common impulse, and still absolutely silent, as was also their strange guest, they both turned and gazed straight at the open door.

It was certain that they could see nothing, for Lily, standing in the passage, was shrouded in deep shadow. Yet on each of the faces now turned towards the hidden watcher was an awful expression of suspense and acute fear—more marked in the Countess's strong-featured countenance than in that of the Count.

"There is no one there; it must have been Cristina."

Uttering these words in a low tone, the Countess got up and shut the door, and, as she did so, the sleeve of Lily's cloak was plucked by Cristina's thin fingers, and she was gently and silently pushed towards the steep staircase.

Lily crept upstairs, opened her bedroom door, and lit a candle. She felt excited and ill at ease. She wished that horrible old man would go away. What could he have said or done to make his host and hostess look like that? Had he some hold over Beppo Polda? Lily's heart was beating with a strange sense of vague disquiet and—yes—fear.

After she had got into bed she began to read one of her English magazines. Somehow she felt she could not go to sleep till the visitor had gone.

She had been reading for about a quarter of an hour when there came over her that peculiar sensation of being companioned which seems to have no reference to sight or sound. She looked up. The Countess was standing just inside the door, with a glass in her hand.

"Cristina has told me of this unfortunate thing that happened tonight. I'm so sorry," she said in a low tone, "that you have missed the gala performance! I feel sad, too, to think of my beloved Beppo's disappointment. I've brought you up a glass of Sirop and water. I remember that you liked it the other day."

"Thank you so much, Aunt Cosy."

"Your Uncle Angelo is seeing off his Dutch friend," went on the Countess, coming up close to her bed. She hesitated a moment. "He is—what do you call it in England?—yes, a rough diamond. So we were glad that neither you nor Beppo were here—Beppo is so very particular. Do not mention to my son that we had a visitor tonight."

Lily took the glass from the Countess's hand and began sipping. Yes, it was certainly very nice; rather too sweet for English taste—like jam dissolved in icy cold water. She drank it all up, however.

"Sleep well, dear. We shall have Beppo out here early, full of apologies. Do not spoil those pretty eyes by reading in bed."

As she uttered the word "bed" there came from outside the house, on the very steep and rough road which lead to the real door of the villa, the loud snort of a motorcar drawing up. Then the bell rang violently.

The Countess was so startled that she dropped the empty glass she was holding in her hand, and it fell, shivered in a dozen pieces.

She walked over to the bedroom door and opened it, and at once Beppo's rather high voice sounded up the staircase. He was evidently telling his father what had happened to their party.

"It is only Beppo!" But the Countess still seemed extraordinarily disturbed. "I will go down and tell him that you are fast asleep, and that he must not make such a noise. I do hope he has not brought any strangers into the house! We are not prepared for visitors."

She shut the bedroom door, and a few minutes later the girl, who had turned very sleepy, heard the car starting again.

* * * *

When Lily awoke the next morning the strong morning light was filtering through the chinks in her dark curtains. She did not feel refreshed, for she had a bad headache. Perhaps the food at the Hotel Hidalgo had been too rich, and yet the other day she had felt all the better for a much more elaborate meal.

She jumped out of bed. It was late—a little after nine o'clock. Putting on her dressing-gown, she prepared to wend her way to the peculiar spot she used as a bathroom; but when she got to the kitchen Cristina barred the way.

"You cannot have a bath today, Mademoiselle. The Count bought some plants yesterday and put them into the bath. I dare not disturb them."

And then Lily noticed something which very much astonished her—yet it was such a little thing! She perceived that the old woman still wore the rather elaborate muslin cap and apron which she was accustomed to put on only in the evening, and only when there was a visitor to dinner. Was it conceivable, possible, that Cristina had sat up all night? She certainly looked very wan and tired. Somehow Lily did not like to ask a question which she felt sure would not be answered truthfully, if what she suspected had happened. But something of what was in her mind perhaps showed in her frank face, for Cristina looked distressed, as if caught out in a shameful action.

"I will boil Mademoiselle an egg and make her a cup of tea," she said nervously.

"No, no, let me do that! But, first, I will go upstairs and manage as well as I can with that little basin."

Lily felt vexed. It was too bad of Uncle Angelo to have filled up the bath with plants, when he must know perfectly well that she used it every morning!

Lily to voice.... Lil........... of Uncle Ang.... to have filled up the bath with plant... what do you know... people well mar.... sed as a very much........ing!

CHAPTER 19

The last time a visitor had dined at La Solitude the guest had been Beppo, and Lily had helped Cristina to clear away the next morning, and then to wash up the beautiful china and glass which were only brought out on special occasions.

She supposed that that would be her programme this morning, and she was glad to think there would be something to keep her busy, for she felt strung up, excited, and ill at ease, curiously unlike herself.

For the first time she felt an eager, instinctive desire to leave La Solitude. In vain she argued with herself that the kind of feeling which now possessed her was unreasonable and absurd; the more so that since the arrival of Beppo at Monte Carlo both the Count and Countess had been very much nicer to her than before he came. In fact, Lily could not doubt that Aunt Cosy was becoming really fond of her! But it was very disagreeable to feel that she was always being *spied on*. Again she grew hot at the thought of Aunt Cosy reading her letter from Angus Stuart. Well she knew that the Countess, with her curious, narrow ideas would think it a very peculiar letter for a girl to have received from a young man! Beppo was right about his parents. They were odd, eccentric people, very difficult to know.

It was in no happy or contented mood that Lily went downstairs, prepared to help Cristina clear away the remains of last night's supper.

Instead of going first to the kitchen, she walked along the short passage which led to the dining-room. There, to her great surprise she found that everything had already been cleared away. Somehow—though that perhaps was hardly reasonable on her part—this confirmed Lily's belief that Cristina had not gone to bed last night.

As she stood just within the empty, windowless room, there surged across Lily Fairfield an uncannily vivid memory of the extraordinary old man who had been sitting last night at the round table now before her.

What could he have said that had made the Count and Countess Polda look as they had looked when they had turned and gazed with such an expression of stony fear at the open door?

Again Lily asked herself uneasily whether that horrible old Dutchman—for so she now described him in her own mind—had any hold over Beppo? The Countess had said that the two men were engaged in some sort of business together, but Lily could not help remembering the almost insolent manner with which Mr. Vissering had treated Count Polda. And she now remembered another thing which struck her as very strange. This was that Beppo's name had not once been mentioned during that awkward three-cornered conversation in the dirty little smoking-room of the Hotel Utrecht.

And then all at once there came over a Lily a most peculiar sensation—it was that of being companioned by the strange old man who had just been so strongly in her thoughts. She felt as if he were here, close to her! It was a most disturbing and odious sensation, and with an overmastering desire to be quit of it, she almost ran into the passage.

But the feeling persisted, and, turning round, she gazed through the open door into the room beyond. So vividly had she visualised just now the Count, the Countess, and the large, black, slightly bent back of their uncouth guest that she half expected to see them there! But of course she only saw the round polished table under the skylight, and the carved gilt chairs in their usual places against the tapestried walls.

Feeling shaken and frightened she went slowly on into the kitchen.

"Is Mademoiselle going into the town this morning?" asked Cristina.

She caught at the suggestion. A walk would chase away these morbid fancies and visions from her brain. Also she had several little things to do in Monte Carlo.

"I'll start at once!" she exclaimed. "Is there anything you would like me to get you in the town?"

But Cristina shook her head.

Lily went quickly up to her room and put on her plain black coat and skirt. Then she took her cheque-book out of the only bag she ever kept locked, and caught up a pretty fancy basket, which had been a present from M. Popeau. He had bought it, full of fruit, at Marseilles, and she found it very useful when she did any little shopping either for herself or for Cristina.

As she opened the door of her room, she heard her name called out in Aunt Cosy's voice: "Lily, Lily!" The voice was low and urgent, and seemed very near; probably Uncle Angelo was still asleep.

She looked up, a little startled. The bedroom opposite to hers, that which she knew to be Cristina's bedroom—though as a matter of fact, she had never seen the old woman either enter it or leave it—had its door ajar, and through that door the Countess, clad in a dressing-gown, now emerged. She had a small, flat parcel in her hand.

"I fear," she said nervously, "that you will think what I am going to ask you to do is very strange, my little one. It is to go to the Hotel Hidalgo, and deliver this parcel into Beppo's own hands. It is of great importance and value. I ought to have given it to him last night, but his coming was so unexpected that I forgot all about it."

Lily was indeed more than surprised at this request, for by this time she had come to realise how very particular foreigners are as to what a girl may or may not do. And that she, Lily, should go to the Hotel Hidalgo, and ask for Beppo was just the sort of thing that all foreigners, Aunt Cosy included, would regard as a very improper thing to do. But she allowed nothing of what was passing in her mind to appear in her manner.

"It will be quite easy for me to go there on my way to cash a cheque!" she exclaimed, and held out her hand for the parcel.

The Countess's face cleared. Then all at once a comical look of dismay came over it. "Why, that melancholy black coat and skirt?" she asked. "I would not like Beppo to see you looking—what is that expressive word?— dowdy! Put on one of your pretty frocks, my dear."

But Lily, reddening, shook her head. Though she was, deep in her heart, sorry that she had not put on something a little more smart than this old dress, she did not feel inclined to change just because she was going to see Beppo!

"Perhaps I shan't see him," she said, smiling. "He mayn't be up. It's early, you know, Aunt Cosy."

"If you do not see him," said the Countess sharply, "then you must bring this parcel back at once to me! I thought I had made that quite clear, Lily?"

"I'm so sorry! I'll be sure to deliver it to him."

And then, to Lily's surprise, Aunt Cosy suddenly drew her into her arms and kissed her with real affection.

"I feel, my little Lily, as if you brought good fortune to La Solitude! God knows I don't want to be unfair to the Marchesa Pescobaldi, for she has been in some ways a good friend to my beloved son. But it is quite true that she has the Evil Eye! Look at what happened yesterday. There was no reason why they should have had that breakdown in the mountains—depriving Beppo of a delightful evening with you! I am very, very glad indeed that the Marchesa is going home tomorrow. *You* are our true mascot!"

Lily was touched and amused by these odd remarks. They had in them a thrill of reality, of truthfulness, which was very rare in Aunt Cosy's voice and manner.

"I'm so sorry Beppo has to go away, too, tomorrow," she said sympathetically.

"We shall see—we shall see! Perhaps it will be possible for him to stay on a little longer after all," answered the Countess. But now she was speaking, or so the girl told herself, in her old, false, affected voice.

Lily took the precious parcel, and put it at the bottom of her basket. Then she went downstairs.

"Well, Cristina, is there really nothing you want me to do?"

"I would like a pound of rice," said Cristina hesitatingly. "And if you could get me such a thing, four fowls' livers; that is all, my little lady."

After the girl had started on her solitary expedition, she debated with herself whether she should go off straight to the Hotel Hidalgo or take it on her way back. She finally decided to go there first.

When about half-way down the hill she saw a woman coming slowly up towards her. But not till they had passed one another did Lily realise that the stranger was Mme. Sansot, who kept the Utrecht Hotel, and who had spoken with such suspicion and dislike of Mr. Vissering. She felt sorry she had not said good-day to her, in the courteous French fashion; still, it was probable that Mme. Sansot had not known her again in her severely simple black coat and skirt, and plain round hat.

It took Lily longer than she had expected to walk to the Hotel Hidalgo, and it was nearly eleven o'clock when she found herself in the hall where she had waited so long and so impatiently last night. Feeling a little shy, she went to the bureau and inquired for Count Beppo Polda.

The clerk, who had not been there the night before, looked at the young English lady with a good deal of curiosity.

"I do not know if you can see the Count," he said hesitatingly. "He is not down here, he is upstairs in the Marchesa Pescobaldi's sitting-room. Does Mademoiselle wish to be shown up there?"

Lily was in a dilemma. "No, I do not think that will be necessary," she said, rather uncomfortably; "I have brought a parcel for Count Beppo from his mother. She wished me to give it to him in person. Perhaps you would let him know that Miss Fairfield would like to see him in the hall for a minute?"

She spoke very decidedly, and the man scribbled something on a card and sent it upstairs. There then followed what seemed to the girl a very long wait. But at last, to her surprise, Beppo and the Marchesa appeared together.

The Marchesa's face was flushed. She looked both angry and disturbed. So did Beppo. As they came into the hall it was quite clear that neither of them recognised Lily. They were talking together animatedly. Then she heard the Marchesa utter an exclamation of surprise, and they both advanced towards her.

"The Marchesa kindly suggests that you should come upstairs to her sitting-room."

Beppo tried to speak pleasantly and naturally, but it was plain to Lily that something had upset him very much.

"Yes," chimed in the Marchesa, "we hope, Miss Fairfield, that you will come upstairs. It will be quite easy to arrange a private interview between you and Count Beppo. My husband and I will leave you alone together. That is more suitable than that you should ask for a private room down here."

"But I only wanted to see Count Beppo to give him a parcel from his mother! I would have sent it up, but Aunt Cosy made me promise I would give it to him personally," exclaimed Lily.

The Marchesa's face cleared as if by magic. "What stupid messages hotel people do give!" she observed. "The message we received was that Miss Fairfield was downstairs, and desired to see Count Beppo Polda alone and secretly—I feared something dreadful had happened at La Solitude!"

"I knew perfectly well that nothing had happened," said Beppo crossly, "you might have let me come down alone, Livia!"

Lily blushed and laughed. "I said nothing about 'secretly,'" she exclaimed. "But I *did* say that I must see Beppo in person; Aunt Cosy made me promise that I would."

She handed the parcel to Beppo, and then they all shook hands.

"Do, please, Miss Fairfield, come back to luncheon with us here. It would give us great pleasure!" The Marchesa spoke with real, eager cordiality, and, as Lily hesitated, she added: "Do ask her, Beppo? She will perhaps do it if *you* ask her. We will send up a message to the Countess explaining that we have kept you."

"Yes, please do!" said Beppo.

"Walk with her to the door, my friend, and put her in the way she wishes to go to do her shopping," said the Marchesa kindly and pleasantly. "I must run up to my husband again and tell him our apprehensions were not justified."

She waved her hand, leaving the two younger people together.

"The Marchesa was afraid that one of my parents was ill," explained Beppo awkwardly. "She has a very warm heart. I am so glad you are coming back to *déjeuner*."

He kept fingering the parcel. "Mamma did not want an answer?"

"No, I'm sure not."

"In any case, I will write my mother a note explaining that you are with us, and telling her that I will escort you back to La Solitude myself this afternoon."

They were out on the road by now. "How I wish I could come with you, Lily, and assist you in the shopping. But, alas! I must leave you here."

She walked off, feeling that foreigners were indeed inexplicable beings.

Without the softening effect of her toque and veil, the Marchesa Pescobaldi had looked a good deal older this morning than she had done the other day, and there had been an unbecoming flush all over her face.

Lily walked on, half glad, half sorry, that she was going to the Hôtel Hidalgo to lunch. Glad she was not going back to La Solitude—sorry that she was to be the guest of the lady with the Evil Eye. In spite of herself Aunt Cosy's words about the Marchesa had impressed her.

Monte Carlo is a very small place—though a place of large, clear spaces; so it was not perhaps as wonderful as Lily thought it was that she should run straight into Captain Stuart.

"This is an answer to prayer!" exclaimed the young Scotsman, and though he smiled, he spoke as if he meant what he said. "I suppose it was presumptuous of me to hope that if you had received my letter you would have answered it?"

"Please forgive me," said Lily penitently. "But yesterday was so full, I hadn't a minute! And—and—"

"Yes?" he said eagerly.

"I'll answer it now," she said, "by telling you that I thought it was very kind of you to write it, and—"

"And?" he repeated.

"That I haven't forgotten my promise! I'll come at once to you if anything else happens to—to upset me again. Not that I expect anything to happen, but still, one never knows."

"I want you to do me a kindness," he said abruptly. "Popeau has entertained me very often, and I've never entertained him yet. Will you lunch with him and with me this morning? I've found quite a nice restaurant. Not as good as the Hôtel de Paris, but quite a decent place. Do, Miss Fairfield? I shall take it as a real kindness—the act of a friend!"

Poor Lily felt sorry indeed that she had engaged herself to the Italian lady.

"I wish I could," she said ruefully. "But I've promised to go back to the Hôtel Hidalgo. The Marchesa Pescobaldi, who is a great friend of the Poldas, begged me to come, and I said I would. I don't see how I can get out of it now—"

He remained silent.

"You do understand, don't you?" she said pleadingly.

"Yes, of course I understand. But I'm sorry."

"I'm sorry too," said Lily in a low voice.

"Forgive me, Miss Fairfield. I'm an ill-tempered, cantankerous fellow! But I was so disappointed—just for the minute. What are you doing this afternoon? May we call for you at the Hôtel Hidalgo after lunch?"

"I'm afraid Beppo Polda will expect me to go out with them," said Lily. "I always used to think I had a firm character till I came to Monte Carlo, but now I'm just like wax; I do whatever I'm told. It's awfully difficult with foreigners—they just make up their minds to do something, and one has to fall in with their plans."

"Count Beppo Polda is going away tomorrow, isn't he?" asked Angus Stuart abruptly.

"Yes, I believe he is."

"I'm glad he's going away."

"Why?" asked Lily.

"I don't care for the fellow—that's all."

"*I* rather like him," observed Lily.

Captain Stuart lifted his hat and walked away.

Then he suddenly came back. "As you can't come to lunch, could you come to dinner tonight, and go to the Club?" He said these very simple words in rather a fierce tone, and Lily suddenly felt as if she must obey him.

"I think I can manage that!" she exclaimed, "Though it is impossible to tell what Aunt Cosy will or will not allow me to do."

As she saw a look of annoyance, almost of anger, flash across the young man's face, she added hurriedly: "Of course, I am now quite free to come and go as I like in the daytime, but I don't know if she would consider it the thing for me to go out to dinner by myself. However, I can but try."

"Are you going back now at once to the Hôtel Hidalgo?"

"No," said Lily frankly. "I am going to call on the English chaplain and ask him if he can't find me something to do. There must be voluntary work of some sort where I could put in a few hours each day."

"But you came here to rest!" he exclaimed, in a dismayed tone.

Lily laughed. "I feel quite well again now. But sometimes La Solitude gets on my nerves. I can't imagine how an energetic woman like Aunt Cosy can stand it as she does. She wouldn't if she wasn't so fond of her husband—they are wrapped up in one another. The real reason why she was so awfully angry with me about Mr. Ponting was because he was so upset. She really is a devoted wife!"

She felt that the man walking by her side had a deep, she thought an unreasonable, prejudice against the Countess Polda. She wanted to show him that there was something good in Aunt Cosy, something better than he thought for.

When they reached the chaplain's house Lily held out her hand. "Good-bye—I hope only till tonight!" she exclaimed.

Captain Stuart shook hands with her rather stiffly, and walked away—this time without turning round and coming back as he had done before.

As to Lily's proposed voluntary work, everything was settled in a very few minutes. She was told that there was a Convalescent Home just outside Monte Carlo, where they would be more than grateful for occasional help.

As she left the chaplain's house Lily felt that she quite looked forward to this opportunity of doing some real work. It was true that the long, dull hours spent by her at La Solitude got on her nerves. Hence that strange, unnerving experience in the dining-room this morning.

It was to her an extraordinary experience to be living in a house into which there never came a book, or even a newspaper of any kind, excepting the odd little sheet published in Monaco itself! That contained practically no news of interest to an English girl—though the long lists of visitors to the various hotels were studied carefully by both Count and Countess Polda.

At first Lily had supposed by the way the Countess talked, that people would come in and out as they did in England. But, with the exception of the unfortunate George Ponting, and of her own two friends, M. Popeau and Captain Stuart, no strangers had been near La Solitude till last night, and then, as Lily knew quite well, the old Dutchman had only been asked because it was hoped that he would be useful to Beppo.

It was strange how Mr. Vissering's sinister, disagreeable personality haunted Lily. When she thought of him she hastened her footsteps, nervously afraid lest she might suddenly run into him.

She wondered if the woman who kept the Utrecht Hotel had been on her way to La Solitude with a message from the Dutchman? Perhaps she was bringing a return invitation from old Mr. Vissering to the Count and Countess. If he had included her—and Lily somehow felt quite certain that if he asked them he would ask her too—then she made up her mind to say quite plainly that she would not go.

CHAPTER 20.

"And now, my good friends, you two had better take a turn in the sunshine, while I carry off Miss Fairfield to my sitting-room for a little rest and a little chat,"—so quoth the Marchesa Pescobaldi to her husband and to Count Beppo the moment lunch was over.

They had had *déjeuner* downstairs, in the hotel dining-room, and it had been a pleasant meal. And yet all the time, while eating, listening, and talking, Lily had felt uncomfortable—very unlike her usual eager, interested, happy self.

The Marchesa had come down to the dining-room dressed as if for going out, in the plainly-made black coat and skirt and elegant toque she had worn on the first occasion that Lily had seen her; yet once more the English girl was struck by her beauty. She was evidently older than Lily had at first thought, but of her pre-eminent loveliness there could be no doubt. Among the many exquisitely dressed, and, in many cases, very pretty and attractive women there, the Marchesa Pescobaldi looked and moved like a goddess among mortals.

By this Italian lady's side the English girl felt very young, very insignificant, and yes, very badly dressed, in her three-year-old black coat and skirt, and plain white linen shirt.

The other three talked a great deal during the meal. Even the Marchese, whom Lily did not really feel she knew at all, addressed a great deal of his conversation to her. Lily was told of a visit he had paid to England long years before, and of a delightful Derby Day experience, when he had won five thousand francs on an Italian horse, at ten to one odds!

Out of compliment to their guest, they all talked English, which the Marchesa spoke extremely well, almost as well as Beppo. Her husband made up for his lack of knowledge by his somewhat elaborate courtesy to the young lady who was his guest.

All at once, as they were sipping their coffee, something was said by Beppo which implied that he was not leaving Monte Carlo as had been arranged with his friends the next day. Perhaps he caught the look of surprise on Lily's face, for he remarked quickly:

"I have had news from Rome which makes it possible for me to stay on here for at any rate another ten days or so."

Lily wondered why he hadn't told her this morning, but all she said was: "How delighted Aunt Cosy will be!"

"I hope that you will not be sorry," he exclaimed jokingly, and Lily, smiling, shook her head. She had certainly enjoyed herself since Beppo's arrival at Monte Carlo. Also his presence had quite altered Aunt Cosy and made her much nicer.

After they had finished had come the brief advice—nay, it was a command—from the Marchesa to the two men to go out and to leave her and Lily for a while by themselves.

"Your rest and chat must not last too long if we are to have the drive we promised ourselves," said Beppo. He took out his watch. "I will come up and fetch you at a quarter-past two. I hope that by then both you ladies will be ready to start?"

"You need not come upstairs," said the Marchesa quickly. "You can send us a message when you are ready. But pray give us a *full* half-hour! There's nothing more disagreeable than motoring just after a meal."

A few moments later the lift was swinging Lily Fairfield and the Marchesa Pescobaldi up smoothly, almost noiselessly, to the top of the hotel.

As they stepped out of the lift the older woman affectionately thrust one of her jewelled hands through Lily's arm, in almost schoolgirl fashion.

"Now that we are alone," she exclaimed, "I want to tell you that I hope you and I, Miss Fairfield, are going to be friends! May I call you Lily? It is a sweet, a delightful name—pure and simple, as I am sure you are yourself. Will you call me by my name too, dear? I am called Livia."

"It is very kind of you to want to make friends with me—Livia," said Lily shyly. "I have always longed to go to Rome some day."

"But, of course, it is because you will live in Rome that I want us to be friends," said the Marchesa, rather quickly.

As she spoke she withdrew her hand from the other's arm, and, opening a door, she stepped back to allow Lily to pass through into a very light, gay-looking sitting-room in which were many bowls and vases filled with exquisite flowers.

"You see," she exclaimed, "how both my husband and Beppo spoil me!"

By far the most beautiful thing in the room was a big nosegay of white lilac, rising from a blue jar which was in itself a thing of beauty.

The Marchesa went up to the lilac and sniffed at them delicately.

"This was Beppo's gift to me this morning," she said. "He went out after seeing you, and got them for me—partly, I suppose, to console me for the fact that he will not be our escort back to Rome tomorrow!"

While she spoke she went on moving about the room, and Lily suddenly told herself that her companion was like a beautiful, restless, untamed animal. Her wonderful eyes—they were like pools of light in her pale face—were darting this way and that. And again the English girl asked herself with a kind of apprehension whether the Marchesa had indeed the fatal maleficent gift, which the superstitious believe may bring sorrow, and even shame, on those its possessor loves best?

"I think we will sit over here," said her hostess at last. "But first, my dear Lily, excuse me a moment. I will take off my toque, for it is heavy. Even the best Parisian modistes have now lost the art of making a hat sit lightly on the wearer's brow. I shall be more comfortable without it. I have a headache. Yesterday's adventure in the mountains was very tiring."

She left the room, and Lily, who had been sitting down, got up and walked, hardly knowing what she was doing, over to a big writing-table. One of the drawers was open, and she could not help seeing that within the drawer was the wrapper of the parcel she had brought for Beppo.

The Marchesa came back. "We will sit in the window," she observed, "so that while we talk we can enjoy the glorious view."

She pushed two easy chairs toward the bow window, so arranging them that while she herself was in the shadow, Lily's face was in the full light.

"And now," she said, "sit down! We have not got very long. I think that Beppo did not like leaving us alone, eh? Men are like that. They detest realities, they do not like the truth!"

Lily would have liked to combat this rather unkind view of the stronger sex, but her hostess was speaking with a kind of suppressed energy which made her feel she could not interrupt.

"Yes, I am all for the truth! I do not believe in the French proverb, 'All truth is not good to say,' and I know that English people always tell the truth?"

She gazed with an eager, rather questioning, look into the girl's open, guileless face.

"Do not think me impertinent," she said suddenly, "but before I go away there are one or two puzzles which I wish much to solve, and you, Lily, alone can help me to solve them. I beg you to believe that I shall be asking these questions in no spirit of idle curiosity, but because for many years past Beppo Polda has been"—she hesitated, and then she went on firmly—"the closest friend of my husband and myself. Can you wonder that I want you and me to be allies?"

She stopped speaking. It was clear she wanted Lily to say something—but what was there to say?

"I know you have been very kind to Beppo," said the girl earnestly. "Aunt Cosy spoke very gratefully of your kindness to him the day I first met you."

That was perhaps somewhat stretching the truth. But still, it *was* the truth.

"My kindness to her son has not made the Countess love me, Lily," said the Marchesa drily. "That woman hates me! Again and again she would have liked to have done me an injury; again and again, not lately, but in the past, she has tried to detach Beppo from his best friends."

Lily began to feel exceedingly uncomfortable. She knew that what the Marchesa said was perfectly true—Aunt Cosy did not like the Pescobaldis. But that was none of her business. When all was said and done she, Lily Fairfield, was really a stranger to them all.

The Marchesa was looking at her intently, evidently willing her to speak again.

"Of course, Aunt Cosy is a very peculiar woman," began the girl awkwardly. "She is so devoted to Beppo that one feels she would be jealous of anyone he really cared for. The other day I could not help feeling that she was actually jealous of dear old Cristina!"

"She has reason to be jealous of Cristina," said the Marchesa slowly, "for Beppo, very rightly, is devoted to that noble woman, who has given up her whole life to him. Do you suppose Cristina would stay one moment with the Countess were it not that it gives her the opportunity of being of service to Beppo—and of seeing Beppo?"

Lily was amazed at the bitterness with which these words were uttered.

"Still, after all, Aunt Cosy is Beppo's mother, and she does love him with all her heart!" she said impulsively. No wonder Aunt Cosy disliked the Pescobaldis if they hated her so, and perhaps tried to set her son against her.

"If you are wise," said the Marchesa impressively, "you will see very, very little of the Countess Polda during the course of your future life. She is likely to live to be a very old woman, and she will wreck your happiness if you are not careful."

Lily stared at the speaker with astonishment and discomfort. What did this beautiful, sinister-eyed woman mean by saying that?

"You know—or perhaps you do not know—that Count and Countess Polda are not really my relations," she said at length. "I am only staying with them till February or March. They are very kind to me, but I don't suppose, once I have got back to England, that I shall ever see them again."

"Surely Beppo is not going to live in England after he has married you?" exclaimed the Marchesa in an agitated voice.

She started up from her chair, and gazed down into Lily's upturned face.

"Oh, Lily!" she cried. "Do not ask that of him! It would be a terrible sacrifice! Believe me, he would never be happy, however rich, in England. He's an Italian through and through! I do not say this to you because of my own strong sentiments of affection for him, but because it is the truth. If you do not care for Rome, then live in Venice, or in Florence—nay, even Paris would be better than London, for Beppo!"

Lily also got up. She felt exceedingly angry.

"I am not going to marry Beppo." She uttered the words very distinctly. "I cannot imagine what can have made you think such a thing? Why, I have only known him two or three days!"

She felt not only very angry, but also disgusted. In fact, so violent was her emotion and her surprise that she found herself trembling all over.

"Sit down, Lily," said the Marchesa slowly. "And forgive me for what I said just now. I do not speak English really well; I ought to have said '*if* you marry Beppo.' It is, after all, a possibility—is it not? It would be absurd to deny—surely you do not deny—that he is in love with you? That is why I said that about the Countess."

But Lily, even in the midst of her agitation, could not help noticing that the Marchesa's manner, as well as her voice, had changed; there was no longer in her words the thrill of sincerity that there had been.

"I'm sure that Beppo is not in love with me," said the girl firmly. "He has not known me long enough to fall in love with me. He has a pretty, coaxing, kind of manner—"

"He has indeed!" broke in the Marchesa sarcastically, but Lily was determined to finish her sentence.

"—But his manner is just as pretty to Cristina as it is to me," she concluded.

She felt as if she were on the brink of tears. How dare this foreign woman insult her so!

And then something else happened which amazed the English girl more than any of the other amazing things which had gone before.

The Marchesa Pescobaldi sank gracefully upon her knees, and from that lowly posture she looked up into Lily's face. She clasped her hands together, and there seemed to be nothing affected or even out of the way in the gesture. The surprised girl felt that now, again, the woman kneeling there was quite honest, quite sincere.

"Forgive me!" exclaimed Livia Pescobaldi. "Forgive me, Lily! I see that I have offended and distressed you—that I have outraged your modesty. But you must remember that we Italians fall in love far more suddenly than do the cold-blooded English and the calculating French. I saw at once that Beppo was fascinated—also that the Countess Polda, who never acts without a motive, was quite willing, nay, desirous, that you and he should become good comrades. So I put two and two together, as you say in England. I see now that in this case my two and two made five—not four, as I thought! I apologise with deep humility for having said what I did."

As Lily still remained silent, the Marchesa went on pleadingly. "Come, be generous! The English are generous. It is one of their finest qualities."

"Of course I forgive you," said Lily, trying to smile. "Perhaps I was silly to be so—so put out! I know what you say is true—that foreigners fancy themselves in love very easily."

"Not foreigners only," said the Marchesa, rising slowly, gracefully, from her knees. "Would you be surprised to learn, Lily, that an Englishman once travelled with me in a train for three hours, and that before the end of the journey he had asked me—nay, implored me—to marry him? He thought I was a young girl, yet at that time I had already been a wife six years!" She laughed mirthlessly.

Lily exclaimed, "Oh, but you are different! You are so very, very beautiful!" She said the words from her heart, and they touched the older woman.

"You are generous!" she said, "generous and kind, little Lily. And now that we are friends again, I want to ask you one more question. It is an indiscreet and impertinent question, but I ask you to answer me truthfully. You can do so more readily if, as you tell me, you are not really related to the Count and Countess Polda."

"A question about them?" Lily said hesitatingly. "I don't expect I shall be able to answer it. I know Aunt Cosy and Uncle Angelo so very little."

The Marchesa went on as if she had not heard the interruption.

"I want to ask you," she said impressively, "how the Countess Polda makes her money? I say the Countess Polda, for the Count, as you can see, is a mere cipher."

"The Countess Polda does not make any money," replied Lily quickly and confidently. "Little as I know about them, I do know that!"

The Marchesa's question had shocked the girl. In some ways Aunt Cosy was not a nice woman, but she never pretended to be better off than she was. In fact, she often spoke of her own and the Count's changed fortunes. It was strange indeed that one who was by way of being an intimate friend did not understand how really poor the Poldas were.

"In one sense, of course, I know that they are poor," said the Marchesa Pescobaldi impatiently. "Every time I come to Monte Carlo I miss something from La Solitude. We went into the drawing-room for a moment last night, and I at once saw that there was only one ebony cabinet where there used to be two. Next time I come doubtless the mirrors will have gone! Yes, I realise that in a sense the Poldas are poor. But what I want to know is, where do they get the money with which they supply Beppo?"

She looked very searchingly at Lily Fairfield. And, as in a flash, Lily remembered that strange, painful interchange of words she had overheard between Beppo and his mother on the day of his arrival—how he had taunted her with not having sent as much money as he had expected. But for that she would have denied absolutely that Aunt Cosy and Uncle Angelo could ever send Beppo money.

"You know, I suppose, that at irregular intervals they do send large sums to their son?"

"No, I did not know that," said Lily.

She spoke in no very determined voice, and the Marchesa, looking at her flushed face, made up her mind that she was not telling the truth.

"Well, Lily, whether you know it or not, it is so! They have ardently desired, ever since I knew them, that Beppo should marry a very rich woman—" She stopped dead and looked straight into Lily's eyes. But the girl's expression did not alter; she evidently did not see into the speaker's heart—or could it be that she was very, very cunning, with a marvellous power of keeping her own counsel? The Marchesa could not make up her mind.

"Up to now Beppo has disappointed them," she went on. "I have done my best—that I can swear! For, at any rate, the last three years I have done my best to find him a rich wife. Meanwhile, I do not say often, I do not even say at regular intervals, but now and again, Beppo receives from his mother a considerable sum of money. I have an important reason for wishing to know where that money comes from."

Again she looked searchingly at Lily, and at last the girl answered in a low, reluctant voice, "Honestly, I can't tell you; in fact, I can hardly believe that they can ever give him what I would call a considerable sum of money. They live so very simply; they are so obviously poor."

It made her uncomfortable that she and a stranger should be discussing the Count and Countess's private affairs in this way.

"What does their son think himself?" she said at last, "surely he must know!"

"Beppo has no idea at all," said the Marchesa impressively.

Lowering her voice a little, she asked suddenly, "How much money have you lent the Countess Polda since you arrived at Monte Carlo?"

"I have lent Aunt Cosy nothing!" cried Lily vehemently. "She has never asked me to lend her a farthing!"

"Then where did she get the money she sent by you to Beppo this morning?" exclaimed the Marchesa imperiously.

"She didn't send me with any money this morning," exclaimed Lily. "She simply sent Beppo a little parcel."

"A little parcel?" mimicked the older woman. "And what do you think was in that little parcel?"

"I don't know," said Lily, bewildered.

"Then I will tell you. In that 'little parcel' were twenty-five thousand francs in Bank of France notes! Do you seriously tell me that you had no idea of the very valuable parcel you were carrying? There was a letter in the parcel," continued the Marchesa slowly, "and that letter I made Beppo show me."

She walked across to the writing-table, unlocked a long narrow drawer, and took from it a letter:

"My dear Son,
      "Here is some of the money I promised you. I have more, but I am afraid to send it in this way.
                                                            "Your Mother."

There was a pause.

"Then you had nothing to do with it? Will you swear that, Lily?"

"No," said Lily quietly. "I will not swear anything. My word is good enough. I had nothing to do with it at all. Surely Beppo does not think I had?"

"I admit that the thought did not occur to Beppo. You see, he knows how often his mother has sent him money before. But it did occur to me."

"And I suppose *you* thought," said Lily slowly, "that I would not have lent the Countess the money were I not going to marry Beppo?"

"That is so. You see what passed in my mind exactly."

The Marchesa felt rather surprised. Then this young English girl was not quite as simple as she looked?

There came a quick knock at the door, and Beppo, opening it, stood smiling before them.

"I've just run up to say that the car has come round. Are you ready? Have you had your rest and your secret talk?"

He looked sharply from the one woman to the other.

"Yes," said the Marchesa. "And I think that we are friends forever!"

As she turned to Lily there was an urgent appeal in her lovely eyes.

Lily answered a little shyly. "Yes, I hope we shall be real friends—always."

And, oddly enough, in spite of the trying moments she had gone through, and in spite of the rather mixed feelings with which she even now regarded the Marchesa, she did feel that this strange woman would henceforth be more to her than a mere acquaintance.

Even so, as she followed the Marchesa into the lift, as she answered more or less mechanically Beppo's gay little remarks and questions, she felt bewildered and oppressed.

Lily Fairfield had always lived among very straightforward, simple people—people, too, who were conventional, who never indulged in intrigue. And now she felt that as long as she lived she would never forget seeing the beautiful Marchesa Pescobaldi sink down on her knees and beg so earnestly, so pathetically, for forgiveness.

Many strange thoughts jostled themselves in the girl's mind while the three made their rapid transit downstairs. Twenty-five thousand francs? A thousand pounds? She felt a little frightened when she thought of her somewhat lonely walk from La Solitude that morning. Aunt Cosy ought to have given her at any rate a hint that she was carrying something valuable!

As to how the money had been obtained, she, Lily, told herself that, after all, the Poldas must have some fortune of their own, if not very much. Take her own case. She knew that now she was twenty-one she could, if she chose to do so, sell out certain securities from which came her income. All that had been explained to her, very carefully, by Uncle Tom, and by his solicitor, Mr. Bowering, who had charge of all the Fairfield family business. No doubt the

Countess, whenever she thought Beppo hard up, sold out certain securities, thus making herself, of course, the poorer, but doing it for her son's sake.

CHAPTER 21.

It was a wonderful drive. Beppo, who acted as chauffeur, was skilful and daring—the unkind would have called him reckless. He took the old, almost worn-out, motorcar where most drivers would have feared to venture, but Lily, physically, was very brave, and once or twice when the Marchese uttered a word of remonstrance she was surprised, and a little amused.

She was still absorbed in what had happened, and in going over and over again every word of her strange talk with the woman who now sat, absolutely silent, by Beppo Polda's side.

Certain passages of the conversation remained far more vividly in Lily's mind than others. Thus, while she hardly gave a thought to the question to which the Marchesa attached such tremendous importance—the question of how Aunt Cosy procured the money which she now and again sent or gave to her son—the English girl kept thinking of what the other woman had said about her, Lily Fairfield, and Beppo.

She felt a good deal disturbed, and at the same time thrilled and moved. Was Beppo really in love with her? Certainly his manner was very, very different when they two, by chance, found themselves alone, even for a few moments. He then either became at once ardent and deferential—or coaxing, affectionate, and delightfully confidential.

This last had been his attitude during the drive he had taken her the day before yesterday, and it was the mood in which she liked him best. When he gazed with burning eyes into her face, the while paying her outrageous compliments, she felt shy, and very ill at ease. At such moments he seemed to be trying an experiment—trying, that is, to rouse in her a feeling her whole being denied him the right to exact. And yet—and yet she did find him an exciting and stimulating companion, and she could not help being glad he was staying on in Monte Carlo....

All at once the motor began to slow down. They were going over the yellow, marshy piece of rough road where they had stopped during the first drive Lily had taken with Beppo and his friends.

The Marchese exclaimed in his careful English: "It is a spring under the earth. Never dry here!"

Once they were safely across the marshy place, Beppo began driving along what was little more than a path cut through a big olive grove, which brought them, far sooner than Lily expected, to the front door of La Solitude.

"There is no short cut around here that I do not know," the young man said, as he helped her down; and almost at the same moment the Marchesa called out: "I cannot do myself the pleasure of coming in to see the Countess, for a friend is coming to tea. Will you return to dinner tonight, and then accompany us to the Club, Lily?"

"I've promised to dine with M. Popeau. But I believe"—she hesitated—"that he is going to take me into the Club."

"Then we shall meet once again—so? I am glad!"

* * * *

To Lily's relief, Aunt Cosy made no objection at all to her spending the evening with M. Popeau and Captain Stuart. In fact, she seemed pleased rather than otherwise that the girl should be going to do what must yet seem to Continental ideas a very unconventional thing.

But perhaps because she now knew that her son intended to stay on for a little longer in Monte Carlo, the Countess's manner was extraordinarily effusive. She seemed excited, unlike herself—indeed, her air of contentment, almost of joy, was in curious contrast to Cristina's overcast countenance. The old woman looked nervous, unhappy, and ill at ease; and when fastening up Lily's pretty evening frock she gave a long, convulsive sigh.

"Is anything the matter, Cristina?"

"No, Mademoiselle. There is nothing more the matter than there has been for a very long time," was the cryptic answer.

At a quarter to eight M. Popeau called for Lily, and during the rapid drive down into Monte Carlo he observed suddenly:

"The Countess does not look like herself tonight. I wonder what has happened to so excite and please her? *Have you any idea of the reason?*"

He asked the question in a very peculiar tone, and Lily, surprised, answered: "Beppo is staying on in Monte Carlo. He may even come to La Solitude for a few days. That is quite enough to account for Aunt Cosy's good humour."

"Are the Pescobaldi's leaving tomorrow?"

"Yes, and it's because Beppo can't get the room he wants at the Hidalgo Hotel that he is thinking of honouring his mother by paying us a short visit!"

Lily could not help a sarcastic inflection coming into her voice. She liked Beppo very much, but she had no sympathy with his love of luxury, and of having everything "just so" about him. After all, what was good enough for his father and mother—to say nothing of herself—ought to be good enough for him!

"So, so," said M. Popeau thoughtfully. "The young Count is not going away?"

Lily looked around quickly. M. Popeau spoke in a singular, preoccupied tone.

"I had occasion today to look through the private telegrams which have arrived at Monte Carlo in the last twelve hours—" he hesitated, and then added slowly, significantly: "and I saw a telegram which I believe contained news which more than accounts for the Countess being so joyous tonight."

"Really?" said Lily uncomfortably. "How very strange."

Somehow it shocked her very much that M. Popeau should have the right to look at private telegrams sent through the Post Office. It seemed to her a very improper thing to happen! No doubt the telegram concerned the Countess's mysterious money matters—those money matters concerning which the Marchesa Pescobaldi had shown such intense interest and curiosity.

"Do *you* know anything of such a telegram?" asked the Frenchman.

He asked the unexpected question very gravely, and as Lily shook her head, a look of relief came over his face.

"I'm glad of that!" he said. "Somehow I did not believe that you had seen the telegram I have in my mind. But I regard it as almost certain that the Countess will show it you either tonight, or tomorrow morning."

Lily was rather taken aback by these mysterious words. But she regarded M. Popeau as being rather fond of saying mysterious things and of making mysterious allusions, so she remained silent; and soon she was far too much absorbed in the amusing, brilliant scene in which she found herself at once a spectator and an actress to give any thought to what he had said.

The Old Casino—as habitués of Monte Carlo have fallen into the way of calling it—has now been given over for some years to the ordinary tourist. Not so the so-called Sporting Club. To the Club any man can obtain admission who can prove that he is a member of a reputable club in whatever may be his own country.

Lily was astonished to see the grandiose way in which everything was conducted there. All the diners in the restaurant of the Club wore evening dress, and the great rooms had a palatial splendour about them, while the decorations were in very much better taste than those of the rooms at the Casino.

They had found Captain Stuart waiting for them, and after they had finished dinner the three went off and looked on at the already high play going on at the tables.

The Club was far more Lily's original idea of a famous gambling resort than had been the Casino. The people about her looked, too, of a different class from those she had seen in the other place.

After they had strolled about from table to table, Monsieur Popeau now and again risking a sovereign or two, Lily saw Beppo Polda and the Marchesa Pescobaldi coming slowly towards her.

When the necessary introductions had been made, the Marchesa began to talk eagerly to the Frenchman, whom she at once remembered having met before the war.

Angus Stuart, with something like a scowl on his face, moved away from the two couples, but he was still near enough to hear Beppo Polda murmur: "I have never seen you in evening dress before, Lily—how lovely you look!"

"What a cad the man must be to say such a thing!" Angus Stuart almost said the words aloud.

Lily laughed nervously. "I have never known anyone pay so many compliments as you do, Beppo! If any of my old friends heard the things you sometimes say they would think you were making fun of me—"

"They would be fools! You *do* look beautiful tonight—so beautiful that I am not going to risk my luck at the tables. I should be sure to win, and if I won I should be in despair!"

Of course Lily knew that Beppo meant to imply that the gambler who is lucky at play is unlucky in love. Again she laughed nervously, but in spite of herself she felt that there was something alluring in her companion's deep voice and absorbed ardent gaze.

"I can think of many good reasons why you should not play, Beppo!"

She uttered the simple words coquettishly, and Angus Stuart bit his lips. This was a side of Lily Fairfield he had not known was there, and a sudden, passionate wave of anger and disgust swept over him. But instead of moving away, as he would have been wise to do, he moved just a little nearer to the tall, distinguished-looking foreigner and the fair, flushed, English girl, whose delicate beauty was certainly set off to great advantage by her pale grey gown and quaint-looking evening cloak.

The young Scotsman heard Beppo Polda say in a very low voice: "You know that from tomorrow I stay at La Solitude?"

"I'm glad of that," Lily said smiling.

"Is that really true? Your words make me so happy—happier than you know, Lily!"

Beppo was gazing down eagerly into her face, and Angus Stuart felt a wild impulse come over him—if only he could knock the fellow down.

"I'm glad you're coming to La Solitude, because I know it will please Aunt Cosy. You know that I have always thought it unkind of you to have gone to the Hidalgo Hotel when she was expecting you to stay with her," and this time Lily spoke quite seriously.

"If I had known who would be at La Solitude I should have come there straight," Beppo answered.

And Angus Stuart again felt that hot, unreasonable rush of rage possess him. How dare this fellow talk in that intimate way to a girl of whom he had seen very much less than he, Stuart, had done? And why did Lily seem to enjoy those boldly turned compliments?

Captain Stuart told himself bitterly that women were all alike; also that he had made a mistake—that Lily was not the kind of a girl he had taken her to be. What would have been more easy than for her to snub Count Beppo?

He remembered how she had snubbed dear old Hercules Popeau on their long journey from Paris, when the Frenchman, presuming on his age, had been perhaps a thought too familiar in his manner; and yet she allowed this—this bold brute to say what he liked to her!

"When I am at La Solitude," went on Beppo in a low tone, "I shall be a good boy, and never come down to Monte Carlo! We will go up each morning to the golf club and have a round. In the afternoons I will take you drives among the mountains. I have already managed to hire a two-seater for a week."

Lily felt a little startled by his eager, intimate tones; also she had caught a glimpse of Angus Stuart's face.

"I shan't be able to be idle all day long," she said hurriedly. "I have asked the English chaplain here if he can't find me something to do. I've already had a month of complete holiday, and somehow I find that idleness doesn't suit me."

Beppo Polda looked extremely surprised and, yes, displeased.

"What nonsense!" he exclaimed.

"Oh, but it isn't nonsense." Lily was speaking very decidedly now. "There's a convalescent home for English soldiers near here, and I have already arranged to go there and help with some of the work. I'm quite looking forward to it!"

"Does mamma know of this foolish plan?" asked Beppo.

"No, I haven't told Aunt Cosy yet. But she and I quite understand one another." Lily looked up at him a little defiantly. "She knows that I am an English girl, and that I am used to doing what I wish—and to going about by myself."

At that moment the Marchesa Pescobaldi detached herself from M. Popeau and came smilingly towards them.

"I fear I must leave this charming scene," she exclaimed, "for we make an early start tomorrow morning—my husband and I."

She bent forward, and, to Lily's astonishment, kissed her warmly. "Goodbye, my little friend!" she said in French. "Perhaps next time we meet in Rome? Do not forget what I said to you today. You and I are friends—*whatever happens*—henceforth!"

Lily felt a sudden feeling of recoil from the beautiful woman. She wondered—wondered—wondered whether the Marchesa really had the Evil Eye? Feeling a little ashamed of herself, she made the curious little symbolic sign with her finger and thumb which M. Popeau had once told her was supposed to avert ill-luck.

Beppo bowed ceremoniously. "A demain, Lily," he said quietly. And then he escorted the Marchesa out through the mass of slowly-moving people.

Lily watched them threading their way among the crowd; then she looked round, and felt a little bewildered and surprised to find herself close to a table where a big duel was going on between a small group of players and the bank.

Suddenly she saw that M. Popeau and Angus Stewart were standing apart near one of the now closely-curtained windows. They were talking earnestly, and Lily would have been very much surprised had she known what M. Popeau had drawn Angus Stuart aside to say.

* * * *

"At the risk of offending you, I beg you to forget yourself, my friend. Believe me, she is in danger!"

"I am not thinking of myself," said Angus Stuart in an angry tone, "and I am trying not to think of her! If Miss Fairfield is in danger, it is her own fault. How can she allow that fellow to make love to her in that open, impudent way?"

"She is a child, and, though intelligent, has no knowledge of life at all," said M. Popeau slowly. "Let me remind you of the truest of our French proverbs: 'To know all is to forgive all.' I lay claim to know, I will not say everything, but a good deal that I do not feel I can say to you. I regard her as being in real danger of having her life wrecked by a number of cruel, selfish, and unscrupulous people, who care for her as much as I do for that piece of paper on the floor! I refer, of course, to the Count and Countess Polda; also, incidentally, to the Marchesa Pescobaldi, who, in this affair, is proving once again that even a heartless woman may be a sublimely unselfish lover. I did my best the other day to warn Miss Fairfield. I was, as they say in England, snubbed for my pains!" He laughed a little ruefully.

"Seriously, Stuart, I have learnt something today which makes it quite clear to me that the Countess Polda—there is something sinister about that woman, I wish I could find out what it is—will make a tremendous effort to attach this English girl to her son. Should she succeed—I say it in all solemnity—that sweet child will soon be changed from a happy, joyous young thing into a grief-worn miserable woman! I speak of what I know. I am an old man, and I have become attached to you."

He paused, and Angus Stuart muttered something under his breath. Was it, "You're a good chap, Popeau"?

The Frenchman went on, speaking much more slowly than was his wont. "You have your chance today. Remember what Shakespeare says, 'There is a tide in the affairs of men.' That tide has come to you *now*. Take her back to La Solitude, my friend, and speak to her on the way. It is a fine night. Why should you two not walk up there, through the scented orange groves? I always look at a woman's feet, and tonight I noticed that Miss Lily was shod in good strong shoes. I was surprised, but glad," he concluded quaintly.

"But what shall I say to her?" asked the other.

M. Popeau looked at him shrewdly.

"I do not press you to speak to her of your own feelings. That is a matter that every man must settle for himself. But I want you to put her on her guard. Beppo Polda is a charmer of women." He saw that his words made the young Scotsman wince.

"It is a great mistake when one is thinking of things as serious as is this thing, to avoid looking at the truth. Beppo Polda, I repeat, is a charmer. And, unfortunately, he likes and admires Miss Lily. I go farther, I say that she is Beppo Polda's ideal of what a man's wife should be. But does that mean that he would be kind or faithful to her after the first few weeks of married life *if temptation came his way*?"

He paused—then answered his own question. "No, of course he would not be! He would always respect her, no doubt, but respect does not satisfy an Englishwoman, as it so often does a Frenchwoman or an Italian. Married to Beppo Polda," concluded M. Popeau very solemnly, "our little Lily would wither like a flower put into a hot gas-oven."

It was a quaint, almost a grotesque, simile, but somehow it impressed Angus Stuart deeply.

"From tomorrow," went on M. Popeau, "Beppo Polda will be living at La Solitude. They will be together all day long, and he will make love to her all day long. His mother will help and abet him in every conceivable way possible."

"But what am I to say to her? She will think me impertinent—and she will be right! I have no standing in this matter. Popeau—would to Heaven I had!"

"In your place," said Hercules Popeau impressively, "I would sacrifice myself for her."

"Heaven knows I am willing to do that!"

"Are you really willing, my friend? Are you willing to put your pride in your pocket? Are you willing to tell her that you love her, and that it is because you love her, even without hope, that you are entitled to warn her against this man? Though the Scotch, as I have found out many a time during the late war, think themselves in every way superior to the English (I do not say that they are, or that they are not, but that is their conviction), still you and she are bound by a common language. Implore her, above all, to do nothing in a hurry. Do not let Beppo Polda go back to Rome engaged to be married to Lily Fairfield."

The matter-of-fact words made the young man feel sick with apprehension, anger, and jealousy. Why, Popeau spoke as if the matter was already almost settled!

"It has not occurred to you, I suppose, that Beppo Polda may be making love to her with no thought of marriage?" Angus Stuart said slowly.

"I confess that was my first conviction. When I spoke to Miss Lily a few days ago I thought Beppo Polda was simply amusing himself—nothing more! But I have a very good reason for having changed by mind."

As he uttered these words he walked across to where Lily was still standing watching the play, and feeling, deep in her heart, forlorn, and a little depressed.

"I have now to go off to see a friend on business at the Hôtel de Paris, so Captain Stuart will escort you home, Mademoiselle."

M. Popeau spoke with a touch of rather unusual formality, and Lily looked round at him surprised. "I am entrusting you to the care of a good and faithful friend," he went on in French. "Be kind to him tonight."

Stuart was now slowly walking towards them, and his face, which had been set in grim lines, softened as his eyes rested on Lily.

The two walked out of the club in silence. She looked distractingly pretty, but also what Stuart had never seen her look before, that is, ashamed—ashamed as a child looks who knows she has done wrong, and yet, while longing for forgiveness, does not want to ask for it.

CHAPTER 22

When they were in the open air they both stopped, and Lily said, almost in a whisper: "How beautiful Monte Carlo is at night!"

The now waning moon silvered the great white buildings and shed shafts of delicate, quivering light across the dark sea to their right.

"I wonder if you'd mind our walking up to La Solitude?" said Lily's companion suddenly. "Were they expecting you back early?"

"No; they didn't think I could be home before eleven."

They made their way across the great open space in front of the Casino, and started walking along one of the deserted paths which led through the gardens. It was indeed a very fairyland of mysterious beauty. Through the high feathery trees could be seen the vast star-powdered sky.

At last Angus Stuart began to speak, but there was something cold, almost icy, in his voice.

"I know I haven't a right to interfere with anything you do, still less to criticise your behaviour, Miss Fairfield—"

"Why do you say that?" She felt sharply hurt and also angry. It did not look as if her companion was going to give her any opportunity of being "kind."

The man walking by her side was looking down into her upturned face with lowering eyes. She had not known that Angus Stuart could look at anyone as he was looking at her now. It was almost as if he hated her! Her lip quivered. She made a great effort over herself—she must not show him how pained she felt.

"The truth is," he said abruptly, "I couldn't stand the way that fellow Beppo Polda behaved to you tonight. I thought him such a cad to talk as he did! Popeau has found out that he hasn't at all a good reputation in Rome. He makes love to every woman he meets!"

While he was saying those words the speaker was cursing himself for a fool. This was not the way he had meant to speak. He had meant to warn Lily in quiet, measured accents of the danger she was running.

"M. Popeau is prejudiced against Beppo Polda." She spoke with a good deal of spirit, though she felt on the brink of tears. "As for his manner, a great many foreigners have that sort of manner. Look what absurd compliments M. Popeau used to pay me on our journey from Paris! Beppo may have a bad reputation, but the Pescobaldis are devoted to him. I've made friends with the Marchesa—she's quite a nice woman."

"Is she indeed?" There was a depth of wordless scorn in the Scotsman's now steadied voice.

"Why, you don't know her—you know nothing about her! You're very prejudiced too," cried Lily.

"Perhaps I am prejudiced," he said curtly.

"You must not be offended with me, Captain Stuart, if I say that with regard to Beppo Polda you are also very unfair!"

"If you think me prejudiced and unfair, it's no use my saying what I meant to say," he said coldly.

"You can say anything you like to me," said Lily impulsively. "After all, where's the good of our being friends if we can't say what we like to one another!"

And then, to her surprise, Angus Stuart burst out: "Of course, I know that Popeau thinks I'm jealous. Frenchmen are like that. But I'm not jealous—at least, I hope not! It's your true interest, and that alone, that I have at heart."

"I never thought you were jealous," said Lily. Then she rather wondered at herself—she was generally a very truthful girl—for saying such a thing.

He turned to her: "You may not have thought so, but—I'm not going to lie—and it's true that I'm very, very jealous! I'm jealous of Beppo Polda—I'm jealous of your being fond of him—but far, far stronger than my jealousy, is my fear that you, Miss Fairfield—"

He hesitated, and she said in a low tone: "What is it you're afraid of?"

"I'm afraid that you may be cajoled into making a very unhappy marriage," he blurted out.

"I don't know why you should think such a thing." Lily spoke in a hesitating, troubled voice.

"It's clear to me—as clear to me as it is to Popeau, who is a shrewder man than I am—that those people, the Count and Countess Polda, want you to become their son's wife."

Lily remained silent. She asked herself agitatedly whether, after all, this might not be the simple truth. She could not but see that the Countess was doing everything she could to throw her and Beppo together.

Captain Stuart hurried on: "The young man is a ne'er-do-well; something of an adventurer, too, if Popeau's information is correct."

He felt surer of himself. He had feared Lily would be very angry with him, but he could see that, though deeply troubled, she was not angry.

"The man leads a completely idle life! Sometimes he has plenty of money to fling about; at other times he appears desperately hard up."

"The thing *I* do not like about Beppo," said Lily, in a low voice, "is that he didn't fight. I thinks that's such an extraordinary thing!"

And then Angus Stuart did a noble thing. He might have remained silent. Instead, he said quickly:

"You mustn't blame Beppo Polda for that! Even Popeau admits that wasn't his fault. He wanted to go to the front, but his mother and the Marchesa Pescobaldi were determined he should run no risks, and so they pulled strings. I think ill of the fellow, and I want you to be on your guard against him. But I don't want you to think him worse than he is."

They had now left the gardens, and were making their way through the dark streets.

Tears were rolling down Lily's cheeks.

"But what can I do?" she said at last. "Surely you don't want me to leave La Solitude just because Beppo Polda is going to stay there for a few days? He's not always as silly as he was tonight. When he and I are alone together he's quite different, and much nicer."

She did not see the look that came over Angus Stuart's face, as he asked himself whether, after all, his words of warning had not come—as such words are so apt to come—too late.

"Perhaps I'm on the wrong track. If so, forgive me! After all, Popeau may be prejudiced. But, oh, Miss Fairfield, don't be in a hurry! Take time to consider whether life in Italy, as an Italian's wife, would be really a happy life for you. I do feel that your whole future happiness may depend on what happens in the next few days."

Angus Stuart was speaking very agitatedly now. He thought he saw, at last, into Lily's heart. He believed that after all she did care for Beppo Polda, and the bitterness which had filled his heart melted away into a great selfless pity and concern. She looked so very young—almost like a child, and even in the dim light about them he could see the tears in her eyes.

"Look here!" he exclaimed. "I dare say the man's not half a bad fellow. Try to forget everything I said!"

"I don't want to forget what you've said," exclaimed Lily—and then she went on, hesitatingly: "Sometimes—tonight, for instance—I feel as if I almost hated Beppo; and then, when he and I are alone together, and he speaks so kindly of his people, and of dear old Cristina, then I tell myself that he *is* nice, after all!"

"Still," said Angus Stuart slowly, "you do enjoy his beastly compliments."

Lily blushed a little, and sighed. "Every girl likes having pretty things said to her. I sometimes think that Englishmen don't say enough pretty things, Captain Stuart. I can't imagine any Englishman paying his mother or old nurse the sort of compliments Beppo pays Aunt Cosy and Cristina!"

"I wish a Scotsman could say the sort of thing you like—the sort of things Beppo Polda said tonight," he muttered ruefully.

"Oh, I shouldn't like *you* to say such things at all!" Lily smiled up into his face.

They were now engaged in the lonely road leading to the heights above Monte Carlo, and they seemed alone in a moonlit enchanted world of beauty, and exquisite night scents. They walked on in silence for some moments. And then Lily just touched her companion's arm.

"I am grateful to you," she whispered, "for having said what you did to me tonight! And I want to tell you that I'll follow your advice. I'll—I'll snub Beppo! I won't let him say the sort of things that you think are horrid—and which perhaps *are* horrid."

There was a tremor in her voice. And all at once he turned on her. Why shouldn't he follow Popeau's advice? Why not burn his boats?

"Look here!" he exclaimed. "I don't see how you can help knowing— knowing—" He stopped.

"Yes?" whispered Lily. "Knowing what?"

"That I love you! I dare say it seems absurd, considering what a little we've seen of one another, and how very seldom I've had a chance of talking to you alone. But there it is! I suppose I fell in love with you at first sight—in fact I know I did;—in that big, grey, dirty Paris station. I've been a lonely chap—a bit cantankerous, too. But there it is! I've never cared for anybody else. And I don't mind how long I wait—if there's the slightest chance that in the end I'll succeed. I oughtn't to speak like this now, for your people don't know anything about me."

He stopped speaking for a moment, then he began again in a slow, thoughtful voice: "I'll tell you what I'll do—"

Lily felt as if she must burst out laughing and crying together. She had never thought that *this* was the way a man proposed.

"I'll write out this very night an account of myself. I'll say where I went to school—what my people were like—what I've done—and what I hope to do. And then I'll ask you to send it to your uncle—I mean to that man who's exactly like your father. Tell him I don't mind how long I wait, if only I can win you for my wife! If it's true that you're not thinking of marrying Beppo Polda then—do give me a chance!"

He spoke in a quick, urgent, muffled voice, and all at once he turned, and took hold of her two hands.

"I can't expect you to like me yet—you don't know me well enough—"

And then Lily suddenly said in a very low, clear voice: "I do know you well enough!"

She was shaking all over. It had been a terrible effort to her to say those six words, but somehow she felt that she ought to say them.

He dropped her hands.

"I say," he said earnestly, "you're not playing with me? Do you really mean that? Will you allow me to hope that in time I shall be able to persuade you to do more than like me?"

He bent forward and then, after he had heard her whispered "Yes," he suddenly understood.

In less than a moment his arms were round her, he was straining her to his heart, and raining kisses on her face. Then—but Lily did not know it—he did a rather fine thing. He drew back.

"Forgive me!" he exclaimed. "That was wrong! But a man can't always do right. For—and I'm quite serious, mind you—we're not to consider ourselves engaged till you've written to your uncle, till you know a little more about me, till—till"—he could not say "till you do a little more than like me!" for he knew now that she did.

They walked on a little way in silence, both extraordinarily happy, yet both feeling extraordinarily shy.

"I'm not a bit jealous of Beppo Polda now," he said suddenly. "But, oh, darling—*darling*, I wish that instead of taking you up to La Solitude I was taking you—well, anywhere else. Somehow I'm afraid of that place! I—I simply hate the Countess Polda!"—he spoke between his teeth. "Do you remember that first visit that Popeau and I paid there, when she forced me to tell her all sorts of things about myself—?"

"I thought you managed very well," said Lily, smiling in the darkness. "I shall never forget your saying you felt as if you'd known me a lifetime!"

"That was quite true," he said seriously. "And, after all, there is a limit to the impudent questions one is obliged to answer truly. I saw her, without her seeing me, a few days ago—I suppose the day that she and Count Polda came down into Monte Carlo to meet their son—and I thought she had such an evil face, a face, too, full of such tremendous determination! I am certain she wants you to marry her son. Must you stay on at La Solitude?"

"I fear I must—" Lily hesitated. "But—but—" she did not know what to call this man who now meant all the world to her, so she called him by that little English word which may mean so much or so very little. "I promise you, dear," she said, "that I won't allow Beppo Polda to flirt with me. I *am* ashamed of the way I went on tonight; I oughtn't to have done it! But somehow something seemed to draw me on, in spite of myself."

He took her hand and held it tightly in his, and, like two happy children, they walked on—Lily in a maze of surprise and of mingled feelings, in which perhaps *comfort* was the one which predominated. It was such a comfortable thing to feel that she had a friend as well as a lover, in the strong, dependable man now walking by her side. She had felt terribly lonely sometimes—now she would never feel lonely anymore.

"Look here!" he said suddenly. "I can absolutely depend on you to tell me everything? I gather you had a pretty bad time with that woman after you found that poor chap's body?"

"Yes," said Lily in a low tone. "I had a very, very bad time. She terrified me. I had never seen anyone so angry."

"If anything of the kind happens again will you manage to get a message sent to me?"

"Nothing of the kind is in the least likely to happen again, and don't feel worried about the other thing; I think I can manage Beppo."

He winced a little at the confidence with which she said those simple words.

They were now standing on the little clearing just below the gate of La Solitude.

"Please don't come up to the house," she said nervously. "Let's say good-bye here."

And then—for, after all, though a man of honour, he was also a man of flesh and blood—Angus Stuart took Lily Fairfield in his arms again, and kissed her—kissed her—kissed her!

CHAPTER 23

With her whole being in a whirl of new sensations and feelings, the happy girl made her way up slowly through the plantation of olive and orange trees. More than once she stopped walking, and pressed her hands to her temples. Was it, indeed, she, Lily Fairfield, who had just gone through that wonderful experience with a man of whom she had never heard a month ago, and yet whom she now knew would be henceforth the whole world to her?

Like most girls brought up entirely with older people, there was something at once childlike and mature about Lily Fairfield. She realised dimly that only an exceptional man, one with a very high sense of honour, would have said to her what he had said tonight. He had not tried to rush her into an immediate marriage as almost any young man who cared for her as he seemed to care would have done.

As to his having taken her in his arms and kissed her—Lily loved him all the more for that. It showed her that he was human after all! Perhaps it was the training of fastidious, old-fashioned Aunt Emily—perhaps it was something in the girl's own nature—but ever since she had begun to think of such things, which was not so very long ago, Lily had always thought of a kiss between a man and a woman a sacred thing. No man had ever kissed her till Angus Stuart's lips had first trembled on her lips a few minutes ago.

Oddly enough, there came to her tonight a memory of the sudden repulsion she had felt for a young man, whom otherwise she had thought a very jolly kind of boy, when he had once observed laughingly, perhaps a trifle boastingly, that he only cared to go to a dance where there was a conservatory in which he could kiss the girls!

Yet it was a comfort to feel that she need not consider herself "engaged" to Angus. It would take a long time for her letter to reach Uncle Tom, and for his letter to reach her, and then she would be within sight of the time when she was due to leave La Solitude.

Perhaps because of what Angus Stuart had said, as she drew nearer and nearer to the house, there came over her an overwhelming desire to go away as soon as possible from La Solitude. With the easy generosity of youth she asked herself why she shouldn't simply hand over to Aunt Cosy the money which she would have had to pay had she stayed on till March? It was the five pounds a week Aunt Cosy valued, not her company—though that the Countess was fond of her in a way, was clear to the girl.

How strange to think that a dwelling-place which had brought her such immeasurable happiness—for had she not come to La Solitude she would never have met the man who had just left her—yet filled her with a curious sense of foreboding and discomfort.

As she emerged on to the lawn and saw, in the bright moonlight, the long, low house, there came over her just the feeling she had had this morning—a feeling of acute, unreasoning discomfort—and again with that disquieting sensation seemed to be coupled the odious personality of the old Dutchman, Mr. Vissering. Perhaps because of that silent, fleeting meeting with the woman who kept the Utrecht Hotel, she had thought of him several times that day, half fearing she might come across him.

Now, tonight, the thought of him was overwhelmingly present, though she had no reason to suppose that she would ever again be brought face to face with his strange, sinister, and, yes, insolent personality. She hoped with all her heart that Beppo was in no way in his power.

She walked up on to the terrace and knocked lightly on one of the drawing-room shutters, for so she had arranged to do with Cristina. What seemed a long time, perhaps five minutes, went by, and she knocked again, a little louder this time. And then, at last, she heard the window within being opened, and the shutter unbarred.

It was Aunt Cosy who let her in—Aunt Cosy, who so very seldom sat up after half-past nine.

"I thought Beppo would have returned with you," said the Countess, and there were both regret and relief struggling in her voice. "I have been listening for the sound of a motor, though I did not expect you to be so soon back, dear child."

Lily felt rather guilty, nervously afraid lest Aunt Cosy should cross-examine her as to how she had got home, and who had brought her back. She told herself desperately that if she was thus questioned she would take a leaf out of Aunt Cosy's own book and say that M. Popeau had brought her back!

But Aunt Cosy asked no questions. Instead she only said in a preoccupied way: "And now we will go to bed."

"I'll go to the kitchen, and get my candlestick," Lily said, but Aunt Cosy stopped her with a peremptory: "I have your candlestick here," and sure enough, to the girl's secret surprise, she saw that there was a candlestick put ready for her on Uncle Angelo's card-table.

After they had made their way up the narrow, steep staircase together, Lily turned to receive Aunt Cosy's usual good-night embrace, but the Countess exclaimed: "I will come into your room for a moment, my dear!"—and when they were inside the door, she shut it quietly.

"I have a piece of news for you," she said slowly; "it is bad news, Lily." There was a very curious look, certainly not a look of sadness, on the speaker's face. "I did not wish to spoil your pleasure this afternoon, or I should have told you then," she added.

Every vestige of colour drained itself from Lily's face.

"Has anything happened to Uncle Tom?" she asked in a low voice.

The other shook her head quickly. "Forgive me, dear child! Of course your thoughts naturally fled to your adopted father. No, no! As far as I know, Tom Fairfield is quite, quite well. No—the news I have to break to you came in a telegram after you had gone this morning. I felt sure you would not mind my opening the telegram?"

She paused.

Lily stared at her. A telegram for her? But there was no one who could have anything to telegraph to her about, excepting Uncle Tom!

"The telegram," went on Aunt Cosy slowly, impressively, "was to tell you that Miss Rosa Fairfield is dead."

"Cousin Rosa dead?" repeated Lily mechanically.

She was very much surprised and yet Uncle Tom and Aunt Emmeline had always been expecting Miss Fairfield's death, talking about it as if it was likely to happen soon, for the old lady was much over eighty.

Yesterday, nay, this morning, the news would have excited and moved her, but what was Miss Rosa Fairfield's death compared with what had happened in the last hour—to that great coming of love which was still absorbing her whole being?

"Here is the telegram."

The girl put down the candle which she had still in her hand, and opened out the piece of paper. Yes, there it was in printed characters: "Miss Rosa Fairfield died yesterday morning. You are her residuary legatee, but no necessity for you to return. Letter follows.—Arnold Bowering."

Lily stared down at the words.

"Who is Arnold Bowering?" asked Aunt Cosy.

"He is our friend, as well as Cousin Rosa's solicitor. I've known him all my life," answered Lily slowly.

"You do not look particularly excited," said the Countess. "I suppose there is no doubt about your heritage? I do not quite understand the term, 'residuary legatee.' Can that mean that Miss Rosa only left you what will be left after some other person has been paid?"

The words can hardly be said to have penetrated Lily's brain, so, "I really don't know," she answered vaguely. "To tell you the truth, Aunt Cosy, I don't care much!"

There had come over her a feeling of keen regret that she had not gone to see Cousin Rosa before leaving England. There had been some talk of her doing so, but the old lady had not seemed really anxious to see her. Lily wondered if she ought to have told Angus about Miss Rosa? Somehow she was glad she had said nothing about it. There would be plenty of time to tell him when next they met—if they had nothing more entrancing, more exciting to talk about—

"We will wait till this Mr. Bowering's letter comes, and we will then judge whether it is necessary or not for you to procure mourning," said the Countess thoughtfully.

Lily felt a slight thrill of disgust run through her. "I'm already in mourning," she said a little coldly, "for Aunt Emmeline."

"Yes, but if you've been left a fortune by this old lady, then surely you should wear all black for at least a month?" observed Aunt Cosy reprovingly. "I should have thought, Lily, that your own good heart would have told you that."

Poor Lily! It was with difficulty that she prevented herself from bursting out laughing. What an unconscious hypocrite Aunt Cosy was!

She longed to be alone, longed intensely to be free of what she felt to be such an alien presence as that of the woman who was still standing there, before her.

"Well, dear child, I will now say good-night. But before I go I should like to see you drink up your Sirop. As a matter of fact I require the glass. We are short of glasses, for I broke mine today. If you will drink up your Sirop I will take the glass away and wash it, and then I will have it for myself. I generally drink a glass of water during the night."

Lily was not particularly thirsty, but she would have done anything at this moment to get rid of Aunt Cosy. So she took up the glass which Cristina had left by her bedside.

And then there came in Uncle Angelo's familiar fretful voice the words "Cosy! Cosy!"

The Countess turned quickly and, leaving the door open, went down the passage.

Lily rushed over to her tiny basin and ewer. Breathlessly she poured the Sirop into the ewer. Why should she drink this rather sweet, sickly stuff if she didn't feel she wanted to do so?

She felt a little bit ashamed of her sly act, but Aunt Cosy's ways induced slyness in those about her.

She went to the door and held out the glass; it was taken quickly from her hand, and then Lily shut the door with considerable relief.

She hesitated a moment—and then something, she could not have told you what, made her turn the key in the lock. It was the first time she had ever done this at La Solitude, or indeed anywhere else.

She undressed. She said her prayers. She got into bed. She blew out her candle. But try as she might she could not fall asleep! She was extraordinarily excited—at once happy and oppressed.

After what seemed to her a very long time, she began to feel that strange, intangible feeling of drowsiness which heralds sleep. And it was at that moment that she realised that the curtains of her window were not drawn. It was a small matter, but it surprised her, for Cristina was very exact and particular as to such things.

Ought she to jump up and draw the curtains together? No, she felt too sleepy to do so.

And then, instead of falling into the healthy, dreamless sleep to which she was accustomed, Lily slid off into dreamland; and in her dream she was far, far away from La Solitude and Monte Carlo. She was back at The Nest at Epsom. She was telling Aunt Emmeline about Angus Stuart, and Aunt Emmeline was looking at her with a rather anxious, troubled look. At last, to her great joy and infinite relief, she heard the measured, slow, kindly, familiar tones:

"From what you tell me, Lily, I think he must be a very worthy young man. Your account of him reminds me of what your Uncle Tom was like, when I first met him."

And then suddenly Lily woke up. For a moment she actually thought that Aunt Emmeline was here, in the room! She seemed to hear the kind, loving, rather prim words echo in her ear.

She was not frightened, yet all her senses were sharply on the alert, and all at once the stillness, the intense, brooding stillness which always hung over La Solitude at night, was broken by some stealthy sounds rising from the yard which was just below her window.

Lily sat up in bed and listened intently. Even now the sounds she heard were less real to her than had been Aunt Emmeline's voice in her dream. Perhaps she was still dreaming? But no, for again she heard those curious stuffless sounds.

She began to feel a little alarmed. Who could have gained access to that narrow yard below? True, there was a big gate which gave on the rough road outside, but it was a gate which, as Cristina had told her, was hardly ever opened.

She jumped out of bed, and, going to the window, pushed it open, and leant cautiously out. As her eyes grew accustomed to the starlit atmosphere, for the moon had set, she thought she could just see that to the right the great gate was open tonight. What an amazing and extraordinary thing! She listened intently, but the stuffless sounds had ceased. So she got into bed again.

After what seemed a long time, she again heard the same sounds. Perhaps some animal had wandered in from the mountainside above? Yes, that was what it sounded like—as if some goat or donkey, finding the gate open, had wandered in, hoping to find something to eat or drink. It was as if some biggish creature was dragging itself along over the uneven brick floor of the yard.

There was only one door giving into the house that side, the door which led to the kitchen, and which was always kept locked. Only unlocked, indeed, when Lily herself went into the yard to the outhouse to have her bath each morning. That door led only into the yard, it was not used as a back door, as it would have been in England.

Lily fell asleep again; and she could not have told you whether it was a few moments or an hour, later, that she was awakened, this time by the loud, unmistakable sound of the gate in the yard below being swung to.

What an extraordinary thing! She jumped out of bed. This time she rushed to the window, and craned her head out to see in the light misty haze of earliest dawn that the gate was shut now, and that everything below looked as it always did.

It must have been a human being, not an animal, which had penetrated into the yard during the night.

She pulled the curtains together and fell asleep again, till she heard Cristina's light step in the passage. Then it wasn't night anymore, it was early morning now? Why did poor Cristina get up so early—perhaps to go to the first Mass up at the chapel? There was a priest staying near there who had the strange habit of saying Mass at five o'clock. Cristina often got up to attend it. Lily always knew, for the old woman looked so dreadfully tired on the days when she had done this.

CHAPTER 24

There are moments in life, not, alas! very many in number, when everything about us takes on a wonderful radiance, and when all that happens seems merged in joy.

All through Lily's curious, disturbed night there had shone the golden flame of her love for Angus Stuart, and of his love for her. It was that miracle which filled the whole of her being and absorbed all her thoughts. When she got up the next morning she scarcely remembered that poor Cousin Rosa was dead, and that she was now a very rich young woman.

"The bath is quite ready," said Cristina eagerly. "And I have already emptied some buckets of hot water in it for Mademoiselle."

With her hand on the key of the door which led into the little yard, Lily turned round: "Oh, Cristina, something so strange happened in the night. I'm quite sure that the big gate outside here was opened, and that someone came in. I heard such curious noises on two separate occasions, but though I looked out of the window it was too dark for me to see anything."

The old woman looked apprehensively towards the door which gave into the house.

"There are many bad characters about," she murmured. "It makes the Count nervous. Do not say anything about this to him, Mademoiselle, or to the Countess. They would only be angry with me."

"Angry with you?" repeated Lily, surprised.

"It is possible that I left the big gate undone. The only time that gate is open is when they are bringing in the wood and the charcoal for the fire. Some was brought a day or two ago. I may have left the gate unlocked," she repeated, in a troubled voice.

The girl hurried out and ran across the yard. The outhouse had evidently been tidied up by Cristina that morning. Somehow it looked different.

Lily glanced round. What was it that made this strange little place look other than usual? Then all at once she knew—the curious-looking trolley, which as a rule stood just opposite the door, was now pushed back alongside the further wall. No doubt it had been used yesterday by Uncle Angelo when moving the plants he had bought two days ago to the garden.

And then, all at once, it struck Lily that it must have been Uncle Angelo who left the gate unlocked. Every time that trolley was moved out from the outhouse the gate must of course be unlocked to let it through.

The water in the high, narrow zinc bath was still very hot, and Lily did not want to go back into the house to get a pailful of cold water. So she walked about, stamping her little feet to keep warm, for it was rather cold in this shadowed, outdoor room where no sun ever penetrated. At last she went close up to the trolley—she could think of no better name for it—and then she noticed that the big bicycle wheels were splashed with yellow mud.

And then, all at once, there rose before her mind that patch of yellow mud into which the Pescobaldis' motor had sunk. She recalled the Marchesa's explanation that there was a spring under the ground. It was clear that the trolley must have been dragged across there very recently.

* * * *

"I want you and Cristina to go down into the town this morning. There is something I desire you to do for me at the English bank."

Before Lily, who had just had her breakfast, could answer, the Countess went on: "I want you to get some money changed for me there."

The Countess went quickly out of the kitchen, and Lily heard her go upstairs into her bedroom. In a few moments she was back again with a small work-box of old Italian workmanship.

"I have here some English notes," she said, "that I want changed into French money. As you know, there is a good rate of exchange, especially if it is done through an honest banker." She paused, and then said firmly: "I want you to say that these notes were sent you from England in a registered letter."

Lily flushed up, and the Countess exclaimed: "It is a very small, a very white, lie!"

"Why should I say anything?" said Lily uncomfortably. "Of course they will think I got the money from England."

"What hypocrites the English are!" The words were uttered very bitterly. "They think nothing of saying 'Not at home' when they *are* at home, but they hesitate about a small thing like this to oblige one who loves them."

Poor Lily! She felt overwhelmed with discomfort. It seemed to her that Aunt Cosy was making a fuss about nothing, and trying to make her, Lily, lie for the sake of lying.

"Very well," she said at last. "If I should be asked—which I don't think likely—then I will say that I got them from England. After all, they did come from England originally!"

She held out her hand. She supposed Aunt Cosy was going to hand her three or four five-pound notes.

But the Countess drew out of the pretty box a thick wad of paper money.

Lily felt much taken aback. In this wad of bank notes which the Countess was holding in her hand there must be some hundreds of pounds—that is, supposing each note was worth five pounds.

"It is not necessary to count them," said the Countess quietly. "There are here—I have reckoned it all out—a hundred thousand francs, my child. That is—let me see?"—she waited a moment—"four thousand pounds of English money."

"Four thousand pounds?" repeated Lily. She was thoroughly startled. "What a tremendous lot of money, Aunt Cosy!"

"Yet I should be sorry if I thought that Miss Rosa had only left you that tremendous amount of money?" exclaimed the older woman drily.

"Each of these notes must be worth a great deal," said the girl slowly.

"They are fifty-pound notes," said the Countess quietly, "and there are here eighty of them."

"The bank manager will be very much surprised," said Lily hesitatingly. Somehow she did not at all like the thought of doing this job for Aunt Cosy. "He will think it so extraordinary that I should want so much French money. Mayn't I say it is for Uncle Angelo?"

"On no account do that, Lily." The Countess looked much disturbed. "The money, as a matter of fact, belongs to a friend of mine, and Beppo is going to invest it."

She waited a moment. "Just now English people are sending their money to France because of the good rate of exchange. The banker will not be as surprised as you expect him to be."

"I should just like to ask you one thing," said Lily timidly.

"Yes, my dear, what is that?"

There was something forbidding in Aunt Cosy's voice.

"I've only been wondering, Aunt Cosy, whether these notes were paid through the bank where I have my account. If so, of course they will know that I cannot have received them from England."

Countess Polda, not for the first time, was startled at this, as she thought, unusual display of intelligence on Lily Fairfield's part.

"You can feel quite comfortable," she said deliberately. "These notes have only just arrived in Monte Carlo by registered post. But if the slightest difficulty is made, then bring them straight back to me. Is that understood, Lily?"

The girl felt relieved. "Yes, of course, Aunt Cosy."

"I shall be very glad if you will start at once," went on the Countess, "for I expect Beppo and his luggage early this afternoon. He will first see his friends off, and then he will come straight here. I need hardly say that you and Cristina must drive back. In fact, you had better engage a carriage as soon as you see one disengaged, and drive in it to the bank."

"Why should we do that?" asked Lily.

The Countess told herself that the girl was a fool after all!

"Because it would be very dangerous for you to leave the bank on foot with so much money on your person. Bad characters hang about banks to see what money is drawn out—then they snatch the bag or purse into which it has been put."

"I see," said Lily slowly. She felt extremely, horribly uncomfortable at the thought of what she was going to do for Aunt Cosy.

"While you are at Monte Carlo, would it not be well to send a telegram to Mr. Bowering, just to say that you have received his communication? It might be well also to instruct him to purchase a handsome wreath. After all, you owe that, dear child, to dear Cousin Rosa!"

Lily made no answer to that suggestion, and a few minutes later she and Cristina started off for the town. The money, contained in a huge envelope which was fully addressed, as Lily noticed, to *herself*, at La Solitude, lay at the bottom of the big market basket carried by the old waiting woman.

They had been walking for a few minutes when suddenly Lily's companion slipped, and would have fallen had not the girl caught her strongly by the arm.

"You ought not to have come out today, Cristina!" exclaimed Lily. "I saw this morning that you were really ill."

"I got up too early, Mademoiselle," said Cristina in a dull tone. "So I am very, very tired. Still, I am glad to be with you, and away from La Solitude!"

"Surely it isn't necessary for you to go to church, especially on a week-day, so very early?" said the girl impulsively.

"I ought never to go into a church." Cristina was speaking in an almost inaudible voice. "I am not worthy to enter the House of God. But, Mademoiselle, I feel so safe there. As you know, the Devil hates holy water. He cannot follow me past the porch."

She spoke in such a suffering, troubled tone that Lily had not the heart to smile at her extraordinary words. In a sense she was awed and moved by the sincerity of Cristina's faith, even if she, Lily, thought it a curiously superstitious faith.

"I am quite sure that only angels surround you, Cristina," she said, now smiling outright. "The Devil is much too busy looking after his own to trouble about you!"

"And what if I were to tell you that I am one of his own?" said the old woman, looking round fixedly into the girl's face.

And though the sun was shining, and Lily's heart was full of joy, there did come over her a strange, eerie feeling of fear.

Cristina's life in La Solitude, a life which must have been extraordinarily lonely before she, Lily, had come there, had evidently affected the poor old soul's brain....

There are a good many lunatic asylums round Epsom, and among Uncle Tom's friends was a very clever doctor attached to one of these institutions. He had sometimes told the Fairfields pathetic stories of his patients, and of their strange, uncanny delusions.

Lily's thoughts turned instinctively to M. Popeau. She must ask him what could be done to rescue Cristina from a life which was evidently slowly driving her mad. There must be almshouses and homes of rest in France, as there are in England, suitable for such a case.

She took Cristina's hand. "Look here!" she exclaimed. "It's wrong to feel like that—really wrong!"

And then, as Cristina shook her head, she added, rather shyly: "I know you believe in the good God. Surely you do not think that He would allow evil spirits to surround you? Why, it's a terrible thought!"

Cristina gazed at Lily with a strangely pathetic look.

"Forget that I said anything," she whispered nervously. "If the Countess knew that I had said this to you, Mademoiselle, well—useful as I am to her, I think she would kill me! I am terribly, terribly afraid of her!"

Lily's heart beat with pity and concern. It was quite clear that Cristina, while fond of the Count in a way, and obviously adoring Beppo, hated her mistress.

"Of course I shall say nothing to Aunt Cosy—I shouldn't think of doing such a thing!"

They walked on in silence.

And then, suddenly, Cristina began to talk in quite a cheerful voice of the food she was going to buy for that night's supper. It was clear that her mind had gone off to Beppo, and to his coming stay at La Solitude.

Suddenly she asked: "Why has Mademoiselle got on a black dress and a black hat? Today is a joyful day in Mademoiselle's life!"

Lily was puzzled by these words. Cristina couldn't possibly know that today, the first day of her secret engagement to Angus Stuart, was indeed marked with a white stone.

She blushed and laughed. "I am happy, though I have had some sad news, Cristina, news that ought to make me sad. An old cousin of mine, who was very kind to me, is dead. The news was in the telegram which came for me yesterday."

"Ah!" said Cristina, drawing a long breath. "Mademoiselle has relieved my mind. The Countess took the telegram from the man, and I was afraid perhaps that Beppo was in some trouble!"

They were now close to the entrance of the town, and the old woman put out her small, thin hand and touched the girl lightly on the arm.

"You have been the good angel of La Solitude!" she exclaimed. "And now it is owing to you, to your being with us, that Beppo comes to pour fresh life into three withered hearts."

She waited a moment, then added slowly, almost reluctantly: "I should not have spoken as I did of the Countess just now. She is not entirely bad, for she is devoted to her son. This morning she told me she believed that hence-forth all would be well with him."

"Indeed, I hope it will!" said Lily.

But still, there came across her a slight twinge of discomfort, for poor Cristina was looking at her with such a strangely adoring expression on her face. Her sensation of discomfort deepened when the old woman added:

"And it is to you—to you, that we owe everything! I always feared that Beppo would marry a haughty, ugly woman, whom he would detest, from whose hand it would be bitter to take anything!"

"I hope he will not do that," said Lily, getting very red.

"We know he will not do that. He is going to marry an angel!"

Lily felt a sharp thrill of annoyance and dismay shoot through her. Aunt Cosy felt so convinced that she could force her, Lily, to marry Beppo, and Beppo to marry Lily, that she had actually confided her intention to Cristina!

The girl hastened her footsteps. She felt embarrassed and angry. But somehow she did not believe that Beppo would lend himself to such a plot, if plot it was.

Perhaps something of what she was feeling showed in her face, for several times Cristina looked at her with a nervous, apprehensive look, though she said nothing.

Things seldom turn out as one expects in this world. The bank manager, while professing himself quite willing to exchange the notes, yet offered her much fatherly counsel on the unwisdom of play. He apologised for what he called his impertinence, explaining that he had daughters of his own; and then he proceeded to tell her one or two sad stories about English ladies who had come to Monte Carlo and risked and lost the whole of their fortunes. Lily did not know what to answer. It seemed best to obey strictly Aunt Cosy's injunctions, to listen to all he had to say, and to make no comment.

* * * *

When Lily came out of the bank she suddenly made up her mind that she would drive to the Convalescent Home, and arrange about work there. Something told her that it would be easier to persuade Aunt Cosy to let her do as she wished if the matter were settled.

The place was a good deal further from La Solitude than the chaplain had given her to understand. In fact, it was in France, quite a couple of miles from Monte Carlo proper.

But Lily found that she was eagerly expected by the good-natured, jolly-looking matron. It was arranged provisionally that she should go there three times a week, arriving about ten in the morning. "And we shall always be pleased to give you lunch," the matron said, smiling into the girl's pretty, happy face.

After they had left the Convalescent Home and were driving back towards Monaco, Cristina suddenly exclaimed in a pleading voice, "I wonder if Mademoiselle would mind taking me for a moment to the Convent of the White Sisters? It would not delay us more than ten minutes."

Lily assented, pleased that she could do something to give the old woman pleasure.

In her eagerness, Cristina got up in the open carriage and touched their driver. He looked round, without slackening their breakneck pace.

"The Convent of the White Sisters," she exclaimed, and the man nodded, and whipped his horses up to go yet faster than they were going.

Up the steep road leading into old Monaco the little carriage rocked and swayed. They swept past the lovely garden of which Lily now had a poignant memory, and then they started going down more slowly a very narrow, quiet street of high stone houses, and finally they drew up opposite a huge closed iron gate.

"Here we are!" exclaimed Cristina in an eager voice—a voice quite unlike her own. "My mother died when I was only five years old," she whispered, "and I was here a great deal, both as a child and as a young girl. Indeed, this convent was my real home."

Lily was very much surprised; she had always supposed Cristina to be Italian born and bred. Then she was a Monegasque, after all?

A postern door opened, and Cristina motioned Lily to pass through into the courtyard round which the convent was built.

Everything up on the rock has to be on a small and rather confined scale, but even so it was a fine and spacious courtyard, and Lily was surprised to see that there were four huge blue pots, exactly similar to the two at La Solitude. Perhaps Cristina saw the surprise in the English girl's face, for she said quickly, "These were presented, as well as the geraniums growing in them, by the Count to the White Sisters. There is a close connection between the Polda family and the White Sisters."

"Yes, indeed," chimed in the nun who had admitted them. "Our holy foundress was a Countess Polda."

Lily could not help smiling at the image evoked. With the best will in the world it would have been impossible to associate the epithet "holy" with the woman she knew as Countess Polda!

The two visitors were shown straight into a small, lofty hall, of which the window overlooked the sea and the rugged coastline towards Nice. Just below the window was a narrow, terraced garden.

"I will inform the Mother Superior that you are here," said the sister ceremoniously; and as soon as she had left them Cristina hurried across to the window. "It is down there," she said, pointing to a path which ran along the top terrace, "that I used to play during Recreation!"

The door opened, and a nun dressed all in white, a commanding, almost a splendid, figure, who looked to Lily's eyes as though she had stepped out of a mediæval pageant, walked in. Cristina curtsied, and the nun put out her hand and clasped that of the old woman.

"So this is your young English friend," she said, and she fixed a pair of penetrating, dark eyes on Lily's face.

"I have brought her to receive your blessing," said Cristina, "and I hope to bring Beppo before many days are past." She added, rather nervously, "Mademoiselle is a Protestant, but that, no doubt, is a misfortune which will in time be remedied."

And then there came across the old nun's face a very charming look. "An old woman's blessing can only do Mademoiselle good!" she exclaimed; and then she took Lily in her arms and kissed her.

The girl felt extremely moved, and, yes, interested by this, to her, surprising experience; but she felt vexed and also annoyed by the reference to Beppo Polda. It was obvious that Cristina meant to associate them, Beppo and herself, in the mind of the Mother Superior.

"A sorrow has befallen the community," said the nun in a sad tone. "We have lost our beautiful cat! Every effort is being made to find him, but we fear he found Monaco too dull, and that he betook himself off one morning to gay Monte Carlo."

The Mother Superior accompanied them across the courtyard. When they reached the postern gate Cristina burst into sudden tears.

"How I wish I was going to stay here, with you!" she said, sobbing.

But the old nun patted her on the shoulder. "Come, come, Cristina, you must not be foolish! How often have I told you that it is a privilege to serve God in the world."

Cristina dried her eyes, and Lily saw her make a determined, almost agonised, effort to regain her usual quietude.

For a time they drove along in silence, and then Lily said affectionately: "I am sure the Mother Superior would agree with what I said to you today, Cristina—that God is far too good to allow any evil spirits to some near you."

"No doubt she would say that," answered Cristina sombrely, "but, like you, Mademoiselle, she is not in a position to know how God treats those who neglect to keep His laws."

And then Lily suddenly remembered with dismay that when making her arrangements with the matron of the Convalescent Home she had forgotten all about Beppo's visit to La Solitude! Perhaps, after all, she had better start going there regularly after he had left.

What had happened the night before had altered the whole of life for Lily Fairfield. Everything, excepting Angus Stuart, his love for her, her love for him, seemed out of focus. She felt ashamed of the interest she had felt in Beppo Polda. She had looked forward to his visit at La Solitude, but now she regarded it with indifference, mixed with a certain apprehension—an apprehension which had deepened since Cristina had uttered those curious, ambiguous words to the old nun. Cristina obviously hoped, with all her heart, that she would marry Beppo, and without any doubt the Countess hoped so too, now that she, Lily, had become residuary legatee to Cousin Rosa.

But somehow she no longer felt afraid of Aunt Cosy, and of Aunt Cosy's plans. Even in England people often want a marriage to come to pass—and it just doesn't!

What would Lily have felt had she known that Aunt Cosy had taken from the postman that very day a bulky letter addressed to "Miss Lily Fairfield," and, further, that after having carefully perused it, she had decided that it need never be delivered to its lawful owner?

CHAPTER 25

"I love you, Lily—love you passionately! Why should you be offended at my saying this? Surely you can understand that we Southerners are not like cold, calculating Englishmen? We say what is in our heart. You laughed just now when I told you that you had been my ideal woman for years, and yet, Lily, it is true!"

Beppo's voice was broken with what seemed to be real tears, and Lily, in spite of herself, felt moved and thrilled by his ardent words.

It was the first evening of the young man's stay at La Solitude, and the two were alone in the garden. After dinner it was Lily who had suggested that they should go out of doors. She had done so quite simply, thinking that the Count and Countess would, as a matter of course, come out too. But they had both stayed in the stuffy salon, only opening one of the windows for a moment to watch with eager, benign eyes the two young people go off together, alone, into the moonlight, to the right, where there was a grass path which led to the confines of the little property.

It was there, pacing up and down almost within earshot of the house, that Beppo, soon throwing away his cigarette, had begun pouring out ardent declarations of love....

At first Lily had tried to treat what he said as a joke, or as a half-joke, but he had soon forced her to take him seriously, for he became more violent, more passionate in his utterances.

Now she was just a little frightened. How would she ever get through the next few days, if whenever they were alone Beppo talked and, what was far worse, acted as he was now doing? For suddenly he had seized her hands, and now he was pressing burning kisses on their upturned palms.

Perhaps he realised he was frightening and offending her, for, with that curious mixture of real ardour, passion, and cool, calculating intelligence, which is so marked a trait in most Southerners, he suddenly dropped her hands.

"Forgive me!" he cried pathetically. "I have been precipitate and selfish tonight. You are so good in allowing me to be your friend! It is well to begin with friendship when one aspires to love."

And, as he had expected her to do, Lily eagerly met him half-way.

"I have always hoped you would be my friend," she said sincerely. "Ever since I came here, ever since Aunt Cosy began talking about you to me, I hoped that if ever we met we should be real friends, Beppo."

"I too hoped it," he said earnestly. "Do you remember that drive we took, only a few days ago? As we talked I felt that my soul and your soul were one! We spoke so intimately; we said so many things that as a rule a young man and a young woman do not say to one another!"

"I don't quite know what you mean," said Lily uncomfortably.

"Surely you remember my telling you how little I understood papa and mamma? Should I have said that to one I did not trust? And then you told me of your lonely childhood, Lily,"—his voice dropped; it became very soft and caressing and gentle—"and I felt that we were truly friends henceforth!"

"Yes," she said slowly, "I enjoyed that drive very much. And it's quite true, Beppo, that I do like you very much more when you are—what shall I say?—sensible, than when you talk as you did just now."

"My pure angel!" he exclaimed ecstatically. "You do not know what it means to me to hear you speak like this!" He added in a lower tone: "It shows me what, of course, I already knew—that no man has ever made love to you, my exquisite Lily. You are a fragrant flower, who, till now, has bloomed alone!"

And though Beppo's words seemed to the girl walking by his side exaggerated, and even absurd, he uttered them in such a serious way and again Lily felt oddly touched. Poor Beppo! Perhaps he had never had a chance of a straightforward, happy friendship with a French or Italian girl.

They were standing now at the extreme end of the grass path. From there, in the daytime, was a beautiful view of sea, sky, and coastline, towards France; and Beppo began telling her some curious stories of his ancestors, who had been almost as great people through the ages, when the Riviera belonged to Italy, as were the Grimaldis on their frowning rock.

At last, at her suggestion, they turned and walked slowly back to the house. The Countess had sat up for them, and as they came into the salon, she looked eagerly into Lily's face, only to see, with disappointment, that the English girl looked her usual quiet, unemotional self.

After Lily had gone upstairs, Beppo lingered on a moment or two with his mother, and at last he answered the mute inquiry in her eyes.

"I think I have made a good beginning," he whispered. "But, mamma, it is no good being in a hurry with Englishwomen! They do not understand! They are frightened and made uneasy if they are what the English call 'rushed.' But that, mamma, is no disadvantage in the long run."

"In the long run?" echoed his mother, puzzled.

"A man does not wish the damsel who is to be his wife to be too forthcoming," he said, quoting an old Italian proverb.

She nodded. What Beppo said was perfectly true.

* * * *

Lily got up long before Beppo was astir, and her heart was soon singing for joy, for she had gone to meet the postman, and had received her first love-letter.

Angus Stuart had compromised with his conscience by having no beginning to his letter, but he had not been able to keep back what was now filling his heart, and to Lily it was a perfect letter. He had added a long postcript: "I had no intention of trying to see you today, but Papa Popeau is determined to see Count Beppo Polda at close quarters, and so I couldn't prevent his making the proposal that we should all meet at lunch."

There had also come for her an elaborate little note from M. Popeau proposing that the whole party at La Solitude should meet him and Captain Stuart at the Golf Club, and lunch there with them today.

Lily could see no reason why they shouldn't all be together, and she did so long to see her lover. There was no fear that Angus would betray himself, though secretly she would have liked to tell Beppo the truth. She had felt such a hypocrite last night!

Then, for the first time, it suddenly struck her as strange that Angus Stuart had not enclosed the little statement as to himself which he had pressed her so earnestly to send to Uncle Tom. However, that was a very small matter! For her part, she had no wish he should ever send it to her. She had quite made up her mind. Even in the very unlikely event of Uncle Tom not approving, nothing he could say would make the slightest difference to her!

Thrusting the letter of her lover in her bodice, and with M. Popeau's note in her hand, she went slowly back to the house, just in time to see Beppo, clad in a wonderful-looking dressing-gown, going, with an air of deep disgust, into the kitchen on his way to his bath. She could hardly help laughing outright.

What a very singular creature he was! What a mass of contradictions! During dinner the night before there had been mention of a hunting expedition he had taken the spring before, during which he had endured, or so he hinted, untold hardships—and yet it was clear that he found the trifling discomforts associated with life at La Solitude almost intolerable.

Lily Fairfield felt very happy as she went out into the garden to wait for the others to come down. The day had opened radiantly well for her, and she could not help putting down a little of her feeling of happiness and content to the presence of Beppo Polda. Not only the Count and Countess, but Cristina also, seemed transformed. It was as if the atmosphere of the lonely house were changed, making all those in it happy—no longer gloomy, preoccupied, and anxious.

When Aunt Cosy came down, Lily handed her M. Popeau's note, fully expecting that she would say, in her decided way, that she could not go to the Golf Club, and that she did not suppose the Count would care to join the party either. But—"It will be a pleasant expedition for us all, Lily! We have only once gone up to the golf course since it was laid out. How glad I am that Beppo had the good thought of ordering a taxi to come this morning. It would have been quite impossible for me to walk."

Her satisfaction at the thought of the forthcoming expedition was apparently shared by Uncle Angelo, but Lily at once saw that Beppo was not at all pleased. He obviously would have preferred going up to the Golf Club with her alone; but, still, he fell in with the plan and he made himself very pleasant during the drive.

M. Popeau had ordered an excellent luncheon, and was himself in exceptionally high spirits. The only two members of the party who did not contribute much to the general conversation were Angus Stuart and Count Polda, but they were both, by nature, silent men.

To Lily's secret relief, Beppo behaved perfectly. He paid her, that is, no more attention than was due to this mother's guest. And when, after luncheon, the younger members of the party played a round in company with some English people with whom M. Popeau had made friends at the Hôtel de Paris, he rather went out of his way to be attentive to a young married woman. Even so, Lily and her lover were not able to exchange more than a very few words alone together. Still, those moments were very precious.

Poor Angus Stuart! Lily could not see into his heart—could not divine, closely as she felt in sympathy with him, how he longed to be with her, far away from all these tiresome people. All he said was: "Will you be coming down to the town—I mean alone, as you used to do—during the next two or three days?"

Lily shook her head regretfully. "I'm afraid not! But Beppo Polda isn't going to stay very long at La Solitude. He's mixed up in some big money scheme, and he will have to go back to Rome in a few days."

The young man's face darkened as she mentioned Beppo, and Lily saw the change in his face.

"It's all right!" she said quickly. "He's been really very nice. But—but I do wish you'd let me tell him!"

"No," he said sharply. "I beg you not to do that—" and then under his breath he whispered the word, "darling"; adding, "You see, I don't want *anyone* to know till you've heard from your uncle. Oh, Lily—" and then he muttered, "Confound it!" ferociously for the Countess was coming towards them with a very determined look in her face.

"Lily!" she exclaimed. "I wish you would explain to me this strange game? I feel that you, dear child, with your clear mind, will be able to make me understand it."

Angus Stuart scowled at the speaker, and she caught his look and put a black mark against him—or, rather, she added a black mark to the several she had already registered with regard to this disagreeable, plain, young Scotsman who apparently thought he had a chance of beating her son at the great game at which Beppo had always been an expert and a lucky player, and he, Angus Stuart, a mere tyro—the human game called Love.

Why, even if Lily had received and sent on that peculiar dry statement and formal covering letter which she, the Countess, had burnt in the empty grate of her bedroom yesterday, there was time enough for Lily and Beppo to be engaged and married ten times over before an answer could have come to it from Tom Fairfield.

The only perfectly happy and contented member of the whole party was Hercules Popeau.

He was intensely interested in what he regarded as the drama now being unfolded before his eyes. He had no doubt at all that the Count and Countess Polda intended their son to marry Lily Fairfield. He was equally convinced that they would fail. Also, though Angus Stuart had not said anything to him, his practical refusal to discuss what he and Lily had talked about during their long night walk to La Solitude, made him certain that something had been settled between the two young people.

Count Beppo's attitude interested and rather puzzled him. Was the young man playing a double game? His manner to Lily was simply civil and deferential. Indeed, it was hard to believe that the Beppo Polda of today was the same Beppo Polda who had showered such extravagant compliments on the girl at the Club two nights ago. The shrewd Frenchman wondered whether Lily Fairfield had confessed to an understanding with Angus Stuart—thus convincing Beppo Polda that she neither would nor could ever marry him. If so, the Count and Countess were evidently not in the secret.

About an hour later Angus Stuart and Lily were again alone for a few moments.

"I don't know how I shall be able to get through the time till you've heard from your uncle," he said in a low tone. "Oh, Lily—I wonder if you know how much I love you?"

She was on the point of telling him that there was not the slightest necessity to write out that account of himself to which he had referred. And yet at the very back of her mind there was a good deal of surprise that he had not enclosed it in his letter to her that morning. He had made such a point of it— had said so very decidedly that they must not consider themselves engaged until Uncle Tom knew something about him, and approved—

"I do so hate that fellow being in the same house with you!" he muttered.

Lily felt distressed. "He really is being quite, quite sensible!"

"I did notice that he behaved decently at lunch." The words were said grudgingly. "If he hadn't, well—"

He stopped abruptly, for the others were now moving towards them, and so he turned away.

It was clear, Lily admitted it to herself regretfully, that there would never be any love lost between Angus Stuart and Beppo Polda. And then, perhaps because the sun was shining, because she was near her lover, because everything seemed to be going just as she wanted it to go, Lily cast a little tender thought towards Beppo Polda.

She did like him! She couldn't help it! But perhaps it was just as well that henceforth their paths would lie far apart. She knew she could never, never make a friend of any man whom Angus really disliked.

The days that followed were like a happy dream. Every morning brought Lily a letter from Angus Stuart. In the sunshine of his new-found happiness the ice of the young Scotsman's reserve broke down, and his long letters filled her with delight, though she sometimes found it impossible to read the new one right through till she had locked herself in her room at night—for, somehow, she was never alone!

Beppo was her shadow—so much so that one day, to her annoyance, Cristina observed with a smile: "I once read a book when I was a young girl, Mademoiselle. It was called 'The Inseparables.' You and the young Count remind me of the title of that book."

On the fifth morning of Beppo's visit Lily made up her mind to go off to the Convalescent Home, and she actually did slip away before the young man was down. But she had only been at the Home an hour when she was told that a gentleman wished to see her, and in the hall she found Beppo smiling, and a little apologetic.

"It is such a lonely walk," he explained, "that mamma thought I had better come and fetch you."

She made him wait a full half-hour while she finished the letters on which she was engaged, and then on the way back to La Solitude she rebuked him gently:

"You know, whatever Aunt Cosy may do, that in England girls always go about by themselves. It's absurd to say that it isn't safe here—it's absolutely safe! I've never met a man, woman or child who looked as if they would harm a fly! Before you came to La Solitude I constantly went down to Monte Carlo by myself, and more than once I came back during that strange change that takes place each afternoon, and which only seems to happen here—I mean when it's daylight one moment and night the next—"

"You will have plenty of time for your good works when I've gone back to Rome," said Beppo firmly. He added, after a moment's pause: "You would not deprive me of one minute of your company if you knew how much it meant to me."

He said these words very simply and sincerely, without garnishing them with any absurd compliments. And again Lily felt touched. What an odd being this man striding along by her side on the lonely hillside was! So boyish in some of his ways, so mature in others. Such a man of the world, and yet now and again so very simple.

During those days of Lily's life Monte Carlo might have been a hundred miles from La Solitude. Beppo did not seem ever to want to go into the town; he was quite happy at the Golf Club, or taking Lily for drives in the funny ramshackle little motor which he had hired for a week.

Two or three times Aunt Cosy had suggested that they should go down and have lunch or dinner in one of the big restaurants, but Beppo had refused.

"If we do that," he objected, "I'm sure to come across people I know, and then my reposeful little holiday will be over."

As for the Countess, she more than once said that she had never been so happy as she was just now.

Once, when they were alone together, his mother asked Beppo if he really *must* go back to Rome just yet, and he answered very seriously:

"You know, mamma, that the money you have so kindly given me should be invested so as to bring in the very highest return. My chance of doing that is to be in Rome with the man of whom I told you. But do not be afraid. I shall very soon come back. All is going well, if slowly."

"I suppose you are wise in going slowly with Lily?" said the Countess doubtfully.

Beppo looked at her thoughtfully: "It is a great trial, but I have no doubt of the wisdom of my course, mamma. Believe me, clever as you are, I know women better than you do."

And she answered with a smile and a sigh, "I do not doubt that, my Beppo! And, after all, there is plenty of time."

"Yes, mamma. Thanks to your cleverness and goodness, there is!"

The Countess lowered her voice:

"Lily had a letter today from the lawyer. I asked her to show it to me. There is no doubt about the money. It is a fortune! Ninety-six thousand English pounds, according to what the man calls 'a rough estimate'; but she will not receive it yet awhile."

"So much the better!" exclaimed Beppo. "You may laugh, mamma, but I am really and truly mad about her! Would that I were a millionaire, leading her penniless to the altar! Then would I scatter diamonds and pearls, rubies and emeralds, before her feet!"

His mother laughed. She could not help feeling a little twinge of jealousy, but still, she was becoming really very fond of Lily Fairfield.

Countess Polda, like so many people, was always apt to admire what belonged to herself, and she now regarded the English girl as being practically her daughter-in-law.

Even so, she noticed uneasily that Beppo was not making much way with Lily, and now and again there would come a moment of discomfort and doubt, when she would ask herself, with real uneasiness, whether the girl and Angus Stuart were in correspondence? There had certainly been no harm in the rather formal, dull letters the young man had written to Lily from Milan during the early days of their acquaintance. But Countess Polda did not consider it at all proper that a girl should be receiving letters from a member of the other sex. It seemed to her unfitting and unnecessary.

Twice, while Lily had been out with Beppo, the Countess had searched her room very thoroughly in order to discover whether there were any new letters there from Angus Stuart. She had found nothing but a couple of notes—one from a friend of Emmeline Fairfield, the other from a girl who had evidently been at school with her correspondent.

And so the days went by very quickly for all the inmates of La Solitude, until one day, at luncheon, Beppo suddenly exclaimed regretfully that a great Paris financier with whom he was in touch was to be in Rome four or five days from now, and that it was important he should see this man.

"I have sent off a telegram to find out exactly when he will be there," he said. "I do not mean to be long away, mamma!"

The Countess saw a look of surprise, and not altogether one of pleased surprise, pass over Lily's face, and that look disturbed the older woman. Did Lily regret the probable quick return of Beppo?

The anxious mother began to wish ardently that something might be settled between the young people before Beppo left. Drawing her son aside, after luncheon was finished, she said, a little nervously: "I hope you are not going too slow, my boy. You do not seem to me to be making very much way with our dear little friend."

But he said: "Leave it to me, mamma. I will choose the right moment! Do not interfere."

Even so, when she stood by the little gate on which were inscribed in faint characters "La Solitude" and saw the two start off for what had now become their daily drive in the beautiful hilly country which lies behind Monaco, she had a sensation that something was going to happen, and she was filled with doubt, anxiety, and suspense.

How terrible to think that the future of so great and ancient a family as the Poldas should depend on the whim of a foolish girl of twenty-one!

CHAPTER 26

"You are frightening me, Beppo! We have been out long enough. Let us go home."

Lily Fairfield was speaking in a very quiet, level voice, but her face looked white and strained.

Beppo had stopped the motor beside a steep and lonely mountain gorge; and now he was pouring a torrent of violent, passionate words of love into her ear. As soon as his hand was free he had grasped her left wrist as in a vice, and now he was trying to force her to look round at him.

But she went on staring before her, a look of endurance and growing fear on her pale face.

"There is nothing to be frightened of, Lily. Do you not understand that I love you? I love you as an Indian devotee worships his idol! You are in no danger from me. I should not have spoken to you today had you not seemed so gentle and so kind. I thought your cold heart might be melting a little— that you might be feeling touched by my silent devotion! Now that I am going away so soon—surely I may speak? What is there between us—what is that menacing shadow that always rises up when I speak to you, God knows with infinite reverence and respect, of my love for you?"

He was speaking in broken, agitated, pleading tones, and yet there was an underlying touch of fierceness in his voice which in very truth did terrify the girl. And the expression on his face had so changed that he seemed a savage stranger, rather than a friend.

She knew that they were miles and miles from La Solitude—for all she knew, miles and miles away from any human habitation—and she was sick with fear and distress. She felt as if she was dealing with a madman.

She asked herself, in a kind of agony, if it would be right to temporise, to soothe him down, to tell him that perhaps in time she would become as he wished her to be.

And then the image of Angus Stuart rose before her. No, she could not be, even for a few moments, false to their love.

"Only tell me that I may hope," he reiterated urgently, "and I will compel you to love me! Nay,"—as he saw her shrink back—"I will teach you most gently, most devotedly, to allow *me* to love *you*! That is all that I ask—it is not much, surely?"

She turned round and faced him, but seeing his convulsed face and blazing eyes, her heart almost stopped beating with fright. She forced herself to say, very quietly: "If you will let go my hand, Beppo, I will speak to you."

He relaxed his strong, painful, grip of her soft wrist.

"Forgive me!" he exclaimed. "I fear I hurt you—but Lily, I am mad—mad for love of you!" and he covered his face with his hands.

"Believe me when I say that I am grateful for your love—"

Poor Lily! She stopped dead, for she did not know what more to say. She would have given years of her life to end this painful, to her this agonising, scene. And the still, lonely beauty of the country round her seemed to mock her distress.

"God bless you for saying that!" exclaimed Beppo fervently. "Lily! My sweet snow-like angel—do not be angry if I ask you to grant me one great, supreme favour—"

Lily looked at him wonderingly. He spoke more like his old self, but he was gazing at her with supplicating eyes. What was he going to say now? He had already implored her to marry him—already implored her to try and love him—to allow him to love her—to give him time to prove his love for her! What was there left to ask for? A supreme favour? What a strange expression! He had been talking—for how long was it? she had lost count of time—ten minutes, a quarter of an hour, half an hour?—it had seemed an eternity to her—in so extravagant and wild a way that there seemed nothing left for him to say.

"What is it?" she asked uncertainly. "I would do a great deal to please you, Beppo, if only—if only"—her voice faltered—"if only you would be reasonable."

He was looking at her now intently, almost as if he were trying to hypnotise her, with those strange, brilliant blue eyes of his.

"The favour I ask," he said at last, and in a very low voice, "I ask, Lily, as a man prays for a saint's intercession—on my knees. Do not be offended—do not be what you in England called 'shocked.' It is not a very great thing that I ask of you—yet to me it will be the greatest thing in the world. It is a thing which many a woman is quite willing to give—a friend."

He stopped, and Lily, looking at him puzzled, asked hesitatingly: "What is it, Beppo? You know I would do anything in reason to please you."

"All I ask for," he said at last, "is the privilege—"

"Yes?" said Lily. "What privilege, Beppo?"

He did not answer at once, and when at last he spoke, his voice had dropped almost to a whisper.

"The privilege of taking you in my arms and kissing you just once, Lily! That is all I ask. Is it not possible that at the contact of our lips your hesitation, your coldness, will melt? May I not teach you what a man's love means to the woman he adores?"

As he ended his quick, rapt, low utterances of these, to Lily, extraordinary and unexpected words, he suddenly got up, pulled her to her feet, and threw his arms round her.

And then, in the little motor, there began a terrible, wordless struggle between the two. Lily was determined—absolutely determined—that he should not kiss her. Rather than that, she would wrench herself free and leap into the gulf to the edge of which they were now so perilously near.

Did Beppo Polda suddenly see into her terror-stricken mind? Or was it that at last he felt the horror and repugnance with which he inspired the girl whom he held closely pressed to him? Be that as it may, there swept over him, like a great tropical storm, a feeling of acute shame and self-loathing, as well as a determination that he would win her yet!

He relaxed his hold, but as he did so a wild blind rage rose up in his heart. Beppo Polda had never seen in a woman's face the look of physical repugnance he now saw in hers.

"You are not the pure angel that I thought you to be," he said hoarsely. "You are keeping your kisses for another man. Is not that so, Lily? If the answer is 'yes,' then I will drive you and myself over the precipice! I have lived my life—I should not mind dying with you!" He was lashing himself up into more and more furious anger. "What a simple-minded fool I was! You are not the first English girl I have known, Lily. But I put *you* on a pedestal. I did not think you were a flirt—now I know you are! And you have succeeded in making me behave as I never thought to behave to a woman."

She sank down, back in the corner of the little car—white and trembling all over, but feeling that Beppo's madness had passed. But with what horror, what loathing, what fear she still regarded him!

"I offer you my humble apology for what has happened," he said in a bitter tone. And then he started the car.

They drove along, in dead silence, for some time. Suddenly he slowed down, and turned towards her.

"Lily," he exclaimed, in a humble, deeply troubled tone, "I implore you to forgive me! I behaved as I should never have thought myself capable of behaving to any human being, least of all to her whom I adore. Will you forgive me, Lily?"

And as she remained silent, for she was still in no state to speak, he went on: "I'll do anything to atone. Impose the heaviest sentence, but do not look at me, Lily, as you are looking at me now!"

She made a great effort over herself.

"I do forgive you, Beppo," she said in a low voice. "But I don't want ever to think about what happened today, again. Try and forget it too. I see," she tried to smile, "that my leaving England at all was a mistake. I don't understand foreigners and their ways. Perhaps I was to blame. Please don't tell Aunt Cosy anything about it," she looked at him pleadingly.

"I am not going to stay at La Solitude long," she went on. "I've been thinking for some days that after you were gone I would make an arrangement with the Convalescent Home—they'll be glad for me to stay there for a while."

He felt utterly dismayed. "Do not punish my poor father and mother for my evil deeds! Lily, that would not be like you—that would be most cruel and ungenerous! Most humbly do I beg your pardon. But—but, Lily, forgive me if I ask you—you do admit that I love you, do you not?"

There was a long pause. And then Lily said, "Yes, Beppo, I do believe you love me—though you show your love in what seems to me a very strange way."

Her frankness took him completely by surprise—and somehow gave him hope.

"If I were to go away," he said suddenly, "and then come back after a long time, is there any, any hope that I might find you different?"

She shook her head, and then, for the first time, she burst into tears.

Beppo stopped the car. He took her hand—very gently this time.

"Lily," he exclaimed, "I shall never, never forgive myself for what happened today! Some demon whispered in my ear that if you would allow me to kiss you all would come right. It was a foolish and an arrogant thought. But I was going away—and, Lily, you admit that you know I love you!"

"Yes," she said in a low tone. "I do know that. But let us try to forget what happened today—we have been so happy, so comfortable together, since you came to La Solitude!"

"Do you think you will ever feel happy and comfortable with me again?" he asked.

And she said slowly, "Yes, of course I shall—as soon as I can forget what happened just now. Let's get home, Beppo. And, if you don't mind, do promise me never to speak to me of it again!"

"I do promise you," he said solemnly. And then, to Lily's secret astonishment, Beppo seemed suddenly to slip back into his old pleasant, easy way with her! It was almost as if what had happened on the edge of that great wooded gorge had been a dream—horrible, unnerving to look back on, but still only a dream.

Even so, she felt she would never forget, not even if she lived another fifty years, that awful moment of wordless, passionate struggle in the little car. She shuddered as she remembered how she had told herself that could she only free herself from Beppo's strong arms she would leap out into the void rather than endure the further contamination of his touch.

When they were close to La Solitude Beppo suddenly turned round. "Look here!" he exclaimed, "I think I'll go down to Monte Carlo this afternoon. A fellow I know asked me to meet him at the Club this evening. Good

Madame Sansot will give me a bed at the Utrecht Hotel." He paused. "Perhaps your thoughts will be kinder tomorrow?"

He said those words so humbly and sincerely that poor Lily felt troubled.

"Won't your going away upset Aunt Cosy?" she asked timidly.

"No, not a bit! I shall come up in the morning. But this is our last drive in this little car. Would that it had been a happier one for you! Tell them that I have gone down with the car, Lily, and that I may or may not come back to dinner."

They were now on the clearing below the house, and then, so strange is human nature, Lily, in spite of all that had happened, felt just a little sorry that Beppo was going to leave her to go up alone to deliver his message at La Solitude.

"Won't you come up to the house?" she said nervously. "They'll think it so odd—your going away like this."

And at once he said, quickly and reassuringly: "Yes, of course I'll come up! I thought you would prefer that I should not do so."

She made no answer to that remark, and as they were walking up through the wood he asked. "Lily? Am I forgiven?"

"Yes," she said, "you are forgiven, Beppo, and I really mean it. But never speak of it again. Perhaps I was foolish to be as upset as I was."

"I was mad!" he muttered, "absolutely mad! When I am like that I lose possession of my senses—I forget what I do. Did I say anything very terrible to you?"

She tried to smile. "I can't remember," she replied evasively. "Don't let's think about it anymore, Beppo—please—please!"

And so it was an apparently very friendly couple who came up to the house. But the Countess had almost second sight where her son was concerned. She saw at once that there had been some kind of trouble; still, she pretended to see nothing, and accepted Beppo's news as to his forthcoming evening at the Club, and his night in Monte Carlo with apparent equanimity.

He kissed his mother and shook hands warmly with Lily. "I shall be up tomorrow morning," he said. "Not very early, but in time for lunch."

Lily went up to her room; she washed her face and she scrubbed her hands. And then she did what she could not remember ever having done before—she locked her door and lay down on her bed.

She lived through every moment of that awful time. If only it had not happened! It had spoilt her pleasant relations with Beppo she felt—forever. Also, it would and must remain a secret as regarded herself and Angus Stuart. She could never, never tell him of what had happened today!

She looked at her wrist; it was still swollen. But Beppo had not known that he was hurting her. At one moment of their struggle the pressure of his arms had been so strong that she had thought he would suffocate her, that she would faint—and she had been quite determined not to faint. She remembered with what a sensation of physical repulsion she had struggled—even after he had released her so suddenly the feeling had persisted for some time.

And now that feeling had become transferred, in a strange kind of way, to Aunt Cosy. When Aunt Cosy had come near her just now she had felt as if she must scream! Her nerves were thoroughly upset.

A few minutes before she knew supper would be ready, Lily got up and changed her dress; and then she cast a longing look at the now growing packet of Angus Stuart's letters. How right he had been when he had said that he wished she would leave La Solitude!

She made up her mind that tomorrow morning she would slip off to the Convalescent Home, and ask if they could put her up for a few days. When there she would be able to see Angus, and arrange never to go back to La Solitude again.

Though Lily tried to behave exactly as usual during the evening that followed, the Countess was well aware that something was wrong. She kept looking at the girl with a kind of furtive, anxious scrutiny.

"Did you have a pleasant drive?" asked Uncle Angelo. And Lily was able to answer, with some appearance of naturalness, "Yes, for we went a new way, and came to a most wonderful gorge. I thought it one of the loveliest spots I had ever seen!" And then she stopped, suddenly overcome by the recollection of what had happened there.

"You do not look well, Lily," said the Countess anxiously. "You look very tired, my dear. Would you like to go up to bed at once, after dinner?"

Lily gratefully accepted. She hoped that very soon La Solitude would have become a memory—a memory of strangely mingled pain and pleasure, of regret and happiness. But now pain, regret and, yes, a hidden fear, predominated, and she longed, with a kind of desperate longing, to escape—now, at once, in the darkness, down to the Hôtel de Paris, to kind, sensible Papa Popeau, and to the man who loved her, and whom she loved!

For one wild moment she actually thought of doing so. And then she felt ashamed. After all, both Aunt Cosy and Uncle Angelo had been very kind to her, according to their lights. And she knew only too well how hurt and angry Aunt Cosy would be when she learnt that Lily had no intention of staying on at La Solitude all the winter.

CHAPTER 27

"I insist on knowing what is the matter, Beppo?" The Countess Polda gazed apprehensively at her son. Not even when he had been going through acute money trouble had he looked as moody and miserable as he looked now.

He had just arrived at La Solitude to hear that Lily had gone off to the Convalescent Home for the morning.

"I do not know that very much is the matter," he answered deliberately, "but perhaps I ought to tell you that I fear you are going to have a big disappointment. As you are such a clever woman, as well as an unscrupulous woman," he laughed disagreeably, "very often what you desire to happen *does* happen. But as regards Lily Fairfield you are destined to meet with failure."

The Countess felt a shock go through her. Instinctively she put her hand on her heart. But she answered him at once, in a calm, good-humoured tone:

"You are such a child, Beppo! And like most young men you are vain and impatient. I never supposed that Lily would fall into your arms at once, as no doubt a great many pretty ladies have done ere now! Believe me, when you are married to her you will be glad that she was not what you want to find her now—eager and ready to be made love to. Perhaps without knowing it you have startled her. English girls are sometimes very prudish, you know."

The Countess was looking fixedly at her son, and she saw that she had guessed right. They had evidently had some kind of a scene yesterday.

"I allowed you to behave a à l'Anglaise," she went on—"I mean taking those walks and drives together—because I thought I could trust to your good sense. But I fear I was wrong, Beppo."

"I lose my head when I am with Lily!" he exclaimed. "Her coldness excites me! I do not want to make a mystery about it, mamma. I see you have guessed that I was a fool!"

As he saw a look of keen dismay come over her face, he added lightly: "Nothing very much happened. But yes, it is true that while we were out yesterday we had something of a quarrel. I told her that if she refused to let me kiss her I would send the car over the edge of the precipice!"

He saw the colour recede from his mother's face. She suddenly looked like an old woman—old, and desperately tired. He felt strangely touched.

"Come, come, mamma, don't be frightened! Years ago, when I was younger, I might have been so mad, but I am an older and a wiser man now."

"Then you did not kiss her?"

"No, mamma; I could have done so, as, of course, she was at my mercy. But—well," he shrugged his shoulders. "I never have kissed an unwilling woman."

"Her conduct is strange," said the Countess thoughtfully, "for she certainly seems to like you." The speaker still felt very shaky, but she was trying to pull herself together.

"I wonder if it has ever occurred to you," said Beppo, "that there is already a man in Lily's life? I taunted her—for, mamma, I quite lost my head—and now, looking back, I remember that she said nothing. She did not deny it—as a modest girl would have done."

As the Countess remained silent, he went on:

"In one of your letters you said that Lily had solemnly assured you she was not engaged, and that you believed this to be the truth. But mamma, has it ever occurred to you that the curious, silent young man, that Captain Stuart who is staying down at the Hôtel de Paris, may be in love with her? If he were a Frenchman I would call him out," added Beppo fiercely. "We would have a duel, and I would kill him!"

"The girl hardly knows him," she said slowly.

"I cannot help suspecting that I have a rival! Yet till yesterday I would have sworn that she was as pure as the flower from which she takes her name!"

"You can still swear that," said the Countess firmly.

She made up her mind to remain absolutely silent as to the little she knew about Angus Stuart and his friendship with Lily Fairfield. After all, there was only that letter—that rather short, formal letter, enclosing those notes on the writer's life. Still, she had thought of that letter and of those notes very often, as she had watched the girl during the last few days, much as a big, wily cat watches an unsuspecting mouse. She was fairly sure that Lily had not sent any letter out of the house, apart from the one she had written to her uncle. It was true that the girl went to meet the postman every morning, but in Monaco postmen are not allowed to take letters to the post, and the post-box was some way down the hill. The Countess was certain that Lily had not been down there alone during the last few days.

Still, the thought that her carefully-laid plans for her son's happiness and prosperity might go wrong because of a silly flirtation between Lily Fairfield and a casual train acquaintance made the Countess Polda feel as if she would go mad with disappointment and rage. She began to hate the girl whom only the previous morning she had almost loved.

"Beppo," she said, and her voice trembled, "do you truly love Lily Fairfield?"

"Yes, I love her," he said sombrely. "And I have never wanted anything so much, mamma. It is quite true that her money—if, indeed, she is certain to have the fortune in which you so confidently believe—would transform my life from that of an adventurer to that of a successful and happy man,"—he was speaking very seriously now. "But, apart from that fortune, even with only the few thousands we know she possesses, I would accept her as a gift from Heaven, on my knees!"

And if rather ashamed of the emotion he had shown, he added in a lighter tone: "It is time that I settled down. Livia Pescobaldi is always urging me to do so! She was disappointed that I did not marry that ugly American girl last winter."

There was a pause, and then the Countess said solemnly:

"Has your mother ever failed you, Beppo?"

He was startled, and again he felt oddly moved.

"No, mamma. You've performed wonders! And I've often racked my brains to know how you did it!"

"I promise you that Lily Fairfield will *in time* be your wife. But do not be in too great a hurry, my son. Carry out your plan of going to Rome in two or three days, and stay away a little longer than you at first intended to do. Then come back, but not to La Solitude; go to the Hôtel Hidalgo—"

"I am sick of the Hidalgo!" he exclaimed. "If I do what you wish, mamma, I shall ask Madame Sansot to put me up again at the Utrecht Hotel."

"Not the Utrecht Hotel!" cried his mother hastily. "Surely you have never stayed there? It is a very common, low kind of place."

"I slept there last night," said Beppo quickly. "And perhaps because, thanks to you, I now have all that money, mamma, I have become a miser! I want to take care of this money—to make use of it. I do not want it to slip away in hotel bills!"

"It will not slip away," said his mother quietly. "And thanks to this money, there is no need for undue haste. I swear to you, Beppo, that if you are patient you will win Lily at last."

"Perhaps you are right, mamma—you are so often right! I will go back to where I started with Lily. She told me not many days ago that I was almost her ideal of—what do you think, mamma?"

"Tell me?" cried the Countess eagerly.

"Of a brother—only that!" he laughed rather harshly. "At any rate she shall be my dear little sister till I go away the day after tomorrow."

"And do not give a jealous thought to that dull Scotsman," said his mother lightly. "His French friend is going back to Paris very soon, and I have an idea that he will then go away, too. Without being vain you can tell yourself, Beppo, that you are very much more attractive than Captain Angus Stuart!"

He was surprised to hear her pronounce so easily the curious Scottish name.

"I am not really jealous of the man. She hardly knows him—I know that," he said in a satisfied tone.

And his mother was glad indeed that she had not told him the little that she knew.

"You have made me feel quite happy again mamma! I know that you are right, and that I was a fool to be so impatient. But it is hard to be forced to go slow, as the English say, when one adores a woman!"

Beppo put his arms round his mother and gave her an affectionate kiss.

"There is no one in the world like my mamma." He said contentedly. There was a moment's pause, then: "Would you advise me to go to the Convalescent Home now, this morning, as I did the other day?"

"No," said his mother, without hesitation. "I think that would be a mistake."

"By the way, there is something I can do to fill in the time till she returns!" he exclaimed. "The Utrecht Hotel"—he did not see just a quiver of discomfort and anxiety cross his mother's face as he uttered the name—"the Utrecht Hotel," he repeated, "is in the most tremendous state of excitement! There was an eccentric old man staying there who disappeared mysteriously some days ago. Well, mamma, his body has been found! I had a most interesting talk about the whole thing with Bouton—you know, the Chief Commissioner of Police. He and that man Popeau are much excited about the matter. For it appears that the old man was no gambler. He was a strange old fellow, and always carried an enormous sum of money about his person—some of it sewn up in his clothes. Well, though Mme. Sansot swears she never told anyone the fact it evidently became known to some band of robbers. He was waylaid—"

"A sadly common story," observed the Countess. She was staring across the lawn towards the sea, and she spoke in an indifferent tone of voice, as if thinking of something else.

Beppo felt rather put out.

"The body was found very near *here*," he said impressively.

"Near here?" she repeated mechanically.

"Yes, mamma, close to that place where there is a spring under the ground. But for the accident that the owner of the land there had to move some hurdles, the body might have lain undiscovered for months."

"That is certainly curious!" exclaimed his mother. She had turned away, and was obviously about to go indoors.

"Let me tell you the rest of the story," pleaded Beppo eagerly. "It is really very interesting—and full of curious, mysterious points."

His mother turned and looked at him. "Tell me quickly, dear child, for I have things to do this morning."

He went on, eagerly: "Mme. Sansot did tell the police of the old man's disappearance; but he was so exceedingly eccentric, and paid his bill from day to day—so the police made up their minds that he had slipped off to Nice. The shabby portmanteau which he left at the hotel—I was shown it this morning—was not worth more than thirty or forty francs and only had a change of linen in it, and an old pair of boots."

"Pray do not talk of this painful affair before your father," said the Countess in a low voice. "And I need hardly warn you not to say anything about it before Lily either."

"I don't see why I should not tell papa," said Beppo quickly. "I think it would interest him very much. There is nothing more exciting, mamma, than a murder mystery. I confess that among the most interesting hours of my life were those spent by me at the Murri trial. You will remember that Livia was determined to go to it, and that I escorted her on that occasion."

"Yes, and I thought it horrible that a woman should wish to be in any way associated with such an affair!" exclaimed the Countess. "It is one of the things about our dear Livia that I have always remembered with distaste and disapproval."

The young man shrugged his shoulders. He was sorry he had mentioned the Marchesa Pescobaldi.

"Your father is not well," went on the Countess, "and I should not like him to hear, even less to see, anything of a painful nature."

"He is bound to hear of it," said Beppo positively. "The whole of the Condamine is ringing with the story. You see, it is not in any way mixed up with the Casino, and therefore no great effort is being made to hush the matter up. However, I will do as you wish—I will say nothing about it. But you must permit *me*, mamma, to be interested in the affair! In fact, with your permission, I shall go off now and investigate the spot where the body was found."

He waved his hand, and smiled at her, telling himself with a little pang of concern, for he was an affectionate if a selfish son, that his mother had grown very much older in the last two or three years. It was she who looked ill today—not his good, easy-going papa.

And then, after he had disappeared round the edge of the terrace, the Countess walked a little gropingly, as might have walked a blind woman, through into the drawing-room.

There was no one there, and she gave an involuntary sigh of relief. She had a disagreeable communication to make to her husband and to Cristina, and she was glad that she would not have to make it at once. She was going to propose something that she knew would annoy and frighten both of her house-mates, and yet it was something which, though disagreeable, had to be done. For the matter concerned Beppo—and would take a danger and an obstacle out of her son's way, make the future for Beppo smooth. Surely Angelo would understand, and not involve her in a long, tiring argument? Still, she would begin with Cristina.

She left the drawing-room, and went slowly to the tiny kitchen.

Cristina was sitting at the small table, doing nothing. She looked up with unsmiling eyes at one whom she regarded as an intruder on her domain.

And, on meeting that look, the Countess felt a pang of exasperation and pain. It was not her fault that Cristina's help was required! Often in the past she had felt that she would have given anything in the world if she could have carried through her schemes unaided. But there are things which no woman, however clever, however determined, however physically strong, can do alone. And the thing which the Countess had made up her mind must be done within the next few days was one of those things in which the co-operation of at least two other human beings was required.

Five minutes after the Countess had entered the kitchen she left it, wiping a few drops from her forehead as she did so. She was not a nervous woman, but the five minutes had tried her nerves severely. For Cristina, to her horror and surprise, had begun by refusing to accede to her wishes.

"I would rather kill myself!" the old woman had said. "And what is more, I *will* kill myself if you drive me too far. Whether I go to hell in the next few days, or in the next few years, does not matter much to me. For the matter of that, I am in hell already!"

And then, after the Countess had answered these wild, extravagant, and foolish words very quietly, making an appeal to Cristina's better feelings, and to her love for Beppo, the other had bowed down her head over the table, and, sobbing bitterly, had confessed herself conquered. Yes, for one more time, she would do what was required of her. But it must be the last time, for she was at the end of her strength.

"And what do you think *I* feel?" the Countess had asked passionately. And then she had gone into her own sitting-room and sat down.

Opening a drawer she took out of it a box of little heart pills, which had been given her six years ago by the specialist at Marseilles whom she had gone to consult about the state of her health. She took two of these, waited for their effect to begin, and then, as she gradually began to feel calmer, she got up and, opening the door, went upstairs to find the Count. It had been her suggestion that the patience table should be taken up there, so as to leave the drawing-room free for Beppo and Lily to talk together in the odd English fashion.

Beppo would have been extremely surprised had he heard the words she uttered as she entered the room where her husband sat playing patience. Those words were:

"The body of Vissering has been found, Angelo. And we must be prepared for some kind of interrogation. I do not feel we can absolutely trust Mme. Sansot. She has been most sensible and most loyal up to now, but still, one never knows—"

Count Polda got up—a sure sign of agitation with him—and came towards her.

"It is no use to build a bridge for trouble," he said slowly. "Unlike you, I am not afraid of Leonie Sansot. I think she will keep faith with us. The more so that it would only be a complication were she now to admit she had not told the truth at first! Also, she knows so very little. Only that the old brute dined here the night he disappeared."

His words consoled the Countess considerably. She suddenly made up her mind that she would not tell him yet of the perilous task which lay just in front of them. There would be time for that a little later on.

By the time her son and Lily came back to La Solitude, she was her own genial, rather garrulous self again.

CHAPTER 28

It was Beppo's last day, and what had happened forty-eight hours ago now seemed to Lily Fairfield like a bad dream.

Beppo was once more the kindly, good-natured, almost brotherly friend of his first week's stay at La Solitude. And though Lily could see that Aunt Cosy was unlike herself, for she looked oddly disturbed, anxious and gloomy, she had taken very well the news that Lily had accepted an invitation to stay with the matron of the Convalescent Home for a few days.

Poor Lily! She felt ashamed of her duplicity, for she knew, deep in her heart, that she had no intention of coming back, at any rate for more than a day or two, to La Solitude.

Beppo was taking the afternoon train to Italy, and it had been arranged that the carriage which brought the Count and Countess back from seeing their son off should take Lily and her luggage to the Convalescent Home.

While all these kindly arrangements were being made, and especially when she heard Cristina say: "I shall miss you, Mademoiselle. Do not stay too long away," she felt as if she *must* come back just for a few days. But all that could be settled later on.

Meanwhile, she was determined to do everything in her power to make the last hours of Beppo's stay at La Solitude pleasant. She wanted him to feel that she had really forgiven him that wild, strange, terrifying scene in the mountains. So, when he asked her to take a last walk with him, she willingly assented.

They had been out for nearly an hour, and were on their homeward way, when they stopped a moment on a path which seemed as if cut out of the mountain side.

Below was a sloping carpet composed of the tops of olive trees, and Lily felt a sensation of delight come over her as she looked at the wonderful panorama spread out before them.

"While you are at the Home," said Beppo suddenly, "do not do what I am told many of the English nurses did here during the war—that is, take a walk all by yourself each afternoon. It is not safe to do so."

"Surely you exaggerate the danger," said Lily, smiling.

"A mysterious murder was lately committed just below the spot where we stand," observed Beppo impressively. "I mentioned it to mamma, who was much upset and begged me to say nothing to papa or Cristina. So will you keep what I am going to tell you to yourself, Lily?"

"What a dreadful thing!" exclaimed Lily.

She told herself that it really did look as if poor Mr. Ponting's friend had been right, and that there was a gang of bad characters—brigands, as the Countess called them—who lay in wait for any passer-by who looked as if he had money in his possession!

"The affair has specially impressed me," went on Beppo, "because the man was staying in the hotel where I stayed a couple of nights ago. It is an hotel kept by a person in whom we Poldas have an interest, for she is the daughter of an old servant of my grandfather."

Lily was startled by Beppo's words. That must, of course, be the Utrecht Hotel, where that horrid Mr. Vissering was staying.

"It is a commercial hotel in the Condamine," went on Beppo. "Nothing smart about it all, but a respectable place, with a Dutch connection."

His companion felt a sudden, unreasoning thrill of surprise and discomfort run through her. Standing there, in the sunshine, with that marvellous view spread out before her, it was as if she had been suddenly borne on a magic carpet to the sordid, dirty, little smoking-room where she had met that sinister old Dutchman! Beppo, absorbed in himself, and in the story he was telling, did not notice the look of apprehension which flitted across her face.

"Listen to what I am going to tell you," he said earnestly. "It will prove to you that my warning as to your lonely walks is by no means foolish or exaggerated."

He waited a moment and then went on:

"About a month ago there arrived at the Utrecht Hotel a rich Dutchman. He had made a lot of money out of the war, and he had come to Monte Carlo to see a little life. After a while the woman who keeps the hotel—her name is Sansot—discovered that the old fellow had with him a great deal, in fact an enormous lot, of money. He kept most of it on his person, sewn into his clothes, and in deep pockets he had had specially made for the purpose. He was an odd individual, and he did not care for gambling, in fact he very seldom went into the Rooms at all—"

"Did you know this old man?" asked Lily in a low voice.

Beppo shook his head.

"I? Of course not! But when I went down to the Utrecht Hotel the other evening I found the place in great commotion."

"Why that?" asked Lily. Her voice had sunk almost to a whisper. "Has anything happened to—" she nearly said "Mr. Vissering," but stopped herself in time!

Her heart was beating, she felt filled with a kind of strange shrinking apprehension; why had Aunt Cosy and Uncle Angelo told her that lie—as to Mr. Vissering being a business friend of Beppo's? She longed, and yet she feared, to hear what Beppo had still to say.

"Let me tell my story in order!" went on Beppo importantly. "About ten days ago or so the old Dutchman disappeared. He had gone out to dinner somewhere, and he told Mme. Sansot that he would be sure to be back early. *But he never returned!* Luckily for herself, the woman informed the police the next day. She was nervous, owing to her knowledge that the man had so much money on him—though she declares that she never told anybody of the fact. Well, Lily, to cut a long story short, this Dutchman's body was found down there"—he pointed vaguely to a spot among the tree-tops just below where they were standing.

"His body was found?" repeated Lily mechanically.

"It is probable that he had had supper in one of the villas which are scattered about on the mountain side, but what happened there is still a complete mystery. Perhaps his murderers followed him from the villa where he had dined and brutally did him to death in a lonely spot, or, if your friend Popeau is right, he was murdered in the villa and his body conveyed to where it was found, after his death."

"How—how terrible!" whispered Lily.

She felt as if everything was going round her, as if she was about to faint. Her hand clutched convulsively the iron railing in front of her.

"The body was found under a heap of hurdles," went on Beppo, "and it was only owing to the fact that the peasant to whom these hurdles belonged had sold them to a neighbour that the corpse did not lie there undiscovered till next spring. Though the body was almost naked, the clothes were neatly arranged under it. They had been ripped open and all the money taken away!"

As Lily made no comment, he added:

"You can imagine the sensation the affair has made in the hotel! While I was there one talked of nothing else. I myself went along to see the Commissioner of Police, a very decent fellow named Bouton, and he told me that there are points about the story which may make it a *cause célèbre*."

"What are those points?" muttered Lily.

"One curious point is that the man appears to have been drugged. If true, that is a very curious fact, for it disposes of the idea that he was set upon and killed by a gang of men who had never seen him before. The object of Bouton, and of the detectives he has put on the case, is to discover where the old fellow spent his last evening. That is still shrouded in absolute mystery! Mme. Sansot declares that she does not know. The Commissioner is sure she is telling the truth, but Popeau—who, as of course you know, Lily, is a distinguished French secret agent—is convinced that the woman *does* know, and will not tell. He is even inclined to believe that she knows more of the murder than she is willing to admit. But that neither I nor mamma think likely. Altogether it is a very exciting affair!"

Lily could not speak. Her mind was in a whirl of miserable suspicion and questioning fear.

"Perhaps you do not realise," went on Beppo, "that the spot where the hideous discovery was made is only about two hundred yards from La Solitude!"

"Surely we're much farther off than that here!" exclaimed Lily.

"Yes, walking homeward as we are now walking, we are at least a mile from La Solitude. But do you remember, during our first drive, how we went by a short cut through the olive woods?"

"Yes," remembered Lily, "I remember that."

"The Dutchman's body was found," said Beppo impressively, "just above the kind of yellow morass into which, as you may remember, our motorcar sank."

Lily gave a long, convulsive gasp. She saw as if it was indeed there, in the air before her, the trolley pushed up against the inner wall of the outhouse, with its big bicycle wheels *stained with yellow mud*.

And then, all at once, her companion saw that she was extraordinarily disturbed. He felt both astonished and alarmed; the girl looked on the point of fainting.

"Forgive me for telling you this horrible story!" he exclaimed. "I had no idea it would frighten you so! And yet, Lily, I shall not be sorry that I told you if it means that you will be careful—"

"I will be very careful," she whispered.

And then they both turned, and walked slowly on. But so frightened, so shaken, was she by the story she had just heard that at last she had to take Beppo's arm, and cling to it.

And always Lily will remember how very kind and considerate Beppo was to her during the half-hour that followed. The young man was puzzled and distressed. Somehow he had not realised that Lily was so sensitive! But he knew that there are people to whom the thought of any crime of violence is extraordinarily painful and disturbing. It was clear that this English girl, whom in his way he so truly loved, was one of them.

And then, suddenly, Lily took a desperate resolution. She felt she could not go back to La Solitude filled with such a hideous, agonising suspicion.

"Beppo," she said pleadingly, "I want you to do me a great kindness. I want you to go on with me *now* to the Convalescent Home, and to arrange for my things to be sent on to me there this afternoon."

She saw a look of surprise and discomfiture come over his face, and she went on, hastily:

"I feel so ill—I know I'm foolish, but I can't help it, Beppo—that story you told me has made me feel sick and faint. If I were to go back with you now, Aunt Cosy would feel worried, and would ask me a lot of questions."

He was impressed by the agitated way she spoke, and by her curious pallor.

"I will do as you wish, Lily," he said in a soothing tone. "I am never at a loss for a good lie! I will say that we met one of the nurses and that she forced you to go back with her to see a girl friend just come out from England."

"That will be good of you," she murmured gratefully. She added, "Perhaps Cristina will put the few things I have out in my room in my trunk. It was arranged that the carriage which brings your father and mother back from the station should come on to the Home."

"Yes, that will be quite all right!" said Beppo cheerfully. "But, Lily, only one thing troubles me—are you fit for that further big walk?"

"Yes, I am quite fit for it," said Lily.

She straightened herself, already feeling better and calmer. And, as she walked slowly on, she told herself how amazed she would have been two days ago had an angel descended from heaven and told her that a time would soon, very soon, come when her heart would be filled, not only with affectionate gratitude, but also with the deepest pity, towards Beppo Polda.

Then she strove to fix her mind on the real foundation for her wild, disordered thoughts and horrible suspicions. She longed to be alone, free to think things over. But still, deep in her heart, she felt she *knew* now that the Count and Countess Polda were cold-blooded murderers....

It was impossible for Beppo Polda to remain silent for any length of time, and during that last half-hour they spent together he talked a great deal, trying to tell Lily things that he thought would interest her about his English friends in Rome. And she answered him with a word now and again, her heart wrung with pain for the man by her side, as there crowded on her memory many of the little scenes of the last ten days—Aunt Cosy's pride and delight in her handsome, good-humoured, attractive son—Beppo's pretty, caressing ways to his mother and to Cristina.

Cristina? Lily remembered the old woman's strange and awful self-accusations. Cristina surely—surely was a good woman?

"Beppo," she said suddenly, "I wish you would tell me something about Cristina."

"About Cristina?" To her surprise he looked disturbed and uncomfortable. "What is it you want to know, Lily?"

"What sort of people did she come from originally? She is so unlike what I should have supposed servants of her class in Italy or France to be."

"You have asked me a question, and I will answer it truly, Lily." He spoke very seriously. "Cristina is not what she seems."

Lily turned and looked at him. She felt surprised, even startled. For a moment she forgot the terrible thoughts which had been filling her mind. What took their place was an overwhelming curiosity.

"Cristina," said Beppo deliberately, "is not a servant. She is my father's sister—not, as mamma probably told you, his foster-sister."

As an exclamation of astonishment escaped Lily he went on: "That woman is an angel! She adores my father, she adores me! When many years ago, papa lost his fortune, and my parents were in very truth terribly poor, my Aunt Cristina offered to come and live with them literally as their servant. Time went on, and we became gradually less pinched. To do mamma justice, she then desired that Cristina should take her proper place in the family. But Cristina refused! She preferred what she calls her independence. It is no secret to you, I feel sure, that she does not like my mother—would that she did! But there it is. They are too utterly different to like one another."

Lily was amazed by what she had heard—amazed, and then, quickly, there was added a feeling of trouble and dismay to her amazement.

"I suppose," said Beppo slowly, "that you are very much surprised, Lily?"

She drew a long breath. "Yes," she said dully. "I am very much surprised—and yet in a sense, Beppo, I am not surprised at all."

The truth escaped her in spite of herself. Whatever there was to know, *Cristina surely knew.*

"I have told you this, Lily," said Beppo impressively, "because to you I will not lie. The only person now living who knows the truth is the Marchesa Pescobaldi. Her family and mine were friends through generations, so she has always known the strange story of Aunt Cristina."

As she spoke there came back to Lily the curious, ambiguous words the Marchesa had used as to Cristina being a noble woman and doing what she did for the sake of Beppo. Had she done a great deal else, which neither Beppo nor anybody else in the world but she, Lily, suspected—also for the sake of Beppo?

They were now close to the entrance of the Home, though still out in the open road.

"Beppo," said Lily very gently, "I should like to say good-bye to you here."

"Certainly, if you wish it," he said, and then he added: "Forgive me for saying I hope you will not go in and begin work at once. You do not know how ill and tired you look, Lily. I shall never forgive myself for having told you that horrible tale!"

"I know you meant it in all kindness," she said.

And then, all at once, she added something which astonished the young man, for, "I've changed my mind," she said tremulously. "I'd rather you came with me through the grounds to the front door. I feel so frightened, Beppo."

"But of course!" he said quickly. "I am enchanted to be in your company a little longer!"

They walked up through some beautiful flowering shrubs till they stood at the door of the house. A few moments later it was opened by the matron.

She uttered an exclamation of surprise.

"I thought you wouldn't mind my coming rather earlier than I said," said Lily. "My luggage will be sent on this afternoon."

She turned round, and held out her hand to Beppo Polda. He took it in his. "Good-bye!" he said. "Good-bye, Lily—or rather—I should say au revoir."

"Good-bye," she repeated. And then she lifted up her face and, with a surprise which his good breeding enabled him completely to conceal, he realised that she expected him to bend down and kiss her, in front of the Englishwoman who stood by, looking at them curiously.

He did kiss her—he kissed her as an affectionate brother would have done. "Thank you, Lily!" he whispered.

He felt very much moved and touched. She was an angel after all! But deep in his heart he realised something else—that this was to be their final parting—that she did not intend that they should meet again.

He turned away, and Lily walked through into the hall.

"Is anything the matter?" asked the matron uneasily. "You look very ill, Miss Fairfield. You look—"

She took hold of the girl's hand and brought her gently forward to a window.

"You look, my dear, as if you'd had a shock! Has anything happened?"

"I have had a shock," said Lily dully. "But I can't tell you what gave it me. It isn't my secret. It's because I feel so ill that I came here earlier than I meant to do."

"You did quite right! And now you had better go straight to bed. I'll send you up a little lunch on a tray."

And then Lily began to cry—very quietly.

These kindly, commonplace words reminded her of Aunt Emmeline, and her old untroubled life in England, which now seemed so infinitely far away.

There are hours in life when everything but one central, concrete point of fear, suspense, or pain, disappears into nothingness. As a rule this state of mind lasts but a little while. If it goes on too long it kills the human being experiencing it, or breaks down the frail barriers between sanity and insanity.

As she lay in bed all through the afternoon which followed her walk with Beppo Polda, Lily Fairfield felt as if she were going mad. She asked herself, indeed, if the awful thoughts and suspicions which crowded her brain were not, in very truth, a proof that her brain had given way, and caused her to become suddenly insane.

Horrible images haunted her mind. She thought of La Solitude, that sinister, lonely house, as being full of the ghosts of those who there had met with a hideous death.

Deep in her heart she knew that the Countess Polda had used her as a cats-paw, and once she heard herself say quite out loud: "Aunt Cosy killed George Ponting, and she killed Mr. Vissering, and each time I helped!"

Her thoughts took another turn. What ought she to do? Was it her duty to betray Beppo's father and mother? Nothing could bring George Ponting or the old Dutchman back to life. On the other hand, how prevent the Count and Countess having new victims?

There floated hazily through her mind a memory—a memory of having been told a strange and frightening story of how a woman who was suspected of having committed two murders was stopped, when on the eve of a third crime, by receiving an anonymous letter, warning her that if she ever committed a third murder she would be arrested. Could she, Lily, do something of the kind with regard to Aunt Cosy?

At last, most mercifully, everything about her became shadowy, indistinct, and she fell asleep.

"Would you like to come down to supper, Miss Fairfield?"

She turned on the electric light—a bright, good light, very unlike the guttering candles of La Solitude.

She sat up, and looked about her. On a table lay her hat, and with the sight of her hat she suddenly remembered—she could not have told you why—M. Popeau.

These people were very kind, but Papa Popeau was her friend, her dear, kind, clever friend. He was leaving Monte Carlo tonight, but late, quite late—she knew that. Why not go to him *now*, and put her suspicions, her almost certainties, before him?

Before doing so she would make him promise to forget that he had anything to do with the police. She would tell him that if he could not make her that promise then she could not ask him for advice. But she felt sure he would understand.

As for Angus, she did not want to bring him into this terrible business at all. There would be plenty of time to tell him everything afterwards. Everything? No, not everything. She would never, never let him know that poor George Ponting had stayed on that night simply because it was a pleasure to him to meet an English girl.

And never, never would she let anyone know either about that horrible old man, Mr. Vissering! She knew—she had always known—that he had come up to La Solitude on that fatal night because he wanted to see her again, and for no other reason.

She went downstairs and then it was as if things were being made easy for her. The matron, on hearing that she wanted to get into Monte Carlo, told her that the motor was going in there to meet a train. But did she feel really well enough for the little expedition?

And Lily said yes, she was all right now, and that it was on really important business that she wanted to see a friend at the Hôtel de Paris.

CHAPTER 29

Hercules Popeau and Captain Stuart were walking up and down in front of the Hôtel de Paris. Stuart held a letter in his hand. It had been left for him late that afternoon, but it had only just been given to him.

He held the letter out to the other man, and M. Popeau read it, slowly and carefully. It was written on the Hôtel de Paris paper:

"Dear Captain Stuart,

"I had hoped to find you in, and so convey my invitation in person. We hope that you will come and share our simple meal tonight at La Solitude. Miss Fairfield is not at all well, but she tells me that she will be able to come down this evening. I do not include Monsieur Popeau in my invitation, as I understand he leaves Monte Carlo today.

"Yours sincerely,

"Cosima Polda."

"It's very decent of the Countess to ask me. I don't see why I shouldn't accept the invitation," he said hesitatingly. "You don't mind my leaving you, old chap?"

"I wish I could divine why the Countess Polda has asked you to dinner tonight, Stuart," M. Popeau uttered these commonplace words in a hesitating, anxious tone.

"Perhaps Miss Fairfield suggested it," said Stuart a little awkwardly.

"She may have done so."

Then came a long pause between the two quaintly contrasted friends.

There was a soft spot in Hercules Popeau's heart. Some thirty-five years before he also had had his innocent, beautiful romance. He had been engaged to a girl he loved, and just before their marriage she had developed consumption.

His most precious possession was a bundle of her simple, formal, and yet how infinitely pathetic, little letters, each of them beginning, "Mon cher fiancé," and telling him of the everyday, dull, quiet life she was leading in the Mentone of the late 'eighties.

He had never spoken of that piteous episode in his past life to any living being since his own mother's death, but now, all at once, he made up his mind that he would speak of it to his companion—to this young Scot, who, though he liked and trusted him, had never confided in him.

"Stuart," he said, "I want to tell you something. You think me a cynical old fellow, but I, too, have loved—I, too, loved a beautiful, pure, sweet-natured girl. She died within a very few miles of where we are standing now. I did not feel, after her death, that I could build up my life again in the good, solid, sensible way which is the only right way for a man to do. That is why I am a bachelor. I know in my heart that you love Lily Fairfield as I loved my little Aimée, and that has much increased my affection for, and interest in, you. I will tell you frankly that I am somewhat uneasy. You trust Miss Fairfield entirely—I do not doubt that she is trustworthy. But still she has now been for many days given to the influence of that Italian lady-killer whom that sinister couple wish her to marry. Why has the Countess Polda asked you there tonight? Especially if Miss Lily is not well? Is it to make to you some disagreeable announcement? I fear so."

"I shall soon know," said Angus Stuart, "for I mean to go."

He was touched by the Frenchman's confidence, but too shy to say so.

"Well!" exclaimed M. Popeau, "I will say no more! Accept the invitation, and good luck attend you. I may be a suspicious old fool after all!"

Again there was silence between them, and then M. Popeau observed: "I wish I were staying on, for this Vissering affair interests me intensely. It is so strange that there should have been another mysterious disappearance, and the discovery of a second body, so soon after that of poor Ponting! I had a suspicion some time ago, but now I confess that I am at fault."

"What did you suspect?" asked Angus Stuart. He had been too absorbed in his own affairs to give much thought to the mystery which seemed to interest Hercules Popeau so deeply.

"It would not be fair to tell you what I suspected. But I will tell you this much. Yesterday Bouton and I had a talk with Count Beppo Polda about the affair. I had a half-suspicion that he knew Mr. Vissering, but it became perfectly clear to me that he had never even heard the Dutchman's name. By the way, he will not be at La Solitude tonight, for he left Monte Carlo today."

"I am glad of that," said Stuart shortly. "I do not care for the fellow."

"There are worse people than Beppo Polda in the world," said M. Popeau mildly. And Angus Stuart felt rather disgusted. Why, it was Popeau who had first set him against the young Count!

"So long!" he said quickly. "I think I'll buzz along now. It isn't good-bye for long."

And Hercules Popeau answered quietly, "No, my friend, for I may still be here when you come back; they keep early hours at La Solitude."

* * * *

This conversation had taken place nearly three hours ago, and now Hercules Popeau was sitting in the hall of the Hôtel de Paris. He had had a delicious little dinner, and was smoking a good cigar. In about half an hour he would be starting for the station.

He kept looking at the door, for he hoped that Angus Stuart would be back before he left the hotel. For the tenth time he asked himself why the Countess Polda had gone out of her way to do the young Scotsman a civility? It would have been more natural to ask him, Popeau, to dinner, for, after all, he had entertained the Count and Countess to luncheon at the Golf Club. They were curious people, but since he and Beppo Polda had had that talk about old Vissering he had liked the young man better.

And then while these thought were flitting through his mind he suddenly uttered an exclamation of astonishment and of dismay, for coming quickly towards him was Lily Fairfield.

Among the brilliant, gay-looking groups of men and women scattered about the hall, some going to, some coming from the Club, she looked a strange, pathetic little figure.

Was it the fact that she was dressed in mourning that made her look so unnaturally pale? And what could have happened at La Solitude? A thrill of sharp apprehension went through him.

"Yes it is I, Monsieur Popeau. I want to see you in private for a few minutes. I have something to tell you—to ask you to do for me. I want your advice."

She was looking round her nervously, like a hunted creature.

"If possible, I don't want Captain Stuart to know that I have come to see you tonight. Can we go somewhere just for a few minutes, where he is not likely to see us?"

"But—he is up to La Solitude, Mademoiselle?"

"At La Solitude? Oh no! Surely not?"

There was surprise and terror in the tone in which the girl repeated the name of the lonely house.

"Let's come out of doors," she exclaimed. "I—I hardly know what I am doing, Monsieur Popeau!"

He followed her, full of unease and acute curiosity; what *could* have happened up at La Solitude, to make Lily Fairfield look as she was looking now? And where was Angus Stuart?

"Surely you left Captain Stuart up at La Solitude?" he exclaimed, when they at last found themselves standing alone in the open air, gazing at one another in the half-darkness.

"I have not come from La Solitude. But even so, why should you think Captain Stuart is there, Monsieur Popeau?"

She asked the question in a voice she tried in vain to make natural and calm.

"The Countess called here this afternoon and left a note asking him to come to dinner either tonight or tomorrow night. She said you were not well, but that you would be down for the meal."

"But she knew that I was at the Convalescent Home and that I am not coming back to La Solitude till next week!"

"That makes what she did appear very strange," said M. Popeau slowly, and he began to feel very much alarmed and puzzled.

There was a curious pause. He took the girl's hand.

"What is it?" he asked. "You frighten me! Though I am a man of mystery, I hate mysteries!"

"We must go up to La Solitude, now, at once!" she whispered, and he saw, he felt, that she was shaking all over.

"They are murderers, Monsieur Popeau! They killed Mr. Vissering—and I think they killed Mr. Ponting. They may be doing—something—to Angus now—"

"No, no! He is probably quite safe. But we will go and see now, this moment!"

He called out to a passing taxi on its way back to Nice.

"We shall be there very soon," he said, and patted her hand. Somehow, his matter-of-fact manner comforted and steadied her as he said to the driver rapidly in French: "This is a hundred-francs' job for you, my friend, and less than half an hour's drive!"

He helped Lily to get into the cab, and then briefly ordered the driver to go to the Condamine.

"You know the house of the Commissioner of Police?"

The man nodded. He did not look at all surprised. Monte Carlo is a place of unexpected happenings, of great and small tragedies.

M. Popeau put his fat right arm round his companion's shoulder.

"Come, come," he said. "Do not be frightened, my dear child."

"Must you go to Monsieur Bouton?" she exclaimed. "Can't we go straight to La Solitude?"

"I am not going to tell Monsieur Bouton anything. I am simply going to ask him to lend me two good stout fellows in case we should require help."

They arrived in the quiet, solitary street she remembered so vividly in a very few seconds, but after M. Popeau had gone into the house she waited, quivering with impatience, in the darkness, for what seemed a long time; but at last he came back alone. "It's all right," he said briskly.

He did not add that he had told M. Bouton that he believed he was on a new track connected with the Vissering affair.

"I've arranged for two intelligent, strong young fellows to follow us in two or three minutes in a police motor, but they won't come into the grounds of La Solitude unless I whistle for them. And now," he said, "would it trouble you very much if you were to tell me why you came to see me tonight, and also why you made that—that very serious allegation against the Count and Countess Polda?"

And Lily did tell him a broken, confused way what she feared, nay, what by now she felt sure, was the dread truth.

"Perhaps I'm being very foolish about Angus," she said in a low voice. "After all, he has no money, thank God!"

"No, but he has you," said M. Popeau very gravely. "Have I not guessed right, my dear child?"

As only answer Lily pressed the hand which held hers in so protective and kind a grasp.

Through both their minds there flashed simultaneously the same thought—that Angus Stuart was indeed a formidable obstacle to the Countess Polda's wishes.

But how could she have found this out? She had hardly ever seen the two young people together. Besides, even he, Hercules Popeau, had not felt *sure* till just now, when the girl sitting by his side had squeezed his hand in answer to his question.

The Frenchman began to feel far more uneasy than he allowed Lily to know. For one thing, it was so strange that Angus Stuart had not come back long ere now to the Hôtel de Paris! On the other hand, they might have just missed him. Another possibility was that Stuart might even now be on his way down to Monte Carlo. Once they got clear of the streets M. Popeau instructed the driver to look out for a gentleman. But as they rushed up the steep, winding road it remained absolutely solitary till at last they heard the police motor coming up behind them.

"I suggest that we stop the taxi some way below the grounds. Our object is to take them by surprise. Remember, Mademoiselle, that if our suspicions are justified we shall have to deal with desperate people."

A few moments later they were creeping softly, swiftly, up through the orange grove. It was very dark, for the moon was now but a slender crescent, and their footsteps sounded unnaturally loud.

Lily and M. Popeau were leading, with the two police agents three or four yards behind them.

All at once M. Popeau stopped walking, and listened intently. Yes, there was a curious sound coming from where they knew the house to be. But it was an outdoor sound, caused by something moving over to the right, where a clump of bushes hid the front door of La Solitude from that end of the terrace.

It was as if a big broom were being lightly brushed along the ground, and now and again there came the rustling of branches. The Frenchman told himself that it was probably some animal which had padded in from the mountainside.

They all walked slowly on, still in the same order. It was very dark, very unlike the brilliant moonlit night when the strange old Dutchman had dined at La Solitude. Still, even so, as they emerged on to the edge of the wood they could dimly see the lawn before them, and the long, low outline of the house.

All at once there came over those watching there, in the shadow of the dense grove of low trees, a feeling that there was something moving, processionally, on the terrace.

Taking Lily's hand, M. Popeau walked forward on to the rough grass of the lawn.

Yes, there could be no doubt about it now, a group of people, propelling something along, were moving noiselessly across the front of the house.

The dim grey group passing so slowly, silently by, reminded M. Popeau, most incongruously, of a wonderful series of shadow pictures he had seen as a young man at a famous café in Montmartre, in which a vivid drama was enacted by silent, noiseless figures in action being thrown upon a screen. What did that sinister procession mean?

He hesitated as to what he should do—whether to give the signal to the two men to rush up and throw their searchlights on that group who were now advancing across the terrace right in front of where he and Lily stood breathlessly watching them, or to wait yet a little longer.

And then, all at once, something small and white leapt off the terrace and came running across the grass straight at the unseen watchers!

M. Popeau stopped and put out his hand. What on earth was this? Had the Poldas a dog? But his hand sank into thick, soft fur.

It was Mimi, the huge cat, pressing herself against Lily's black skirt, purring loudly the while, glad at having found a friend who perhaps would take some notice of her, unlike her other, more familiar friends, who were too much absorbed in their strange business to notice her.

And still M. Popeau delayed to give the signal to the men who were behind him. For one thing he was afraid of what he was about to discover— afraid as he had never been in his life before, for he had come to care for Angus Stuart.

Slowly the moving shadows disappeared to the left. They were evidently now engaged in the broad path which led from the left of the house to the edge of the little property, with naught beyond but a wild bit of mountainside.

The Frenchman, still holding Lily by the hand, moved up after the sinister group, and then, all at once, he blew his whistle.

At that signal all four rushed forward at right angles across the lawn on to the end of the terrace. M. Popeau uttered loudly the one word "Maintenant!" and two powerful torches were turned full on the strangest sight which even the famous secret agent had ever gazed upon.

On a long, low trolley with high bicycle wheels lay Angus Stuart, looking as if asleep—M. Popeau thought him dead.

The trolley was being propelled by Count Polda, and at the foot of the trolley walked the Countess, backwards. Cristina stepped lightly, phantom-like, by the further side.

For the space of what seemed a long time, though it was only for three or four seconds, the group remained, brilliantly lighted up, in stark and terrified immobility.

Then two shots rang out. The Count had turned the weapon with which he had meant to kill Angus Stuart against himself.

At once there followed a scene of awful confusion. The Countess began fighting as if for her life with one of the strong, agile men provided by M. Bouton. His companion was bending over Count Polda, and Lily, with trembling fingers, was following M. Popeau's directions and trying to undo the insensible Angus Stuart's collar and shirt. But since he had exclaimed, in a tone of infinite relief, "Be of good courage! He is not dead," she no longer troubled as to what was happening about her.

And then, while all this was going on, Cristina vanished like a wraith, in the night. But no one saw her go, or indeed noticed that she had gone, till long afterwards—as length of time was counted on that strange and awful night.

"Do you think you could go into the house and find me a candle?" muttered M. Popeau.

"Oh yes, of course I can!"

Lily set off running towards the house.

"Not so fast!" panted M. Popeau close behind her. "Stuart is only drugged," he exclaimed. "He will be quite himself by tomorrow morning. But we only came just in time. You saved his life!"

Lily stopped, and looked at the closed shutters of La Solitude.

"I wonder how I can get in?" she murmured.

"Are you afraid to go into the house alone?" he asked.

"No, no," she cried, "not a bit afraid! Never afraid anymore!"

She ran along the terrace and so round to the back of the house—yes, the gate which gave access to the yard was wide open!

She opened the kitchen door. Cristina's little oil lamp was burning, and she felt a vague sensation of surprise that everything looked just as usual.

Taking up a candle and a box of matches she rushed back again through the yard and round to the terrace.

She found M. Popeau alone by the trolley. After Lily had lit the candle, "Yes, it is as I thought—they could not make him drunk, but they gave him some form of strong narcotic, probably in water. We will take him down to the taxi, and so back to the hotel. He will be all right by the morning."

The man whom Lily had last seen struggling with the Countess Polda came forward. "I have got her tied up," he said apologetically. "There was nothing else to do, Monsieur!"

"You had better take her into the house, and stay there with her till M. Bouton sends up instructions."

"We fear Count Polda is dying—"

"And where is the old servant?" asked M. Popeau suddenly.

The man looked taken aback. "She can't have gone far," he exclaimed; "we'll soon find her, Monsieur!"

* * * *

Beppo Polda sat in his bachelor rooms in Rome finishing the frugal supper his excellent day-servant had left out for him. He had only arrived about an hour before, and he felt pleasantly tired after the long journey.

He was in a very cheerful state of mind, for he had found awaiting him a cordial letter from the great financial authority he had come to meet. And also he had had time to forget the at once solemn and rather painful impression Lily's farewell had made on him. Nay, more, he had half persuaded himself by now that that strange good-bye kiss had been a sign that she was softening towards him. His mother was not only a clever woman, she also had a shrewd knowledge of human nature. She was probably right in thinking that if he were only patient he would win Lily in the end.

He was hesitating as to whether he should go to bed, or saunter along to his club, when he heard a low knock at the door which opened on one of the landings of the huge old house where he had his rooms. Feeling rather surprised, for no one yet knew of his return, he went and opened the door—and then a thrill of irritation shot through him, for a slim, deeply-veiled woman stood out there, in the dim light cast by the staircase lantern.

He knew, only too well, who his visitor was.

"This is really wrong, and most imprudent, Livia," he said sharply. "I should not have told you the hour of my arrival had I known that you would do this mad thing!"

She threw back her veil, and he was startled at the look of strain and anguish on her pale face.

"What is it?" he exclaimed. "Has anything happened to—to—"

"No, nothing has happened to my husband; and he knows, Beppo, that I am here."

"He knows that you are here?"

He was thoroughly startled and alarmed now. What was it she had come to say?

He drew her gently through into his ante-chamber. Then he shut the door. "Now tell me, Livia," he said, "what brings you here tonight?"

She answered in an almost inaudible voice, "During the evening four different reporters came at different times to ask if we knew where you were."

"Four reporters?" Beppo looked astounded.

"Then you have heard nothing? No one has been here?"

"The notice telling of my absence is still on the door downstairs. But why am I sought for?" he asked, bewildered.

The Marchesa Pescobaldi was trembling violently now; it was if she had the ague. He took her cold hand in his.

"Come, Livia, calm yourself! I have done nothing—I swear it!"

"Of course I know that you have done nothing," she whispered, and then she held out with shaking fingers a strip of thin paper.

Beppo Polda did not know that it was what all the world over is familiar to newspaper men as "flimsy."

He took it in his hand, and turning away from her held it close up under a lamp which hung from the high ceiling.

On the piece of paper was written in pale characters and in a plain, round hand:

A TERRIBLE AFFAIR AT MONTE CARLO.

An amazing affair has just taken place at Monte Carlo. The Count and Countess Polda, highly-respected residents and natives of the Principality, are both in prison since last night under the charge of having committed a series of singularly cold-blooded and infamous murders.

The Count lies, dangerously wounded by his own hand, in the infirmary of the prison. The Countess has had a series of heart attacks, and it is thought probable that she will escape justice.

A search is being instituted in the neighborhood for their servant, who is believed to have been their accomplice.

Their last victim, a rich young Englishman staying at the Hôtel de Paris, was only saved by the fortunate accident that a friend, having business with him, hurried up to the Polda's villa late at night, to find the miscreants on the point of killing him. His grave was already dug.

The affair is of peculiar interest to Roman society, as Count Beppo Polda, the well-known sportsman, is the only son of the Count and Countess Polda.

Count Beppo, who had been staying with his parents, left Monte Carlo yesterday. Every effort will be made to find him, as it is thought that he is an accomplice.

CHAPTER 31

Four days had gone by, and Lily was sitting out in the sunshine with Angus Stuart. The effect of the poisonous drug which had been administered to him the night he had dined at La Solitude had not passed off as quickly as Papa Popeau had believed it would. Still, he was now by way of being well again, and for the first time Lily felt she could ask him to tell her what had happened during the evening which was to end in so terrible and tragic a fashion.

He waited for a while before answering her, and then he said very quietly:

"There is curiously little to tell, darling. The one outstanding thing I remember is how surprised and annoyed I was that you did not appear. The Countess Polda is a wonderful actress—"

Lily shuddered. "She is indeed," she whispered.

"I remember that when she came out to meet me, as I walked up to the terrace by the usual way cross the lawn, she explained that you were not quite so well, and that she had persuaded you to remain in bed until after dinner. Looking back, I suppose she intended me to say—'I hope Miss Fairfield won't come down at all.'" He waited for a moment, then went on: "But, Lily, I was selfish, and I wanted desperately to see you! I had a kind of apprehensive feeling about you. Popeau had said something which had made me feel vaguely anxious, and I didn't believe it would do you any harm to come down for a few minutes—so I simply answered that I was glad you would come down after dinner."

"What happened then?" asked Lily.

"Nothing particular happened, that I can recall. They were both very civil, in a formal, affected way, and I was astonished at the splendid spread to which we ultimately sat down. Still, there was a certain amount of delay, and as I look back I cannot help suspecting that their old servant—"

He saw a curious expression pass over Lily's face, but he had no clue to what lay behind, so after a moment he went on:

"What was I saying? Oh yes—I cannot help thinking that the old servant wanted to convey some kind of warning to me. Twice, when she was standing in the only place where neither the Count nor the Countess could see her face, she stared at me in the most peculiar fashion, as if trying to attract my attention; and then after we had some hot soup—the rest of the meal was cold—she dropped a lovely but very small decanter on to the floor, and it broke into three or four pieces. It had had in it some liqueur the Count wanted me to taste, and I wondered today—for today is the first time I have really thought the whole thing over—whether that liqueur was drugged? Though the Count and Countess took the breaking of the decanter very well, and really made no fuss about it, I could see that they were extremely angry with the poor old soul. In fact, the Countess told her that henceforth we would wait on ourselves, and that she need not come back into the room."

Again he stopped speaking for a few moments. Then he began again: "The Count went out of the dining-room for some more of this special liqueur, and he brought back some of it already poured out in two rather big wineglasses. I confess I thought it was quite delicious, and made, I should judge, of very old brandy."

"And what happened after you had finished dinner?" asked Lily in an almost inaudible voice.

There had risen before her the scene Angus had described so simply—the unhappy Cristina trying to save Angus, and of course failing, utterly.

"To tell you the truth, Lily, I felt very tired and stupid. The Count had filled up my wineglass rather often," he added, smiling. "That does not mean that I was drunk. But still, I did feel rather odd!"

"You mean after dinner?"

"Yes. And yet I was very much alive to the fact that you had not fulfilled your promise to come down, and twice the Countess went upstairs to hurry you. Each time she came back she said you were just coming, and of course I believed her. And then—and then—well, Lily, I suppose the drug they had managed to convey to me, either in the food, or in the wine and liqueur, began to act. As I sat on in the drawing-room, I got desperately drowsy, but I cannot tell at what exact time I fell into the sort of sleep which was practically insensibility."

"I wonder they didn't kill you in the house," said Lily in a strained voice.

"It was much safer to put a bullet into me by the side of the grave they had dug, and then tumble me in," he said in a matter-of-fact way. "Popeau is convinced that I was the first of their friends they had ever thought of burying. The others were all so arranged as to convey in each case the impression of suicide."

Lily Fairfield drew a long breath.

"You have told me everything I wanted to know," she said, "and we'll make up our minds, here and now, never to speak of it again!"

"I agree," he answered quietly. "Popeau knows all I have told you, and he didn't want me to go into it with you, but it would only have worried you to go on wondering what had happened."

* * * *

Reader, have you ever thought what it would be like to be in any way associated with a great criminal case—what the French call a *cause célè-bre*? Lily felt herself the cynosure of a hundred eyes wherever she moved or showed herself; yet very few of the people gazing so curiously at the pretty English girl knew how really closely associated she had been with the awful events which had taken place in the last few weeks at La Solitude. But the mere fact that she had stayed there as the guest of the Count and Countess Polda invested her with a morbid interest in their eyes.

The principal public excitement was concentrated on Cristina, and on that unhappy woman's mysterious disappearance. She was being searched for high and low, but it was as if the earth had swallowed her up.

And now, today, Lily Fairfield was expecting Mr. Bowering, who had been at once telegraphed for by Hercules Popeau. Though everything had been done to save her pain and distress, she had had to submit to a long inter-rogation on the part of three famous French lawyers, and M. Popeau was now secretly absorbed in the task of devising a way by which his young friend could be spared the terrible ordeal of appearing as a witness at the Countess Polda's forthcoming trial.

Count Polda was dying, and the hope of finding out where Cristina had hidden herself was being gradually abandoned.

All at once M. Popeau ambled up to where the two young people were sitting.

"Would you like to walk down to the station and meet your English friend?" he said persuasively to Lily.

The girl got up obediently. She moved like an automaton. "I will, if you think I had better do so," she said dully. The story Angus Stuart had just told her was becoming intolerably real to her.

While walking down the broad road leading to the station Lily suddenly startled M. Popeau.

"There's something I *must* ask you," she said in a low tone. "I want to know about Beppo Polda. Does poor, poor Beppo know?" There was a sob in her throat. "If he does, how strange it is that he isn't here! Or is he here, after all? Have they arrested him too? I seem to know nothing now of what is *really* happening!"

The Frenchman hesitated for a moment, then he said gently:

"You do not need to trouble yourself about Beppo Polda. By a strange and wonderful piece of good fortune for him, poor fellow, he killed himself accidentally in a shooting gallery the very night he arrived in Rome—before there was time for him to have learnt the awful truth."

Lily's lip quivered, the tears ran down her face. And yet—yes, she was glad!

"And Cristina?" she ventured. "What do you think has *really* happened to her, Monsieur Popeau?"

"I think I know what has happened to Cristina," he said mysteriously. Then he stopped walking, and looked round, but there was no one near enough to hear what he had suddenly made up his mind to tell her. He knew that he could trust her.

"I am quite sure that the unhappy woman fled on that awful night down to the valley, and then up to old Monaco, to the Convent of the White Sisters," he said in a low voice.

Before Lily's inward vision there rose up the great forbidding-looking iron gates which gave access to the sunny courtyard beyond. She saw again the stately Mother Superior, heard her reprove poor Cristina, kindly but firmly, for the wild way in which she had spoken of herself.

"The Order was founded by one of Cristina's own ancestresses," went on the Frenchman, "and there has always been a close connection between the Convent and the Poldas. It is possible, but I do not say it is likely—for after all, women are women, even when they wear the Holy Habit—that the nuns have not yet heard the story of what has happened at La Solitude, though all Monaco is ringing with it! But in any case, the nuns would never give Cristina up to justice. The poor soul will spend her life henceforth in work and prayer, repenting of her part in her wicked sister-in-law's crimes, and praying for Beppo Polda's soul."

"I cannot understand how Cristina could ever have allowed herself to be used in that way," said Lily in a deeply troubled tone. "She was so very kind and gentle."

"I have little doubt that at first she was but an unconscious accomplice, and that at last the Count and Countess had to take her into their confidence. You may think of her now as being happier than she has been for years and years, for her life must have been one long torture. Yes, during the last two days I have liked to think of poor Cristina in that quiet old convent on the hill," he said meditatively. "There must be wonderful views of both sea and land from those of the nuns' cells which overlook the sea."

"Two days ago?" said Lily suddenly. "Then did something happen two days ago that made you feel sure that Cristina had taken refuge there?"

Monsieur Popeau again looked round. He even came a little closer to his pretty companion.

"I took a walk up to old Monaco quite early in the morning two days ago," he said hesitatingly. "I walked past the gardens where I once left you alone with Captain Stuart, and then, when I was at the extreme end of the rock, I looked up, and on a little piece of wall which I now know to have been the wall of the convent garden, I saw—"

He stopped, and Lily exclaimed breathlessly, "You saw Cristina peeping over?"

"No, I did *not* see Cristina peeping over—but I saw—Mimi!"

"Mimi! the cat?" exclaimed Lily.

"Yes, Mimi, the cat—walking along the top of the wall, already beginning to look as if he felt at home there! In fact, I will confess to you, Mademoiselle, that I tried a little experiment. I called out very quietly and tenderly, 'Mimi, Mimi, come hither, my friend!' and at once he jumped down, and rubbed himself, purring loudly, against me."

"What an extraordinary thing!" exclaimed Lily.

"Without doubt poor Cristina caught up the cat, and fled with him. And now, as I said before, you may think of the poor woman as being happier than she has been for many, many years. She was the hapless victim of her wicked sister-in-law."

As Lily gazed up into his face, a thousand questions trembling on her lips—questions that yet she shrank from asking—he went on, slowly:

"Bouton and I have been making certain calculations, and we are convinced that old Vissering was the Countess's ninth victim. But, of course, till the last few weeks, when circumstances proved too much for her, she was very prudent—she allowed, that is, plenty of time to elapse between each of her crimes. Towards the last, the complete immunity she had enjoyed made her feel that she need never fear to be suspected. Hers was the master mind. We have some evidence that the Count and Cristina were unwilling accomplices. On two occasions men afterwards so foully done to death received anonymous letters which we know could only have come from La Solitude."

CHAPTER 31

Lily sat up in bed and rubbed her eyes. She had been dreaming—dreaming of home, of Aunt Emmeline, and of kind Uncle Tom. And then, all at once, she remembered everything. This at once familiar and unfamiliar place was her bedroom, in the Convalescent Home where she had been treated with such wonderful kindness during the last ten days.

Only ten days since that awful night? It seemed to her a year. Sometimes she still felt as if it was all a dream. And yet—and yet—

All at once she covered her face with her hands. Today, incredible though the fact still seemed, was to be her wedding day!

It was Hercules Popeau who had worked the miracle—for it still seemed a miracle to the two most closely concerned. It was he who had persuaded the cautious English lawyer, Mr. Bowering, that if Lily Fairfield were to be saved from the terrible ordeal of giving evidence against her pseudo-aunt, she must become, before the trial of Countess Polda, Angus Stuart's wife—the chattel of her husband, compelled, that is, to follow him where he ordered her to go.

There had been a good deal of rather anxious discussion. For one thing, Angus Stuart had been unwilling to take advantage of the strange position in which Lily found herself. But once Mr. Bowering and Hercules Popeau had overcome his scruples, Lily had been profoundly moved to see how ecstatically happy her lover had become. Almost as happy, she now whispered, as she was herself!

There came a sudden knocking at the bedroom door, and the matron, walking in, pulled up the blind.

"Am I too early?" she asked solicitously.

Lily shook her head, smiling.

And now, with the sun streaming into the room, for the very first time the awful nightmare which had always been there in the background, even during the last few joyous days, seemed to fade away. Lily forgot the past and thought only of the future.

How wonderful to know that she and Angus were going off alone, this afternoon, to Italy for their honeymoon! It seemed, somehow, too good to be true.

"A large box has come for you from Paris. I wonder what can be in it?" said the matron, smiling.

"But I don't know anyone in Paris!" But even as she said the words one of the V.A.D.'s with whom Lily had made friends during the last few days brought in a large box, covered with that curious black shiny paper with which French people do up parcels.

"I don't think it *can* be for me," exclaimed Lily doubtfully.

"Oh yes, it is. It's been expressed by passenger train."

"How very, very strange!"

She jumped out of bed, and looked down eagerly at the mysterious box. It was addressed "Mademoiselle Fairfield."

The V.A.D. cut the stout cord, and lifted the wooden lid. Layer after layer of tissue paper was taken out, and then, finally, a beautiful ermine coat emerged, together with a quaint little ermine toque, in which nestled a sprig of orange-blossom and of myrtle!

It was the matron who finally espied a visiting-card, on which was written in tiny characters:

"With the donor's sincere good wishes. Papa Popeau hopes that Mademoiselle Lily will honour him by wearing his wedding gift on her marriage day."

Lily's eyes filled with tears. How very good this quaint, whimsical, elderly Frenchman had been to her!

* * * *

Looking back, as they often do look back, to their strange wedding-day, both Angus and Lily Stuart always agree that in many ways it was Papa Popeau, rather than the bridegroom, who had seemed the hero of the occasion. It was he who appeared the central figure of the quaint little group gathered together round the temporary altar which had been set up that day in the hotel where the British chaplain, during that first winter after the War, officiated.

As was but fitting, the Frenchman was best man to his Scots friend, and to everybody's amazement he had appeared garbed in ancient dress clothes, with, on his breast, the Cross of the Legion of Honour and the Military Cross!

It was Papa Popeau also who presided at the wedding feast which took place just after the wedding in a private room at the Hôtel de Paris. It was he who put the bride, looking radiantly happy and wearing her superb ermine coat over her old frock—for she felt as if she never wanted to see any of the lovely clothes she had bought with Aunt Cosy again—into the luxurious motor which somehow or other he had managed to procure for the happy pair at very short notice.

In fact, so extraordinarily brilliant were Papa Popeau's various improvisations, and so artful the way in which he had managed to persuade everybody to do exactly what he wanted done, that Mr. Bowering muttered to Angus Stuart: "I begin to see why France won the Battle of the Marne."

But it was fortunate, perhaps, that Lily did not overhear the final words which Hercules Popeau exchanged with the English solicitor after the two had watched the motorcar containing the now married lovers speeding towards Italy:

"And now, dear sir, while you go back to the fogs of Albion, I will return to the more congenial task of seeing that the Countess Polda is well and truly guillotined!"